THE
PILLARS
OF
ROME

A ROMAN REPUBLIC NOVEL

THE
PILLARS
OF
ROME

DAVID DONACHIE

McBooks
Press
Essex, Connecticut

McBooks Press

An imprint of Globe Pequot, the trade division of
The Rowman & Littlefield Publishing Group, Inc.
4501 Forbes Blvd., Ste. 200
Lanham, MD 20706
www.rowman.com

Distributed by NATIONAL BOOK NETWORK

British Library Cataloguing in Publication Information available

Library of Congress Cataloging-in-Publication Data

ISBN 978-1-4930-7395-5 (paper)
ISBN 978-1-4930-7396-2 (ebook)

♾™ The paper used in this publication meets the minimum requirements of
American National Standard for Information Sciences—Permanence of Paper
for Printed Library Materials, ANSI/NISO Z39.48-1992.

To Nick Webb,
A star!

PROLOGUE

It was a prank, one of those pieces of devilry which Lucius Falerius treasured; one his best friend Aulus Cornelius feared because of his more potent respect for the power of the gods. How could two twelve-year-olds know that what they would experience on this night would have a bearing on the rest of their lives?

Both were dressed in manly gowns, appropriated so they could visit a famous Sybil, an oracle who inhabited a cave in the Alban Hills close to Rome, a privilege forbidden to mere boys. The lifting of those garments had shown that for all his strength and prowess at games, Aulus could easily be bested where deception was required. In his father's country villa, dealing with his own family slaves, his way would have been to rush in, grab what he wanted, and flee. Lucius, a guest, swept in with a proprietary air and emerged with the garments neatly folded over his forearm, seemingly unconcerned about the whipping both they and the slaves would receive if the boys were caught. Clothes formed only part of the disguise and in this Lucius could again best his friend. Aulus had the nose of his race, prominent and straight, full cheeks and the makings of a noble forehead, but he struggled to get his thick, black hair into anything resembling an adult style. Somehow Lucius, smaller, with features softer in every respect, managed to look older merely by the superior way in which he held himself.

It was daunting, entering that poorly lit cave; penetrating cold, the swish of bats wheeling about their heads, dripping water the only sound to disturb the silence. Under a guttering oil lamp coins were handed over to a veiled acolyte, supposedly an offering to the power of the Sybil, though Lucius, in his customary irreverent manner, whispered it was more like a bribe. Aulus could not look at his friend then, nor could he say anything; his heart was pounding so much he felt sure it must be visible, like the sweat he could feel just below his hairline. Lucius would not sweat, and he could speak without even a trace of a tremor in his voice.

They were shown into a chamber hacked out of the rock, lit by flickering torches, a place reeking of bat droppings as well as human and animal waste, that mingled with a heady smell of incense. The detritus of dead creatures littered the space between them and the Sybil, sat on a high stone pedestal, staring straight ahead with what seemed like sightless eyes. Neither youngster was willing to examine the bleached bones at their feet to see from what source they came, but the impression, very firmly imparted, told them that to trifle with the gods was to end up like these, mere skeletons lying at the feet of the oracle. In a voice much deeper than his natural tone, Lucius calmly asked for a prediction of their future.

The answer was a hiss from the Sybil, an aged crone with a face more deeply lined than the bark of an ancient olive tree. Staring straight ahead, she demanded their own names as well as those of their ancestors. Both boys, well versed in the histories of their respective families, named noble progenitors who had helped not only to found the Roman Republic, but had acted to make her the greatest power in the known world. What followed was a silence that seemed to last for a half-glass of sand, one that deepened the air of mystery.

'You are but youths,' the Sybil finally wheezed, running her uncut, ragged-edged fingernails through matted grey hair. 'It is for men to plead the oracle, not boys.'

'We have made an offering,' Lucius replied. 'If it is forbidden for boys to plead, why was that not rejected?'

'You will be the Falerii.'

'I am,' Lucius replied, his voice almost defiant.

'You think beyond your years. The Cornelii is pious, you are not.'

'Should we fear you?' Lucius demanded.

Aulus sucked in his breath and his whole frame shook. Lucius might not suppose that this priestess could strike them dead on the spot, but he did; the bones that littered the space between them made him believe that others had suffered such a fate.

'You should fear what I may say, Falerii.'

'If you, Sybil, can see my future, then it is already decided. What need then have I to fear it?'

A finger was used to summon a hunched, unidentifiable figure, who knelt before the Sybil holding a framed papyrus. She, with no more than that index fingernail, executed a series of strokes. The light from the torches behind her framed the thin material, so both boys saw, as silhouettes, those strokes translated into some kind of drawing, this as she hissed her prophecy.

'One shall tame a mighty foe, the other strike to save Rome's fame, neither will achieve their aim. Look aloft if you dare, though what you fear cannot fly, both will face it before you die.'

A sweep of the hand detached the papyrus from its flimsy frame, causing it to roll itself like a scroll, which the Sibyl took and threw at their feet. Lucius bent to pick it up, opening it to reveal a drawing of a bird in blood red, crude, but clearly an eagle with wings outstretched in flight.

'What does this mean?' demanded Lucius.

The laugh was high and humourless, a cackle that echoed off the walls. 'You are clever, Falerii, you decide.'

Lucius might be impious, but what happened next dented even his studied pose. He let out a strangled cry as the papyrus began to smoke in his hand and the hole of a burn appeared in the centre, spreading rapidly, a brown-edged nemesis consuming the document, but not before that crude red drawing was burnt with equal force into their minds. Just as it singed Lucius's hand, forcing him to throw it to the ground, all the torches in the cave went out, plunging them into darkness. Aulus began to howl incantations to *Jove*, the greatest of the gods, seeking protection for both himself and a friend now clutching his arm in a painful grip. The lantern-light that appeared behind them offered a salvation that both boys took with alacrity and they stumbled out of the cave of the Alban Sybil, following a light that they could never catch.

That night, in the glim of a shared bedroom, they kept the lantern burning low as they talked of the Sybil, the cave, the smells, the acolytes, but mostly of the prophecy. What did it portend? Each word they examined and repeated over and over again, searching for meaning. "One shall tame a mighty foe, the other strike to save Rome's fame." How could they do that and not achieve their aim?

'What is our aim?' asked Aulus.

'Glory for us, our families, and the Republic.'

There was no boast in Lucius's words, just the ambition of every well-born Roman boy. 'The Sybil must be wrong,' he whispered, his soft brown eyes fixing his friend, as if by doing so they would make fact of speculation.

'Can an oracle be wrong?' Aulus was desperately hoping that Lucius, so much wiser in the ways of the world than he, would say yes, but his companion did not oblige, he merely repeated the last part of the Sybil's prophecy. 'Look aloft if you dare, though what you fear cannot fly, both will face it before you die.'

'Does that mean we will die together?'

'It might,' Lucius said in an uncertain tone.

'All I ask is a noble death.'

A platitude to an adult, it was a truism to any twelve-year-old. 'We can face no other, Aulus, we are Romans.'

As the night wore on, Lucius recovered his poise, that air of certainty which, however questionable, he carried off with a composure beyond his years. He suggested that they use a knife to exchange blood and to swear eternal friendship that would surely act as a talisman to ward off any evil spirits. Were the gods not fickle, prone to behave like humans, to take sides, to change sides even? Fate could not ever be unalterable! Lucius Falerius, in his steady seductive voice, began to question the certainty of the prophecy. As noble Romans they could consult the priests of every temple in Rome, sacrifice birds and animals and have the signs within the entrails read; what fear could they have of a bird that could not fly? The burning papyrus was mere trickery. Aulus Cornelius tried hard to match his friend's growing disbelief, but he knew his own voice betrayed his failure to do so.

The image of that blood red drawing, that eagle in flight was behind his lids, to scare him every time he closed his eyes.

Brennos could conjure up an image of his impending fate and no amount of knocking his head on the smooth walls of his underground prison could erase the horrifying vision; only days before he had taken his place in the circle of massive rectangular stones to ritually do the same to another. Taller than ten men, when the sun rose on a clear day those huge granite blocks cast shadows that ran black to the edge of the world. Robed in white, Brennos had helped form the circle of priests surrounding the flat altar on which lay a recumbent male, eyes glassy from drinking an infusion of sense-dulling herbs. The priests had assembled in the grey pre-dawn light and waited in silence till the first sign of that blood-red ball of fire rose in the east, the moment when the giver of life dragged itself away from the souls of the dead to be greeted by bright blood. But on this day, at this sunrise, it would be his blood and his agony. There would be no drug to dull his feelings and his face would carry no ecstatic smile. The knife would cut out his heart while he was fully conscious, his body so arranged that he could watch it happen; that was the fate of a condemned Druid.

He had worked hard for what he was about to lose. To be a priest of the cult was to walk the earth like a god. As shamans to the greater part of the Celtic world, Druids held much power: they could impose peace or start a war, bless a union or damn the new-born child of a tribal chieftain. The common herd went in awe of their powers and gifted to their island temple treasures that were the envy of their world. Yet like all bodies created by men, the priesthood was awash with personal rivalry. Brennos was nephew to Orcan, who had sought to advance him quickly, while his rivals wanted the young heart to kill off an enemy before he became too potent in his own right. He would die for his own and his uncle's ambition.

In frustration he raised his arms and, with the very ends of his fingertips, pushed against the heavy rock that acted as the roof of his cell, one that had taken six men to put in place. His breathing stopped as it moved aside, easily and silently, so that above his head the stars shone in the sky, silhouetting a hooded figure. A hand reached through, jerking nervously that he should take hold, which he did and as he leapt, he was hauled clear. The hooded figure helped him to his feet, pressing something into his hand.

'Orcan bids you depart, Brennos, since he fears words won't save you, that those who oppose him will prevail. In your hand is a gift from him, taken from the Sacred Grove. It will protect you, aid you and give you purpose.'

Brennos held it up by the chain. Even in the glim of the starlight it shone, a gold charm, shaped like an eagle, wings spread as if in flight. As a priest entitled to enter the Sacred Grove he had seen it before, knew that once it had been lodged below Mount Olympus in the Temple of *Apollo* at Delphi until that shrine was sacked by a great Celtic multitude. It had belonged to the man after whom he had been named, the leader of an army that had ravaged the land of the Greeks, and even held Rome itself to ransom, a talisman that carried with it a prophecy, though one couched as a riddle. It was said that one day a chieftain would arise who had the right to wear it, for he would be even greater than the man who stole it from the Greeks. The prediction was that he would do what the Great Brennos had failed to do, and take his sword to the very inner temple of the Roman Gods.

There was another prophecy, another enigmatic story, one that had a less pleasant interpretation, talked of in hushed whispers in the Sacred Grove. It said that one day Rome would expand to hold sway over all the lands of the Celts, to subdue not only the tribes but their priests as well, burning bodies and temples and driving them to the very edge of the western sea. Surely both could not prevail? Which was a true reading of the future?

'Your uncle entrusts it to you, with a message. Leave now, go to the very edge of our world where you will be beyond the reach of your enemies. He has seen you in his dark-hour visions, wearing this, standing in the Roman Temple of *Jupiter*. He has seen that you have the faith to confront Rome and thus the power to fulfil the prophecy.'

'When did he dream this?'

'Brennos, I was entrusted with the message that I have given you and no more.'

That said, he departed, leaving the freed prisoner to wonder at what fate awaited him: to wonder also where the men who had been set to guard him had gone, at the power of thought that had made the moving of that massive stone covering something he had achieved with his fingertips. He lifted the eagle once more, glinting in the moonlight, looking at the shape; the proud head, the extended wings, before slipping the chain over his head.

Brennos did not run away; having invoked the blessing of the Great God *Dagda* and his companion, the Earth Mother, *Morrigan*, he walked. If there was to be a pursuit, he would have to hope that the gods would confound it. Before the moon was renewed three times he had left the northern island and crossed the narrow strip of water to the huge expanse of Celtic lands that ran forever towards the rising sun, most ending at the point where it met the arrogance of Rome or the barbarity of the godless eastern tribes. South and south again he journeyed, with many a remark on his passing, the red-gold hair on his head, in a country of dark and swarthy folk, being as unusual as his height. As a young traveller in a Celtic world he wanted for nothing, with each hearth obliged to treat him hospitably, until finally he reached the point where his world ran up against another.

Brennos stood on a long escarpment, looking down on to a settled agricultural plain, criss-crossed with neatly ordered fields. In the distance lay a white-walled town, red-tiled roofs catching the rays of a sinking sun. Behind him lay thousands of Celtic tribesmen, warriors who could obliterate these Roman settlements, all they needed was a leader. He raised the eagle to his lips as he had done every day since his escape and made a vow; that one day he would return to the lands of the north, not as a fugitive but as an all-conquering head of an army; that one day he would stand in that circle of stones and, keen knife in hand, cut out the hearts of those who had sought to slay him.

CHAPTER ONE

———•———

The tiny chapel off the atrium was packed, though the number of people in the confined space was small. There was no need in normal times for this private family room to hold a multitude; it was the dimensions of the chamber rather than the number of guests that created the impression of overcrowding. Some were family, others important friends, fellow senators or clients, while one distinct group stood close to the altar, dressed partly in goatskins. On the day of the Festival of *Lupercalia*, these men had stopped on their way to the sacred cave on the Palatine Hill, wearing the skin of the animals they would sacrifice in the rituals of their cult. *Lupercalia* being the God of Fertility, no child could ask for a more propitious day to be born.

Those dressed, like their host, in purple-bordered togas and red sandals made up the bulk of the assembly: Roman senators, they had come to witness the birth of a child to Lucius Falerius

Nerva, one of the leading men of the city-state, and by their presence to affirm their allegiance to both the man and his cause. Lesser mortals filled the atrium, intent on laying claim to a share of his gratitude that the gods should bless him so, a share in the power the Falerii could command in these troubled times. In the streets of Rome, just a few feet away, few men dared to walk alone; the city was split into warring factions, as the ill-bred supporters of Livonius fought the Senate for control of the most potent state the world had ever known.

Tiberius Livonius, plebeian tribune, was bent on forcing his reforms through the assembly, the *Comita Tribalis*; acts that appealed to the basest sectors of Roman society, an alteration to the voting qualifications that would spread authority through the ranks of the thirty-five tribes, so even the meanest, ill-bred member would stand on a level with the richest and most aristocratic. Patrician nobles, members of the oldest and most illustrious families, like Lucius Falerius and those assembled to witness this birth, opposed such moves with all the considerable energy at their command. For such people power could only be entrusted to men of quality and wealth – anything else was a surrender to the mob.

They had stood quietly, faces set, just like the death masks of the Falerii ancestors that lined the walls, sweating in their uncomfortable garments

while out of sight the midwives worked diligently in
the bedchamber, muttering incantations for the
intercession of *Lucina*, the Goddess of Childbirth.
Each invited guest had stoically ignored the cries of
Lucius's wife, Ameliana, as she struggled, strapped
in to her special delivery chair, to bring forth the
child; that was in the nature of things and not a
cause for comment. No flicker of emotion crossed a
brow as the cries of the child took over from the
painful screams of the mother. The master's body
slave Ragas, tall, muscular, his shoulders glistening
with oils, crossed the atrium, imperiously elbowing
his way through the throng, to whisper in his
owner's ear.

The guests remained still and expressionless,
while Lucius, having acknowledged the message,
moved to the end of the room, his fine-boned,
intelligent face as expressionless as his deep-set
brown eyes. Each craned forward as their host
made an offering at the altar dedicated to the *dio
domicilus*, a sacrifice to the family Genius, for it
was by this *Lares*, this household God, that a man
such as Lucius Falerius, and his ancestors before
him, achieved immortality. They knew by the
sacrifice of a black puppy that Ameliana had been
delivered of a son. Moments later, like a well staged
appearance in a drama, the child, carried by a
midwife in a wicker basket, wrapped loosely in a
swaddling cloth, was brought into the chapel, still

yelling mightily, the small puckered face bright pink with fury and the coal black hair which capped his head still glistening from the scented water in which it had been bathed.

Ragas took the basket and approached his master, so the true moment had arrived; a man's wife could be delivered of a child and that child might be a boy, but he was not yet the son of Lucius, not yet a true descendant of the Falerii, who could trace their line back to the days when Aeneas, fleeing from the ruins of Troy, had founded the city of Rome. In the period between the birth and what followed the child was an orphan. If the next stage of the family ritual was omitted it would remain so and shame would fall on the head of Ameliana Falerius from this day forth. Tension was heightened by a sudden pause, as the slave held up the basket, close enough for Lucius to see the child, but just too far away for his master to touch. The guests could only wonder at the way the pair locked eyes, the slave smiling, his master frowning, before the basket was inched a fraction closer. Lucius did not move a muscle, almost teasing his audience in the way he examined the child, carefully lifting the swaddling cloth to confirm his sex, daring someone to break the spell.

Raising his head he looked around the room, inspecting each face in the flickering light. Suddenly he frowned, for the one person he had hoped to see

was absent. Young Quintus Cornelius was there, in
the uniform of a military tribune, his face like the
others covered in a sheen of sweat, but the boy's
father, Aulus Cornelius Macedonicus, had not
answered the summons, even though he had
returned to Italy from Spain. What of the bonds
they had sworn as children, sealing them in blood,
oaths renewed through years of friendship; that
they would always attend upon each other in any
hour of need or celebration?

Nothing counted as much as the birth of a first-
born child, quite possibly a son, especially for a
man who had been married without issue for nearly
twenty years, but it was more than that. His
greatest friend and staunchest political ally, absent
from Rome for two years, had not come to aid the
patrician cause at a time when he and his class were
under threat, when a real possibility existed that a
conflict might break out between the rival factions
seeking to control the power of the Roman State.
To treat Lucius so was a grave breach of obligation,
made more so by the help that the perpetrator had
received in pursuit of his own ambitions. Aulus
would never have been given command in Spain if
Lucius Falerius had not used all his prestige, and
marshalled all his adherents in the Senate, to secure
the appointment. Yet the beneficiary, Rome's most
successful soldier, declined to appear at a moment
when his mere presence might tip what was a very

delicate balance. With the nagging thought that his friend was less committed to the cause than he, and had no care for the effect his non-appearance had on wavering senators, the timing of this absence smacked of a deliberate insult.

The murmuring of his guests, like a low but rising moan, brought Lucius back to the present and he felt a flash of anger, immediately tinged with regret for what might be an over-hasty judgement, as he conjured up a series of images of himself and his childhood companion; playing just out of infancy, growing up together at a time when he could still wrestle Aulus with some chance of winning, even risking damnation in that prank in the Sibylline cave, sharing terror at the prophecy and relief when that fear abated as they grew to manhood, till at least he, Lucius, could make jokes about eagles, unlike his friend, who could not even observe one in flight without calling down *Jove* to aid him. He had stood with Aulus when his own two sons had been born, his happiness at his friend's good fortune tinged with regret that he himself was childless.

They were different he knew, and not just physically: Aulus had none of the cynicism of his more worldly friend. He had a simple soldier's view of things, unable or unwilling to grasp the subtlety necessary to achieve success in the political arena and he seemed to take good fortune as his due. Did he appreciate how much Lucius had aided him, helping to keep his armies in the field, assisting him to commands that gave him an arena for his manifest gifts? Sometimes Aulus angered him by his artlessness, his desire to see both sides of an argument, yet always that same trait – his palpable honesty – had brought forgiveness. Would it be so easy to forgive him for this? It was with some difficulty that he put both memories and irritation out of his mind. Lucius leant forward and with a swift motion lifted the child from the basket. He then raised it, arms fully extended, acknowledging to all that this boy was the fruit of his own loins, his son and heir. Great cries of joy erupted from the assembled guests and they pressed forward to praise the father and bless the child. Next door, the midwives, still praying to the Goddess *Lucina*, struggled in vain to save the life of a mother who, they all thought, at thirty-five, was too old to be bearing her first child.

Aulus Cornelius Macedonicus stood alone by the undecorated turf altar, dressed in a simple white garment, worn short and loose in the Greek fashion. The muffled moans of his wife, attended by a single young midwife, seemed to cause him an actual physical pain he struggled to contain. For all his pre-eminence as the foremost general of the Roman world, no guests attended this birth and no supplicants crowded the room. The walls of this borrowed villa were as bare as the altar and the single tallow wad guttering in the sconce lent the colonnaded room a ghostly feel. None of the normal rules of celebration were to be gifted to the birth of this child and the fact that it was taking place on the day of the Festival of *Lupercalia* was something that mocked rather than honoured the event.

'Hot, honeyed wine,' said Cholon, his young personal slave, proffering an unadorned stone goblet. Aulus shivered slightly in the chill of the early spring air as he took the drink. 'Your cloak, master?'

'No, thank you,' Aulus replied automatically, his voice a hoarse whisper.

His servant was unsure if he had heard him right, though he never doubted any response would be polite. It always was, whether the person addressed was a common soldier or the noble monarch of a Roman client-state. No one exemplified more than Aulus Cornelius Macedonicus the virtues of which Rome was so proud; he was upright, honest and brave, a soldier's soldier revered by his men. The fickle Rome mob cheered him too, as a man who paid more than lip service to ancient freedoms, yet when his city was in turmoil and he was desperately needed in Rome, here he was skulking in this empty country villa. The mob would not cheer him for that!

Cholon knew that lesser men, enmeshed in the dirty world of politics, sneered derisively at what they saw as his master's arrogance. They would hold that a senator and ex-consul showed insufficient gravitas when he discarded his home, his responsibilities, his friends, even his toga on such an occasion, but the general who had humbled the heirs of Alexander the Great and brought powerful Macedonia to heel, so that it was now a vassal-state to the Roman Republic, could ignore and withstand the disapproval of anyone. His family was as ancient as any in Rome: the death masks of his ancestors stood proud in their decorated cupboards. These lined the walls of the family chapel in the home of the Cornelii on the Palatine Hill, situated right above the broad avenue of the *Via Triumphalis*.

Had he been in that chapel and sensed the disapproval of those ancestors at this clandestine birth, he would have looked at their masks with disdain. Aulus Cornelius Macedonicus was the greatest of his tribe, the foremost exemplar of the family Genius. His mask, on his death, would take pride of place above the family altar when future generations gathered for prayers. He prized his reputation as much as the next man, just as he felt keenly the need to maintain his honour, yet he would not see another suffer to retain that, especially one he loved. He could not bear that his wife should be shamed in public for something he held to be entirely his own fault.

Marcia, feeling nervous, stifled a yawn as she sat watching the nameless woman cradle the child to her breast, encouraging it to feed, but the infant, having already taken its fill, did not respond. Occasionally the lady moaned, exactly reproducing the sounds she had uttered in labour through the tooth-marked leather strap, now discarded. She had given birth, fists clenched, several minutes earlier, flat on her back like a peasant. An inexperienced midwife, who had never before attended on a birth unsupervised, Marcia knew that very few deliveries would be as uncomplicated as this, yet for all the ease of the birth, things seemed set to change. The girl sensed trouble and the manner of her summons to attend this lady provided little reassurance. She had been dragged from the Lupercalian celebrations, so pertinent to her trade, with the promise of a rich reward if she came at once.

Since the baby came quickly there had been little time to spare for curiosity. The woman had fought with enormous will power to hold her cries as the child emerged from her womb, her voice never rising above the labour moans that she had emitted with increasing frequency. Marcia had been forbidden to slap the baby's feet and the exhausted mother had waved away her attempt to bring the child to life with a sip of wine. Once the cord was cut the woman immediately suckled the infant, which fed greedily and silently, leaving Marcia to wonder anew at the strange circumstances surrounding the whole affair. It would be something to tell her friends, since she had never heard of a child being born in silence. Then with a slight shock, Marcia realised that she could tell no one; before being admitted to this barren bedchamber she had sworn the most frightful oaths to the Goddess *Juno*, never to reveal anything about this event.

Oaths or not, nothing could abate her curiosity. There were strange things to ponder, not least the fact that Marcia's attempt to summon the slave, so that the husband who had administered these oaths could be told, had been abruptly halted; she found herself ordered by a violent gesture from the mother to remain still. The whole affair was a deliberate mystery and the person paying her fee, pacing to and fro next door, wanted it kept that way. The young midwife knew she was in the presence of nobility; the bearing of the man, despite his plain unadorned dress, left her in no doubt and the woman, this lady, was high-born too; it was obvious by her well-dressed hair, her expensive clothes and her demeanour. She had been given no names and her attempts to question the Greek slave who had summoned her to this house, pressing on her the first part of her fee, had met with a sharp and unpleasant response.

'Attend upon the lady, deliver the child, and ask no questions. Be assured that the man who pays you this gold will not hesitate to kill you should you break any oath you are required to give.'

Come to that she did not even know the name of the slave! The child, half-asleep, was offered again, taking the teat in his mouth automatically, but still showing little enthusiasm for milk. The russet-gold hair and striking blue eyes were unusual, in sharp contrast to the jet-black hair and dark pupils of the boy's mother and father. You could never tell with these things; Marcia knew, better than most, that families often threw up children who bore little resemblance to their immediate parents.

The woman moaned again as though she had not yet given birth. It was all so strange; they really should take him to his father. Then, with another slight jolt, the young midwife understood: this child was not to be acknowledged. Could this infant, this changeling, be the result of an adulterous union? Was the lady, seemingly so noble and refined, really no better than a common whore? The mother, still moaning, opened her clenched fist to reveal a glistening object, which she then wound round the infant's puckered ankle. The gold of the chain

flashed as it swung by the baby's foot, causing
Marcia to crane forward to see the charm. It was
gold, shaped like an eagle in flight, with the wings
delicately picked out to show proud feathers. As
soon as it was securely attached the lady covered
the whole of the small body in swaddling cloths.
Then, kissing the child gently on the forehead, she
pinched him hard. He immediately awoke from his
contented state and in the way of all babies
proceeded, in a very noisy fashion, to let the world
know of his arrival.

Throughout this charade, Aulus had paced the
barren atrium, cursing himself for the events of the
past two years. His mind went further back to the
triumph, celebrated at the successful conclusion of
his wars on the Greek mainland, where, in a part
fulfilment of the prophecy, 'he had tamed a mighty
foe', having brought Perseus, King of Macedon, to
Rome in chains, to be hauled along behind his
chariot. Others carried the male children of that
same king's court, who would be educated as
Romans and held as a blood bond for the behaviour
of their fathers. The city had never witnessed such a
triumph; not even the defeat of Carthage had
introduced such wealth to the Republic. The slave
beside him in his four-horsed war chariot might
caution that all glory was fleeting, but the cheers of
the crowds added to the unstinting praise of the
Senate made it both hard to hear and impossible to

comprehend. There was not a soldier in the legions that marched behind him on that day that did not feel immortal.

Aulus had brought back more than Alexander's heir. The wealth that Perseus's great ancestor had plundered from Greece and the Persian Empire came too, in a train of carts that took two whole days to wend its way from the city gates to the Capitol. Hundreds of finely wrought and valuable urns, full to the lip with gold coins, were carried in procession behind him. Still others followed, brimming with jewels and precious objects, all borne on the shoulders of men who had once been Macedonian soldiers, the most feared army in the world. Now they would be sold in the market-place and in such quantities that the price of male slaves had plummeted.

Alexander the Great's armour came too, in his own war chariot; breastplate, helm and shield, which held an almost mythical significance for the whole civilised world. His sword, which no man dared to wear, lest such impiety caused him to be struck down by the angry gods, lay atop the pile. These were the possessions of the greatest conqueror the world had ever known and who had overturned his descendants? None other than Aulus Cornelius, styled now, by order of the Senate and the people of Rome, Macedonicus.

The triumph was complete when Aulus hauled

his royal captive to the steps of the Temple of *Jupiter*, made obeisance to the greatest of the Roman gods, then used the rope that had dragged him through the streets to ritually strangle Perseus before a howling and delirious mob.

Cholon stood near the entrance to the bedchamber watching his master, reflecting that some men could never rest on their laurels. Who else could they blame if the gods, having so favoured them, chose to demonstrate the pitfalls of excessive pride? As an Athenian, he had been glad to see the Macedonians humbled; his city had suffered much at their hands, yet he could not understand these Latins. Having conquered all of Greece they desired nothing more than to speak his language with fluency, to discuss Greek philosophy, read Greek writers and watch Greek plays while spouting endlessly about the benefits of liberty. For barbarians these Romans were not savage enough.

With the Macedonians at his mercy, and having killed more than enough enemies in battle to ensure his triumph when he returned to Rome, Aulus had halted his legions. Those who surrendered he spared, taking only hostages, as well as a token number of captives as slaves. Cholon, being Greek and somewhat wiser, would have killed them all, the land he would have laid to waste instead of handing it back, telling those who had owned it that they were safe provided they paid enough tribute to the Republic and obeyed the rule of law. They would, in time, rise again and another Roman army would have to be despatched to subdue them.

'You wait and see if I'm not right!'

This was said under his breath. He was much given to taking liberties with his master but he knew this was not the time to indulge in such behaviour. Cholon Pyliades considered himself a pious man, so if the gods chose to desert the Macedonians and their allies by allowing victory to go to the barbarian Romans, then his master, who had the power to do as he wished, should have punished them properly and having done that he should have lived in honourable retirement and not gone back off to war at the very first opportunity.

As the young slave entered to collect the child, Marcia examined him, staring again at his carefully curled hair, held by the braided band. He had a pale, almost girlish face, soft full lips and a slim, graceful figure, which caused her to wonder at the relationship between him and the man outside. He stood over the woman for a moment waiting for her to hand over the bawling child. Where would they expose it? That was obviously what was intended. The secrecy seemed unnecessary since exposing children was a common enough thing, even among the well-born, who could afford to feed a large brood. Would a hint regarding a good spot be welcome? After all, the woman desired the child to live, regardless of her husband's wishes. She had put that charm around the child's foot to identify him, a sure sign she would want him back at sometime in the future, with perhaps a handsome reward for the person who had reared him. But then she reasoned it would be best to stay silent. There were only so many places round these parts to expose a child; someone would find him and for a tenth of the fee she was getting tonight they would gladly give him up.

'Cholon!'

The sharp command cut through her thoughts, as well as the child's cries, like a whiplash. The man stood in the doorway, a black look on his face. Even after the strain of child-bearing the mother's youth and beauty shone out in stark contrast to the countenance of her older husband. Marcia tried to guess how greatly the couple differed in age, which led her to further speculation, since such unions often ended in tears. The slave, responding to his master, bent down and took the child, slipping through the space left in the doorway. That was when the angry face softened: the man's straight prominent nose and thick black eyebrows lost their menace, the full lips parted and he smiled at his young wife. Not a joyous smile, more one of relief that her ordeal was ended, but this changed his face completely, and when he spoke to Marcia his voice, soft and gentle, matched his changed mood.

'Your work is done, child, yet I would ask you one more thing. Stay with the lady until I return, then my servant will see you safely home.' Marcia just nodded, too awed by his presence to speak. She could see, as he could not, that the mother was fighting hard to hold back her tears. 'But do not pry into matters which don't concern you.'

His face still had the same smile but his black eyes bored into her, warning her of a fate that was certain should she disobey him. Then he spun on his heel and left. She busied herself, making her exhausted charge comfortable and the lady, who gave free rein to her sobs as soon as the husband departed, actually cried herself to sleep. The young midwife sat silently by her makeshift bed, her mind whirling with thoughts of what she had witnessed, and what the future might hold for her after the events of the night.

Cholon was already mounted, the sleeping child slung in a saddlebag by his side, when his master came out of the villa, leaping on to his horse with the agility of a long-serving soldier.

'Where to?' asked Cholon.

There was a half-mocking tone in the reply, for now that the child was born some of his master's natural humour had resurfaced. 'Don't tell me you've no suggestions to make, Cholon? You usually do.'

'There are several likely spots nearby, General, reasonably close to villages. If we lay him on a hillside they will find him as they go out to gather wood.'

The voice became hard. 'We go south, Cholon. And I want a spot that's miles from anywhere. I don't want him found, ever!'

With that he kicked his horse and set off, leaving his servant behind. Cholon nudged his own mount and leant over its withers to follow. As soon as the horse moved the child awoke and the Greek found himself staring down into the steady gaze of a pair of bright blue eyes. He looked up quickly lest he be tempted to pity, and not for the first time uttered a soft curse aimed at his master, now some distance ahead.

CHAPTER TWO

Aulus rode hard, trying to block out the memories of the last two and a half years, a vain hope given the picture of that period never left him. A widower, he had decided to remarry, taking as a bride the daughter of an old army comrade, a girl twenty years younger than himself. As a frequent visitor to her father's house, he had known Claudia as a pretty and precocious child; meeting her again aged sixteen it was very evident that she had blossomed into a beauty, surrounded by ardent admirers. Was it foolish for a man of his age and standing to fall in love with such a girl, even more imprudent to ask for her hand? His eldest son was older than she, the other not so very much younger, but he had consulted the augurs, made sacrifices aimed to ensure good fortune, and all, according to the priests, had been encouraging. The irreligious in the slums of Rome thought him a fool, a great warrior bewitched by a slip of a girl, which gave rise to much ribaldry and obscene graffiti between the day when the betrothal was announced and the ceremony by which Claudia became his wife.

What followed was as close to bliss as Aulus had ever experienced. At first in awe of him, his young wife melded within weeks into a companion of the kind he had only ever heard of but never experienced, even though he could claim his previous marriage to be a good one. Besides her beauty, Claudia had wit and charm and at no time did the difference in age seem to intrude in their relationship, especially in the bedchamber. She was passionate, willing as well as obliging as a wife, and a surprise delight when it came to dealing with the majority of his friends, who were naturally of his age. Aulus had never been so happy, and swore to anyone who would listen that he would trade his Macedonian victories rather than lose her.

The nuptials were less than six months past when news arrived of serious trouble in Spain. The Celtic tribes of the Iberian interior, hitherto kept at bay by the Roman ability, mixing bribery and flattery to keep them divided, had come together under a new and enterprising chieftain called Brennos. That was a name to strike fear into Roman hearts; they had faced a Celtic Brennos nearly three hundred years before, a barbarian leader who had sacked most of Greece and all of northern Italy before appearing before the very gates of Rome. One legend had it that a stoic Roman defence had forced him to withdraw; a less heroic tale maintained that he had been bribed with sacks of gold to depart after he had burnt most of the city. Now his namesake was terrorising Roman Spain and this time the fractious mountain tribes were not merely raiding the rich coastal plains in search of booty. Reports suggested that they were being organised into an army that threatened to conquer the whole country, which could not be allowed to pass. Too many senators, Aulus included, had possessions in Spain; farms, mining concessions and profitable monopolies, as well as the valuable slave labour that worked them.

No Roman nobleman worth his salt shirks his responsibilities, regardless of how rich and respected past campaigns have made him, nor was his recent marriage allowed to interfere. With the full backing of his new wife, who was inordinately proud of his military achievements, Aulus Cornelius Macedonicus immediately made it known that, as Rome's foremost soldier, he was available if required. It was an offer that pleased a number of his contemporaries, yet troubled many others in a society that was far from stable – when the norms that had governed Roman life for centuries seemed under threat from some of the very people entrusted with upholding the state.

Factionalism was rife, so even some of those senators who stood to lose from the depredations of this new Brennos demurred when offered the services of such a man, frightened to entrust a campaign to one who had already garnered such glory. Would another success make Aulus too powerful, a man to be feared rather than admired? Certainly he was known for his personal probity, but men not themselves free from temptation found it hard to believe that there existed anyone untainted from the vice of ambition.

In the past, when the state faced a threat too difficult for the normal consular system to control, one man had been given supreme, temporary power, a crisis measure that lasted only as long as the emergency it was created to face. Such a thing had been brought about by the need to confront an external enemy but now it seemed to many that the enemy was within. A temporary Dictator would divide the factions even more, if that were possible. Senators like Tiberius Livonius were agitating for change; apart from tribal voting rights they wanted to extend Roman citizenship to the suppliant states of Italy, once Rome's enemies, now her allies, a source of manpower in war and tax revenue in peace. To others the notion that such people should be given equal status with those who had defeated them was anathema. Roman citizenship was a prize worthy only of those born to it; to dilute such a privilege was nothing but a prelude to state disintegration.

If that had been all, it was enough, but Livonius and his supporters had other plans that struck at the very heart of the city-state. Rome had grown fat on the spoils of empire and in the process it had become the magnet for everyone seeking a fortune and in many cases those in search of no more than the food necessary to survive. The city was crowded, with huge wealth living cheek by jowl with acute poverty. In fear of riot it had been agreed that a dole of corn, enough to sustain life, should be issued to the poorest members of the population, but that was not enough for the reformers; they now wanted to give farms to the landless peasants who filled the slums as a way of clearing them out of the city, land that would have to come from those who owned it, the wealthy elite that governed the city and had made vast fortunes from Rome's conquests. Egging on the mob, who had most to gain from his proposed reforms, Tiberius Livonius threatened to make Rome ungovernable.

Such ideas must be fought and defeated, but politically, not by some successful soldier at the head of fighting legions, who were barred from entry to the city. It was over four hundred years since the leading families had founded the Republic, expelling the Tarquin kings, yet the memory of their despotism still lived on, making men suspicious of success, lest too much fortune tempt anyone to seek supreme power; to overthrow the Senate, suborn the Republic and reinstate a royal tyranny. Aulus Cornelius Macedonicus, attached as he was to the patrician cause, with one great campaign to his name, given another, might see personal rule as the best method of restoring order, and having done so, the best method of keeping it so by a continuation of that rule. Lucius Falerius, who knew the man in question better than anyone, had used his considerable oratory to ridicule such fears.

'I fear I must remind you, my fellow senators, of how much this august body and the people of Rome owe to Aulus Cornelius Macedonicus. Is this some upstart seeking advantage? No. He is a man who has no need of further military success. Is he so poor that he needs to go on campaign to load the state with his living expenses? Hardly, given the treasure and slaves he brought back from Greece, he is one of the wealthiest men in Rome and I suspect many present have had occasions when they have needed to borrow from him. I fear that some of our members have transferred their own level of base thinking to a fellow senator whose principles are so elevated over theirs as to be incomprehensible.'

Aulus was cheered inwardly at the memory of the protest that accusation had set off, with the very people both he and Lucius knew to be the most venal, the loudest in their denials. He recalled the magisterial look on his friend's face then, one that made him proud of their close association. Lucius appeared his best at moments like these, his eyes alight, face mobile enough to match his rich and varied voice, driving home his point, his tone just the right side of mocking. Privately, he might have become a touch tiresome of late, irritable and impatient even with his close friends and adherents, hardly surprising given the workload he undertook, but when it came to the collective pulse of the Senate, Lucius was the man who could feel and respond to it. Aulus gave special attention to examining the faces of those men he and Lucius rated as allies, those senators who shared their political views, yet had expressed themselves troubled at his friend's recent imperious behaviour. He wanted to say to those who carped, 'Observe this, and ask yourself, given this body, the Roman Senate, disparate, fractious with more scoundrels on its benches than upright individuals, could you command it with half the ability of this man?'

'The task outlined by the Senate,' Lucius continued, 'demands no conquest, only that the Celtic-Iberian tribes should be defeated, dispersed and sent back into the mountains from which they came. There is therefore little glory to be garnered on this campaign, only hard fighting and the risk of death. Given that, I demand to know who else would volunteer?'

He was answered only by silence; that he

expected from those who supported him. It was his enemies and the uncommitted he was challenging, the latter the key to a majority. Lucius stopped short of calling them cowards, though not very far short. He clinched their support by reminding them that he, in his second term as a reigning consul, had the right to command the army, but, just as he had for the war in Macedonia, he was willing to put aside his claim, as was his junior colleague, to secure a quick victory as well as a return to normality by sending to Spain, as proconsul, the man he trusted most with a military command. Lucius took Aulus's hand and raised him so that he could consent to the agreement of his peers, knowing his friend would, in humility, stammer his acceptance. The Senate was not the natural arena for Aulus: he liked simple chains of command, orders given and obeyed. Not for him, thought Lucius, the balancing of political weight, or the need to persuade or terrorise a reluctant senator so that he could see where his best interests lay.

Aulus did surprise Lucius by adding one stipulation; that, as he was going to a Roman province with proconsular powers to contain a rebellion, his family, including his young wife, should accompany him. Everyone now looked to the man who had moved the motion to give him the command to see if he would demur. Privately,

Lucius had made quite a few salacious jokes about the way that his old friend was smitten, had even secretly admired the pornographic graffiti with which the slum dwellers of Rome were wont to tell their betters what they thought of their actions. Personally he found Claudia gauche and the sight of Aulus drooling over her embarrassing, but he saw no harm in the notion and nodded his assent. After the drubbing the doubters had just received none in the Senate had dared protest at a general taking his family on campaign. In reality forbidden, it seemed a small price to pay to secure his services.

Besides, matters were serious and time was short; these barbarians must be both punished and pushed back, forced to make peace or die. Aulus, once the Senate had approved his appointment, took ship for the southern coast of Gaul to join the four legions, two Roman, the others auxiliaries made up of Italian allies, already marching towards Iberia. Within two weeks he crossed into the province of Hither Spain, accompanied by his sons, the youngest, Titus, riding alongside him, mounted on a small white cob; Claudia was with the baggage train between the two auxiliary legions, comfortable in a litter, surrounded by her husband's personal bodyguard. Quintus, his eldest son, a year older than Claudia, rode ahead with Nepos, the cavalry legate in command of the advance guard. Within a week they would be in the provincial capital of Saguntum, ready to begin the task of defeating Brennos. At that moment, everything in his life seemed perfect, his happiness unassailable.

Aulus, trusting his horse not to stumble or leave the roadway, closed his eyes tightly as less pleasant memories surfaced, recollections of a truth he had ignored. A slave had stood behind him in his war chariot as, face painted red, dressed in the deep purple toga of a victorious general, he rode down the *Via Triumphalis* responding to the cheers of the crowd gathered to celebrate his Macedonian victories. The man was there to remind him, by whispering in his ear, that all glory was fleeting: that he needed to beware of the sin of hubris; that the gods would bring low any man who dared to forget he was a mere mortal, that they would not be mocked.

Doing battle with barbarians was very different from engaging the disciplined army of a state like Macedonia. Formal combat, in which he would confront the entire enemy host was not something Aulus expected, despite their numerical superiority. His informants confirmed that the Celt-Iberians, at his approach, had withdrawn from the coastal plain and taken to the hills. This underlined his belief that it would be a war of ambush and raid. He had set himself for a difficult task, with his legions broken up, operating in centuries and cohorts, trying to destroy the means by which the rebels sustained themselves. They would need to be ruthless and cruel, burning villages and destroying pasture and crops, taking hostages and enslaving women and children if the insurrection was to be brought under control. He in turn would need to be tough, to prevent his troops from descending into a rabble, if required, killing some to maintain discipline. Necessary in Macedonia, such measures, in Spain, would be even more indispensable.

That whispering slave who had stood behind him had been right! It was foolish to assume anything in war, to be so sure that his enemies would wait in the hills for him to attack, just as it was unwise to rely upon his reputation to fight his battles for him. His name meant little to the Celt-Iberians and nothing to this Brennos, who was clever, and more powerful than the Romans had imagined. Somehow he had achieved what they thought impossible, the welding together of the notoriously cantankerous Celts into a single fighting unit. He had no intention of leaving Aulus to march peacefully to his base camp, appearing suddenly at the head of a multitude of braying tribesmen to attack an army that had not even begun to pursue him, an army strung out on the march.

By their disordered tactics, really just a melee in which those who could engage did so, the Celt-

Iberians had managed to split his forces, separating the auxiliary legions from the Roman troops. With his command structure shattered, disaster threatened, so putting himself at the head of his heavy infantry Aulus had ridden to the rear, cutting his way through, and rallied the Italian allies under his personal command. Now his experience and legionary drill told. Facing them about in copybook fashion, he fought his way back to join the remainder of his Romans so that they could present a united front to their adversaries. Nepos, well to the fore and out of touch with Aulus, had shown both courage and good sense when he declined to force-march his advance guard, which included the legion's Numidian cavalry, back towards the main body. That would have brought him into contact with a massive screen of tribal warriors waiting to engage him.

Instead he took his cavalry in a great arc, into the very foothills from which this Brennos had attacked, catching the Celt-Iberians unawares. An irresistible charge on their rear, with his son Quintus well to the fore, had broken the order of the attackers. Aulus now formed his whole army into a cohesive whole, ready to advance in any direction and engage, but a loud horn blew twice and the enemy evaporated, with a discipline no Roman fighting a Celtic army had ever encountered, leaving him no one to fight. Worse still, his baggage train had been plundered and in the process he had lost his wife. He had to march past the site of that as he sought to pursue the enemy, forced to gaze on the broken wagons, scattered possessions and the dead from the engagement. His position, the on-going battle and the need to appear in control debarred any notion that he could stop and examine the wreckage to see if the body of Claudia was amongst the dead. Only later, as the sun sank low in the west, was he able to establish that she was gone and that every man in his Praetorian Guard had died trying to defend her. That evening he received private word that she was alive, the personal prisoner of Brennos, who demanded no less than the withdrawal of the Roman legions as the price for her freedom.

That was a bargain he could not even begin to accept. If her life was to be forfeit, then so be it. He called his sons to him, swore them to secrecy, then told them of the demand and of his decision. Quintus, too old to have much attachment to his stepmother, did not even allow himself the flicker of an eyelid as he agreed. Titus, younger, and less the stern Roman, assented with tears in his eyes, but both were obliged to attend the ceremonies that followed, in which the auguries were taken in an attempt to see what the future held, even pious Aulus surprised by the positive signs they revealed.

A despondent Aulus Cornelius had achieved more than he knew. His enemies had anticipated an easy victory and had convinced themselves that they would destroy his army and leave their bones to bleach in the sun. His prompt action in uniting his force, plus the steadfast defence of the legions, had destroyed that illusion, which forced the Celts back to their usual tactics of raid and ambush. Yet this Brennos seemed capable of inspiring the varied tribes to an unprecedented level of resistance and it took two campaigning seasons to bring them to heel. No more battles of any size, more an endless series of hard fought skirmishes with an enemy that faded away at the first hint of real danger, often to the sound of that same horn that had been heard in the first battle.

Needing to be ruthless, Aulus led by example, and the blood he spilt, the men he crucified, both his own and the natives, the women and children force-marched into slavery, testified to his determination. No pity was allowed, and that cruelty he increased as the war dragged on, only being ameliorated when it would have the effect of detaching support from his enemy, Aulus discovering that Brennos laboured under as many problems as did he. The Celtic leader never managed to repeat the effect of that single initial battle, in which he had united the clans under his personal discipline. Outright success would have made his position unassailable, partial failure exposed the endemic differences between the tribes and their leaders. Not all the chieftains were content to accept his control and quite a few, bribed by Aulus, deserted his cause, so that Rome had good intelligence about both the man and his methods.

Brennos had come from the misty regions to the north, from the cold windswept islands that were the spiritual home of the Cult of the Druids, a priest as well as a warrior, and this gave him great stature, for he could weave spells and cure the sick, bring rain to parched crops and tell long Bardic tales of Celtic bravery that went back to the very beginning of time. The man was able and cruel, possessed of a silken tongue, and, it seemed, a stone instead of a heart. Utilising his religious powers, this northerner wove a cunning tapestry before an audience only too willing to believe his prophecies. He told them that the Romans could be defeated in battle, foresaw the day when the legions would be ejected from Hispania, leaving the Iberian tribes as masters of their own lands.

But he held out an even more tempting prospect; once that goal was achieved, it would be time to unite all the Celtic nations, a race that ringed practically the whole of the Latin conquests, all in opposition to the power of Rome. He reminded them that the Celts under one Brennos had invaded and sacked the city, convinced them the time had come to do so again, and on this occasion to destroy the greedy Republic, to take back from Rome all that it had stolen from their world. It was heady stuff for a race of men noted for their excitable nature and their love of plunder.

Nothing he heard about this stranger made Aulus feel secure, either as a husband or an army commander, especially the fact that Brennos was right. If he could unite the Celts and lead them in a disciplined campaign, then Rome could be beaten; it had happened in the past when the Republic was faced with an organised enemy. The fractious nature of their foes formed the basis of Roman success and Aulus placed great faith in the notion that, for all his abilities, Brennos' plan would founder on the character of the warriors he led. At least in that area the auspices were good, with Brennos, by his arrogance, contributing to the destruction of his own aim.

After the first battle when the chieftains were celebrating what they perceived as a triumph over the legions, Brennos had interrupted their feast to berate them, calling them failures. Full of drink and in the middle of great boasts about their individual exploits, they had not taken kindly to his hectoring tone, yet faced with a man of seemingly supernatural power, few dared to argue. Two chieftains had tried, so Brennos killed them both during the night then ordered their entire families, including women and children, to be put to the sword, his own hand contributing to the deed. Others, no less offended by his words and his deeds, but with the sense to remain silent, thought it prudent to desert and take Roman bribes. It was these men and the information they provided that enabled Aulus to contain his numerically superior enemy.

All along he had his personal burden to carry, one he could share with no one. Claudia's youth and beauty, plus her station as his wife, made it only too easy for him to conjure up in his fevered mind an unpleasant fate, a plaything to be used and abused at will by her captors. Often he wished her dead rather than suffering the things he imagined and such thoughts drove him hard, and he knew, made him cruel. He denied both himself, and his legions, proper rest, while Brennos, in turn, taunted him. In nearly every encampment they found and destroyed, discreet signs that his wife had been there were deliberately left to goad him.

Finally, eighteen months after she had gone missing, with the snow thickening on the foothills of the mountains in the north, his eldest son rode alone into the camp, requesting his father's Quaestor, the Legate Nepos and the tribunes to leave his command tent so that they could speak privately.

'You, too, Cholon,' said Quintus, as the slave poured him a cup of hot wine from a gold and silver Corinthian flagon.

The Greek looked to his master; as Aulus's personal valet he was not to be ordered about by anyone, even the man's son and heir. Having seen the look in Quintus's eye, his master jerked his head to indicate that the slave should obey. Cholon put the flagon down a trifle more sharply than necessary to signal his displeasure but the two men were locked in a mutual stare and failed to notice.

'Claudia?' asked Aulus softly. Dread welled up at the nod of assent, there being no relief in his expression. 'She is dead?'

'No, Father. Your wife is alive. We surprised a party of enemy spearmen on the move. They were escorting a covered wagon. I knew immediately that there had to be something valuable in that wagon, since they chose to defend it rather than run away. They all died for that, just like your bodyguard. When I entered the wagon the Lady Claudia was there.'

Images of a sick or maimed woman flashed through Aulus's mind and his black eyes bored into those of his eldest son. 'There is no joy in you, Quintus. If you're the bearer of bad tidings it would be a kindness to tell me.'

His son's shoulders sagged and for once he dropped that rigid Roman demeanour which was the core of his being. 'Is it awful news, Father? The Lady Claudia is well and wishes to see you.'

Aulus was surprised. 'Not wounded or hurt?'

Quintus squared his shoulders once more, looking at a point just above his father's head and fighting to maintain his composure. 'I carry a message from her to you. The wagon we captured and in which I found her stands at the same spot, surrounded by the bodies of our enemies. She bids you come so that you may speak. Until then she does not desire to move from there, and will neither set off for, nor enter, your camp, until you have spoken.'

'What do you mean?' snapped Aulus, goaded by the impersonal military voice his son had used. 'How dare you address me in such a manner?'

Quintus did not flinch, keeping his eyes away from contact, nor did his tone of voice change. 'I carry her message, Father. She bade me deliver it and swear an oath to say no more. I cannot think that you would wish me to breach such an undertaking.'

It was insolence and Aulus raised his hand to strike. Quintus did not flinch as the balled fist froze above him. Then Aulus gave a huge shout. 'Cholon. My horse.'

He stared hard at his son for another second, then pushed past him out of the tent. Quintus, with his father's body out of the way, stared at the rear of the spacious tent. There sat the altar, loaded with regimental symbols and those Cornelii family vessels brought from Rome. Silently he prayed to the gods that what he suspected was not true, yet he was old enough and man enough to be sure it was and with a sinking heart he turned, following his father's footsteps.

Claudia Cornelia, sat in the back of the wagon where Quintus had left her, heard the pounding hoof beats, first distant, then growing in volume until they seemed to fill her head. She dreaded what was to come, a confrontation she never thought would happen, which made her rub a hand fearfully over her already swelling belly, trying to feel the kick of the child inside. Then she remembered the eagle charm on her neck, hidden from Quintus under her cloak, an object that might become visible to Aulus. Quickly she removed it, feeling as she touched it an almost physical connection to the power it embodied. A last look, before concealment, had her recall the very first moment she had set eyes on it: for the first time in nearly a year, her mind went back to her capture, and the events that had changed her life.

CHAPTER THREE

The first sounds of battle, the trumpets blowing, shouted commands that sought to organise the defence of her husband's Praetorian Guard, had been just a precursor of the confusion that followed. Claudia's father had told her, many times, of the madness of battle, of the fog that surrounded everyone from commander to common soldier, that for a successful soldier luck was often more vital than skill. She had thought him indulging in modesty but that day Claudia Cornelia learnt the truth. Disobeying the request to stay in her litter with the curtains drawn, she had alighted to see what was happening, it being too exciting to miss. The army had been strung out in a long shallow valley, the Roman legions ahead, Italian auxiliaries to the rear, struggling to form up against a mass of tribesmen rushing downhill to engage them. With a father kind enough to indulge an intelligent daughter, she had known enough about tactics to be aware that the general who held the heights held the advantage. That did not lie with Aulus, but such was her faith in the superiority of Roman arms and the skill of her husband that it had never occurred to her that the legions could lose.

Metullus, the centurion in command of the praetorians, had yelled furiously at the muleteers to get their wagons into a circle then arm themselves and it was only then that Claudia realised how great the gap had become between the baggage train and any support from Aulus's army, the forward elements of which were barely visible. It had been the same to the rear, for marching in line had allowed the tight formation of the morning to extend itself, leaving the centre section, her and the baggage, isolated.

'Lady Claudia.' She had turned at the voice, loud and close enough to drown out the noise of trumpets and screaming defenders, to face a young soldier holding a horse by the reins. 'I am commanded to get you on to this horse. Gaius Metullus suggests that you ride forward to join your husband. Stop for nothing and no one.'

Claudia had looked around at the scene: with the circle of wagons Metullus desired half-formed, they were already slaughtering the oxen, dropping them in the shafts to act as obstacles in the gaps. The ring held soldiers young and old; the servants of the army, cooks, carpenters, metalworkers, maids, seamstresses, slaves and some of the personal servants of her husband and his officers. How could she just up and leave them? Her own natural courage had combined with the thought of what Aulus would do in a like situation. He would never desert any responsibility; that and his modesty were what defined him. Therefore, as his wife, neither could she.

'You take the horse. Ride hard and tell my husband how exposed we are, but assure him that his soldiers will hold until he can rescue us.'

The young soldier had hesitated, but faced with a command from someone as elevated as his general's wife, he could not refuse, so he jumped into the saddle, and headed out through the rapidly closing gap as the circle of wagons became complete. Gaius Metullus had yelled after him, before turning to face her, but he must have seen in her expression that she had ordered the youngster to go and he had lifted the blade of his sword to his lips in salute. Surrounded by panic, screaming women, men, servants and drovers running around like headless chickens, Claudia had never felt so useless. She had seen Metullus arranging his soldiers, half to man the perimeter, the other forty members of his century forming up in the middle to provide a mobile reserve. From deep in her memory Claudia had dragged out the stories her father had told of fighting and the things a soldier thought about when engaged.

'The mouth goes dry, your tongue becomes like leather. You think of the need to drink more often than the need to stay alive.'

'Get the water out,' she had shouted, before grabbing several servants and pushing and cajoling them into obedience. 'See if there are any spears in the wagons, or swords, axes, anything that will serve as a weapon.'

Time had seemed to stand still, the whole effect of her words played in a slower motion that reality and she heard rather than saw the first probing attack by a detached band of Celt-Iberian tribesmen; the clash of swords on shields and metal, the hiss of spears and arrows as they sped through the air, the screams of unidentified victims as they were wounded or killed mingled with the triumphant cries of those who had delivered the blow. Claudia had been too busy to follow the course of the contest, supervising the unloading of the water butts, too occupied with buckets and ladles, organising a line of supply to the fighting men that would ensure that they had water to drink. Every sharp tool in the baggage train had been put in the hands of a person who could use it, practically doubling the number of fighters Metullus had at his disposal. And to all she had repeated the same thing.

'We need not hold for long. My husband is at this very moment on his way to rescue us.'

It had been a while before the truth dawned. Through the dust kicked up by the tribesmen seeking to break into the circle of wagons, it was just possible to observe that the Roman legions had formed up in a hedgehog defence, shields up to the front, the rest over their heads to protect against arrows, the whole forward-moving assembly bristling with protruding spears. What they had not seen was the *hastari*, Aulus's best troops, moving past the baggage train, not towards it, going to the rescue of the allied legions. Claudia could not know that on receipt of her message, her husband had had no choice but to save his army before he could think of saving her.

Inside the circle of wagons the death toll had risen inexorably. Metullus had fought as well as he could, husbanding his men, waiting till the last moment to close any breach that the attackers had gained, but each counter-attack stepped over the bodies of fallen comrades; each success in repulsing the enemy had been bought at the expense of casualties, diminishing a force that was already too weak in numbers. The wounded had fought alongside those who could still walk, well aware that death would follow defeat and in the background, above all the shouting, cursing and clash of arms they had heard trumpets, Roman trumpets ordering manoeuvres that they prayed were to aid them.

Metullus had pulled his men back just as collapse was imminent, when three sections of his wall of wagons had been breached so that the last thirty surviving soldiers had formed a shield around the wagon that contained the personal baggage of Aulus and his family. Inside that shield crowded every one of the non-combatants of the army. Some had wailed, others cried silently, a few looked so shocked as to be unaware of what was happening, but most, men and women, Romans in the main, had stared at the enemy with undisguised contempt and had prayed to *Fortuna,* the Goddess of Fate.

'Lady Claudia, it is my duty to offer you the use of my sword.'

Claudia had looked into the blood-covered face of Metullus, at the gashes on both arms from sword cuts, as well as a great slash across his forehead that had left a flap of skin hanging over one eye. Dust had coated the blood, as well as the rest of him, armour included. Claudia had whipped off the embroidered linen shawl that covered her head, and pushing that filthy flap of skin upwards, had wrapped it round Metullus's head so that he could see properly.

'You need your sword to defend us, Gaius Metullus.'

When she could see both eyes, she saw a pain in them greater than that which came from his wounds, for like him she could see how the Celt-

Iberian tribesmen had crept cautiously through the gaps in the wagons in numbers too great to contest.

'Be aware of what awaits you, Lady.'

'It awaits all we women, Metullus. I would not have you spare me the fate of the rest.'

'Then I shall kill you all.'

'Do you not know that some of my ancestors were Sabine, Metullus? They survived and so shall I.'

Metullus had actually smiled then at the reference to the Rape of the Sabine Women, a piece of Roman folklore known to every citizen of the city-state, a story of brutal Roman soldiers who had assaulted the defenceless wives of their defeated enemies.

'Face your destiny, Metullus, and I will face mine.' Pearls were embroidered into her shawl, now wrapped round the soldier's head. She had pulled off two and handed him one. 'Pay the ferryman with this in place of a coin. That should ensure that your journey over the River Styx to Hades will be a comfortable one.'

The cry behind, as well as the low moan from those around him had told Metullus the final assault was coming. For the second time that day he had raised his sword blade to his lips, to salute the bravery of the young wife of his general, then he had turned as they charged, his voice rising to a yell, his sword set forward to engage the enemy. He had fought well, killing three or four tribesmen before a spear took him in the neck. By that time all his men were dead, and within the space of a few seconds the killing of the non-combatants had begun.

Claudia had sought to get to the front, prepared to take the killer blow that would end things, the pearl under her tongue seeming like a huge stone, but it was as if everything, people and events, had combined to block her path. That allowed her to observe that only the men, the cooks, carpenters and ostlers were dying; the women were being dragged to the first clear space, to be thrown to the ground once their clothing had been ripped from their bodies, several already being raped. Faced with the reality, and with a sinking heart that had her wishing she had taken Metullus's offer, the same fate approached her. Grabbed by several tribesmen, the one who had her hair exerted the greatest force to drag her out to a place where the ground was clear of blood and bodies. Her garments, of a finer quality than those that had suffered before her, had been ripped with ease, her attempts at modesty as she sought to cover her nakedness causing her assailants great mirth.

With her curled hair and fine clothes they must have known she was special, and they decided to toy with her instead of indulging in an immediate violation. Claudia found herself spun round, punched and pushed back and forth, trying to shut out of her mind the leering faces, the spittle-flecked lips and the hoarse cries she could not comprehend. Somehow she knew there was an argument going on as to who should have the privilege of violating her first, the greatest prize, a very young woman who had been exquisitely clothed and, now naked, showed the full figure and smooth skin of a true beauty.

Whatever bargain was struck she was eventually grabbed by two individuals, her arms pinned as she was hauled to the ground. One look at the man who had won her had been enough to make Claudia want to close her eyes; yellow teeth, dark bronzed skin ravaged with smallpox, eyes like a small pig, but she fought against that. Whatever her fate, Claudia had had to look it in the eye, to let this barbarian beast know that whatever they did they could not break her Roman spirit. The glare of her look, and the pearl she spat into his face made him hesitate just a second, so that neither he nor she heard, from behind him, the swish of the *falcata*. The great steel blade of the Celtic sword had appeared in the corner of one eye like a flash of lightning, and the look had died in those piggy eyes as the head was lopped off the body, to jump free from the trunk like some child's toy, that followed by a fountain of blood that drenched her, forcing her at last to close her eyes.

The shouting had stopped, and so had the

screaming. Claudia had opened her eyes again, to see that everyone who had surrounded her had fallen back bar this one silhouette framed against the blue sky, a big man, even taller and broader than Aulus. The hair was long, and as he had leant forward, hand outstretched to raise her up, it had turned from silhouetted black to a red-gold colour, but, more than that, the talisman her saviour wore, which had fallen from his bent neck almost to her face, took her eye.

Gold, and as his shadow had cut out the brightness of the sun it allowed her to see that it was shaped like an eagle in flight, with the wings picked out in delicate engraving.

The moment when Claudia's eyes met those of her husband was a sad one; he looking for the degree of affection he had known before, she unable to give it to him. Yet she felt a tenderness that came to her as a surprise, which meant that most of the words rehearsed for this confrontation remained unsaid. What followed was hurtful, just as much because she chose to lie rather than tell the truth. Aulus, seeing her condition, had struggled to hide his lacerated feelings, yet such was his open nature that he could not succeed. Claudia lacked the heart to wound him further, yet half-suspected that her actions were prompted as much by the fear of what Aulus might do if she told him the truth. At all costs she must protect the child she was carrying.

'I will not have you speak of disgrace,' Aulus had said, wiping the tears from his eyes. He knew that to display his emotions was wrong, but so wounded was his heart, so sure was he that he was to blame, that he could not help himself. He wondered why Claudia seemed strangely calm, as if, having practised for this meeting, she had used up all her emotion before he arrived. He could not know of the turmoil that filled her breast, could not know of the strain she was under when she replied in an even tone.

'I cannot think what to call it, husband. What is the bearing of another man's child, if it is not disgrace? I prayed that you would not find me, prayed that you would never know.'

He had raised his reddened eyes, as if trying to see through the canvas roof of the wagon so that he could ask the gods for help. He knew what he should do, adopt the same lack of sentiment with which he had campaigned all his life, the same obligation to his race that had him personally strangle the Macedonian King in front of the Temple of *Jupiter Maximus*; he was a Roman soldier and he should behave like one. How many women with child had died at the hands of his legionaries, how many children would be born as slaves who had been conceived in freedom? He had a choice, to kill Claudia or to disown her, both actions the society of which he was a member would applaud. How could he be so strong in battle, so callous when necessary in conquest, yet so weak in his private affairs? Would the gods not damn him for such frailty?

'I will not put you aside, in any way.'

Her voice was still even, masking disappointment. 'So all you have achieved will come to nought? The great Macedonicus, a laughing stock, because his wife bore the child of a barbarian Celt?'

Aulus had taken her hand then, his voice thick with emotion, but his mind was active, seeking and arriving at a solution, daring the deities to object. 'There is a way, my love, there is a way.'

Bending to kiss that hand, he had failed to see the look of deep pity in her eyes.

Aulus put his wife in the care of Cholon and a villa was found on the coast where Claudia could remain out of sight, with temporary, local servants who were not told of her identity. There she waited, her belly continuing to swell, while her husband sought a final victory over the man who had so abused his wife. For someone who had fought so long and hard, the end came quickly; it was almost as if the Druid's powers had deserted him. He seemed incapable of winning a single engagement and failure only accelerated the decline in his military fortunes so that many of his warriors, lacking either plunder or trophies, were led away by their disgruntled chieftains.

Aulus encouraged them and used his already successful tactic to detach them completely, even lenient enough to free some hostages and slaves already captured, at a huge personal cost in terms of money lost. As long as they swore an oath to Rome, and promised to observe the peace, he left them to settle back on their tribal lands. The Averici and the Bregones, who had fought the hardest, were the last tribes to depart. The former, deadly dangerous on their swift ponies, simply disappeared into their mountain fastness, wanting no truck with Rome. Masugori, the Bregones chieftain, took the wiser course. Even although his tribal lands were deep in the interior the young chieftain, newly elevated to the leadership through the death in battle of his father, took the trouble to make a formal peace with Rome, having been advised by his priests that such a thing would in the future protect both him and his people. Aulus, just as keen, treated him as an honoured guest and entertained him in his tent, even invited him to take part in his family prayers, a mark of real respect. Titus was ordered to consort with the senior Bregones warriors, to learn some of their language and study their method of fighting.

But it was the chief who mattered. Masugori was

small, swarthy, with soft brown eyes. The gold and silver objects he wore to proclaim his wealth and power, flashing in the light from the dozens of oil lamps that lit the army commander's tent, seemed too big, too heavy a burden of ornament for such a slight frame. Yet Aulus sensed a degree of acumen, one obvious pointer the fact that Masugori had taken the trouble to try to learn Latin. The proconsul sought to tempt him into an alliance with Rome, but the young chieftain obviously saw that for what it was, a ploy to place the burden of tribal containment on the Bregones, thus relieving Rome of the need to keep troops in Spain. It was with some subtlety that he manoeuvred his way out of the various snares and temptations Aulus put in his way to end up with what he wanted; not a confrontation with his neighbours, just peace with the main coastal power that would allow his tribe to trade from the interior in peace and ensure a degree of prosperity.

Of more interest was the man Aulus had been fighting, and here he had a young man who knew Brennos well. The physical description he already had: tall, blue-eyed with red-gold hair and simply dressed, eschewing the display in which Celts were prone to indulge. No torque or valuable breastplates adorned Brennos, he wore only one decorative charm around his neck, made of gold and shaped like an eagle in flight, said to be a trophy taken by the previous Brennos from the sack of the Temple of *Apollo* at Delphi, and to be blessed with magical powers.

Hearing that made Aulus fearful; the words of the prophecy he had heard as a youngster had never left him. What Masugori was describing sounded very like the drawing that had burst into flames in Lucius's hand and this was most certainly an eagle that did not fly. Did it mean that he would meet this Brennos and that would be the day of his death? Aulus found the thought strangely comforting, being less fearful of something known than something mysterious and as a soldier he had long ago ceased to worry about death, only concerned that the manner of his end be appropriate. So be it, if the gods willed it, such a thing would come to pass, but he silently vowed that he would take with him to Hades the man who had caused Rome, and himself, so much difficulty. More troubling was what Masugori went on to say; the notion that Brennos was not truly beaten.

'He will not accept that the Romans are too powerful.'

'You said this to him?' asked Aulus. The young chieftain nodded, his nose wrinkling as he picked up the scented odour of a Greek slave, leaning forward to refill his goblet with wine. 'And how did he reply?'

'He insists he has spoken with the gods of our

race, and the message is clear. We Celts have ten men to every one of yours...'

The youngster's black eyes took on a fearful look as he conjured up the image of the eagle charm that the Druid had then taken into his fingers. He called it his talisman, the harbinger of his destiny. How many times had Masugori listened as Brennos had told him that the man who wore this would conquer the legions. Like so many prophecies, it had not come to pass; someone, somewhere, had misread the omens.

'He refuses to believe that we cannot fight you and win.'

Aulus had asked his next question with some hesitation, feeling, deep in his being that he already knew the answer. 'And what does he intend now?'

'Not surrender. He has gone north into the mountains. A man like Brennos will want to question the gods from a place close to the sky, but he will return. He swears it is his fate to confront Rome, only the means and the method elude him. Nothing has happened to dent that belief.'

The sun had been behind Brennos as he had uttered his parting words, framing his red-gold hair like a halo. Even in shadow his bright blue eyes had blazed with anger while his parting words, which had sounded so much like a prophecy, were seared into the young chieftain's brain.

'Go, make your peace, Masugori, but before

either you or I are dust, every man who accepts Rome's word will end as bones on a bloody battlefield, heaped high to bring glory to a Roman general.'

Those were the very last words Brennos had uttered, as he lifted the golden eagle and put it to his lips.

CHAPTER FOUR

The Falerii house was empty now, the guests gone, leaving Lucius alone. Outside the atrium was cold from the air of late winter. It was rare for a man of his eminence to be afforded such solitude, but the death in childbirth of his wife had forced even the most ardent supplicant away from his door. He stared at the papers before him, untouched on his desk, and allowed himself a quiet smile. The last to depart had been his closest political allies, all famous men, all noble and some of the best brains in the Senate, yet not even they guessed what was about to happen. With exquisite timing his band of hired thugs, wrapped in heavy, hooded cloaks, had been led in via the servants' quarters by his Dacian body slave, just as the last senator had exited through the front gate. Their leader, Gafon, manager of a gladiator school who had lost everything gambling, saluted Lucius Falerius with his sword as he emerged from his private study.

'Leave your men here,' said Lucius sharply, indicating to Ragas that he should watch them lest they be tempted to pilfer something.

'As you command, Lu...'

Gafon was not allowed to finish as the senator cut across him. 'I shall not use your name, be so good as to avoid using mine.'

His eyes flicked past the object of this rebuke to the shadowy group of men. Their leader bowed, sword still held in salute, but he was looking obsequiously at Lucius's back. The older man had already spun on his heel to re-enter his study. Gafon turned to his men and with a shrug sought to play down the insult, seeking to convey that for what they were earning tonight, the purple-striped bastard could be as snooty as he liked.

'Would that you had come alone,' Lucius said, warming his hands at the brazier before finally raising his deep brown eyes to engage those of his visitor.

'I didn't see the need, your honour.'

The eyes closed and the body tensed as Lucius tried to control his anger, the effort making his slender frame shake slightly. Normally the most controlled of men he was surprised at this reaction, even more alarmed at the thought that he was actually nervous.

'It is not for you to see anything!'

'If we do right tonight no one is going to have too

much doubt who's behind it. No band of drunken youngsters is going to kill a man like...' Gafon hesitated, not wishing to use the name. 'Regardless of how far gone they are.'

'There is a difference between cackling rumour in the market-place and evidence sufficient to lay before a praetor.'

That last word made Gafon swallow hard; the mere mention of a magistrate was enough to remind him of how close he stood to being sold into debt bondage. Winter was no time for games and gladiator fights. If he did not come up with some money soon his creditors would take over his property and sell him off as a farm labourer to some distant rancher.

'What is important is that the deed is undertaken unseen. If you are observed, and you are connected to me, I will pay the penalty for your misjudgement.'

The debt-ridden manager had a sudden fear that the commission was going to be withdrawn, which was not something that would go down well with the party of cut-throats he had gathered. If they found out that they had emerged from their slums for no reward they might just decide to take it out on him.

Lucius Falerius was considering abandoning the whole affair. He had a personal matter to settle as well as a political one, so a degree of self-examination was required to separate the two and ensure that one was not overshadowing the other. This idiot was right; if he and his band succeeded tonight, few would hesitate to lay the blame for what happened at his door. The idea that some of the drunken patrician youths who infested the streets and taverns, with too much money and too little sense, would murder a plebeian tribune was risible. Would it have been wiser to hang onto a few of his guests, so that they could swear he was home, grief stricken and wailing at the moment when Tiberius Livonius breathed his last?

No! Evidence from his friends would not be believed; if anything it would only serve to convince the rumour mill of the truth of their speculations. His best defence lay in avoiding such a contrivance and he would rather rely on his word alone. It had to be done; a formal break that would force men to decide which camp they adhered to. Some senators, either from a belief that the ideas of Tiberius Livonius would enhance their prospects, or even, in a very few cases, from misguided ideology, backed proposals that Lucius knew to be inimical to the safety of the Republic. Once let Livonius alter the balance of power in the *Comita Tribalis,* and it would be lost forever, turning what was an easily bypassed talking shop into a legislature to challenge the Senate.

His so-called Agrarian Law, limiting the amount

of public land a citizen could hold, struck at the very heart of the faction Lucius represented. That was bad enough; the idea that the same land, sequestered to the state, should be divided up into small lots and gifted to the landless scum who filled the poorest quarters of Rome, was nothing less than a bribe to the mob. To Lucius that was a recipe for endless trouble, because the mob could never be satisfied; to give in to their demands once was to open the door to an endless run of fresh claims.

Worse was the plebeian tribune's desire to extend Roman citizenship to the whole of Italy, which would permanently dilute patrician power by widening the franchise. This would strike at the wealth and political authority of the same class by allowing inter-marriage, as well as extending to such people the kind of trade concessions that buttressed senatorial wealth. With a keen sense of history, Lucius Falerius knew that empires were unstable constructs, with no gods-given right to continued existence. What was being proposed would weaken the Roman state, and once the spirit of the Goddess *Discordia* was let loose, there was no telling where matters would end. Tiberius Livonius had to be stopped, and the best way to kill off the body of such ideas was to chop off the head.

He cared nothing for himself in this; the power and majesty of Rome was everything to Lucius Falerius. He had given his every waking moment for a full thirty years to increasing that Imperium so would gladly give his last breath to maintain it. To his mind only the *optimates* could be entrusted with such a task; they were the men who had supervised the creation of the empire; they must combine to fight off the *populares* who, by appealing to the base greed of the lower orders, would drag Rome down, as other empires had been, by a fatal weakening of the structure of authority that had brought about success. Nothing counted against that single object, certainly not the life of one senator. Without doubt they would point to him, but who would believe that a man just delivered of a son, with his wife newly dead because of it, would choose that moment to murder his greatest political rival?

For the first time in two decades that Sibylline prophecy surfaced, and he recalled that night in the cave, as well as the terrors and reflections that had followed; Aulus so fearful, he determined to be rational. His childhood friend had certainly tamed his mighty foe; was this the moment he would strike to save Rome's fame? Was there some truth in that Sibylline nonsense after all? The image of the eagle he had never forgotten, but surely it did not apply to a man like Livonius, unless the gods saw him as a bird of prey bringing down the Roman state. No! His enemy was no taloned eagle, more a twittering sparrow needing to be silenced.

'Here,' said Lucius, throwing Gafon a small leather bag full of coins. It was caught and weighed by a person well used to calculating the contents of a purse, a man who knew that what he had in his hand was either his whole agreed fee, or something very close to it. 'We agreed half your fee in advance. You will already have ascertained that the purse contains more.'

'Does it, your honour?' Gafon's eyes were wide, and larded with insincere surprise.

'I have another task for you.' That changed the innocent look to one of barely disguised suspicion. 'It is nothing like as dangerous, but it is, to me, just as important. It therefore qualifies for a substantial reward.'

His hired assassin was thinking that if there was another fee, it was one of which his thugs would know nothing, therefore payment of whatever was required, if he agreed to it, would be for him alone.

'I have a slave who has betrayed me,' said Lucius, fingering a tightly rolled scroll of paper. 'I could of course just kill him, I have the legal right to do so, but that would not send out the message that I require.'

'He could die beside Livonius.'

Lucius shook his head. This Gafon was stupid, but he dealt with that every day, quite often with men who held high rank, so masking the thought came easily. 'Nor would his body in the street point out what's required, quite apart from his obvious association with me.'

Lucius waited for Gafon to draw the conclusion he sought to convey; that this household slave was in some way connected to the party of *populares* who supported Tiberius Livonius; that his death had to send a message to them as well as the rest of Rome's slaves; that spying on their masters would result in only one fate; not just death but total oblivion.

'You want him to disappear?'

'Yes. How that is done I leave to you. I am about to call for him and give him some instructions relating to your task. He will readily understand that I distrust you, with the same arrogance that makes him think I have complete faith in him. I will ask him to accompany you, and watch to make sure that you carry out my instructions to the letter. How you do it and when I leave to you, but I want him disposed of, yet some sign of his demise to be publicly visible. Carry out that, as well, and your fee for the night's work will be increased substantially.'

'I accept,' Gafon replied crisply.

'You do not wish to ponder this?' asked Lucius, with an arch, almost amused expression. The owner of the gladiator school, more concerned with his indebtedness than the prospect of another murder, shook his head. 'The slave will have with him a scroll, and that too must disappear.' Gafon nodded, then grinned as the senator continued. 'He will also have some money of his own, which I expect you will relieve him of.'

That Gafon would have to share, but he was more concerned with how to make a dead body disappear.

'Make sure you come back alone to tell me what you have done,' Lucius added. 'You will never talk of this to anyone, at the peril of the same fate as those you will dispose of tonight. And tell those brawlers you have with you to hold their tongues as well.'

Gafon was well aware of the potency of the threat. Armed with a sword he might be, but against the power and dignity of this man he would be impotent. He could plead till he was blue that he had been hired to do murder, but that would just guarantee his own removal. That his paymaster may suffer subsequently was little compensation.

Lucius went to the door and signalled that Ragas should enter. With a last glance at the assembled thugs he did so; coming into the well-lit study it was possible for Gafon to examine him. Taller than both men in the room he carried himself as though he was the lord and Lucius the slave. His skin was discoloured around his neck, stained by the metal of the slave collar he had worn for many years, but even that did nothing to dent his natural dignity.

Loosely dressed in a light tunic, the muscles of his body rippled on arms and breast and he showed no sign at all that the cold of the open atrium had affected him.

Gafon knew enough about fighting men to recognise a boxer when he saw one. It was in the face certainly; the nose which had once been straight and handsome flattened by numerous blows; the scar tissue on the brow and the raised knuckles on the large hands. This man would have acted as bodyguard as well as a body slave, protecting Lucius from assault in the troubled city streets. But Gafon was also struck by a similarity of features in both men. Lucius was like an aesthetic older relation of the sturdier slave. His hair was receding now and no doubt his fine dark brown mop had once been as thick as that of the servant, but it was around the eyes of both men that the similarity was most marked; deep brown yet penetrating pupils under marked eyebrows.

'That will be all,' Lucius said to Gafon, as soon as the assassin had managed to get a good look at his victim. 'Wait outside the door.'

Gafon obeyed, masking his surprise that one so close to Lucius had betrayed him. But it made sense, for the boxer would be with his master more than any other person, both inside the Falerii house and out on the streets. Who would know more about his movements, whom he visited, the senators he spoke with. Given that most men where blind to the presence of a slave, and would talk freely when he was close, what plans he hatched with people whom Tiberius Livonius might assume were on his side.

Behind the closed door the slave was receiving from his master's hand a scroll stating that he had been the property of the Falerii family but was now, by order of the head of that household, free. It was an act that should have been witnessed by either his friends or a magistrate, but since he had held the office of consul he had decided to dispense with anything public for the very good reason that he was not sure he wanted this manumission to be generally known. Lucius was uncomfortable, certainly more so than his now ex-slave. Ragas had always carried himself in the manner to which he had been born, a war leader among his own tribe, which had rendered a troubled edge to their relationship from the day he had been accepted as a gift from Aulus Cornelius. Not one to suffer insolence, Lucius had made the man's life a misery, seeking to rupture a spirit determined to challenge all notions of servitude. It had taken months and he could not claim to have broken him, but he had got Ragas to acknowledge who gave orders and who obeyed, in the process forming, for him, a strange admiration. Lucius did not like Ragas one little bit, but he saw qualities in him; some traits that he had himself, others more physical that he lacked but wished he possessed.

They shared a steely determination, a refusal to buckle under adversity. Where the slave had been physically hard, Lucius possessed a will of iron that could not be deflected from any objective, once set, a trait which had earned him his nickname, Nerva. Beyond those first confrontations, the master had found that his body slave had a brain as well. He learnt Latin with ease, both the written and spoken word, and possessed a devious mind, but it was the attraction of his wife Ameliana for this Dacian which had brought the greatest service of all. The couple had endured near-twenty childless years, not unusual in a Roman family, but galling to a man as proud as Lucius. Adoption was the commonplace solution for a patrician family, yet he was unwilling to take that step, not wishing to open himself up to the gossip of the mob or see ribald drawings on his own villa walls regarding his potency in the bedchamber. Originally furious at the notice his wife afforded to a slave, as well as the nocturnal scrabblings it engendered, his natural pragmatism forced him to look at it objectively. Finally he came to see it as the solution to an intractable dilemma, and to relish the market-place joke that now attached to his name; that he took such a long view of everything that he had saved up his seed over all those years for one mighty endeavour.

'In the end, you served me well, better than either of us could have imagined.'

Ragas held up the scroll that made him both a free man and a Roman citizen. 'For this I would have done more.'

'Will you stay in the city?' That warranted a shrug from a man who now had the right not to respond. 'A man of your abilities will prosper here and you always have my good offices to call upon should you need assistance.'

'We have agreed many times, Lucius Falerius, that haste is fatal. I shall look around me, see what I see, then decide on my next course of action.'

'I have one last job for you, tonight, if you wish to undertake it. Naturally should you do so there would be a fee.' Lucius held up another small leather pouch. The Dacian took it and bounced the leather purse in his hand, causing Lucius to add, 'Those men outside have been engaged for a very special service.'

'The final reckoning. No more debates.'

That brought forth, from Lucius, a full smile. Proud of his own deductive powers he liked to observe them in a man he had some claim to have trained. No expression on his face betrayed the thought that he would miss Ragas, not for his insolence perhaps but certainly for his sagacity as well as his powerful physical and protective presence. But he had the good name of his house to consider, and closure, just as it was for Tiberius Livonius, was the best method of securing that.

'I wish to be sure they do as they are told! Go with them, Ragas. You need take no part, but you can bring back the news that what orders I have given them have been carried out to the letter.'

'No one to survive?'

It was with a wolfish grin that Lucius replied. 'Precisely.'

CHAPTER FIVE

Lucius waited till he was sure they had all gone before making his way to the room of the wet nurse, she asleep by the brazier, her own child cradled in her arms. He ignored her, passing on to look into the cot, which contained the new-born child he had publicly acknowledged as his son. The infant lay at peace, the long black lashes on his eyes seeming to cover a goodly portion of his face. The jet-black hair of his birth would go, but it would come back thick and as strong as the physical presence masked by the soft rounded features of a baby.

Lucius stroked the tiny hand. 'I pray to the gods that you will grow to manhood, and stand as potent as I do as a representative of a noble house. You will be the son I have always longed for. Tomorrow we will commence the ceremonies. Within a week the whole Roman world will know of your arrival.'

With that he turned on his heel and left. On his way back to his study he passed the room in which his wife lay, silent and pale upon a bier, her white bloodless hands folded across her breasts. Lucius Falerius did not spare her cadaver a second's glance.

The streets of Rome were never deserted, but for such a teeming, crowded city they were, on this night, ominously quiet. It was cold and perhaps the taverns were full, and what trouble the wine would bring was brewing within them. Those out, seeing Gafon and his band approach, thought it prudent to choose another route to whichever destination they were heading. There was a certain amount of shuffling of the pack as Gafon tried to ensure that Ragas, like the others in a heavy cloak, led them, while the slave was equally determined to bring up the rear, for the gang leader was gnawing on a tricky problem, whether to kill Ragas before his main task was completed, or after? The mistake Gafon made was to look so hard at Ragas while he tried to decide. For a man that loved to fight, had been a potent warrior and was at his happiest in the boxing square it sent a danger signal that other men might not have sensed. Ragas, noticing the indifference of the other members of the party, wondered if he was not indulging in a fantasy without foundation, but once alerted to a potential threat he could not relax.

Neither man had much time to think, since the Cave of Lupercal, where the rites to mark the cult were nearing completion, was no great distance from the Temple of *Ceres*. Home of the plebeian Aediles, this was the known destination of Tiberius Livonius and his supporters once the ceremonies were over. At least Gafon could be happy, as they skirted the Forum Boracum, they were heading in the right direction, towards the wharves and warehouses of the Port of Rome, a teeming warren of alleys, empty at night, where the dead body of a slave could be carried without causing fuss. He had finally decided what to do; assassinate Tiberius first, then see to his secondary task. Ragas would be decapitated after being killed, his head and body thrown separately into the Tiber. The waters of the river would carry both parts, at differing speeds, all the way downriver, and washed ashore in different places, they would never be connected.

Gafon heard them coming, four noisy individuals who thought themselves immune to the hazards faced by ordinary mortals. Like the men who had stopped on their way to the Cave of Lupercal to attend the recent Falerii birth they were dressed in goatskins. Now the dried sacrificial blood that gave potency to the adherents to the cult streaked their bodies, illuminated by the flaring torches they carried. Gafon had placed three men who would let them pass, and put himself at the head of the other three to intercept his prey. The lights they carried, plus their own noisy conversation, made things ridiculously easy and they did not hear the men who slipped out behind to follow in their wake, and showed little shock when further progress was barred by Gafon. Even when the hidden weapons were brought to their attention, no hint of fear could be detected in their behaviour.

'Do you not know who I am?' demanded the tallest of the group, lifting the goat's mask from his head. Even sweat-streaked and blood-stained there was no mistaking the well-known profile of Tiberius Livonius, the plebeian tribune.

'We know,' Gafon replied.

Tiberius Livonius pointed towards the sword in Gafon's hand. 'Then you will know to even raise that in my presence is to invite eternal damnation.'

'Damnation is something we have already, Tribune. Happen you'll find when you cross the Styx that what awaits you is the kind of life we folk live as normal.'

So sure was Tiberius of his status that he did not even attempt to raise his hands to defend himself and the shock on his face was as much from the dent to his certainties as it was to the blade of Gafon's sword slicing into his bare gut. The eyes opened wide as the body arched towards the gang leader as, with the same skill as he taught his gladiators, the weapon was rammed sideways and up, to tear through the vital organs and ensure instant death. Gafon felt the tribune's blood flowing hot over the sword handle and his hand, watched as the croak of protest turned to a gurgle of bright red as the froth of yet more began to spill out of his mouth. Around him the light faded as those bearing the torches fell noisily to his men, screaming as they were repeatedly stabbed and clubbed by idiots who had no idea how to execute a clean kill.

In the silence that followed, Gafon took up a torch and turned to the alleyway in which Ragas was standing, hood up and cloak held tightly to his body. 'Come, friend, and see that they are all dead. Then you can return to your master and give him the news.'

Ragas declined to move. 'I can see well enough from here.'

'Then you have the eyes of a god. For me, I would rather come closer so that I could be certain.'

Good with a sword, Gafon was less accomplished at the telling of falsehoods, so his words struck a false note that was highlighted by the torchlight and the bodies around his feet. Ragas, looking into Gafon's eyes, saw no humour, no reassurance in those eyes, all he saw was the possibility of his own death. Having committed such a crime, the whole gang should have dispersed instantly. Yet there was still a lingering doubt, for his death would have had to be ordered and he could just not bring himself to believe that even Lucius Falerius would stoop so low.

'Go on your way,' he said to Gafon, 'and I will return with the news of your success.'

'Look at them,' Gafon demanded, jabbing toward the bodies with his sword. Ragas threw off his cloak and ran then, and the voice behind him cried out the words he had dreaded to hear, words that told him that his fears were real. 'Get him. Ten gold denarii to the man who brings me his head.'

The pitch-black alleys of the port were both a help and a hindrance. He was aided by the sheer number, but handicapped by the lack of certainty as to his direction, as well as the numerous objects that lay hidden in his path, objects which saw him more than once crashing painfully onto the hard packed earth. That he had to do silently, so that his ears could alert him to the proximity of the noisy pursuit. There were stars above his head, but not enough to steer a course by, and they were often cut off from view by the overhang of the higher warehouses. Common sense told him to stop on occasions and listen to see if the pursuit had passed him by. Renewed fear made him move, there being no security in noises, the distance of which he could not discern. Several times he nearly ran into one of Gafon's thugs, alerted only by a flicker of torchlight that the route he had chosen was one to take him into danger, not out of it.

His luck ran out after about ten minutes. He saw one torch in front of him, only to find as he turned that another was casting a glow at an intersection to his rear. Ragas felt his heart contract as that glow turned to flame, and he saw behind him a scarred, grinning brawler carrying a spiked club. He was grinning because behind his quarry he could see quite plainly his leader, Gafon, sword in hand and so could Ragas when he turned to look. A boxer has fast reflexes; he has to, when in a bout only a split second separates him from delivering a blow or receiving one. Ragas did not hesitate; he ran at the thug holding the club, knowing that he stood a better chance against that than he did against the sharp blade and lethal point of a gladiator's sword. The thug readied himself, club half-raised to smash in the approaching skull, as, behind him, Ragas could hear Gafon moving in to complete the kill.

The way he launched himself, feet first at the ankles of the brawler, one foot striking home, threw the man off balance. The spiked club was already swinging, but the increased distance to a body now on the ground, added to his own loss of stability, took most of the strength out of the blow. It still broke an upraised left forearm, the crack of the bone going echoing off the alley walls. Ragas had spun upwards, fear making him unaware of the pain; he knew his left arm was useless, but that was not needed by a right-handed fighter. The bare-knuckled punch took the clubman right on the edge of his jawbone and the crack of that going was audible, accompanied as it was by a scream of pain that died in the brute's throat as he was knocked unconscious. Ragas was out from under the collapsing body and running, cradling his broken arm, before the body hit the ground. He heard Gafon curse as he leapt over the inert gang member, as well as the ring of his sword blade as it connected with something solid. It was not any sense of direction that made Ragas turn left, just the need of self-preservation, but his hopes lifted as he saw the silver blue streak of the river ahead of him.

The Tiber was not safety; it was fast flowing and treacherous, at its worst as it ran under the inner city bridges, doubly so to a man with only one good arm, but it was better than the certainty that lay behind him, a sword from which he could in no way protect himself. As he emerged on to the open wharf Ragas dug his feet into the wooden boards to add an extra ounce of purchase to his run. At the edge he threw himself with all the force he could muster, his dive taking him clear of the tied up boats. In the interval between leaving terra firma and the icy water closing over his head, Ragas heard Gafon yell in frustration.

His putative assassin was only ten feet behind the

splash, but for all that mattered it could have been ten leagues. Gafon could not swim, and even if he had been able to nothing would have got him into the Tiber at a point where it was narrow and deep. Instead he stopped, searching the silver sheen of moon-reflecting water to see if he could spot a floating head. One by one he was joined by the rest of his gang, who were sent downriver to look out for Ragas.

'He'll be dead for certain,' Gafon said, when they re-gathered. 'I'm sure I heard his arm go when it took that club. There's no way that he could survive in that river with two good arms, let alone one.'

In some ways Gafon was trying to reassure himself, yet as they made their way back to where the fallen clubman still lay, he reasoned that it made little difference. The odds of the slave surviving went from nil to near impossible, and if he did, would he want anyone to know; the only person interested was the one who had ordered him killed.

'Look at him,' Gafon said, as he stood over the crumpled heap of his gang member. 'Supposed to be a street fighter and yet he gets knocked out by one blow.'

The torchlight picked up the pale cream of the scroll that lay against the recumbent body. Gafon picked it up, handed his torch to another and opened it. He could not read it, but the words of Lucius Falerius filled his thoughts.

'That scroll must disappear too.'

'So it shall,' Gafon reasoned, sensing that in his hand he held a guarantee of his own security. 'Into my strongbox.'

'Right, lads,' he called. 'Get back to your houses. I'll go and tell our stuck up employer that his wishes have been carried out.'

The shock of the freezing water, coming straight off the snow covered mountains of the Apennines, sent a jolt through Ragas's body, yet it was not just the cold he feared but the speed of a watercourse in spate. Tumbling downriver in the teeming cataract, he fought to get his head sufficiently above water to keep air in his lungs, difficult with one arm useless, while with his good arm he sought to stay away from the riverbank. In that Ragas succeeded, but he had forgotten about the Tiber bridges and it was those that did for him. With arches constraining the waters, the speed of the flow increased and he was sent tumbling into a raging torrent that spun him head over heels so that he no longer knew which was up or down.

Still under water, his body going rigid with the cold, Ragas knew he was going to drown, for with only one arm he had not the means to save himself. His mind turned first to the gods he had worshipped all his life to plead for intercession,

aware that they never had in all the years he had
made obeisance to them and that they were not
going to now. But then as his lungs filled with water
he saw the image of that child in the basket as he
had handed it to Lucius, the infant that ensured his
bloodline was safe. So perhaps his gods had not
deserted him after all. He could have, many times,
died in battle, but they had kept him alive till he had
fulfilled that one function. So, if the earth had no
further use of him, he could depart it in peace.

The corpse that washed up downriver was
beyond recognition, naked, battered as it was by
rocks and scarred by sand so that it looked as if it
had been flayed; there was no way to tell who the
man was or from what part of society he had come.
Bodies washed downriver towards the port of Ostia
were nothing new; they could be paupers dead of
starvation, victims of robbery and murder, slaves
killed by their masters, even men in despair who
took their own life.

Those who found it were decent folk, farmers
and fisher folk, and pious enough to appease
Mania, Goddess of the Dead, so they had the good
grace to set up a pyre and give the body some sort
of burial, watching as the soul of this unknown
casualty was taken up to the heavens in the smoke
of his burning corpse.

Gafon returned alone as promised to the Falerii household, to tell Lucius that his orders had been fulfilled, glad that the man who had employed him seemed satisfied enough to gift him another purse of gold for his efforts. But he was not allowed to depart without what the senator called advice, but which he knew to be a threat.

'Be careful how you pay off those to whom you owe money, Gafon. Sudden evidence of wealth, or even claims of unexpected good fortune, makes men wonder, and that causes them to gossip.'

'I shall take care, Lucius Falerius, and if I can ever be again of service...'

'I cannot see that we shall ever need to meet again.'

Gafon felt the scroll inside his tunic, pressed against his belly. They would meet again, all right, when things died down. Lucius Falerius would pay handsomely for that, just to ensure that no one connected the disappearance of his warrior body slave with the murders he and his band had just committed. He exited to streets that were now full of wild people and flaming torches, as those who had supported the plebeian tribune, and saw in him hope for the future, reacted noisily to the news of his death.

CHAPTER SIX

He should not have been there, wherever there happened to be, and as Clodius forced his eyes open, he tried at the same time to focus so that he could locate himself. Normally he woke in the shack, warm when the wind was not too fierce, with the familiar smell of the sod-brick walls, his pig snuffling, chickens clacking and the odour of peat smouldering on the fire. Now he was cold and what little sun penetrated the canopy of trees above his head hurt his eyes. He turned on his side, but the tangled tree roots looked so menacing close up that he threw himself onto his back, stifling a groan as the stabbing pain filled his entire skull. Slowly it subsided to a dull ache, along with the first flicker of memory: an all-night drinking session with his friends. It had not started that way, just a quick snort to be friendly, but one cup of the rough red wine, unwatered, had followed another, until the prospect of Fulmina's anger at his prolonged absence faded. By the time they had started on the grain spirits that was distant indeed, and it continued to recede with each cup, till any concern about what his wife would say finally evaporated completely.

Now such thoughts came back with a vengeance! He lay, eyes still tightly shut, going over in his throbbing head the words he knew would greet him; he had heard them from Fulmina often enough before. Clodius opened his eyes a fraction and struggled slowly to his feet, knowing her wrath would just have to be faced, and the sooner the better. His mouth was as dry as a bone, with his tongue like a piece of leather in the middle and his nose had that painful sensation at the top that feels like the start of a cold. He must have been snoring fit to wake the dead. Gently he rocked back and forth, aware that he was still suffering from the effects of drink, putting his hand out to steady himself against the nearest tree.

'Never again,' he croaked, rubbing his throat, this a vow he often made in the morning when his head hurt, one he struggled to keep when the sun went down. He looked around at the unfamiliar surroundings and his voice croaked again as he berated himself. 'You've done it again, Clodius Terentius.'

Most people, when they got drunk could at least find their way home, even crawling. Not Clodius:

drink made him seek the open air where he could look at the stars and sing melodies to the gods in the heavens. Sweet songs to him, but Fulmina was fond of telling him otherwise; that if he had heard himself singing in his cups, then he would know why the gods never granted him any of his requests. Rubbing his fingers into his temples provided some temporary relief from the ache in his head, but it did nothing for his mouth, or his throat. He tried to swallow to alleviate his suffering, but no fluid came, so he pushed himself off from his supporting tree, letting his weight carry him down the hill to where he was sure he would find water.

'Fulmina.'

His voice felt as though it was full of sand as he croaked his wife's name. Why was it everybody saw her as a good and kind person? He stumbled through the trees, fending himself off as he lost his balance, cursing her and all her friends as he did so, people who were always telling him how lucky he was to have such a wife. Even his men friends did so, forever remarking that she had kept her figure, but they did not have to live with her, and perhaps if she had not been so kind and generous and had avoided feeding anyone who cared to call at their door, they would not have reached the stage, quite so quickly, where everything, including the small farm they had once owned, had had to be sold.

The stream was gurgling, the trees forming a

dark canopy over the clear brook. Clodius walked straight in up to his knees, gasping at the freezing temperature as the water of a melted glacier filled his sandals. He bent down to drink, telling himself that, knowing this river, he would be home before the sand had time to run through the glass. Clodius had forgotten that he had been drinking Dabo's rough spirit the previous night, the stuff his old army chum distilled from grain, a brew much more potent than wine. Worse still, a copious drink in the morning tended to leave you just as drunk as you were the night before. His cupped hands moved rapidly as he gulped down quantities of icy water, throwing yet more over his head. The dryness in his throat eased immediately, but as he stood up, he swayed alarmingly and a warm glow filled his body as the pain in his head evaporated. Suddenly he threw back his head and laughed out loud, his long straggly hair still wet, dripping water down the back of his grubby tunic.

'What an old woman I am!' he shouted, waving his arm as though addressing an audience. 'To be afraid of a slip of a thing like Fulmina.' His round, purple face took on a deep and threatening frown, as he loudly addressed his imaginary audience, *Nemestrinus*, the God of the Woods and the nymphs that inhabited these forest glades. 'Am I not her husband? Is she not bound to obey me?'

Clodius was shaking his fist at the imagined face

of his spouse, but it stopped abruptly as the child's cries rent the air. He staggered slightly, losing his balance as he sought the source, so that the freezing water, coming up to his chest as he fell to his knees, made him wince. Struggling to his feet again, Clodius splashed through the stream towards the sound, till he saw the small white bundle in the tiny patch of sunlight. He also saw the little pink face, screwed up in displeasure, and the wide-open mouth. Bending for a closer look, his bulk cut out the sunlight from the child's tightly closed eyes, which added to its distress. Clodius noticed the disturbed state of the ground around the tiny glade, evidence that it had been visited by men on horseback and as he turned he saw, through the tops of the trees, the distant mountain, an extinct volcano, with a hollowed out top shaped like a votive cup.

Clodius was not much of a father, never had been, yet he had picked up his own sprogs often enough, drunk and sober, to lift this mite. The piercing blue eyes were open, fixed on him in an unblinking stare. He chucked the bawling infant under the chin, and put his hand inside the swaddling clothes, running it up the baby's legs, to feel the small scrotum and penis.

'Well, little fellow,' he said, his voice now clear and soft. 'How did you come to be in a spot like this?'

Clodius bent down and wet his finger, pushing it into the child's mouth. The infant, suddenly silent, suckled greedily, his gums taking a strong hold on the knuckle. When he pulled his hand away the crying started at once. The child's other hand had taken a grip on Clodius's index finger, pulling hard to indicate the need for food.

'Tough little mite, ain't we.' He pulled at his index finger but his charge would not let go. 'And a strong 'un too.'

He ignored the yells of the child as he spoke soothingly, throwing a quick glance at the sun, which, in its limited winter strength, had probably saved the baby's life, and which also told him which direction to go. 'Who'd want to leave a fine little lad like you out here to die, eh? I think I'd better take you home to my Fulmina so she can have a look at you.'

Fulmina would be mad at him for getting drunk and being out all night but he knew her well and had seen, often enough, the way she looked at new-born infants to suspect that this little fellow, with the red-gold hair and the strong grip, would deflect any abuse his wife might throw his way. She would start yelling as soon as she saw him, but once Fulmina had this bundle in her arms and gazed into those bright blue eyes, he would be forgotten.

It was not all plain sailing. She shouted at him all right, first because of his absence, that followed by an instruction to fetch the girl, Prana, from across the field at the back of their hut. She had had a baby the week before, so within seconds of her arrival the child was silent, hungrily feeding from Prana's breast. Clodius felt very weary; the consuming tiredness of man suffering from the effects of drink and he started to ease himself onto a stool.

'Don't sit down!' Fulmina snapped. 'Get some water on the fire.'

'It's nearly out,' Clodius replied, leaning over it and giving it a prod with the broken sword he had brought back from war service.

'Then bank it up. This poor mite needs to be bathed.'

'Take him down to the river.'

Fulmina's face took on the expression she reserved for addressing idiots, one Clodius saw all too frequently. 'Oh yes. You find a child that has been out in the cold all night…'

Clodius replied before he realised that to do so was a grave mistake. 'Didn't do me any harm.'

His wife positively spat at him. 'More's the pity. You could freeze to death anytime and not be missed. Besides, he still has blood on him. Poor thing wasn't even washed after the delivery.'

'Why wash something you don't want to keep?'

The look in Fulmina's eye told him that she would never want to wash him. Not for the first time Clodius wondered what had happened to that sweet slip of a girl with whom he had set up home all those years ago. By the time he had banked up the fire around the blacked clay pot, now full of water, the child was fed and Prana had gone back to her own brood. Fulmina held him over her shoulder, singing softly and patting him on the back while Clodius sat by the fire, occasionally dipping his finger into the pot; if the water got too hot, the terracotta would crack.

The infant gave a loud burp, which brought a big smile to Fulmina's face and she sat down on the other side of the peat fire cradling him in her lap. 'Where did you find him?'

'Upstream, near the edge of the Barbinus ranch.'

That made Fulmina glower, for they had been forced to sell their farm to the wealthy Cassius Barbinus and any use of the name always upset her. 'I won't ask what you were doing up there yourself,' she hissed angrily. 'I dare say you were singing to the gods again, you drunken oaf.'

Clodius wanted to explain that it had been an accident, with one harmless drink leading to another. He had the Feast of *Lupercalia* as an excuse, but experience told him to remain silent on that score. 'It's a good two leagues away from any road. He wasn't meant to be found.'

'What makes you think the people that abandoned him came from the road?'

'Hoof prints. Two horses, at least, I'd say. He must be a sturdy fellow, though he's well wrapped up. If they'd bothered to undo those swaddling clothes, he wouldn't have survived through the night.'

'Poor little mite,' said Fulmina, beginning to unwrap him so he could be washed. 'Is that water warmed through yet?'

Clodius poked his finger into the top of the pot. 'Nearly. It wasn't just the cloth though. There's shade all along that riverbank. They put him in one of the few spots that gets any sun once it has topped the mountains. I think that's really what kept him going till I turned up. The question is, what are we going to do with him?'

Fulmina had the cloths open, exposing the top half of the child's pink body with the stump of the umbilicus red and angry. As she removed the rest she cooed, 'There, there.'

Clodius squatted down and poked gently at the fire, his back to his wife. 'Somebody went to a lot of trouble to hide him. Not much point in raising a bairn that no one wants. Whoever sired him wouldn't thank us for rearing him to manhood and then givin' him back, always supposing we can find out who dumped him in the first place.'

'Somebody wants him back,' said Fulmina. 'And badly at that.'

'Naw!' scoffed Clodius. 'There are any number of places to expose around here if you want the child to live. You certainly don't go hiding him in the middle of nowhere...'

Fulmina spoke without anger, almost gently again, except for the note of urgency. 'Shut up, Clodius Terentius, and look at this.'

Clodius turned slowly, straight away catching the glint of the chain, plus the flash of the eagle in Fulmina's fingers, and stood up quickly to take a closer look. It was beautiful, even to an eye unused to examining precious objects. On top of the gold, all the bird's features were picked out in fine engraving.

'Someone wants this child raised, Clodius. This is a mark to identify him, as well as a sign to tell whoever finds the boy that the person who brings him up is in for a reward when he's taken back.'

'That's gold,' said Clodius, as he took it off her, fingering the feathers on the wing. He felt the small indentation in the back and turned the object over to examine it. Fulmina was looking at him strangely, trying to see if he was playing the fool, for she had only ever seen one piece of gold in her life, a charm on the wrist of the local praetor's wife. It had flashed in the sun the day the magistrate crucified the slaves of a rich fellow who had been murdered. Quite an event that; all the women, young and old, had noticed that golden charm, and conversation was made up, for months afterwards, of endless wishful thinking about a life that could include such luxuries.

Clodius, though, had been a soldier, and that was all old sweats talked about. Booty, generally in the form of gold and silver and usually slipping through their fingers by the merest whisker of fate. Fulmina took the eagle back, emulating Clodius in the way that she ran the charm through her fingers. She gave a small gasp, as if she had hurt herself, but quickly recovered as Clodius leant forward to touch it again, his eyes wide with greed and wonder.

'Perhaps your singing to the gods and asking them for favours hasn't all been in vain, husband. Perhaps we have come into some good fortune at last.'

'I wonder how much it's worth?'

'What?'

Clodius was so busy looking at the gold he mistook Fulmina's surprised reaction for a real question. 'The gold charm. If we sell it, would it provide enough to buy another farm?'

She scowled. 'Tend that pot before it cracks, you fool!'

Clodius hauled the pot out of the fire. Some of the water spilt on his hand and by its heat he knew that he had got to it just in time, which brought forth a sigh of relief. A pot like this, fired in a charcoal kiln, was worth a bit, a valuable item that they would find impossible to replace. Then he smiled; sell that charm and they could probably afford a dozen pots like this, perhaps even a beaten copper one. He turned to carry the water over to his wife, who had laid the tiny infant on the rough top of the wooden table. The baby kicked with both legs and thrust its arms in the air, pushing against Fulmina's hands.

'My,' cooed Fulmina once more. 'We have a little fighter here.'

She proceeded to bathe the little fellow, gently removing the dark streaks of dried blood from his body. Now well fed, the tot seemed to be enjoying it, gazing at Fulmina with those steady blue eyes, and gurgling happily.

'Well, what do you think?' Clodius demanded.

Fulmina didn't take her eyes off the child. 'Think. About what?'

'About what?' said Clodius impatiently, feeling that his good fortune in finding the child allowed him a little licence to berate his wife. 'What have we just been talking about?' He put out his hand and lifted the eagle so that it lay in his palm. 'How much is it worth?'

That made Fulmina stop her bathing. She stood up and stretched to her full height. This still left her a good head shorter than her husband. 'You're a fool, husband. All you can think of is selling this thing so you can have enough money to carry on with your drinking.'

'That's not true. I asked if it was enough to buy a farm.'

'You drank away one farm, Clodius,' she sneered. 'I daresay you could easily manage to drink away another.' Fulmina reached up and tapped the side of his head. 'Think for once and try and see past the first flask of wine. Somebody exposed this child in a secret place so he would not be found, but whoever put this charm on him wanted him to live. How many people round these parts could afford to own something like this?'

Clodius shrugged.

'Not many, husband, and how many of them would have had a child since the sun went down last night?' She stopped talking, watching the slow look of comprehension cross her husband's brow. 'Shouldn't be too hard to find that out if we ask around. Then we'll know.'

'What happens then?'

'One thing at a time, husband. Let's find out who this little fellow is, then we can decide what to do.' She lifted the charm out of Clodius's palm. 'Whoever it is might pay more than the price of this to see him grow up to manhood.'

'Fourteen years is a long time, Fulmina. Another mouth to feed.'

His wife fixed him with a glacial stare. 'We can

manage it, that is if you stay off the drink and get some kind of work. You made a pig's ear of raising our brood, let's see if you can do a better job on this one.'

Clodius knew when he was beaten, knew when it was time to make a tactical withdrawal and his golden rule was always to change the subject. 'Well, if he's staying with us, he'll need a name. What are we going to call him. What about Lupus, since he was born on the feast-night of *Lupercalia*.'

Fulmina looked down at the charm. The eagle flashed, seeming to be truly in flight. 'Not Lupus, husband. With a charm shaped like this, what else can we call him but Aquila.'

They asked all over the district. There were often disagreements about exposing children, even those that were deformed, for in a world where a husband's word was law, it was the father's sole decision, even if the mother virulently disagreed. In that case the wife would arrange for a particular family to "find" the child and pay for them to raise it. With luck, and a discreet approach, they might find someone willing to pay them for rearing Aquila. At the very least they would elicit a promise of a future reward. Clodius was sent as far afield as he could walk in a day, but there was no evidence of a well-born lady, or the wife of some rich merchant or rancher, giving birth in the district.

Travellers and traders on the road could not help either and gradually, as the weeks went by, the search petered out.

By that time Fulmina had begun to have her dreams, all of which featured this foundling child. Clodius was allowed only the barest details of what these portended and even then he was tempted to scoff, but he knew his wife to be a great believer in such things. Then she got together with Drisia, the local soothsayer. Clodius could not stand the woman, a filthy wretch, of uncertain age, who seemed never to wash. To him, being upwind of her was like standing too close to a legionary latrine and since he made no effort to keep this opinion to himself, his distaste was heartily reciprocated. He made a vain attempt to bar her from entering the hut, only to find himself ordered out with scant courtesy, forced to observe proceedings through a crack in the wall.

Drisia made a potion of herbs, mixed with some rough wine. This she rolled around her mouth, with her eyes closed, emitting a low moaning sound. Then she spat it onto the beaten earth of the floor where it formed globules in the dust. Both women leant forward to examine the pattern this created, with Drisia pointing to various shapes. He could see Fulmina nodding, and later, though she refused to tell him what the soothsayer had prophesied, she insisted that the eagle charm had some kind of magical powers to affect the child's future. To Clodius it was all nonsense; that charm, in his eyes, had power all right; the money it would fetch could change his life.

Drisia came again the next day, employing the whole range of her soothsayer's art. Bones were cast on the ground, the way they fell carefully inspected; various wild animals and birds were cut open and their entrails examined. Fulmina became totally attached to her little 'eagle' and any suggestion that he, or his gold charm would have to go, was met with a furious tirade and the threat of eviction for Clodius himself, this while the burden of the extra mouth to feed forced him to find some proper work. He began to curse the day he had found the boy.

Five leagues to the north the young midwife Marcia had engaged in the same quest. She too could find no information about the baby born on the Feast of *Lupercalia*; still had no idea of the identity of the strange lady who had given birth that night. Time, as the days lengthened into months, stilled her enquiries, though every year on the Feast of *Lupercalia* she would cast her mind back to that night, wondering about the name of that stern-faced patrician who could look so gentle when his gaze fell upon his young wife. And what about that effeminate Greek, Cholon, the name spat out in one unguarded moment by his master? Which direction did they take, after the slave took her home? When she returned to the villa, looking for clues, it was deserted and devoid of any evidence of their occupancy. Most of all Marcia ached to know where they had ridden to, immediately after the birth. Where did they go to expose the child, a journey that had kept them away until well after dawn broke the following day?

CHAPTER SEVEN

The house of Lucius Falerius Nerva was, once more, full of people. They stood, in groups, around the waterless fountain and burning braziers in the spacious atrium, their conversation setting up a steady buzz as they discussed the events of the previous two days; Tiberius Livonius cut down along with four companions garbed in his robes as a priest of the Cult of *Lupercalia*. This had led to serious rioting, as the people he represented, the poor and needy, poured out of their slums screaming for retribution, thus giving the patrician party an excuse to respond with their armed retainers, which in turn led to the massacre of Livonius's adherents. Over three hundred had died as the patricians egged on their supporters to kill their political enemies.

Yet their deaths paled beside the effect of the initial assassination. The murder of a plebeian tribune, a hero to the dispossessed, whose person was held to be inviolate, was a heinous crime. All Rome was agog to know the names of the assailants, though few seemed to doubt that the author of the attack was the owner of this house. An angry crowd, defying the danger of another massacre, as well as the orders of the lictors to disperse, had gathered outside to yell obscenities. Those lictors, whose task it was to maintain civil order, were forced to mount guard at the gate. The noise swelled as the outer door swung open to admit another caller, and the room fell silent as Aulus Cornelius Macedonicus entered. A collective sigh rose from the throats of those with a slim chance of an interview with Lucius, for their prospects were so diminished as to have almost disappeared. Everyone else knew that the mere presence of this man would considerably extend the time they had to wait; Aulus would be admitted to the great man's study just as soon as the host was appraised of his arrival.

Properly clad in his senatorial toga, with one fold acting as a cowl to cover his head, Aulus took up position on his own, at a point far away from the entrance to the study. Several men bowed in his direction, indicating that many a conversation was open to him. While courteously returning the bows, Aulus held himself aloof. Likewise those clients of Lucius, who would also wish to avail themselves of Aulus's largesse, he being one of the richest men in

Rome, were kept at bay by the look in his eye, which was not one to invite an approach. Lucius's steward, ushering an elderly knight out of the study, failed to see Aulus and was just about to indicate that another man should proceed through the door when a hurried whisper made him spin round. It was like a scene from a comedy by Plautus. The steward's hand shot to his mouth in a most unprofessional manner and he rushed into the study to tell his master. Seconds lengthened into a full minute before he returned, which had already heightened the tension, but when the fellow ignored Aulus, and indicated that the original supplicant should go through, the air became charged. For quite some time no one could speak; they just stared at Aulus to see what he would do.

The object of their curiosity did not even flick a black eyebrow; there was no reaction at all to this obvious slight, even though, inwardly, he was troubled. Aulus had come with three objects in mind; to celebrate a birth, to mourn a death and to expunge the dread that what the mob protested outside, that Lucius had been responsible for the assassination of Tiberius Livonius, was true. Ruminating in turn on all three, he stared back at his inquisitive audience as if daring one of them to mention what had just taken place; to state the level of the insult that had just been very publicly delivered. No one did and soon the conversation resumed, if anything louder than before, as the gathering tried to make sense of this unexpected shift in the political wind.

In the jumble of thoughts that coursed through Aulus's mind the sight of the child he had exposed kept cropping up, unbidden, a bundle of white placed on the cold earth. He had avoided looking at it too closely, staying mounted on a horse suddenly skittish, not wishing to be haunted by the physical image, but all that meant was that he transposed, instead, the infant faces of his own two sons. Much as he tried to concentrate on the forthcoming meeting with Lucius, which was now bound to be difficult, he could not erase the memory of watching Cholon lay down the sleeping infant with a gentility that was at odds with what was intended. On a clear moonlit night the trees had sighed in the gentle wind, as if in sorrow. As he had gazed at the outline of the distant mountains, with the ghostly outline of an extinct volcano, Aulus had felt the chill in the air as the clear sky sucked what little heat the day had produced out of the earth, the chill that would ensure a slow but painless death.

Two more knights and one senator were admitted while Aulus stood waiting. All the while he kept trying to bring his thoughts back to matters at hand, or to the turmoil that had greeted him and his wife as they had entered the city he loved and had fought for; the sight of bodies in the streets; of armed bands passing him with swords already bloody, and a look in their eyes that promised more killing. The notion persisted that by being present he might have been able to prevent this, but the moonlit glade well away from the Via Appia kept intruding. The body would provide food for some predator, so that the little bones would be scattered. He wanted to shake his head, to destroy the image he had then – why was he so shaken by one death when he had participated in so many – but too many eyes were on him, too many people looking for some kind of reaction to what they had observed.

Finally, with his progress followed by the whole room, the steward made his way across the atrium towards the tall, imposing, but solitary figure. His whispered words brought a curt nod and Aulus, head high, looking neither left nor right, made his way towards the study, hearing the steward, behind him, announce that there would be no more business conducted that day. The study was much darker than the atrium, hardly surprising since what he had left was open to both daylight and the elements. Here the light came from a glowing brazier and oil lamps, with the bulk of their effect concentrated on the owner's desk. It was only then that Aulus realised what was missing; Ragas, the warrior slave he had gifted to this house after his return from Macedonia, a fellow always with

Lucius, who knew as well as anyone that, with the position he held, he could be the target of an assassination.

'Greetings, Lucius Falerius,' said Aulus.

He reached up to uncover his head as a mark of the genuine respect he felt for this man, but the hand froze in mid-air. Lucius Falerius did not even look up, but just kept on writing, his quill scratching across the rough papyrus and for one of the few times in his adult life, Aulus felt foolish, unsure of what he should do. To uncover his head while being blatantly ignored would be undignified.

'It's difficult to know what to do, is it not, Aulus, when you're unsure who your friends are?'

Lucius still had not looked up, leaving Aulus trying to discern something from the voice; anger, guilt or was it just pique? He and Lucius had fallen out often enough – you could not be friends for thirty years with a man like him and not have the occasional spat, but they had been, in most cases, of short duration. Aulus was always willing to admit when he was at fault, while Lucius was gifted with the wit and words to eventually turn any dispute into an object of mirth. On the rare occasions when Aulus thought about their long attachment he would conclude that, though very different in many ways, they balanced each other, the uncomplicated warrior and the wily politician. This, Aulus knew, because of the way he had been left waiting in the atrium, was different.

Faced with such a welcome, kept waiting like some common supplicant, Aulus was forced to confront an unwelcome truth. It was no secret that Lucius had become more acid and less tolerant over the years as the burdens he undertook increased, just as it was known that he was inclined to outbursts which could only be ascribed to jealousy. Some of his comments on the marriage with Claudia, which had been repeated by gossipy tongues, had been far from amusing and Aulus had chided him, before departing for Spain, about the fact that he was prone to treat some of his friends with the same disdain he reserved for his enemies.

As he looked down at the thinning hair on the bowed head, it seemed such an attitude applied to him as well, and for the first time in his life and for all the years he had considered this man a companion, ally and confidant, he was unsure if the words he was about to use were wholly true. 'I have never had cause to doubt that we were friends, Lucius.'

There was a trace of a growl in the Falerii voice as Lucius responded, which made Aulus really bridle for the first time since he had entered the house. 'Then you are more fortunate than I!'

'That is, until now,' snapped Aulus, his black eyes blazing with anger. 'No friend of mine has ever seen fit to humiliate me.'

The top of Lucius's balding head shook slightly, the sheen of his pate catching the light from the nearby lanterns. 'Again you are fortunate.' The voice had softened now, to become almost silky, but still Lucius, as he continued, would not look at his guest. 'A friend of mine did something very like that recently, someone bound to me by a lifetime's companionship as well as the most solemn of blood oaths. Perhaps humiliation overstates the case somewhat, but this friend saw fit to be absent at a time when any true comrade, who has it in his power to be present, knows that he should be. I refer Aulus, to the birth of my son.'

That stung, for the blood oath they had exchanged as children was a covenant that meant a great deal to a deeply religious man like Aulus. He had known as soon as he heard of the birth and death that an important obligation had been broken, just as he knew that his presence on Italian soil, so close to Rome, must have been known to Lucius. The man had cause to be angry. Suppressing his own annoyance at the way he had been treated, he responded in a deferential tone.

'I came here to congratulate you on that joyous birth, Lucius, as well as to commiserate with you on the loss of the Lady Ameliana. Having lost a wife myself, I know how you must be feeling.'

Aulus snatched the cowl off his head at the mention of her name, using the excuse of his genuine grief, when speaking of Lucius's dead wife, to solve an apparently intractable dilemma, while still retaining a measure of his dignity. As if blessed with a sixth sense, Lucius chose that precise moment to look up from the papers before him, eyes narrowed and lips disapproving.

'Yet you uncover yourself, Aulus. Can I therefore assume that my anger is misdirected?'

Lucius was addressing him as though he was an errant child, but Aulus again decided, for the sake of their long association and the death just alluded to, to let that pass. 'If I could have been here, I would. You must know that!'

Lucius frowned deeply, as if such a statement smacked of improbability. 'Perhaps if I were to hear why you were delayed, my hurt would be lessened. For be assured, Aulus, I was hurt. And disappointed.'

The silence lasted for several seconds for Aulus had no intention of lying to Lucius, since nothing could reduce him more in his own estimation than that he should adopt such a course. Yet neither was he prepared to tell the truth: only he, his wife and Cholon would ever know that secret and a true friend, to his mind, would not ask for an excuse if none were volunteered. Again he felt it necessary to suppress a rising sense of anger, found that he needed to fight to control his voice and keep it gentle.

'It ill becomes you to demand explanations from me, Lucius.'

Lucius jerked backwards in his chair. 'I agree, Aulus. One would hope that the companion of your youth would not be required to demand.'

'I came to congratulate and commiserate,' hissed Aulus, pulling himself up to his full, imposing height, his restraint shattered in the face of such arrogance, as well as his own deep sense of guilt. 'I came as a friend, as well, ready to apologise to you for my absence, but my apology will have to suffice. There is no man born that can demand an explanation from me. You go too far!'

The host rubbed a hand over his forehead as though weary. Other people faced with someone as physically impressive might have flinched, but not Lucius Falerius: his response was smooth.

'Perhaps I do, my friend, perhaps I do,' he said, seemingly now intent on being emollient, his voice becoming full of warmth, tinged with hurt and concern. 'But can you not see how our enemies perceive such behaviour. They are always on the lookout to drive a wedge between people like us.'

The word 'us' jarred, for Aulus suspected that Lucius used the word to refer almost entirely to himself. Besides, what had these supposed enemies to do with what was a purely personal matter? The voice was still cordial as Lucius continued. 'If you tell me that you were delayed, and for an honourable purpose, I will enquire no further.'

It was with a tight feeling in his throat that Aulus responded, for he knew that the gods would judge him for what he would say, and that made for an uncomfortable sensation. 'I was delayed, and the purpose was one that I could not, as an honourable man, avoid.'

'Then enough said, my friend,' said Lucius, standing up to come from behind his desk, holding out his forearm. 'Let us join hands, as of old, and put the matter from our minds.'

Aulus stepped forward with relief, clasping Lucius's arm just below the elbow, grateful that he had abandoned his icy hauteur. The man he had come to see, the friend he remembered, responded, and at the same time treated him to a warm smile. 'I fear the burden of my tasks makes me a poor host. It was wrong of me to make you wait, wrong of me to allow my resentment to spill over into so public a response.'

'You do too much,' Aulus replied, with genuine feeling. He wanted to say that Lucius should stop, take time to himself, let others bear the burdens of leading the patrician cause. He did not because he suspected he would be wasting his breath.

Lucius shook his head as if confused. 'I do what I must, my friend, though your concern touches me.'

There was a moment then when Lucius changed,

and a sight of that once-known, engaging youth, resurfaced; the smile, which seemed to draw him in, added to the expression in the dark brown eyes that, when concentrated made you feel as if you were at the very centre of his thoughts. This was the congenial Lucius that could seduce people to agree with him, so far from the cranked one that had existed when Aulus entered, a mood change which he felt allowed him to ascertain something of which he was curious.

'Where is Ragas? I can barely recall ever seeing you without him.'

'I freed him on the birth of my son, Aulus, and do you know he upped and left within an hour, swearing that he would return to his homeland, and get away from Rome, which he hated. He was quite spiteful in his condemnation. A pity, I think he could have had a great future here.'

'Then I must provide you with another, Lucius.'

Lucius laughed out loud, rare for him. 'Must Rome start another war just to gain me a body slave?'

'You know I have many on my estates, more than is needed to work the land.'

Jabbing with a gentle and friendly finger, Lucius replied, 'I know you harbour them carefully, Aulus, and only bring them into the city to sell when prices are high.'

'I sell them, Lucius, when I can recover the cost of feeding them.'

Lucius tugged slightly at a sleeve to lead his friend from the room. 'Come, Aulus. I must show you my son. He is as lusty a little fellow as you're ever likely to encounter.'

He led the way out of the rear of the study and down the colonnaded walkway by the side of the garden. The sound reached them soon enough, and lusty was the right word for it.

The child is yelling fit to wake the dead, thought Aulus.

He immediately regretted his impiety, for the body of his friend's wife was likely somewhere nearby. This, in turn, made him wonder at this unbridled joy, which should surely be mixed with a deep sorrow for that passing, yet there was no sign of grief in Lucius's manner. Indeed, Aulus had been surprised on entering the house to see so many people present, as though this was just a normal day in an important man's life. Never mind what had happened on the streets of Rome, what had occurred within these walls was enough; the place should have been deserted. No one could blame a man, however elevated his status, for refusing to conduct business after such a loss.

The wet nurse, her child on her lap, stood up as they entered. Lucius waved her away, and taking his companion's arm once more, led him over to the cot. They gazed down at the wailing infant. 'Look at him, Aulus. Is he not a fine fellow?'

Again there was the feeling of years dropping away, because Lucius was excited and made no attempt to disguise it. Over time he had, of necessity, become the most reserved of men, consummate at disguising his feelings, ever the politician. It was a telling thought that Aulus harboured then, one tinged with regret; his friend was for once behaving like a normal human being.

'I have sent to Greece for a list of tutors. I wish him to learn Greek as his first language. He shall have the finest pedagogues available in all subjects, no expense spared. He'll learn better than anyone the twin pillars of Rome, the power of the law and the use of the sword. He will be more handsome than his father, and may the gods make him as tall and straight as you.' The child yelled on, oblivious to the enthusiasm of his already doting parent, who babbled on in an animated fashion, arm securely linked to that of his guest. 'I have already consulted the priests, Aulus, and the auguries are excellent. Look at the date of his birth, for instance, the Feast of *Lupercalia*. What better day could a Roman ask to enter the world? He shall be a great magistrate and a great soldier, my friend. He has been bred to plead in the courts and to command armies. In time he will come upon his just inheritance, and another Falerii will stand as consul in the Forum Boracum.'

The father's eyes were alight, gleaming at the prospect of future greatness for his son, and it was an inadvertent thought that made Aulus allude to the boy lacking a mother.

'To spoil him you mean!' snapped Lucius, looking up with a return of his previous sour expression. 'To make him soft like a milksop.'

'Come, Lucius. Mothers can teach boys a great deal. If you do not believe me, ask my sons.'

Lucius permitted himself a half smile. 'Perhaps so, Aulus. Perhaps I shall wed again, like you, but this time I shall require more comfort than this boy's mother ever gave me.'

Lucius had always had within him a callous streak – it was not out of place in the world they inhabited – but to speak so ill of a loyal wife, who had just performed her duty by producing this infant, when she was barely cold, was deeply shocking.

'Take care, Lucius, to avoid blasphemy.'

Lucius actually grinned, for he was always ribbing Aulus about his piety. 'You worry about blasphemy, while I worry about Rome.'

'How do you intend to arrange the ceremonies?' Aulus asked, bemused and slightly at a loss as to how to react.

The response was vague, as though the thought of his twin responsibilities had never crossed Lucius's mind, and there was an element of confusion on the plural nature of the word he used. 'Ceremonies?'

'Custom demands that you bury your wife on the ninth day. That is also the day you're supposed to celebrate the birth of your son and name him.'

'I shall do both, Aulus, never fear.'

'On the same day?'

'Of course,' Lucius insisted. 'But all Rome shall know at what ceremony I have set my heart.'

The wet nurse was called forward to lift the child from his cot. This she did, and prepared to offer the infant her breast to feed.

'Stop!' cried Lucius. 'Let him wait until the appointed time. It does no harm for a Roman soldier to go hungry.'

'Hardly a soldier yet, Lucius?'

That remark was greeted with a look that contained a gleam of fanaticism. 'Let us start as we mean to go on, Aulus. This boy, whom I intend to name Marcellus, is a Roman. He will be taught to behave like one from the very moment of birth. He will know, as soon as he can understand the nickname Orestes, that his birth itself on such a feast-day was so potent that his mother had to be sacrificed to achieve it. That will be the benchmark for his future aims in life.'

'Then he's in for a hard upbringing, Lucius.'

No hint of the inherent cruelty in his words seemed to dent Lucius's certainty. 'He is that, Aulus.'

CHAPTER EIGHT

They made their way back to the study with Lucius still prattling on about the brilliant future he envisaged for his son until Aulus felt the subject exhausted and changed it. He had three objectives to complete on his visit; time to move on to the most troublesome one.

'I am surprised to find you conducting business on such a day.'

As if to underline the truth of this remark, Lucius went straight back to his desk, and his paperwork. Aulus found himself staring at that bald head again as his host bent to his labours.

'Had to, my friend. After the events of the last two days, I couldn't have the mob implying that I was hiding away.'

'Even you are allowed time to grieve,' Aulus replied, as he eased himself into a chair.

Lucius looked up, his eyes steady. 'Am I? No, let those who loved Tiberius Livonius grieve.'

There was a second's pause before Aulus responded, for he had not even mentioned the murders, in fact he had been referring to Ameliana. 'You are aware of the talk?'

Lucius waved his quill, dismissively. 'That it was I who had him killed?'

'Yes,' Aulus replied, his voice tense.

Lucius emitted a rather mannered sigh and carried on writing. 'On the very day that my wife died, I'm supposed to find the time to murder a man whom I hold in utter contempt. His adherents flatter him. No one, Aulus, is that important.'

That shook Aulus, making him think in a manner he wanted to avoid. Lucius had shown no sign of grief at all. No weeping and covering of the head for him, just business as usual today. Was it also business as usual when those assassins had struck down the plebeian tribune: had committed a crime that in its repercussions could set the whole city ablaze? Aulus flattered himself that he knew Lucius better than anyone alive, even his own late wife, yet he was left wondering at this moment whether he truly knew him at all.

'You will not be surprised to hear that some of the gabblers in that same market-place are saying I ordered Ragas to kill Livonius then sent him away. Utter nonsense, of course. What hurts most is that some people think I am as stupid as they are.'

'The accusation still stands, Lucius.'

That made his host look up. 'Surely you of all people give it no credence?'

'I never listen to gossip Lucius and I try not to respond to rumour. But should the accusation be placed in public, someone will have to refute it.'

'I can refute it,' Lucius snapped.

Aulus could see he was annoyed by the way his quill now flew across the papyrus and he nearly stopped then, the prospect of letting matters rest an enticing one, and not only for Lucius. There was a selfish motive as well. He was seen by all as a close friend and ally to this man; if the rumour was not laid to rest he could be tainted by association. He had not fought his wars and gained his triumph to have it sullied by such a possibility.

'Is that wise, Lucius? All of Roman law is based on having another plead your case.'

The head snapped up and those dark brown eyes were cold now. 'I don't need an advocate!'

'I say you do.' Seeing the tightening of the jaw on his friend's face he carried swiftly on. 'I say we all do at times. I will not have you shorn of your dignity to refute such base and false allegations. You referred yourself to enemies trying to drive a wedge between us. Someone is bound to bring the matter up in the Senate, either directly or by allusion. I can't see how it could be otherwise when a person as important as Tiberius Livonius has been murdered. I am, in fact, offering myself for the role of advocate on your behalf.'

Lucius gave him a wolfish smile. 'You think your eloquence outshines mine?'

'Not in a millennium,' Aulus replied sincerely; he had never been able to match Lucius in that department. 'But I hold to my point that it is better to have someone else plead your case, rather than do so yourself.'

The quill was pointing at Aulus now. 'Even if there's no case to answer?'

'You're playing with words, Lucius. Either admit I'm right, or demand I desist.'

Lucius dropped the quill and sat back in his chair, his fingers forming a point below his lips. 'Perhaps you are correct. Some fool may make the accusation in the Forum.'

Aulus tried to drive home his point, unsure, as he heard his own voice, if he had got the tone right. 'I have heard it said that a man feels unclean, even when he has to defend himself from the basest and most unfounded charge.'

Lucius replied in the same pensive mode. 'I doubt I should feel that way, Aulus. Still, you may have the right of it.'

Aulus sat forward, eagerly. 'Then it is settled. If someone is foolish enough to suggest that you had a hand in the death of Tiberius Livonius, I shall speak on your behalf.'

Lucius smiled behind the pointed fingers. 'Am I allowed to advise you as to how you should go about it?'

Aulus returned the smile, though he could feel the tightness in his jaw. 'Of course. Just as you are obliged, for the sake of my honour, to swear to me personally that I shall be speaking the truth.'

Lucius sat absolutely still, yet there was a palpable tenseness as he spoke. 'Why do I feel you've set out to trap me?'

'Trap you!' Aulus threw back his head and laughed, really to avoid looking into those searching eyes, for deep down he knew that was precisely what he had done. He put on his best bluff manner, playing the old soldier, hoping, that way, to draw Lucius further on. 'All I wish to do is defend you and just to show that I have complete faith in you, please don't feel that you have to give me any assurances at all.'

The voice was icy now, the face set and hard, with no trace of any affection. 'Oh, but I shall, my friend. I swear on the bones of my ancestors that I did not kill Tiberius Livonius.'

Aulus laughed again, praying it sounded real. 'Lucius, I doubt that anyone, even the most scatterbrained, thinks you actually struck the blow.'

Lucius waved a finger to indicate the steady drone of noise from the street, the noise of a crowd still held in check by the lictors. 'There are those with insufficient brains to scatter who believe just that.'

'The mob?'

Lucius leant forward, his voice even, formal and controlled. 'I know how careful you are of your honour, Aulus Cornelius Macedonicus. I swear I had no hand in the death of Tiberius Livonius.'

Aulus put his hand over that of Lucius, squeezing tightly, trying to communicate the relief he felt, while still seeking to dissemble with his eyes. This is what he had come for, half fearing that it would not happen and he felt a surge of affection for Lucius, even though he knew he had wounded him. That would pass; they were friends, always had been, and in time, when Lucius came to consider what had just happened, he would realise that Aulus only had his best interests at heart.

'I look forward, Lucius, to routing your enemies.'

The tight smile, brought forth by this tactile act, seemed to be the most that Lucius was capable of. 'I shall listen with rapt attention, to see how much of my style of rhetoric you have absorbed.'

'I have enough words of my own, Lucius.'

'I'm sure you do, Aulus. I'm sure you do.'

Lucius stood up, and his guest followed suit. They grasped hands again and Aulus spoke gravely for he had pushed the bounds of friendship to the limit, and no one was more aware of it than he. 'This is a difficult time,

Lucius. Please call upon me for anything you
need.'

'Thank you, my friend,' said Lucius, bowing his
head with apparent feeling, and, as a mark of
respect, he showed Aulus out of the house
personally. But once the door was shut, he called
loudly for his steward. The man, used to his ways,
sensed he was angry and ran to receive instructions,
to find his master standing rock still, staring at an
oil lamp. Then his face began to move as he hissed
to himself. Lucius felt deceived, felt that the one
person he had the right to rely on had let him down,
and not just on this day. Why? Was it just that piety
for which Aulus was so famous, a probity that was
easy for a man too ineffectual to involve himself in
the grubby world of politics. How easy to keep
your hands clean and let others do the dirty work.

Then the thought occurred that there might be
another cause. Aulus had trapped him, of that there
was no doubt, and he had refused to explain why he
had missed the birth of Marcellus to a person from
whom he had no right to keep a secret. Lucius
Falerius had learnt many years before that you
could never repose complete faith in anyone.
Shocked by the train of his own thoughts, that even
someone as close to him as Aulus might play him
false, Lucius spoke quickly, in staccato fashion, his
voice rising with each word.

'I want to know where Aulus Cornelius

Macedonicus was the night before last. He was not here for the birth of my son and I know that he landed at Ostia a whole week ago. His son Quintus assured me he was not at home either and that means he spent the night somewhere else. I want to know where, but more important than that, I want to know precisely whom he was with!'

The steward bowed as his master's voice rose to a crescendo, still smarting from the need to so utterly disguise his true feelings, as well as swear an oath that was false.

'Spare no expense, for I tell you, I smell betrayal.'

For the first time in his life Aulus felt isolated, a sensation that had the effect of making him feel slightly absurd. Here he was, in his own home, surrounded by family and dozens of slaves all ready to obey his instructions and see to his well being, yet that seemed an illusion. His wife, still feeling the after effects of the birth, was asleep. Quintus was at the house of the Galbinus family, having had dinner with his future father-in-law; he would be gambling now, trying, as he crudely put it, to double the dowry. Titus was doing the same as all young men his age, seeking pleasure in the fleshpots of the city, not that any of them, if they had been present, would have provided the foil he needed to ease his troubled thoughts.

Claudia had been a distant presence since they

had found her in that wagon. She had meekly submitted to his instructions that turned her into a virtual recluse, so that her condition would remain a secret, and had returned to Italy with him after his legions had departed. During that journey, try as he might, Aulus could find no way to lift her spirits, no way to rekindle the joy they had taken in each other's company prior to her capture. The occasion of the birth was not one he cared to dwell on, suffice to say that the final leg of their journey to Rome, the day before, had been accomplished in complete silence. He reasoned that after such an ordeal as the one she must have suffered, it would take time for her to heal the mental scars of the abasement she had been forced to endure. Vaguely he wondered if the Vestal Virgins had some cleansing ritual for such a thing, making a mental note to discreetly enquire.

Relations with his eldest son conformed to the usual pattern; he was shown much respect, while left in no doubt that Quintus believed him to be old-fashioned and out of touch with modern life. Titus, so like him physically, was, he suspected, a little afraid of his father, too awed by his reputation to even consider that his age allowed him some liberty, like that of occasionally treating his parent as an equal. His eyes flicked slightly as he picked up the movement in the corner of his vision. Cholon had come to look again, come to make sure his master was comfortable.

'Cholon Pyliades,' he said without rancour, 'will you please stop flitting about like a chimera, and either stand where I can see you, or take yourself off to sleep.'

'I can do that only when you are settled, master.'

Aulus laughed, but it was not pleasure that he conveyed, more a sardonic sense of bitterness. 'Settled?'

'If you wish to think aloud, I am happy to listen.'

'To what end, Cholon?'

'If I might be allowed the liberty of an observation, master, it is clear that you are troubled.'

Aulus felt some of his tension ease as he smiled, wondering how many of his patrician contemporaries would have thrown something at a slave's head for making such a remark, but Cholon had always been like that, seeing himself as more than just a personal attendant. Yet even if the Greek was willing he could not discuss, with him, the state of Rome; the feeling that the ideas he had supported year upon year were no longer wholly tenable. Worse that he could even entertain the thought that the friend of his youth, who had been so changed by the corruption of power, might stoop to murder to maintain it. The missing body slave troubled him, for although Lucius had told him of the man's conceit and the battle he had had to train him, they had come to form what seemed an inseparable bond. Perhaps Lucius had killed Ragas – such a thing was not uncommon – Aulus himself had had recourse to it with one or two untameable slaves in the past. But if he had, where was the body? Such thoughts led him into areas of further speculation where he did not want to go, so he took refuge in memories.

If the friendship between Lucius and he had seemed natural to them, Aulus knew it had puzzled others, especially when the time had come for both to undertake military service. Lucius, with his slight frame and narrow shoulders, showed no aptitude whatever for the art of war. He had struggled to throw a spear any distance and was an easy opponent to best at swordplay. Finding he lacked the required physical and combat skills for front-line command and being in possession of an acid sense of humour, Lucius had taken to denigrating those skills as a form of compensation. Aulus, secure in his own abilities, had laughed at his jibes; not so others, who had evinced more than once a desire to duck this self-styled humorist in the latrine. Lucius probably had, to this day, no knowledge of the number of times that Aulus had saved him from the consequences of his barbed remarks. Yet that very lack of fighting ability had allowed Lucius to discover his true vocation; he became, quite simply, a superb quartermaster.

No army that Lucius marched with had ever

wanted for anything in the way of supplies and in the process of procurement, bargaining and arguing, he had honed those skills that made his movement into a life of politics seamless. He had filled every public office on the *cursus honarium* with the same efficiency he had shown in the army and much of the subsequent years were spent apart as Aulus pursued his military career in various outposts of the empire. Yet when they had met, their attachment to each other had seemed as strong as ever, with Lucius aiding Aulus to follow him into the various offices of state, and to have such service returned with unstinting political support. They had even served as consuls together, with Lucius, the senior, content to let his friend garner the glory of his Macedonian campaign, while he stayed at home, as he put it, minding the shop.

Recalling that, and what had happened so recently in the streets of Rome, Aulus wondered if others, even Lucius, saw how shaky was the edifice they supported, the Imperium of the Republic. Was it merely vouchsafed to fighting soldiers, looking inward from distant frontiers, to observe that if the centre did not hold, nothing else could be retained; that the whole empire could crumble over disputes between internal political factions? His mind turned back to the Celtic chieftain whom he had so recently defeated. Let a man like Brennos loose in a world in turmoil and there would be no end to the mischief he could make. He certainly made enough in the Cornelii household and in a swift, angry movement, he pulled himself off the couch.

'I shall go to bed, Cholon.'

'Yes, master.'

But he did not sleep, for Aulus had two unpleasant tasks to perform in the morning, one that would, he hoped, protect Lucius and settle the present rumblings surrounding the murder of Tiberius Livonius. But the other was the harder, and had only been decided as he made his way home from his visit to the Falerii house. His friend had made his oath of innocence and Aulus was satisfied, but Lucius seemed unaware that even if he was guilt-free his own actions had engendered an atmosphere in which such a heinous crime could take place. That threatened the very foundations of the Republic. Aulus would not be part of such a thing and he knew he needed to find an avenue by which that could, publicly, be made plain.

CHAPTER NINE

Lucius was at his desk before cockcrow, reading the various missives that had come in during the night. The system of mounted messengers that traversed the empire was one of the pillars of Roman control, giving the reigning consuls the ability to act swiftly in the event of an emergency. That, added to the reports from the governors of the various provinces, gave whoever sat in his place a very comprehensive view of their responsibilities. The thought that this was so made him smile, for it seemed he often knew more of what took place on the frontiers than in the houses of his political enemies, some a mere stone's throw from his front gate. Even his friends could mystify him, the behaviour of Aulus Cornelius being just one example. After a good night's sleep he had no doubt there was a deeper motive behind what had taken place the previous evening, something that he could not see? To Lucius, Aulus was a brilliant man in command of legions;

certainly a good administrator and a supportive junior consul, but not in the least deep and calculating. Aulus would struggle to hatch a plot, never mind execute one.

Yet the possibility existed that after all these years he had been wrong in his assessment; that this simple soldier was in fact devious enough not only to betray him but to do so in a manner that left him perplexed. If only Aulus had been in Rome when he should have been, perhaps he could have routed the Livonian faction on the floor of the Senate. Was his old friend actually not, in part, responsible for what had happened? That thought suddenly seemed absurd; if Aulus had been close he would have had to put aside any thought of killing Livonius until he was out of the city; that well-known Cornelii piety would have been a burden, not an asset.

He sighed at his own folly as he picked up the last report but one from the pile on his desk. This told him that the provincial governor of Illyricum had fallen seriously ill at the port of Brindisium on the way to take up his duties; if the man failed to recover he would have to find a replacement prepared to leave immediately. That should not present much in the way of difficulty, the governorship being an opportunity to profit both in money and reputation. Certain sections of the province, particularly the coastal strip of Dalmatia, were as peaceful as Italy, but inland, in the mountainous terrain, the tribes needed no Romans to provoke a fight. Blood feuds abounded, the original reasons long since overlaid with added death and destruction. Illyricum also had, to the west, a long porous border, constantly raided by the Celtic tribes of Dacia, so keeping the peace was never easy. Yet it was a land full of fertile valleys, which produced an abundance of valuable crops if order could be maintained and the mining concessions in the mountains were equally profitable, so that the tax revenue was substantial, as was the gubernatorial reward. It would not be a hard office to fill.

Lifting that missive had uncovered the last item, the initial reports his steward had produced regarding Aulus Cornelius. They were slim indeed; the man had been unable to find out anything of interest. Still more time would surely produce the information he required, even if he now wondered if it would be worth the effort. Lucius snapped himself out of this reverie. He had to attend the Senate in a few hours, accompanied by his oldest friend. It would be an important day and if in the unlikely event that outright duplicity was in the air, then he would know before the sun reached its zenith.

The session started in total uproar, with no senator, it seemed, prepared to yield the floor to another. Scrolls were waved in furious disagreement, or used as pointers to exaggerate a particular insult. Lucius, with an equally silent Aulus by his side, watched this mayhem with a jaundiced eye, for he had the power to quell this, merely by getting to his feet. His adherents would fall silent from respect, the undecided from curiosity, even his enemies would cease prattling for the mere prospect of hearing the lies they suspected would emerge. Much as he hated disorder, the present display suited his purpose, for one thing Lucius knew about his fellow legislators was their fear of public turbulence. No matter how bad matters became inside the Curia Hostilia they would close ranks to ensure that such disputes did not spread to incite a public riot, something too easy to ignite in the crowded tenements of the city.

Rome's population had expanded alarmingly. Rootless peasants from all over Italy formed a discontented body, denied political rights by their lack of citizenship, willing to follow any leader who promised to alleviate their grievances. But worse than the mob were the citizen farmers, unable to sustain themselves on the land, many soldiers ruined by long service in the legions. They too had come to the city, drawn at first by the corn dole that the plebeian tribune had introduced and this, in turn, had swelled the numbers in the thirty-six tribes that formed the Comitia, making what had been an easily controlled voting body exceedingly unruly. Since the whole structure of political power rested on that assembly of Roman citizens, keeping it's members from mischief was of paramount concern. Once out of control, the whole nature of the way Rome was governed could be altered.

Aulus Cornelius was as aware of that as anyone; the Republic was a fragile concept, always vulnerable, and becoming more so. It required virtue to be the abiding rule of public office, yet that was the one thing that was becoming increasingly rare, ruined by captured wealth, some of which he had had a hand in providing. The whole Mediterranean littoral sent riches to the city, either in cash tribute, taxes, or as gifts of necessity, the cheap grain that supported the corn dole being the most obvious. Senators, knights and astute businessmen had grown rich beyond the dreams of avarice; he had himself by his conquests, and more of his time was taken up lending money at decent rates of interest than worrying about it, or husbanding his slave-holdings to manipulate the market for the best price. Yet they sat above a volcano of dearth and the gap between those who had and those who lacked was getting wider, loosing the bonds that held the state together.

Things were becoming acceptable that would once have been deemed heinous; should it be that the murder of public officials, hitherto a blasphemy, become everyday, then Rome was doomed. Aulus got to his feet, his eyes ranging round the chamber with a cold stare that silenced his excited peers one by one. No one could doubt as he stood there the degree of his gravitas, for, as still as one of the statues that lined the Sacred Way, he had an abundance of presence. The physical aspect, his height, his dark colouring with hair greying at the temples, the strong features of his handsome face were only part of that. Power emanated from him in such a way that it was easy to comprehend how he could command legions, control a battle and demonstrate to his troops that he was as brave as the most courageous of the men he led.

It was odd how small Lucius looked beside him, hunched forward, legs crossed, hand supporting his chin, eyes hooded as if content to merely listen. He was sitting of course, which exaggerated the contrast between the two men, yet even standing Aulus would have dominated the assembly by his physicality. It was an interesting thought for those who cared to consider it; that for all his impressive carriage, Aulus, without an army at his back, had little power, while for all his present hunched insignificance, Lucius on his own had a great deal, which would colour the way they listened to what this speaker had to say. Here was a man to be respected, but not a man to be feared.

Determined to exert total control, Aulus let the hush persist, waiting for a full minute before commencing his speech. Those who had not guessed his intention to defend Lucius must have sensed it now; the way they had entered the chamber arm in arm, the stillness they had displayed during the unruly debate, should have alerted all to the fact that Aulus was set to pre-empt an accusation and face the matter of Lucius's guilt head on. That someone so patently upright chose to do so should be enough to sway a great number of the uncommitted. Senators who, moments before, might just as easily have joined in a clamour that would have seen Lucius Falerius impeached, now sat in silent anticipation.

'It is the nature of debates in this house to allow us to indulge in rhetoric, to demonstrate our skills in those arts which raise a man above the common herd and excite admiration in his contemporaries. I now ask that you indulge me for not attaining the desired standard for, in what I am about to say to the Senate, and considering the gravity of recent events, such delicate methods of speech are inappropriate.'

A buzz ran around the chamber, which died as Aulus held up his hand. 'A noble Roman, a good and honest citizen, a member of this august body, was cruelly murdered three nights past. In the annals of crimes against the state it ranks amongst the worst, equal to the tyranny of the despised Tarquin kings who built this very Curia in which we speak as free men.'

Only those few who were watching Lucius saw his fingers take a tighter grip on the scroll in his hand as he lifted his head and squared his shoulders. No one was close enough to see the way his eyes dilated – either from fear or anger – nor observe the effort it took for him to produce a relaxed smile. He was determined to face them, to look anyone who wanted to accuse him in the eye, so he uncrossed his legs and sat forward, as if prepared to leap to his feet and demand the floor. But he didn't; he merely listened as Aulus continued.

'Yet from things that I hear, sordid rumours bandied about by dim-witted peasants, there is a demand to compound this crime by committing one that is even worse. What could be less becoming to the supreme judicial body of the Republic than this; that the death of one upright man should be followed by the disgrace of someone of equal stature. Rumours abound that one of our number has taken a political difference and transformed it into a criminal act. Rumours, fellow senators, levelled against Lucius Falerius Nerva.'

Those who supported Lucius regardless cried shame, his less numerous enemies aimed their angry scrolls at his heart, but a majority, the permanently uncommitted, stayed silent, content to hear the noble Aulus Cornelius Macedonicus to the end.

'What's to be gained by perpetrating this foul act. Money? Where in Rome will you find a man less avaricious than Lucius Falerius Nerva? Who among you have put aside considerations of personal gain so that you may devote all your energies to the commonweal? My friend may not thank me for saying this, but while many here have increased their wealth a hundred-fold, sometimes at the expense of the state, my noble companion has watched his possessions dwindle through neglect. Why? Because he cares more about the power and majesty of the Republic than he does about himself, or his family.'

That last sentence was greeted by a mixture of nods, violently shaking jowls and the odd senators who threw back their heads in disbelief that anyone could countenance such tripe.

'Then it's rumoured the act was committed to gain power, as if the man does not dispose of enough of that already.'

Some members, trying to ensure that Lucius saw them do so, very vocally cried, 'The gods be praised'. Others again aimed their scrolls at him and damned him as a tyrant. Aulus let the noise go on until it died of its own volition. Changing his voice, he sought a tone of inclusion, not declamation.

'Fellow senators, it is in the nature of this assembly that differences of opinion will surface, sometimes disputes that are serious enough to threaten the very fabric of the polity we are set to defend. What kind of sheep would we be if everyone, here present, agreed on every subject? It is debate that has made us, the very variety of beliefs itself being our strength. This Senate has overseen the expansion of Roman power till no organised state can stand against us. We hold borders that would have caused envy in the breast of Alexander himself.'

Aulus paused to allow them a moment of self-congratulation, as well as to allow his fellow senators to recall his own triumphs. 'And who in this house stands head and shoulders above us all in his ability to command attention on the floor of the house? What man cares more than he that the dignity of the Senate should be maintained? None other that that same Lucius Falerius Nerva. Which member has more ability to bring attention to his principles? Would such a man, with so much in his favour, stoop to secret murder, cause riot and mayhem which could put at risk everything he holds dear for the mere prospect of personal revenge?'

Aulus paused before he thundered his repetition of the word. 'Revenge!'

'Yet the rumours have some basis. There are

those determined to take advantage of recent events to gain a spurious political advantage. That, I submit, ranks with murder as a felony. All I propose to the house is this; that whoever committed this atrocity could not have the well-being of the Republic at the forefront of his concerns. That, more than the vow he personally volunteered to me, exonerates Lucius Falerius Nerva. I humbly ask that the repetition of such accusations should be made a criminal offence.'

Lucius had relaxed, and now his smile was genuine instead of forced. Aulus, in his bluff soldierly way, had played an admirable hand. True, it was not advocacy as Lucius understood it, but the effect was obvious. Even some of those he considered his opponents were pray to doubts and the motion Aulus had proposed would silence them for good. He could nod now to those who supported him most closely, men who probably did not believe a word of what Aulus Cornelius had just said, but could not care less. They had wanted Tiberius Livonius dead as much as anyone, and since that had come to pass they were satisfied.

He was slightly surprised when his defender continued. Aulus had made his case and really there was no more to say. Also, experience told Lucius that once a certain point had been reached, it was better to desist, that there was such a thing as excessive advocacy. It annoyed him that, least of all in the chamber, he was in no position to interrupt, and the frustration showed on his fine boned face.

'Everything humanly possible,' Aulus proclaimed, 'must be done to bring to justice the perpetrators of this heinous crime. Men must know that a plebeian tribune's death will not remain unavenged. They must also be made aware that his ideas and principles do not die with him. I hope and trust that all will share my view; that Tiberius Livonius had the good of the Republic close to his heart, in the same way as my good friend and fellow senator whose case I've pleaded today. Both men deserve to be heard.'

The stunned silence that followed these words spoke volumes to those with the wit to interpret Aulus's remarks. He had done no less than detach himself from slavish adherence to the Falerian faction. He may not have recommended Tiberius Livonius's political nostrums to the house, but he had indicated that he, at least, was prepared to debate them. There was no smile on Lucius's face now, just the look of a man fighting to hide cold fury.

He had to speak; to offer to the man who had defended him his gratitude. Lucius did so, with all the skill he could command, but at the final moment of his peroration the thanks he gave Aulus were offered through clenched teeth. The two men left the Forum separately, Lucius as usual surrounded by supplicants and toadies, all eager to pledge support, Aulus alone, shunning even those who would congratulate him. He felt an emptiness inside, as if he had cut out some vital organ from his body. The following day, Aulus left Rome, sending a message to Lucius that he would regret not attending either the funeral of his wife or the celebration of the birth of his son; that after so long away from Italy, he needed to tour his estates, which, without his personal attention might go to rack and ruin. When he returned three months later, answering a politely couched, though pressing summons from Lucius, it was to a city that had moved on, to a populace to whom the murder of Tiberius Livonius was nothing but a distant memory.

It was with some trepidation that he called and to ensure that he was not humiliated a second time, he sent ahead his steward to arrange an appointment. The relief, as he was greeted like an old friend, was immense. He was taken to the nursery to see how young Marcellus was progressing and back in his study Lucius could even refer to the debate and Aulus's speech without a trace of discomfort.

'As you so rightly observed in the Senate, Aulus, I too have sadly neglected my properties. Now that my term of office is ending, I must undertake the task you've just completed and look to visit my estates.'

On those travels Aulus had had much time to ponder his act of separation, one on which he had no intention of going back, but he did want this man to know that despite what had happened, on a personal if not a political level, he still considered him a friend, still considered himself bound by that oath they had taken years before. Nothing in Lucius's demeanour told him that he was seen as dangerous now, a man around whom opposition might coalesce, just as Lucius would never let on how much his power had been dented by Aulus's defection. He had not lost control of the Senate, but without his old friend's unquestioning support, his authority had been severely diminished. He now had to bargain where once he could command.

'Do you wish me to accompany you?' Aulus asked.

Lucius laughed. 'Never in life. I shall be sadly bored by the need. I would not even think of subjecting you to such a thing, especially since you've undergone months of such torture.'

Aulus was perplexed and it showed, for the messenger Lucius had sent asked that he return to Rome without delay. 'Yet your message implied some urgency.'

'True, and I apologise for it. You must have still been coated with the dust of travel when it arrived.' Aulus shrugged, as Lucius continued. 'You will recall my telling you on the way to the Senate, the day you defended me, that the governor of Illyricum was ill.'

'Is he still in Brindisium?'

'His ashes are,' said Lucius, with a sigh. 'Three months it's taken him to die. Meanwhile everything in the province is on the perish. I need an immediate replacement, on whose abilities I can rely, and naturally my thoughts turned to you.'

'Would the house agree, Lucius?'

His old friend laughed, as if amazed at the naivety he was witnessing. 'You have no idea of how high you stand in the estimation of your fellow senators, Aulus. They see now what I have known all along, that you are a paragon. If you agree, they will!'

Aulus blushed at the word paragon, and as he considered the proposition he knew he should turn it down, given that he had only so recently returned from Spain. To be given another posting, and a lucrative one at that, would cause jealousy in some quarters, and in others, since it came from the hand of Lucius, undermine the independence he was so desperate to maintain. Yet against that was a deep desire to be away from Rome. Titus was on the first leg of a career in military service and Quintus was about to be married. Perhaps the preparations for that event had disguised the deep rift that remained between him and Claudia. The last quarter had been a torture that had nothing to do with travelling round his scattered possessions, more to do with his infrequent, and discreet returns to

Rome. His wife had remained cold and distant and nothing he could do seemed to help. She needed even more time to recover from her ordeal in Spain and that painful birth. His presence clearly hindered that process, and it was an old but valid expression that 'absence made the heart grow fonder'.

'I am always at the service of the state, you know that,' he said.

'Good,' Lucius exclaimed. 'You must dine with me before you depart.'

Aulus nodded as Lucius took his arm in a gesture of friendship that was wholly false. Inwardly he was content; Lucius knew that he must hold close those he did not fully trust but there was more than one method by which he could skin a cat. The death of Tiberius Livonius had stilled the clamour for reform, but it had not killed it off and if anything, Lucius, faced with a multitude of enemies rather than one, had to be even more vigilant. He had a task to perform, to sell all his distant properties and concentrate his holdings around the capital. Never again would he face the need for a prolonged absence and he believed that while he had to be out of the city this one last time, to leave Aulus Cornelius in the Senate was too dangerous an idea to contemplate. Even present, Lucius could not be sure of controlling him.

CHAPTER TEN

'You're not the same fellow, Clodius,' said Piscius Dabo, patting his sweating companion on the back.

The contrast between the pair was telling; Dabo, wiry of build in clean, dust free clothes, Clodius Terentius, sturdily built and unkempt, his hair and smock grey from the powdered chaff. He leant down to hoist another sack of corn, gasping rather than speaking his reply as he heaved the load onto his shoulder. 'I'm older, Dabo, that's for certain, but as the gods will swear, no wiser.'

Dabo followed him across the yard. 'That sounds like Fulmina's words, not yours.'

'I don't get many words from Fulmina these days, few words and precious little else, to boot. If she speaks at all, it's usually to say we need more coin.'

Dabo executed a sad shake of the head. 'That changeling boy has certainly taken over her life.'

Clodius threw the sack on to the rear of the cart, then leant there for a second, hoping the mill owner would be too busy to notice him slacking, as he thought about his past; of how a life that had once had some pleasure now seemed just full of toil. In six or seven years he had gone from being the owner of a farm to paid day labourer. Dabo, whose life had gone in the opposite direction watched him closely, thinking that if his old comrade had an abiding fault he was too soft, and nothing demonstrated it more than the way his life was now ordered to suit a child that was not even his own.

'He's taken over mine, as well, friend,' Clodius sighed. 'Aquila needs this, Aquila needs that. I can't remember the last time I had the means to get drunk.'

Dabo smiled broadly and patted him on the back again. 'You're welcome at my place anytime, mate, you know that.'

Clodius eyed him warily, for to call Dabo a friend was stretching a point. True they had shared many a flagon as they swapped stories about their days in the legions but in the last few years Dabo had prospered, so held himself to be a cut above Clodius the day labourer. Dabo had not only retained his own farm, he had taken over his father's place as well and with the income from both had bought another from the family of some poor sod who had been cut down in Spain. Piscius Dabo was now a man of property and given sufficient drink he would open up enough to boast, to tell all and sundry that he intended to die a knight. He would need a damn sight more than three farms to have enough property to qualify for such an elevated class as the *Equities* and his pretensions were a source of much quiet amusement in the vicinity.

'You don't hand out the invitations like you used to, Dabo.'

The other man looked shocked. 'Invitations! Since when did you need an invitation to visit my place?'

Anytime in the last three years, thought Clodius, but he did not say that his old drinking companion had become stand-offish around the time that the child had arrived. That was also, coincidentally, the time that Dabo acquired his third farm. 'I don't like to just drop in. It ain't polite. An' you might be busy anyway.'

'Never too busy to see an old chum,' replied Dabo, in a jolly tone. 'Why don't you drop round soon, and we'll have a proper wet.'

The voice from the mill cut through the hot morning air. 'What do you think you're about, you lazy swine?' Clodius jumped back to work, dashing across the yard and grabbing a sack from the pile. He practically ran to load it onto the cart, while all the while the voice followed him. 'Why do I employ you? I could get a slave to do your work for the food he needs to eat, instead of parting with hard earned denarii to keep you.'

'Denarii,' gasped Clodius as he passed Dabo.

'I've never seen a coin larger than a copper ass from that bastard.'

'This is cruel work, Clodius,' said Dabo raising his voice so that his friend could hear him as he raced away to the pile of sacks. 'Strikes me that you need somethin' a mite better than this.'

Clodius replied from under another sack. 'I won't argue with that, friend.'

'Best drop over an' see me soon. I can't stand by and watch a fellow legionary in a pickle like this.'

'Will you leave Clodius alone to get on with his work.'

Dabo shouted back at the mill owner in an even louder voice. 'Put a pair of socks in your mouth, you fat slob. Remember, Samnite pig, that you're talking to a couple of citizens of Rome.'

'Citizens of Rome,' whooped the mill owner. 'Some citizens, one with his arse hanging out of his smalls and the other a long-winded fart with ideas above his station.'

Dabo growled, and looked set to go into the mill and box the owner's ears.

'Don't, Dabo,' gasped Clodius. 'The bastard'll only take it out on me.'

The mill owner was treated to a glare and Dabo's eyes were still angry when he turned to talk to Clodius. 'You come and see me, d'ye hear.'

Aquila raced across the dusty yard, his long golden hair flying behind him, as soon as Clodius came into sight. For all his moans about the little fellow, Clodius was fond of him. He was a tyke, into everything and always in trouble, just like his adopted father. Despite the rigours of his working day, Clodius caught him and tossed him high in the air.

The boy squealed with delight and said, 'Gain.'

Clodius puffed loudly. 'Come on lad. Your papa's had a hard old day.'

The boy held his arms out insistently. 'Gain!'

'Just one more, right?'

Aquila nodded untruthfully and made Clodius toss him up in the air until Fulmina stopped him. 'What are you trying to do, addle the boy's brain. If you shake him about much more he'll end up as daft as you.'

He was surprised to see Drisia come out of the hut, less so that she fixed him with an evil look. An infrequent caller since the time the boy had been found, the soothsayer was even more wizened than Clodius could remember. Even so she never seemed to age, nor, as far as he could tell, did she ever change her clothes, which were filthy, smelling worse than a cow byre in summer while her dull grey hair was matted, uncombed and dirty. Clodius suspected that the old bitch encouraged Fulmina's fantasies about the boy, because his wife always seemed to nag him more after the rank one had made a visit.

'Did I ever tell you what we did to some of them Salyes tribesmen, young Aquila?' said Clodius, gathering the boy into his arms to avoid throwing him any more. He made his way into the welcome shade of the canopy where the reed roof jutted out over the door of the hut. Aquila, his blue eyes wide with interest, shook his head. 'Smelly mob, they were. Never washed so you could always tell when they was about to attack, the camp dogs would start whining. On top of that they had this war cry that they never let up with. Noise fit to drive a man over the edge of the world, I tell you. Could never get them to shut up so what we did, when we caught 'em, was to bury 'em in some sand right by the edge of the water.'

'Swim,' said Aquila eagerly.

'In a minute,' replied Clodius, shaking him slightly. He raised his voice to make sure the two women could hear. 'Right by the water's edge, as I say. Then we told 'em to yell their war cry as the water rose. The tide don't rise much in the middle sea, but it certainly came up enough to shut those Gallic bastards up.'

Fulmina knew where the story was aimed. She nudged Drisia as she replied. 'No point in trying that on you, eh! Clodius, you'd just drink it, like you used to do every coin that came into this house.'

Clodius scowled and put the boy down. He liked a drink and could not deny it, but given the way it had been in short supply he felt aggrieved. Aquila looked from one to the other, aware that they were going to be bad to each other again. He didn't understand and it showed in the anxious look on his face. Fulmina spotted it and her whole tone changed.

'Come on, little one, cheer up. Papa's back and he's going to take you for a dip in the river.'

Clodius sniffed loudly, pulling a face and nodded at Drisia. 'Happen that someone else could use a dip in the river.'

Fulmina glared at him. 'Just stay out of the house for a bit.'

More prophesying, thought Clodius, so they wanted both him and the boy out of the way. He entered the hut and grabbed a hunk of unleavened bread off the rough table, stuffing it into his mouth as he re-emerged into the warm sunlit evening. The words that followed were hard to comprehend, but the nodding head told Aquila that Fulmina was speaking the truth. Papa was going to take him for a swim, so he whooped with joy and ran for the river. Both adoptive parents looked after him smiling serenely, then their eyes met and the smiles evaporated.

'Don't be down there forever,' snapped Fulmina. 'The nights are drawing in and I can't afford to feed you by the light of a tallow wad.'

'This is no life for a man,' said Clodius, stomping off in pursuit of the boy.

Fulmina went into the hut, leant over the pot of polenta and gave it a stir. 'It would be nice to come across a real man, just once in my life.'

Aquila had thrown off his smock and dived right in. Even at three he could swim a bit, though it looked more like a dog paddling than the proper thing. His body was golden brown and his gold hair took on a ginger shading when it was wet. Round these parts, where people, including his adoptive parents, had black hair and dark skin, he was the cause of much comment. Clodius murmured a quick incantation to *Volturnus*, the River God, then treated himself to a cooling and cleansing dip; he did not stay in the water long, but sat by the edge and watched the boy splash around in the stream.

There were few times that Clodius could say he was happy, but this was one of them. He had been indifferent to his other children, partly because he had been away on legionary service when they were Aquila's age. By the time he got back they were old enough to argue with him, and Clodius got too much of that from his wife to welcome more of the same from his offspring. Yet even taking that into account, they did not have what this youngster had. Curious they might be, but everyone hereabouts liked him, for he had a way of attracting people. Perhaps it was his gaiety, for he was always laughing, always on the move, and never morose. Even that fat slob of a mill owner had offered Aquila some honey-coated bread the day he had run away to visit Papa's place of work. Fulmina, thinking he had been stolen, had yelled at the boy when she found him, a rare thing, since she hardly ever raised her voice to him, but, without crying, he took her hand, as if he realised that she was only shouting because she was frightened for him.

'It's a bugger bein' poor,' said Clodius, raising his head to address the gods. They had heard precious little from him lately, no nocturnal songs and slurred requests for intercession. 'If you can't bless me with some fortune, then put some aside for young Aquila. Maybe you'll help him to find his real family. They have the money to raise him to be somethin'. I'm damned if I do.'

The soaking wet bundle landed right on top of him, catching him, in his reverie, totally unawares. They rolled over in the grey sand that lined the side of the stream, laughing and squealing, with Clodius pretending to hit Aquila severely, and taking the punches of the boy, hard for a mere three-year-old, in good part. Aquila was allowed to win, and he sat astride his papa, grinning from ear to ear, and saying 'ender ender.'

Clodius surrendered happily.

'Dabo's coming down a bit, to mix with the likes of you.'

'Happen he's realised that true friendship don't lie with money.'

'In a pig's ear,' snapped Fulmina, but quietly, since the child was asleep. 'He's got a whole host of folk to get drunk with. Why choose you?'

Clodius felt that Dabo had hinted at some kind of work, but he did not want to say anything to Fulmina, knowing she would only scoff. 'Well that don't count, since the invitation was plain.'

'So that's it. A weasel like Dabo crooks his little finger and mighty man Clodius runs off to oblige. Well just you make sure you're fit to get to the mill tomorrow, otherwise he might sling you out of your job.'

'He won't,' Clodius insisted. 'The bastard's too mean.'

'He'll get himself a slave if you're late once more.'

'Not him. That would mean layin' out real money. He'd rather give me a pittance every day than put down any of his precious capital to buy slave labour.'

'What worries me, Dabo, is that, if prices drop, the bastard will get himself a slave.'

Dabo nodded, his face full of comradely concern. 'Which they will, mate, as soon as there is a decent war. Price of slaves will go down as it always does.'

'Not much chance of that is there?'

They were sitting just outside Dabo's house; not really a house, more an elevated hut with space underneath for the livestock, but it had more than a single room, so it qualified as a house. Dabo's fat wife had been ordered to bed and the men sat in the warm spring night, drinking steadily but quietly.

'Happen there will be a war soon,' Dabo replied. 'They've started on the *dilectus*.'

'The call up don't affect me, thank the gods,' said Clodius, taking a swig from the large gourd Dabo had given him.

'Then there's some fortune in being poor,' Dabo growled.

It was the way Dabo said it that alerted Clodius. 'Not you!'

'Rumour has it!' said his old comrade sourly. 'They can't fill the levies with the normal methods. I've heard they're planning to pull in men who've already done their time, as long as they meet the property laws.'

'That's sacrilege!'

'It was once, Clodius, but the consuls have got the priests in their pockets, as well as the laws in their hands. They can do whatever they like, and will, just so long as they get enough men.'

Clodius took a swig of wine, before replying, 'I'm sure it's just a rumour.'

'Let's hope you're right.' They sat in silence for some time, each alone with his thoughts and memories. It was Dabo who eventually spoke. 'Not that life in the legions was that bad.'

'It wasn't good either,' replied Clodius, for once dropping the rosy glow that usually accompanied his military recollections.

'The women were willing enough.'

Clodius laughed. 'Don't recall that it mattered much if they were willing or not.'

'Damned right, Clodius,' Dabo whooped. 'We speared 'em anyway.'

'Makes you wonder how many of Rome's slaves are bred from Roman juice.'

'Quite a few, old friend, quite a few,' Dabo gently tapped his fired clay goblet against the wooden gourd in Clodius's hand. It made a hollow sound, so Dabo filled it to the brim before completing the toast. 'The good old days.'

'Back breaking work on the march, and then even more when we pitched camp for the night,' said Clodius ruefully.

'Booty, Clodius.'

'Don't seem to recall mine lasting all that long, Dabo. An' when I came back the farm had gone to ruin. That six years' service did for me.'

Dabo had come back at the same time, but he had brought his farm back to proper fruitfulness, so he reckoned he knew just who was to blame for his companion's failure, and it was not divine providence. 'You had rotten luck, Clodius, an' no mistake. No father to tend your fields and kids too young to pull their weight.'

'I reckon Fulmina did her best,' said Clodius, in a rare expression of praise for his wife.

'Beats me how she kept her looks. For all the work she does, she's still a fine looking woman.'

'Made of stone as far as I'm concerned. I hinted that Aquila could use a playmate.'

'What did she say to that?'

Clodius laughed without pleasure, then took another deep swig. 'Said that it was me grovelling for a playmate. Told me if I wanted one I could do some extra work and buy comfort at the brothel in Aprilium.'

'Sad thing when a woman takes her favours away. Makes for a hard life.'

The drink was beginning to affect Clodius. He laughed properly and drained his gourd. 'You can say that again, Dabo. A sheep's bum is enough to excite me these days.'

'Do you remember that centurion and the goat?'

'Do I,' whooped Clodius.

They were off, swapping well-worn tales and reminiscences, talking of the good times and relegating the bad, capping each story with a cupful of wine, until life in the army seemed the highest thing to which a man could aspire. The drink flowed, with Dabo going into the storehouse below and coming back with an ampoule full of his potent grain spirit. How they laughed. All the old jokes were trotted out and soon they were singing the songs, with their filthy words, that the legions had used since time immemorial to ease the pain of a long march. Dabo, who was drinking a good deal less that Clodius, made sure his guest's gourd was never empty.

They were trying to recover from the pain in the sides after a particularly hilarious anecdote. This concerned an officer who preferred boys trying to persuade his commander to let him raid a nearby town because he had heard it contained an all-male brothel full to the brim of young blond Scythians. He could not say that, of course, and it was not even true, one of the more impudent soldiers having concocted the story as a joke. Everyone had sidled as near to the command tent as they could to eavesdrop on the exchange, which had become increasingly desperate as the man found all his arguments refuted.

Clodius told the story well. He had the officer's high-pitched voice to perfection, as well as the gruff tone to convey the increasingly irritated responses of the commander. Dabo was reduced to hugging his sides, trying to get his breath, while Clodius, laughing just as much, had rolled down the steps, scattering the chickens, and was now crouched over, hands around his stomach, half in pain and half in hysterics.

'What a life eh! Clodius.'

'Golden days,' gasped Clodius.

'You know what we need now, old friend,' said Dabo, staggering down the three steps and helping Clodius to his feet. 'We need a woman. What says we get in that there cart and head for town.'

Clodius started to shake his head, patting his belt to indicate his lack of funds. Dabo threw his arm around his guest's shoulder. 'Pay no heed to that, old friend. This one's on me.'

'Never,' replied Clodius, with profound disbelief.

'Damn women, Clodius,' Dabo slurred. 'You give them a squeeze and they greet you with an elbow in the ribs. Damn them, I say. They don't treat their chickens that bad. If the cock don't perform they get mad, chop its head off and cook it, then go and buy another, but we're not ever allowed to perform.'

'That's right. Mind you, an elbow's better than a chopper across the throat,' slurred Clodius, with a wide, knowing grin.

'Let them hear the sniff of Cerberus on their way to hell, I say. I'm willing to stand you...'

'Stand me. I think I can stand on my own, thank you!' spluttered Clodius, reprising the homosexual officer's arch voice. They both screeched with laughter, doubling up again. Dabo, recovering first, grabbed his friend and bundled him into the cart.

'Aprilium, here we come,' he crowed.

If Clodius had wondered why the mule, which should have been in its stall, had spent the whole night harnessed in the shafts, he was too drunk now to enquire.

Clodius sang nearly all the way to Aprilium, and since Dabo had been clever enough to fetch a flagon of grain spirit along, neither his throat, nor his level of inebriation, faltered. In between the songs and the usual requests for some form of intercession from the gods, Dabo moaned about the prospect of having to go back into the legions.

'I'm a man of substance now, Clodius. I had my eye on another place next door to my father's old farm. Given a bit of luck I can join them all together and go into cattle ranching.'

'That's where the loot is, Dabo. Every moneybags in Rome is well into ranching.'

His host slapped his hand hard on the side of the cart. 'That's right! The last thing I need is another six years in the army. It will throw my plans right out.'

Clodius tried to console him with a pat on the back. 'Shame at that, Dabo. If you was to get on, I could say that I know someone who's a knight. Not many people round these parts can call someone worth a hundred thousand denarii a friend.' He leant over and grabbed the flagon. 'Mind, I hope you drink a choicer brew than this shit when you're rich.'

For the first time that night, Dabo's bluff, cheerful manner deserted him. 'That's just it, you oaf. If I go into the legions I won't be rich. I'll end up like you, on my arse.'

Clodius's mood changed just as quickly. 'Don't say as I take kindly to being called an oaf.'

Dabo ignored him. 'And it's only because I've got a bit that I'm being called up in the first place.'

Clodius put all the sympathy he could into the reply. 'But you're not sure that you are going to be called up.'

Dabo seemed to collect himself, losing his belligerent tone. 'That's right, Clodius. Help yourself to another mouthful, old friend, and right sorry I am for any offence. It's not your fault that you're near potless. That's what sticks in my craw. If they was to call you to the ranks what harm would it do.'

'Depends on who I'm fightin' with.'

'I don't mean that. It's the law that means only men of property can be trusted to fight. Crap I say. If you've got nothing to lose they won't have you. If you own a farm, you're taken into the army, 'cause they reckon you've got something to defend. Your farm goes to seed while you're away, so you end up a pauper who they can't call up, living off the public dole.'

'Blessings on Tiberius Livonius,' slurred Clodius, helping himself to another swig. 'Needed that corn dole on more'n one occasion.'

'Tell me, Clodius, if they called you up, changed the law, like, what would you do?'

'I'd go. What else could I do? Might be better off in some ways, for I tell you, Dabo, I'm fed up humping sacks of grain for a pittance. Not that the pay in the army would keep a pig in scraps. Family'd likely starve when I was gone.'

'That's it!' cried Dabo, putting as much sincerity into his voice as he could. 'If'n you had a decent wage, enough to keep Fulmina and your young Aquila in comfort, how would you feel about the Army?'

'A damn sight better than I would workin' for that tightwad at the corn mill.'

'Drink up, old friend,' said Dabo, placing his hand on the bottom of the ampoule and pushing it up. 'There's plenty more where that came from.'

'You're a fool, Clodius.' Fulmina spoke without rancour. Her voice was resigned rather than harsh, for which her sore-headed husband was extremely grateful. 'Always were, and now you'll go and get yourself killed, most likely.'

'I'm not that easy to kill.'

'You're going away?' asked Aquila, who, by the look on his face, was struggling with this strange concept.

'I'm going to be a soldier again, boy.'

'Can I come?'

Clodius bent down and put both his hands on the boy's shoulders. 'No lad, you have to stay here and look after Mama.' Aquila had heard that too many times as Clodius departed to his job at the mill to be pleased at the prospect. 'Maybe, when you're grown up, you can be a soldier too. And if your papa can just fall in the way of a bit of luck, you might even be a member of the first class, a *principi*.'

His wife sniffed loudly. Drisia's soothsaying had promised much more than that, but it was not something Fulmina discussed with the sceptical Clodius. Even so, she could not let his remark pass. 'Some future for Aquila, and all the while Dabo's eldest brat grows up to be a knight.'

'Dabo's a long way from bein' that,' said Clodius looking up, for once on safe ground with the promise Dabo had given him to support his family while he was away. 'But at least I'm getting some of his wealth to rub off on me. At least, this time, I won't be at the bottom of the pile.'

Then he turned his eyes back to the disappointed child. 'What says Papa makes you a suit of armour, just like the one he's goin' to wear?'

That cheered Aquila up no end. Clodius set too, using twigs and bark, carving the decorations for shield and breastplate with a sharp knife, and he had plenty of time to do it, having chucked in his job at the corn mill. Dabo, as well as providing the equipment he would need on service, had agreed to support him until he was actually called to join his maniple. While he was away, Fulmina would receive food, wine, oil and kindling on a regular basis as a wage for his surrogate soldier. Of course, he had made sure that Clodius fixed his mark by Dabo's name with the recruiting commission, and appended the same to an agreement drawn up by a notary the very night they had gone into town. As far as the Roman State was concerned, Clodius Terentius had become Piscius Dabo.

CHAPTER ELEVEN

Claudia Cornelia sat upright in her chair, observing her husband's eldest son, thinking that, regardless of the way he sought to emulate Aulus, Quintus was totally unlike his father. Virtual strangers since the parental marriage they had finally spent time together the year before, travelling to visit Aulus in Illyricum. Claudia had not enjoyed the experience and she suspected that her stepson had taken from it even less in the way of pleasure. Conversation with Quintus tended to be stilted at best, and quite often disputatious. Even so the journey had been better than the stay, the happiness Aulus displayed on her arrival, after two long years, sinking slowly back into the confused misery that marked their relationship before he had departed Rome.

With the head of the house absent Quintus had moved back with his wife and child to his own family home, a setting that allowed him a greater degree of independence than he enjoyed in the house of his father-in-law. Prior to the meal he had led the family prayers in a sonorous voice and performed the rituals in elaborate fashion. Quintus liked to entertain but tonight was solely a family occasion. Nevertheless it was typical of him to insist on so ritual a dinner for just two people. Claudia had been forced to dress her hair and don a flowing, formal garment. His own wife Pulchra was with child again and unwell, with no appetite for food, so she had been ordered to bed by her unsympathetic husband.

Claudia had been told that Quintus had been a playful boy and a wild youth, popular with his classmates. That carefree spirit, if it ever existed, had gone; he was very much a nobleman now, full of gravitas and conscious of his station in the Roman world. A praetor, Quintus harboured the ultimate goal of standing for the consulship, though he had a good few years to wait before he would become eligible and many offices to fill on the way. The route of honour they called it, yet when Claudia thought of some of the despicable creatures who had climbed that ladder, including a goodly number who had achieved that eminent, supreme accolade of serving as a consul, she wondered if the appellation was appropriate.

'Do I have to initiate all the conversation,' said Quintus from his position on the couch. His voice carried just a trace of that petulance which, combined with arrogance, had become the hallmark of his behaviour.

Claudia greeted this with a slight smile. 'A mere woman speak at dinner, without permission, Quintus? I wouldn't dream of breaching the bounds of what is known to be proper behaviour. I'm surprised that you of all people should suggest such an outlandish thing.'

'Me of all people! What precisely does that mean?'

'Oh come, Quintus. You pride yourself on your manners.'

Quintus swung one foot in an arc, his eyes on the toes of his sandals. 'I do think a stepmother is allowed to open a conversation with her husband's eldest son.'

That avoidance of the appellation stepson was a roundabout way to deliver an insult, meant to underline that Quintus still regarded her as some kind of interloper in the Cornelii household. Claudia responded by treating him to a look of mock horror. 'The gods forbid.'

'You choose to tease me?'

'You do tend to invite it, Quintus.'

He tried to assume a disinterested look. 'Do I indeed?'

His lethargy angered Claudia and she spoke sharply, her tone somewhat harsher than she truly intended. 'Everything you do is undertaken in the light of its effect on your precious career.'

Quintus stiffened slightly. 'Precious? That word makes my behaviour sound suspect.'

'Are you saying that you don't value your career?'

'Of course I do.'

Claudia thought of his browbeaten wife, sent to bed simply because she might embarrass him for her want of appetite and spoke with a trace of sadness. 'More than anything in the world, I think.'

'I refuse to accept the implied rebuke in those words,' he snapped.

Claudia produced a mocking smile. 'Oh dear. I seem to have offended you.'

'Not offended, but I cannot fathom why you mind my behaviour. I cannot think what it is I've done to cause you to speak this way.'

Claudia maintained that mocking smile, her voice taking on a note of irony. 'You have done nothing you should be ashamed of.'

'Ashamed! That's another word that is out of place. I know you're not much given to explanation, Lady Claudia, but I would appreciate it if you would just speak plainly for once.'

'Now you're rebuking me.'

'Perhaps I am, but I would dearly like to know what you're getting at. What is it I have done to earn your barely disguised disapproval.'

Claudia leant forward slightly. 'I don't disapprove of you.'

Quintus swung his feet to the floor, waving aside the slave intent on serving him. Claudia observed that one of his greatest failings was the way he sought the approval of others, even those he probably despised. Aulus, his father, was not like that; he looked at everything with a clear idea of right and wrong, then acted accordingly. Time had even allowed Claudia to see that his actions, when he had come to her in that isolated wagon, sprang from the same trait of natural nobility. That his behaviour had trapped her did nothing to alter the fact; Aulus had acted from the highest of motives, never aware of the despair he had inflicted on her, because there were no circumstances in which she could tell him. Perhaps the lack of years between her and his eldest son exacerbated the natural divide of two people who were basically incompatible. Quintus had apparently been devoted to his mother and always made a point of invoking her memory at prayers. That was as it should be; according to Aulus she had been an upright Roman lady and it was reasonable to suppose her sons would be put out at their father taking on another wife.

Quintus waited until the slave was out of earshot before he spoke again. 'You don't disapprove of me yet you're not proud of me?'

Claudia wondered if he was really asking what she thought, putting to her a question he could never address to his father. Or was he just fishing for praise? Considering the way he treated her, and all women for that matter, what opinions she had should count for nothing. The easy way out would be to say, 'Of course, Quintus.' But she could not bring herself to do so.

'Not unreservedly, no!' she replied.

'That smacks of more equivocation.'

'Please, Quintus. You are much admired by others, let that suffice. You have done nothing to offend me and many things that please your father. Yet he would, like me, wish you were a trifle less serious.'

That did surprise him. 'Serious? No one has ever accused me of that.'

'Parents, especially step-parents, observe their children differently, more closely perhaps than other people.'

Yet she was thinking that no one observed Quintus as much as he did himself; he behaved like a man watching his own image in a play. His younger brother, Titus, was much more relaxed, but the second boy was the very image of Aulus, physically and morally. Quintus was angry, she could see that and Claudia regretted having taken the conversation in this direction. Her stepson lacked a sense of humour, which meant that, at this moment, he needed to say something to restore his self-esteem.

'Children observe their elders as well, madam,

and they don't always like what they see.'

Claudia made a point of sitting upright in her couch, smoothing the folds of her gown, composing her features before replying. 'Such as?'

'Since father is absent, I shall speak freely...'

'Please do!'

Quintus lay back on his couch, aware that he had reasserted his hold on the conversation. 'It seems to me that our visit to Illyricum could have been a happier affair. He certainly seemed glad to see us all when we arrived, especially you, yet within days he was cast down into a deep depression that lasted until our departure. He'll be home before the year is out and should the same thing occur here in Rome, Titus and I might wonder at the relationship between you.'

Her voice was icy. Again, Quintus had made her sound like an interloper in the Cornelii household. 'It's perfectly in order to wonder, Quintus, just as long as you don't pry!'

Her tone seemed to increase the lethargy in his voice, rather than diminish it. 'Who would need to pry? You may think you disguise your coldness to him very well, but you don't. It's plain enough to see, for anyone who cares to look.'

'If you expect me to explain, to you, my relationship with your father, I fear you're going to be disappointed.'

The calm evaporated and his voice became hard.

'I require no explanation, lady. Remember who it was who rescued you from those barbarians.'

Claudia dropped her head, the dark ringlets of her hair cascading forward. 'That I shall never forget.'

'And I'm neither blind nor stupid.'

She raised her head again, looking her stepson right in the eye. 'This is leading up to something, Quintus.'

'It is indeed. I have a concern that nothing you do, or have done, will stain my family name.'

'Don't you mean your name? Or should I say your prospects,' she snapped.

Quintus spoke slowly, deliberately. 'I don't know why father tolerates it.'

'Perhaps you'd best ask him.'

'I think he's suffered enough. He may not have eyes to see, but I have. So has my brother, I should think. If the truth ever emerged about what happened in Spain, our name would be coated in mud.'

'And your precious career would grind to a halt.' Quintus made to speak, but she shouted him down. 'Don't interrupt me. I am from a family that is every bit as noble as yours. While your father is alive I answer to him and to him alone. You asked earlier what it is I disapprove of. Well this dinner is one thing. You are so careful of your dignity, you cannot even dine informally in your own house.'

Quintus was genuinely surprised at an attack on that topic and it showed on his face, but Claudia denied him any chance to respond.

'I hope, and believe, that you esteem your father and wish to emulate him, but I cannot help but think that you lack the one quality he has in abundance, the one quality that makes him a great man, the lack of which will make you mediocre, regardless of how high you climb politically. That quality is natural humility.'

Quintus was stung by the rebuke, though, in truth it was not serious, but he was a grown man, a praetor, and as a senior magistrate unaccustomed to being addressed so. His anger was caused by the dent his stepmother had delivered to his self-esteem rather than anything in the actual words she had used. He stood up abruptly, his round face quivering with suppressed passion, his black eyes full of what looked remarkably like hate.

'He has enough natural humility to abide the daily insult your coolness heaps upon him. If I lack that quality, then I'm thankful for it. In his shoes I wouldn't skulk away in some godforsaken province like Illyricum. I'd end it, one way or another!'

'I would welcome that, if only for his sake,' Claudia replied softly.

Quintus, in his rage, did not hear. He was halfway out of the dining room, kicking off his sandals and calling for his shoes. But he did deliver one last parting shot.

'I rue the day I found you and left you alive for my "oh so humble" father.'

Claudia felt the tears sting her eyes and closed them tight to shut off the flow. No one regretted that day more than she did, herself; no one had the nightly curse of remembrance. Even to open up to someone as unsympathetic as Quintus would have provided some kind of release from the constant mental turmoil that plagued her life.

The shuffling sound alerted her to the fact that the slaves had entered the dining area to clear up. Hastily she rose to her feet, and keeping her head down so they should not observe that she was distressed, Claudia hurried to her own chamber, thinking that if things were bad now, they would be worse soon. Aulus's term as Governor of Illyricum was coming to its end. He would be home, living with her in the same house, a constant reminder by day of the tortured dreams that haunted her nights.

Aulus returned in the Spring, leaving behind him in Illyricum a province at peace, a border quiet if not entirely secure from raids. He was welcomed to Rome by two consuls grateful for the way he had, by his enlightened governorship, eased their burden. He was well aware they were adherents of Lucius Falerius, who had fought hard to engineer their appointment, just as he knew that his real report would be made to him, but all the proper forms had to be preserved to maintain the fiction that the pair holding what was supposed to be the supreme office of the Republic were their own men.

The note from Lucius was also couched in the proper form, with a date and a wish that Aulus would call; that he, as a man who still had an interest in the safety of the Republic, would welcome his oldest, dearest friend, Aulus Cornelius, and would be eager to hear from him the details of what he had found in Illyricum, and what he had left; that, after a gap of fourteen days, no one, not even given the most malicious tongue, could accuse him of interference in the affairs of state. There had been a time, Aulus thought as he read it, that when he came home Lucius would have been at his house to greet him, a degree of warmth that would have been very welcome.

Other senators called on him in between receipt of the note and their meeting, men who were political opponents of the Falerii faction. Some had been supporters of Tiberius Livonius and honestly shared his views on citizenship and land grants to the poor, others were more opportunistic, spouting high principles while hoping to seduce him into backing some cause more to do with their own greed or ambition than proper government. Each, though greeted politely and subjected to all proper hospitality, left disappointed. Aulus would not even consent to discuss the nature of Lucius's power, let alone condemn it; all they had was the constantly repeated refrain that their host was allied to no party, that he was a servant of Rome, with no desire to be or support anyone who sought to be her master.

The meeting with Lucius was cordial without being effusive and both maintained the fiction it was only curiosity that made his host delve so deeply into what had happened during Aulus's governorship, only an aid to memory that had his scribe writing down so many details on crop and mine yields, tax revenues set against expenditure and the state of relations on the borders of the province. Yet it was clear as the discussion progressed that Lucius was less than happy, and Aulus had to gently chide him several times for his rather high-handed methods of interrogation. It was only after one of those that the truth of his irritability began to surface.

Having had no hand in the choice of his successor, Aulus, when asked, refused to cast any opinion on his abilities, something in which Lucius was less restrained, and it was during a peroration on the perceived faults of one Vegetius Flaminus that Aulus realised that he was, in part, being castigated himself, for so weakening the Falerii power that the head of that faction had been forced to agree to the appointment of a man of whom he thoroughly disapproved.

'You know how hard I fought against everything that Tiberius Livonius proposed, but at least, in his own crackpot way, the man was honest. Not Vegetius! He and others like him have taken up the Livonian baton as a stick with which to beat me and don't they just love the way the riff-raff sing their praises and draw me as a beast on the walls. They no more believe in his ideas than do I, but they will happily string along our Latin allies and take bribes from them to bring such measures before the house. You have no notion of how hard I have to work to keep them at bay and when this came up, replacing you. Just to avoid defeat on something far more important, I was forced to concede. Every vote involves a concession to some interest or other. It should not be so, and would not be so, if men who should know better saw where their duty lay.'

'Then retire,' said Aulus, tired of this litany of self-pity mixed with disguised complaint.

Lucius narrowed his eyes as he looked at Aulus. 'Would you leave the field of battle without a victory?' The lack of a response was answer enough. 'No, my friend, you would not, and neither shall I.'

'Lucius, let us dine together and perhaps talk of other things, more pleasant things.'

'I fear I would find that difficult, Aulus, so much does my care for the Republic master my time. At least my candidates for next year's consular elections are relatively safe. If I had denied Vegetius Flaminus they might not have been.'

Aulus repeated his invitation as a way of staying off politics, of which he was bored. 'But you will try to come to dinner?'

'Yes, I will. And it will be pleasant to see again the Lady Claudia, who I must say I have sadly neglected to entertain in your absence, though she did decline more than one invitation from me.'

Claudia did not like Lucius, and both men knew it, for she too had heard about the jokes that Lucius had helped circulate at the time of their marriage. 'With good reason I'm sure.'

'Of course,' said Lucius, with a wide smile. 'Though I must say she is less vivacious since you both returned from Spain. I fear campaigning did not suit her.'

Aulus knew he should not react; Lucius was chiding him too, but he could not keep the terse tone out of his voice. 'I think you have forgotten, my friend, how exhausting fighting in the field can be.'

'It has one great advantage over fighting in the Senate, Aulus. In the field you know precisely who are your enemies and who are your friends.' As Aulus swelled up to react, Lucius added quickly, with an air designed to disarm, 'but I so look forward to an evening spent in the company of you both, and I assure you, politics will not intrude.'

When Aulus invited Lucius to dine, both men knew that it would not be an intimate affair. Quite apart from his own family, the in-laws of Quintus were present, as were Claudia's parents and several of Aulus's old field commanders, each provided with a dining couch. As was the custom they ate without drinking and then drank without eating, watered but still potent wine, which was the point at which matters took a turn for the worse.

Even with all those people to distract him, the evening was not a success. Lucius and Claudia, close together as he was the guest of honour, sniped at each other continually, though each did so with smiles that left the other guests to wonder whether their barbed comments were examples of wit or malice. Aulus knew better, knew that his wife was defending him, because Lucius, despite his promise, could not leave politics alone, something which left him too confused to intervene. Why would a woman who showed him no affection in private be so stoutly defensive of his reputation in public? That she had little time for Lucius, he knew, and that went back to the time of their wedding.

What he did not comprehend was that Claudia

had her own opinion of Lucius, formed in the four years he had been away in Illyricum. She was a member of a set of well-born women who met regularly without the presence of their husbands, and as women do, they talked, mostly relaying to each other the frustrations, aspirations, doubts and certainties of each absent spouse. It was a commonplace jest that if you wanted to know what was really going on in Rome, it would be best to ask the wife of a senator. The actions of Lucius Falerius came up often, how could they not given his political prominence, and they were rarely flattering.

'Probity, my dear Lady Claudia, is all very well in its place, but Rome cannot maintain its conquests on only that.'

If no one understood what Lucius was saying, Claudia did; it was nothing less than a subtle denigration of her husband and his natural decency. She had praised that quality when Lucius sought to imply that any man who stood aloof from affairs of state, though they might see themselves as virtuous, was in fact living in a world of dreams; Rome was run by actions, not contemplations.

'But is that not what separates us from barbarians, Lucius Falerius, the notion that we will do the right thing even if it works against our interests? You of all people stand as an example of self-sacrifice in the pursuit of a well-run state.'

The gimlet look that accompanied those words took away from them any sincerity; Lucius knew that he was being accused of exactly the opposite. 'I work for an ideal, I admit.'

'Which must bring you great satisfaction.'

'All I know is that it gives me much to do.'

'How tiresome it must be, having all day, every day, to remind others of the need for integrity in all things.'

'I think it is time for the musicians, father,' said Quintus, who alone of all the guests knew exactly what was going on. Aulus agreed, indicated that they should be summoned, and tried to change the subject.

'Is Marcellus musical in any way?'

'No, thank the gods,' Lucius replied. 'My son's activities are confined to subjects which will serve him in the field, and make him a good administrator.'

'You should encourage him, Lucius,' said Claudia, in a mischievous tone. 'Music does much to soften the natural coarseness in young boys. It is possible to be both a soldier and a poet. I suggest he learns the lyre.'

'Claudia, enough,' said Aulus, for that play on words was going too far.

She nodded to indicate that she would henceforth be silent, but Lucius was not about to let it go. 'I had no idea, Lady Claudia, that you were so knowledgeable about young men.'

'Perhaps it is greater than yours, given that I am closer to it in memory.'

'I know many women who admire that coarseness you refer to when boys become men.'

'And yet you have not remarried after the death of the Lady Ameliana. That I find surprising, given that many women must admire you.'

That was an insult, to make Aulus sit up, but Lucius was too well-versed in the art of that not to return the compliment in full measure. 'A pity, I know, especially when you and Aulus have set me such a fine example.'

The musicians were assembled, and Aulus, fearing a slanging match, waved at them furiously to begin playing. The opening notes were loud enough to drown out what Lucius said next, so that only Claudia heard him express his sorrow that she and Aulus had not managed to have children. Looking intently at her he knew he had struck home by the look of pain that crossed her face.

CHAPTER TWELVE

⬥

Aulus rolled onto his back with that same angry feeling which had been with him since the first night he came home. The trouble was he could not bring himself to blame his young wife for her lack of interest, he being so much older than she. And that difference in age grew more marked with each passing year, a fact that had been made so much worse by the long separation of his proconsular service in Illyricum. He knew her skin was dry, so the sweat on his body seemed to mock him. She would not perspire, all the effort was from him, and had been for years.

'I'm sorry, Aulus.'

'Why do you sound so sad?'

'Because I am. Because I cannot give you what you need.'

Aulus rolled back onto one elbow, his body above hers. He ran his hand over her firm breast, just brushing the nipple. Claudia, her eyes shut tight, gave an involuntary shiver. 'It's not as though you cannot feel. I thought time would be enough to heal you. I prayed that our life would be as it once was.'

She laughed softly, but it indicated misery, not happiness. 'The perfect Roman couple, both of the finest stock despite the difference in age and a touch of Sabine blood in my past. A mature and garlanded warrior entwined, in the strictest marriage form, with his young bride. I think your old friend Lucius Falerius should be jealous.'

Aulus was perplexed. It was rare for Claudia to offer anything other than the persistent apology. 'Is that not enough?'

'It ought to be.'

His voice betrayed the anger he fought so hard to conceal beneath his habitual calm exterior. 'That's not what I asked!'

She opened her eyes and looked into his, then reached up and touched his face. 'No woman has the right to demand more than a husband like you. You're a gift from the gods.'

'Yet you reject that gift at every turn,' he snapped. 'We hardly speak to each other during the day, you wander the house as though your mind is elsewhere, without guests we dine in near silence and here in bed you're like a statue. Yet tonight, when Lucius sought to reproach my views, you leapt to my defence.'

'I don't know why you bother, Aulus.'

He spoke almost without feeling, determined to hide both the depth of his passion plus the guilt he felt for what had happened to her in Spain. 'I bother because I love you.'

'Any other man would have put me aside, perhaps for another wife.'

His hand wandered up from her breast to her throat. 'I have the right to kill you, Claudia, if I so wish.'

'I won't struggle, Aulus, and I'll gladly release you from the need to return my dowry.'

She had not meant her words to sound churlish, but the right tone for what she was trying to say eluded her.

'Why!' he shouted, stung at last to outright anger, his hand involuntarily closing round her windpipe. 'Why?'

Her shoulders started to heave. Aulus saw she was crying and he released his grip, his head fell on her shoulder and he spoke softly, his words muffled by her skin. 'Why?'

She strained to keep her voice level. 'How glad I am that you are angry, husband. I often wish that you would show anger more often.'

When he replied the thickness in his own throat was obvious. 'I need some kind of explanation, Claudia.'

'Something died in me, Aulus. Something vital! For all your efforts you cannot revive it and I tell you now that is the last word I will say. I shall not speak of it again and if you wish to respond, do so by showing your anger. I hate your pity more than I hate anything in the world.'

With that Claudia turned her back on him, eyes tight shut as she recalled that day of the battle. She thought it odd that she could never remember the faces of those murderous tribesmen intent on raping her, even if she could quite easily recapture the feelings of loathing and disgust she had felt at the time. It was as if the change in her life was so total that she had blocked them out, as if the flashing *falcata* blade had sliced through the two separate parts of her existence, forever separating them. That decapitation had halted everyone, so the only sound she could hear was the sobbing and muffled screams of those women less fortunate than she. As her saviour helped her to her feet, wrapping her nakedness in a cloak of rough wool, his height became even more obvious. She barely came up to his chest and even through the dust in the air and the odour of death which surrounded her she had smelt him, a musky fragrance of fresh perspiration that had never left her memory. Then he had spoken, in perfect Latin, in a deep and harmonious voice to ask her if she was suffering from any pain.

'No,' Claudia had replied, aware, as the aches of her violation began to make themselves felt, that she was lying. Her arms hurt from the way she had been dragged around, her chest and back from the pummelling of the pushing and shoving. She could feel where her hair had been tugged till it nearly parted from her scalp and the throbbing by her eye she suspected had come from a blow to the side of the head.

'Look at me.'

Claudia fought her own inclination to respond, as a way of stating defiance, a way of showing this barbarian she was not there to obey commands, but another force seemed to exert a more telling pressure that brought up her head. What struck her first were the eyes, large, piercing and bright blue, set in a face that was bronzed, not blackened by the sun, his hair golden and long. His hand came up slowly to touch her cheek right at the point where it now throbbed and those blue eyes closed while the face took on a look of deep concentration. Almost immediately Claudia felt the pain ease, and within seconds it had gone completely. He spoke swiftly as the eyes opened again, in a tribal argot she could not understand.

Claudia was subjected to a series of mixed emotions. She knew she had this man to thank for saving her honour – very likely her life – and she could not help but be impressed by his presence, the effortless ease with which he commanded respect, yet he was clearly an enemy, so she felt she should despise him. It was an emotion she tried very hard to conjure up, only to find that when she spoke her voice sounded meek.

'Who are you?'

'I am Brennos, the leader of the Celt-Iberians. I have told them to take you to our camp. You will be treated with all respect. Anyone who harms a hair on your head knows he will have to face me.'

'The other women?' Claudia asked, sure that every man was already dead.

'Are of no interest to me. They do not have a Roman general for a husband.'

Isolation, in an unlit tent made of animal skins, allowed Claudia's thoughts to run riot. She sat in the only chair, every possible scenario played out in her imagination: Aulus riding into the Celtic camp to rescue her; the same rescuer dragged in chains and defeated, to be burnt in a wicker cage before her eyes. In her head armies clashed and both sides won and lost, with her own possible fate mixed with the heat and blood of battle. What would Brennos do with her? Had he saved her from his fellow barbarians only to despoil her at his own leisure? Would she be sacrificed to one of their heathen gods? And through all of this two images fought for supremacy: first the face of Aulus, swarthy skin, black eyes, grave with his pepper and salt hair, concerned for her well-being, and second that of Brennos. It was not so much his face but his presence, a power of personality so great that she could still smell him, still hear his voice and the touch of his healing hand. The sounds from outside grew as night fell, plunging the interior of the tent into a pitch darkness that only served to enhance her disquiet, wandering from being brave to near panic and back again. Sleep proved impossible, every time she closed her eyes the image of those who had died that day leapt up like accusers. Opening them was little better; she felt as if their ghosts were in the tent, crowding in on her, demanding to know why she was alive while they had perished.

The growing clamour outside went some way to alleviating this, her confused and solitary state making it easy to translate the shouted sounds of a language she did not understand into her own native Latin. Individual voices predominated, interspersed with the sudden roars of acclamation. Then there was only one voice, angry, starting out even and rising steadily to a shout, soon to be joined by others in what seemed to be disagreement. More voices were added to the dispute until no one person could be heard, then the tent flap was hauled back, and Brennos, carrying a flaring torch, entered.

He was still coated in the dust of the day's action, the great decapitating sword at his side, dressed in a loose smock and leggings held in place by the thongs of his sandals. As he stuck the torch in a metal sconce Claudia observed again his salient features, mentally recognising that he was extremely handsome, with his height, his broad shoulders and the lean, tanned face. That was before she sharply reminded herself he was the enemy of both her city and her husband. He looked around the tent, at the unused bed covered with a sheepskin, the wicker stand that held a basin and a jug of water, none of which she had used, then back to Claudia, still in her woollen cloak, her sitting pose rigid.

'You are comfortable?'

'I am a prisoner.'

The haughty pose she struck then clearly amused him. 'I have been a prisoner in my time, lady, and it was not like this. When you fear to sleep lest the rats eat your toes you will know what being a prisoner means.'

'My husband?'

'Is alive and still in command of his army.' Brennos sighed then, before adding, with a toss of the head, 'Those fools behave as if we won a great victory. They are telling each other how brave they are.' His face held a strange expression, which Claudia thought, at first, was despair, but closer examination showed it to be frustration. 'Your husband is a good soldier.'

'The very best that Rome has,' Claudia replied, pompously.

Brennos smiled then, for the first time. 'Then I can be sure that once I've beaten him, I have nothing to fear.'

'You won't beat Aulus, and even if you did, another army would arrive next year.'

'And another the year after,' he replied, in a voice that showed no trace of fear at the prospect. 'That is always assuming I stay here and wait to be attacked. Instead of putting them to all the trouble of marching to Spain I'll meet them outside the gates of Rome.'

Claudia had to stop herself laughing then. His words, calmly delivered as they were, still sounded like madness to her. 'You think yourself greater than Hannibal.'

'Not me, lady,' Brennos said, taking the gold eagle charm between his fingers, an act which drew it once more to Claudia's attention. It flashed in the torchlight as he moved it, seeming to have come alive, as if the bird was actually flying. 'But the race to which I belong. Your husband was lucky today, so we will meet again. He has to be lucky once more, indeed every time he fights the Celtic tribes. They only need to be lucky once.'

As he spoke he strode towards a jug and basin,

undoing his sword belt and peeling off his smock. With a start Claudia realised that this tent was his own, obvious really since she was his personal prisoner. She tried to avert her gaze as he picked up the water jug and emptied half the contents over his head, but the image of the muscles moving in that broad, tanned back stayed with her. The flap opened again to admit two girls, one of whom had fresh clothes for Brennos, while the other carried a tray of food, which she laid on the sheepskin bedcover. Neither said a word, yet Claudia observed interest in the way they gazed at him, looks that made her wonder at his own domestic arrangements. Was there a wife or a series of concubines ready to satisfy his needs? Why was she curious?

'Eat,' he commanded.

She was hungry, ravenous in fact, but she also had her pride. 'I have no desire to take anything from you.'

That look of frustration crossed his face again. 'Please don't be foolish. I have sent a message to your husband, saying if he wants you back he and his legions must quit Spain.'

'He will never agree to that.'

'No, he won't. I doubt your being my prisoner will affect a single act of his as a soldier.'

'Then you might as well kill me now.'

Claudia knew she had struck a pose as she said

that, her head turned away, eyes raised in an attempt to imbue her words with a degree of nobility. She stayed like that as he approached her, very aware of his proximity as he stood by her chair. His hand reached out to touch her chin and pull her head round, the contact sending a shiver through her whole body.

'You would face death, I think, with that same look.'

'I hope so.'

'Roman pride.'

'Roman spirit.'

His hand dropped to the edge of her cloak, opening it slightly to reveal her naked flesh. A single finger was brushed across her skin, and all the time those blue eyes held hers, in a locked gaze she could not break. She felt her body react to his touch, a tingling that went down her arms to her fingertips, a feeling halfway between an ache and pleasure that forced her to clench the muscles of her stomach. Two things Claudia knew: that she should not feel like this, it was wrong and wicked; it was also a sensation she had never before experienced, and one that she did not want to stop.

'I would want that Roman spirit maintained, which means you must eat. We brought the wagon with your possessions back from the battlefield. You should wash and dress as well.'

Both physical and eye contact were broken

simultaneously. Brennos picked up his huge sword, with its heavy curved blade, broad at the base and narrow near the handle, then the torch.

'And you should sleep. We leave here at first light.'

Claudia tried, only to find her efforts punctuated by screams and wailing, leaving her unsure if what she was hearing came from her dreams or reality. When Brennos came back his clean smock was coated with blood so fresh and copious that it glistened in the torchlight. Through one narrowed eye she watched him as he stripped again, unable to properly hear the soft incantations that sounded like prayer. With his head back, eyes closed, the eagle talisman at his neck held in one hand, he looked very much like a man asking for forgiveness.

Brennos kept Claudia close to him, wherever he went. The Celt-Iberians moved camp often, rarely staying in one spot for more than the three days it took to strip the country around them of surplus food. Most of the time her world was bound by deep wooded valleys and rocky escarpments, with only an occasional glimpse of the coastal plain controlled by her own people, the one constant being a blazing sun punctuated every few days by tremendous rain-storms full of thunder and lightning. When they pitched their tents she was assigned to his; when they rode, her horse was rarely more than a few feet from him and since he treated her with respect it was impossible not to respond, just as it was impossible, even for someone who could not speak a word of the language, to pick up the hint of the problems that Brennos laboured under.

As they rode out of that first camp the bodies of the slaughtered, men, women and children, were still lying where they had fallen. Over the following days she learnt that these were tribal chiefs and their families, men who thought one battle with Rome quite sufficient and who had wanted to return to their own lands with what they had managed to acquire. She could see the way that those tribal leaders still with him looked at Brennos; there was no love in their attentiveness, more a caution born of a desire to survive. Yet he held them together as a fighting force by some unnamed power, their forays to find Romans to harry always resulting in a return to the camp with booty in abundance. Each sortie would be followed by celebration and the recounting of long heroic tales to follow the feasting and drinking, all watched and heard by a leader who could not keep out of his eye a slight look of scorn. For all that they did as he asked.

Brennos had a quality of command that Claudia had seen in her husband, but he had something else as well: an elemental ascendancy over those with whom he dealt. As the days and weeks went by, she began to realise that a portion of that same power had taken a hold of her. Proximity tempered both her resolve and her pride. It was impossible to be with someone like Brennos and maintain a stiff Roman neck, hopeless to try and avoid conversation with a man so curious about Rome and its ways, who so entranced her with tales of his own past. So Claudia learnt of the land of mists and rain from which he had come, far to the north surrounded by angry water where gold and tin were mined and the people painted their faces blue. She heard of the ordeals undertaken by those like him who wished to serve as Druid priests, scourged by fire, earth and water, during the latter bound to a rock while the great western sea lashed at his naked body; of the vow each took to forsake the company of women for life.

Brennos could recount the history of his race, with stories harking back to beyond the mists of time; tell of battles won and heroes made; invoke the intercession of the Great God *Dagda* and his companion, the Earth Mother, *Morrigan*. He was a man who could describe, in detail, the potions that healed, as well as those which killed, reel off the entire canon of Celtic law, which he had been empowered to interpret. Less and less she thought of Aulus; her husband seemed to recede from her considerations, to become like a distant memory, her thoughts taken up instead with imagined conversations with Brennos, and Claudia, though still only eighteen, was old enough and experienced enough to know that the growing feelings she harboured for this Celt were reciprocated. It was in the way he looked at her, the smile she saw that was given to few others. She could make him laugh too, and took pleasure from doing so, the guilt of that first night, at even speaking with an enemy, weakening as time went by.

As a man Brennos was naturally tactile, much given to touching those with whom he was in conversation. This applied to his tribal commanders as well as her, leaving her to wonder if they felt the same sensation, that feeling that imbued every pore on her skin with an ache of impatience. Claudia Cornelia went to sleep beside her husband recalling that it was she not Brennos who had acted to bring matters to a head. Pointedly she wore that same cloak with which he had covered her nakedness the first day they met. Not a shred of remorse did she feel as she took the hand of her tall blue-eyed Celt, to pull him to her and place her lips on his. There was no image of Aulus when she let that cloak slip from her shoulders to reveal the same naked body. Brennos had resisted, but feebly, unable, despite his vows, to cope with so determined a woman.

It was she who removed his smock, then knelt, her head against his groin, to untie the thongs that held on his sandals. Brennos was half pleading with her to desist, but only vocally. For once, Claudia had the elemental power not him, a power strong enough to lead him to the sheepskin-covered bed, to pull his naked body onto hers. It was her hand on that eagle charm, not his, holding it behind his head so that it would not cause her pain. What came from Brennos's throat as he made love to her sounded very much like that. She remembered it now, just as she remembered the sensations she had undergone, feelings that were as new to her as they were to her barbarian lover.

CHAPTER THIRTEEN

Titus Cornelius returned to Spain not as the youngest son of the great Macedonicus, a boy mounted on a cob, but as a fully fledged tribune commanding several centuries, to the very locality where his father had begun his campaign so many years before. He had even visited the battlefield, that long shallow valley where he had first experienced action. It was hard after so many years and in surroundings so peaceful to recall the thousands engaged, the clouds of dust, the clang of swords, the clamour of battle, the smell of blood and death. What lingered was the memory of what followed: the long, hard campaign; the constant risk of ambush as his father's cohorts pushed their way into the mountains to flush out the enemy; the burning and pillaging that was necessary to suppress each tribe in turn; how his father had borne his own burden in silence, concentrating on the tactics necessary to isolate and finally defeat Brennos. The endless list of tribes and chieftains who had eventually agreed to peace, each one obliged to leave blood relatives as hostages in the Roman encampment until the campaign was over, as a token of continued good behaviour.

Titus had regarded these sons and nephews of the tribal chiefs with all the arrogance of his race, but that mellowed with contact; they were barbarians, uncouth in speech and manners, but they also held a fascination for an enquiring mind. Tentative contact was established after the ritual exchange of a suspicious glare, this encouraged by his father's habit of treating them as honoured guests instead of prisoners. The reasoning was simple; if these young men knew Rome better, they might respect her more.

Facets of their very different life were absorbed during the games they played; mock sword fights in which each side would learn how to parry each other's weapons, short Roman sword against wooden *falcatas*. They engaged in archery and spear-throwing competitions, bouts of wrestling and boxing, horse races at which the Celts excelled and, once the campaign had reached a certain point of success, hunting expeditions. Titus learnt to tell one tribe from another, how to communicate basic expressions in their tongue, while teaching them the rudiments of Latin. They were not content to compete with him, but more intent on besting some rival from another tribe. The interlocking relationships, hatreds and disputes between the various clans were too complex to master, and tact was necessary to avoid offence. In particular Aulus encouraged his son, when peace was finally brought to the frontier, to show respect and friendship to the leader of the Bregones, only a few years older than Titus, but a hereditary chieftain. In this case curiosity was mutual; Masugori could speak some Latin and wanted to know as much about Rome as Titus did about Celt-Iberian culture, and he became the person who tutored the young Roman in the language, local dialects, customs, and more importantly who hated who, knowledge that allowed him to understand more clearly those with whom he had contact.

Listening to Masugori describe the endemic quarrels of the various tribes, of shifting alliances, the way they continually raided each other's lands, stealing cattle, crops and women, made him wonder how this Brennos had ever got them to combine, for it was plain that these Celt-Iberians were not only fractious but their disputes were of long duration. Masugori was not himself immune to this; he had his hatreds for the tribes on the borders of his own lands, as well as many beyond, and he talked of events in a way that made them seem as if they had happened yesterday, only for Titus to find he was speaking of raids and counter raids which had been stories told to him by his grandfather.

On seeing the landscape again, the flat coastal plains interspersed with mountains, Titus was conscious of how much he had forgotten. Yet gradually, through contact with the nearest tribes, some things came back; words and phrases, tribal identification through clothing and the decorations on head-dresses, torques, buckles and the pommels of swords, all of which he found useful in his present task, one which required peace. The duties he undertook, supervising the building of a section of the Roman road from New Carthage to Saguntum was to him just as vital as the notion of combat. It had been drummed into Titus Cornelius, just as it had been drummed into every young Roman, that the roads they built were the sinews of the Imperium, part of the genius of their Republic. By these arrow straight highways their empire would last where others, grown too large to control, had failed.

There had been some confrontations with roving bands, the odd skirmish with small groups intent on plunder, which forced him to keep a mounted mobile force ready at all times. A proper battle had seemed impossible until that morning, an attitude that the events of the last hour had altered dramatically.

Titus bit hard on the leather strap when the surgeon tended the gash in his arm. Despite the pain, he could not help but feel pleased, the memory of the recent action suffusing him with the warm glow of success. It is the moment each soldier dreads, that first taste of real warfare, the time when every nerve in your body screams for safety, yet you know that you must stand and fight and – if need be – die. The Celt-Iberians, hundreds instead of the usual few dozen, had come out of their mountain retreat under cover of darkness, waited, hidden in the nearby pine forests until the soldiers had breakfasted and set about their road-building tasks; then they had attacked. Titus, with his few men armed and mounted, had charged to blunt their progress, finding himself surrounded in a matter of minutes. This was no ordinary band of marauding, local tribesmen, so no shame would have attached to his name if he had turned and tried to escape, for even during his charge, and in the midst of the subsequent fighting, he had registered that he was engaged against men of more than one tribe. But flight was impossible; the men on the road, who would be outnumbered, needed time to get their weapons and shields, time to form up and attack as a disciplined body. He trusted them, and his second in command, to do the right thing. Titus, shouting over the clash of metal, ordered his men to dismount, kill their horses and stand in a circle.

The ploy worked; the Celt-Iberians, with such an

easy prey before them, could not resist the opportunity. Ignoring their real goal and the growing danger from their rear, they tried to get at the surrounded Roman cavalry, slipping in the blood from dead horses and men, as they struggled to leap across the low rampart made by the dead animals. Titus and his party nearly died under the sheer weight of the attack, as those behind the men they were fighting, unable to engage themselves, still pressed forward eagerly, pushing their companions onto the Roman swords, thus increasing the height of the obstacle they had to climb. This, rather than their own defensive strokes, saved the cohort from being overwhelmed.

Gaius Julius, the other military tribune, later confessed that he had written Titus off, along with his men and, instead of worrying about their fate, had concentrated on forming up his own troops without disruptive haste. The sound of the trumpets, as the relief finally advanced, relieved the pressure on Titus at once, as those warriors at the rear turned to fight Gaius's infantry, which actually increased the danger. Now the men attacking him, without any pressure, took more care with their strokes, using the increased space to deadly effect. His soldiers began to die, each one selling his life as dearly as he could, a fate to which Titus Cornelius was himself resigned; Gaius would win, but it would be too late for him.

Whoever commanded the enemy saved him. The

horn blew twice in the distance, two long notes, and with a discipline they were not supposed to enjoy, the enemy broke off the action and streamed north in good order. Titus saw over the bodies of men and horses the approaching Romans, then turned to observe his attackers disappear in a billowing cloud of red dust, taking with them the few trophies they had been able to rip off the dead legionaries.

'How's the wound?'

Gaius Julius was still in full battle armour, while most of his men had removed their breastplates and helmets then gone back to road-building. Another party was stripping bare and piling up the dead tribesmen, separating them from the Roman casualties, who would receive a proper burial. Perhaps in the night the tribesmen would come for their fallen comrades; if not they would be food for the wolves and vultures.

Titus looked at his right arm, with the surgeon busily stitching. 'I fear you will have to write the despatch.'

That produced a frown. 'It will be a short document.'

'We've more to say than you think, Gaius.'

'They raided our lines, which is something they've done often enough.'

'This was different. We've never faced them so numerous or so well-ordered.' Titus could see that his second in command did not understand him. 'If they attack, they do so in small parties, to try and steal our mules or supplies. Not this time. They waited to catch us unprepared, stayed hidden until we'd eaten and started to work. This time they wanted to kill Romans.'

'I've put scouts out to avoid that,' said Gaius. He looked round at the men toiling behind him. 'We'll need to make up the numbers with slaves if we're ever to get this section of road finished.'

'More important was the way they broke off the action.'

Gaius Julius snorted derisively. 'They ran away, Titus. They always do, once we're organised.'

'They didn't run away, they were ordered to retreat.' Titus realised that Gaius Julius had not heard the horn; he thought that the mere act of attacking had forced them to flee. Nor was he aware that the bodies left behind were from different tribes and, as he explained, he could see the face fall. Gaius had been wondering if he would receive some form of commendation for his efforts in routing the enemy and saving his comrades. 'The horn blew twice and they obeyed it immediately, every one of them. I've known that happen once before, when I was campaigning here with my father.'

The surgeon looked up at the mention of the boy's father. He had served with Aulus himself and looking at Titus he was struck with the likeness. It was not just physical; he had the same effortless ease of command, added to the air of a man who would never be anything other than modest about his personal achievements.

'I can't see that it makes any difference,' said Gaius Julius.

Understanding how an award for bravery, especially one for saving Roman lives, could enhance a man's career, Titus explained gently, telling Gaius about his father's campaign against Brennos, as well as the Druid's notions of a great Celtic confederation.

'We used to talk about it and shudder. You would too if you think of the number of tribes in and to the north of the Alps, then add them to those in Spain and Dacia. More men than Rome could ever fight. If they ever combine under a single leader it could be the disaster at the Allia all over again.'

Gaius Julius exploded. 'Did you get a blow on the head, as well! How can you equate what happened this morning with the defeat of four legions over two hundred years ago?'

Titus smiled, then looked to the north-west, where the snow-topped mountains reached towards the bright blue sky. 'You're right, of course, I'm letting my imagination run riot, but something odd happened today, and it is our duty to inform our general of the fact. After all, we don't want the

Celts trying to sack Rome a second time.'

'Just as long as I'm allowed to mention that we won,' said Gaius Julius, with some feeling.

Titus was not really listening, he was still looking at pine-forested hills, wondering if they had, indeed, achieved the easy victory Gaius Julius supposed. It was only when they moved that he caught sight of them on a distant hilltop bare of trees. A small party of horsemen perfectly placed to oversee the recent action and as they moved, a small object at the neck of one of the riders caught the sun, and flashed a sharp reflection that seemed like a weapon aimed directly at him.

One of Rome's foremost engineers, Licinius Domitius sat, eyes blank, looking at a point just behind the tribune's head as Titus made his report. It was known that the only things to totally engage his interest were roads, bridges and viaducts. Evidence of this lay on the table at which he sat, covered, as it was, in plans and drawings. Yet he had served with distinction in the past, as a soldier and a provincial governor, so he could be trusted not to ignore the implications of what Titus was saying. Yet Domitius related the whole affair to the problems of his present construction project; the provision of a road that would run all the way from Spain, along the Mediterranean coast of Gaul, on into northern Italy, to join the road to

Rome. Since senatorial approval for this expensive undertaking had been hard to secure, anything with the potential to disrupt his work caused anxiety.

He had met with the tribal chiefs before starting this section of the road, a decent bribe extracting a promise to leave the builders alone, but Domitius was well aware of the limitations of such a tactic; the Celts would take his money AND steal what they could, but if it was kept to an acceptable level it would be money well spent. Had that undertaking been broken and could such a breach presage future trouble? There was no doubt some of the dead were from tribes who had taken bribes, but were they acting with the knowledge of their chieftains? Did what had been reported justify him in detaching troops from construction work to punish the transgressors? Like all seasoned Roman politicians he decided to compromise, and elected to send his young tribune on a mission to ascertain just how serious this outbreak could be.

'And why not, Titus Cornelius, since you are forever lecturing me on the habits of these barbarians.'

'I admit to a little knowledge, sir.'

'Then get more, young man. I need to know what it is we face.'

There were two methods by which Titus gathered information, both of which involved payment. Some Celts were prepared to sell information on their race, while the Greek traders who dealt with the interior looked for concessions, like reduced tariffs from the people who controlled the routes to their main markets, the Roman governors of the two Spanish provinces. Titus preferred the Greeks since they were less likely to lie. The names of tribes, chieftains and locations, as he listened to his informants, brought back the past into sharper focus. Some of the youths he had competed with eight years before had risen to be leaders. Each was deserving of respect, but amongst those who could trouble Rome, one person stood out above all others; a tall Druid shaman and warrior, with red-gold hair, ruler of a tribe called the Duncani, whose lands lay deep in the central highlands. In a race noted for excessive display he wore nothing but plain cloth and a gold talisman round his neck, shaped like an eagle in flight.

His name was Brennos, the same man who had fought his father and it was he who had commanded the raid in which Titus had been wounded, leading men who had been forbidden to take part by their own, now angry chieftains. As a token of their sincerity, some offered to return Domitius's gold, but Titus declined to accept, first because he suspected it was designed to elicit a refusal and secondly their possession of Roman money was the one thing that bound them to keep the peace. His refusal also had the added advantage of making them quite open about the real threat, creating the impression that Brennos was a man they feared, a leader persuasive enough to wean their own younger warriors from their natural loyalties.

The shaman had acquired a secure tribal base of his own, deep in the interior and he had only essayed from that and come towards the coast to cause trouble. If the chieftains of the eastern mountains had made him welcome, it was because of their tradition of hospitality more than any love of the man and his aims. They too could remember, just like Titus, what had gone before; the rebellion he had led and the brutal way he had exercised command. It was not something they wished to repeat – being so close to Roman power meant they were also first in line for Roman revenge – yet care had to be taken by tribal leaders in a society of warriors, many of whom saw bending the knee to Rome as cowardice. It was of no help to have this interloper stirring up the passions of those who thought their leaders too supine so they were only too willing to recount to Titus how his re-birth as a threat had come about.

After the collapse of his revolt Brennos had retired further west into the interior of the Iberian Peninsula to lick his wounds, to the lands that bordered the great western confederation of the

Lusitani. They occupied a fragmented domain on the eastern side of the Iberian Peninsula that extended all along the rocky coast of the great, heaving, outer sea, sharing only a southern border with Rome around the old Carthaginian port of Gades. It was a relatively peaceful one, since the Romans tended to leave the Lusitani alone; the tribal group was so large and the country so inhospitable that to provoke them would entail a full-scale war in a land that looked as if it would produce little in the way of profit.

Brennos had crossed into Lusitani territory to work amongst the people, employing his skills as a healer, bringing rain to parched crops, telling the future and entertaining the encampments he visited with the long oral tales so beloved by Celts wherever they resided. His reputation spread, until, as a mark of the respect in which he was held as a Druid, the Lusitani chieftains had invited Brennos to officiate at the great festival of Sambain. This was held in a sacred grove, full of tall standing stones like those he had left behind in the north, the home of a temple that was reputed to contain treasures of gold and silver beyond price. From what Titus could glean, the trust placed in Brennos was sadly misplaced, for he had repaid their hospitality by a deliberate attempt to undermine his hosts. Identifying the men who would succeed the present chieftains, hungry for power and not yet wealthy, or tested enough to esteem peace, he preached his previous doctrine of a destructive war on Rome and sought to revive his notion of a great Celtic confederation to smash the power of the Republic.

That was history now. Obliged to move on by the angry Lusitani chieftains, Brennos had taken to travelling once more, returning to the western borders of some of those clans he had led against Aulus Cornelius. He had wandered amongst them, not always a welcome guest, the information Titus was given placing him at some time or other in every tribal encampment in the land as he wandered the length of Celtic Iberia. Finally, he had come to rest at Numantia, home of a clan called the Duncani. Here he had been truly welcomed, with his powers to heal the sick and remove the blight from their meagre crops, for the Duncani were a tribe in decline.

Celtic hospitality had always been the Druid's most potent ally and it was doubly so here, especially since the chieftain, an old warrior called Vertogani, had accommodated him in his own hut. Fond of food, drink and virgins, the old fellow had welcomed someone new to whom he could boast, proud as he was of the arch of skulls that decorated the entrance to his abode. The tribe had been feared once, and so had Vertogani, but he was now old and useless and his people, squeezed between the

Lusitani to the west and the increasingly powerful tribes to the east, who sought to take over their lands, were creeping towards extinction.

Vertogani had lived too long and in the process, through a constant succession of young wives, he had bred too many children, especially sons, each one parcelled out a small piece of tribal land. Tired of waiting, these successors had easily succumbed to the blandishments of greedy neighbours, only to find that promises to elevate them to the leadership of the Duncani tended to evaporate once the aggressors had their land under control. Some of them, prodigals chastened by the experience, had come back to the fold, to be forgiven by their over-indulgent parent. There they waited patiently for the old man to die, so they could lay claim to his title, but they had reckoned without Brennos.

He cast aside his Druid vows of celibacy, married Vertogani's favourite daughter, and immediately began to manoeuvre to replace her father, insinuating his way into the old man's counsel so that in truth he was the real leader. One by one, in mysterious circumstances, his rivals, Vertogani's blood children, died. Other relatives of the old chieftain, including those who had related much of this tale to those passing it on to Titus, had summoned up the sense to leave, so when the old chieftain finally succumbed, only one man stood to take his place.

Titus could not fathom it, and his Celtic informants could not enlighten him. Why should Brennos go to so much trouble to take over a tribe weak in men and wealth? Then, slowly, as more and more information filtered through from the Greek traders, he realised that, for him, the Duncani had one precious asset that outweighed all others. The location of the main tribal fort. Numantia, a huge hill with three steep escarpments, stood in the fastness of the central mountains, at the confluence of two rivers. The Duncani huts sat at the top of this great mound, which dominated all the countryside around it. When Titus questioned the Greeks who traded with Brennos, he began to see the outline of his intentions; Brennos had already begun to strengthen the one side of the hill fort requiring defence, his aim to make Numantia impregnable, clear to those with the wit to see.

The sharp-eyed Greek traders drew sketches of what had been achieved, as well as a decent map of the surroundings, which allowed Titus to add the logical extensions that such work would produce. Brennos still preached his message of war with Rome, one that attracted to him the discontented of other tribes, so, whereas the old leader had shed warriors, Brennos was acquiring them in abundance. Secure in his bailiwick, he had begun to aggressively take back what lands had been stolen under his predecessor and he was in the process, through a mixture of fighting and blandishments, of creating fear amongst his neighbours. The result was an increasingly powerful domain in which, through treaty or by threat, he was the acknowledged leader, one quite open in his intention to widen that sphere of influence in a way that was bound to bring him once more into conflict with Rome.

Titus had so much information about Brennos, it was almost as if the Druid wanted the Romans to know his thoughts. You cannot construct huge outworks, ring upon ring, yet still with enough room inside for an army and expect it to go unnoticed. Nor could he extend his string of alliances without eventually alerting the only power on the peninsula with the means to check his ambitions. His reported utterances all referred to his hatred of Rome, words said so often that they had been reported verbatim to Titus by source after source.

'So there you have it, sir, the stuff of my father's nightmares. First a victory in Spain, then the destruction of Rome by bringing together all the Celtic tribes from Iberia, through Gaul, to Dacia.'

'It's a pretty story, Titus Cornelius,' said Licinius Domitius, 'but I doubt a true one. If you wish to hear three different opinions, all you have to do is question two Celtic chieftains. They never, as a matter of course, agree on anything. Believe me, I know. I've fought them in the foothills of the Alps, which is hard, and made treaties of peace with them, which is worse.'

'He managed it against my father. We fought an association not a tribe.'

'Only in Spain and he lost,' the old senator declared. He looked at the scrolls again, the ones on which Titus had written his report, as if to check his facts. 'This Brennos can spout all he likes, it will take more than words, however potent, to unite the entire Celtic confederation. Their Great God *Dagda* himself, if he came from the bowels of the earth, couldn't do it.'

'I believe their supreme god resides in a tree, sir, not in the bowels of the earth.'

'There you are! His brains are made of wood, just like those who worship him!'

'So we do nothing, sir?'

'We have a road to build, Titus Cornelius.' He picked up the scroll and began to roll it tight. 'And this goes to Rome. We have consuls who decide these things. Let them do their work while I do mine.'

CHAPTER FOURTEEN

Lucius Falerius sat looking at the scrolls before him, a set he had had to search for in the packed cupboards that lined his study. With Aulus expected soon, he had not been able to resist the temptation to refresh his memory. It was six years since he had last looked at them, eight years since the event they described. His steward, now standing silently before him with a worried look on his face, had done everything possible; the sheer quantity of the rolls before his master testified to that. He could not be faulted for his inability to discover the information that Lucius required, though he certainly gave the impression of a man anticipating a rebuke.

With the master absent the Cornelii household slaves had been royally entertained in the wine shops, questioned when drunk and in one case directly bribed, but nothing had come of it. His steward, refusing to give up, had even acted as matchmaker to one of the Lady Claudia's personal handmaidens. A flighty girl, he had introduced her to a handsome Numidian called Thoas, sent to Rome from the Falerii farm in Sicily. This slave, being well over six feet tall and handsome, intended to act as body slave to Lucius, had proceeded to sweep the serving girl off her feet. With his master's permission the steward had arranged a trade, offering the well-built Numidian to the Cornelii household at a knock-down price that Quintus, left in charge, could not refuse. Thus Lucius had ended up with a spy in the very home of the man whose movements he was investigating, yet even with that, and nearly a year of patient enquiry, he still could not find out where Aulus had gone the night Marcellus was born.

His mind turned immediately, at the thought of his son's name, to the boy himself. Much care had been taken with Marcellus's upbringing. Even more care had been exercised in the matter of choosing a suitable tutor. Several had been tried and found wanting, showing alarming tendencies to allow behaviour in his son that Lucius considered inappropriate to a Roman. Of course, each one had come from that damned tribe of educated Greeks so numerous in the catalogues of the slave merchants; that is, if you could afford to pay for them. The one he had finally bought, Timeon by name, an Athenian, had cost nearly as much as his cook, but

Lucius had made a handsome profit by enrolling the children of other patricians so that Timeon taught a whole class of boys rather than merely tutoring Marcellus. This had the added advantage of giving his son fellows of his own age and class to play with, and as the owner of the school, his father was in a position to vet these playmates to ensure their suitability. Ten boys, all from the most noble families, attended every day.

Not that you would know it; Timeon was not one to brook boisterous behaviour. He had a vine sapling as part of his teaching equipment and Lucius was glad to know that he used it, even on Marcellus. He saw, in his mind's eye, the sapling cracking across his son's back. That was the way to raise a Roman; a harsh regime and a strict diet. The steward, seeing the expression on his master's face, as he contemplated the regular punishment of his heir, mistook it for the coming reprimand, and spoke quickly in the hope of deflecting the coming anger.

'As you will see from the last report, master, the Numidian has confirmed that Aulus Macedonicus landed at Ostia, yet he did not actually arrive in Rome until the day after the birth of Master Marcellus.'

'While his sons came home weeks before,' said Lucius, riffling through the papyrus sheets until he found the one he wanted.

'Six weeks before, master. Aulus Macedonicus took ship from Emphorae to Massila, instead of coming straight back from Spain.'

Lucius recalled the time with much more clarity than he had the facts, or lack of them, in the scrolls; the Republic in turmoil, riots as a mob intent on supporting Livonius and his so-called reforms threatened to burst out of their slums. Talk of electing a dictator, with the clear implication that Tiberius should be that man, something he had headed off in the only way he knew. To Lucius, he had not sanctioned murder, he had terminated a conspiracy that would have undermined the foundations of the state. The mayhem that followed had appeared to strengthen his own position, but that was incidental and in any case had lasted only days, until Aulus had made the speech that detached him from the *optimates* cause. He was still having to deal with the results of that defection, still having to deal with a fractious legislature in which he had a constant battle to harness the majority he wanted, often having to give ground not just to his opponents but to men who sought to profit from his need for votes.

Lucius wondered if Aulus knew how damaging his declaration of independence had been, aware that he himself had never underestimated the degree to which the support of such a patently honest man had been in the past. Yet he could also say with certainty that life had been simpler as he and Aulus rose through the *cursus honarium*. The Republic had been on a sound footing; it seemed everyone knew their place in the scheme of things; change, if any was mooted at all, was gradual; a golden time. He felt a sadness then, for hard as he made his heart when it came to the safety of the state, he could not help but miss the one friendship on which he was sure he could rely, actually feeling a burning sensation at the top of his nose, which he pinched, lest tears begin to flow. The images that flashed through his mind were of the companionship they had enjoyed; mock fights, mischief, fishing and hunting together, learning Greek, with Lucius always ahead in that. Realising he was indulging in nostalgia, Lucius forced himself to be pragmatic; romantics would destroy everything with their well-meaning but essentially useless principles, unless, of course, Aulus was not as honest as he wished to appear.

'Even the legions got back before their general,' he said and the steward nodded. 'Since there was no public reason for it I can only assume he deliberately delayed his return to the city at a time when he knew that matters were coming to a head.'

'All his body slaves, except Cholon, returned with his sons, Quintus and Titus Cornelius, master.'

Lucius examined the papyrus rolls again. 'That's what is so odd. He sent them all back. The Lady Claudia reportedly lost her two handmaidens on the campaign, so his wife was left with no personal servants at all. Why?'

The steward ventured the same opinion he had all those years ago, for if he could think of a dozen reasons that would lift suspicion from the man in question, he saw no need to avoid feeding this particular bee in his master's bonnet. It made life easier. 'Because she didn't need them. She, and her husband, both in Gaul and in Italy, were the guests of someone who could provide for all their bodily comforts, someone wealthy enough to have an abundance of household slaves.'

'And from Ostia he could go in any direction. How easy it would be for him to go in to the Campangna hills, which is full of villas which belong to my most persistent enemies? Who did he talk with that so weaned him away from our cause?'

What he meant was, who had exercised more persuasion over his old friend than he could himself? Aulus had always deferred to him in politics, had always trusted his judgement over that of other men. The nose was pinched again, but it was a touch of self-pity that created the need. The steward's shrug, as he looked up, made Lucius angry and he gestured his dismissal, turning to a pile of scrolls, copies of the most recent despatches, just come in from the provinces.

The sapling flicked stingingly, and expertly, against Marcellus's ear lobe. He fought to control his features so that Timeon could not see that he had inflicted any pain. The tutor enjoyed delivering physical punishment and the young son of his master was the prime target. He took more care with the others, lest their parents, angry at their treatment, withdrew them from the class, for the same Lucius Falerius, who would nod with approval as Timeon outlined the number of strokes he had administered to Marcellus, would leap into a towering rage if he lost a pupil and the revenue that loss entailed. The Greek knew how much he had cost to buy.

'I shall ask you the question again, Master Marcellus.'

'Was the answer incorrect?' replied Marcellus boldly.

He noticed his fellow pupils wince, given that talking to Timeon in that insolent tone was a perfect way to invite another blow. The tutor obliged, this time the sapling whacked the youngster across the upper arm. He could not control himself and was forced to shut his eyes tightly.

'How would I know if the answer is correct, you miserable pup!' his tutor shouted. 'I have told you before not to mumble.'

Marcellus always defied Timeon, sometimes even

interceding on behalf of the other pupils and drawing down punishment on himself and, while they admired him for it, they were much given to telling him that he was a fool. Marcellus would reply, his childish chest puffing out slightly, that as a Roman he would not stand by and see punishment inflicted without justification. Most of the time his companions liked him, but when he made pompous statements like that they loathed him. On such occasions they would gang up on him: they had to; singly, or even in pairs, they could not match him for strength and determination.

Timeon had raised the sapling well above his head, a gleam in his eye as he prepared to give Marcellus a cut with all the strength he had, but the figure in the doorway, observed from the corner of his eye, standing silent and still, froze his hand in mid-air. Marcellus had lifted his head to show he was not afraid and when the blow did not come, he too turned to look. Tall and imposing in his senatorial toga, the visitor held Timeon's gaze the way a terrier holds the eyes of a frightened rabbit. All the boys were now looking at him; they saw an adult, a member of a group sometimes considered enemies, sometimes friends. Marcellus, with his romantic vision of the Imperium of his city-state, saw the perfect Roman. The grey hair was slightly curled, the eyes were dark and piercing, the nose prominent and his lips, set in a slight smile, implied a person without fear. The confidence emanating from him was almost tangible; he did not have to speak to impose himself, merely to be. Here was a Roman senator, an ex-consul judging by the thickness of his purple edging, a man who could single-handedly quell a savage tribe, or halt a mutiny in the ranks of a legion, without even raising his voice. He did speak, one short sentence, in a deep attractive timbre, designed to deflate the over-weaning ego of the recipient.

'Should you tire of teaching, my friend, the army always has need of muleteers.'

A quick spluttering laugh was speedily suppressed by Marcellus, while the other boys tried to hide their grins. The man in the doorway turned his head slightly and smiled at Marcellus as Timeon had dropped his arm to his side, not sure what to do. The boy pulled himself upright and looked straight into those eyes, which somehow seemed to be both stern and warm. In the spirit of defiance that was both his major blessing and his major fault, he replied on behalf of the entire class.

'Let the mules be, sir. Surely they know enough already. This teacher would only lead them up a blind alley.'

The lips parted in a full smile. 'You are Marcellus Falerius Orestes?'

If anything the boy became even more erect. Few people used that full name, given it alluded to the circumstances of his mother's death. 'I am, sir.'

The visitor's eyes, visibly hardening, turned slowly back towards Timeon. 'Then have a care, teacher. If anything happens to the boy's father, he will be your master. You may well find yourself praying for a position so elevated as that of a muleteer. If I was he, on coming into my inheritance, I'd have you whitewashing the inside of the sewers.'

The spell was broken by a slave calling the hour, and the man nodded once more to Marcellus and moved away. Timeon spoke in a hoarse voice. 'Lessons over. Tidy the place up before you leave.'

It was a measure of the loss of face he had just suffered that his class ignored him. They all rushed out at once, heading for the alleyway at the back of the house to play. Aulus turned to look at them, thinking of his own sons, who had now grown too old to afford him the pleasure these fellows gave their sires. His eldest was a magistrate with his eye on the consulship, while his younger son was in the army, already, he had heard, in receipt of his first wound after a minor skirmish. That had been months before, and with no further news he assumed his Titus to be fully recovered from what he had described in his letters as a mere scratch.

A copy of the despatch sent by Domitius to Rome, naming Titus Cornelius and his contribution, was amongst the scrolls on Lucius Falerius's desk. This did not come to him in his official capacity as a censor, the reigning consuls had sent the information on, both men being his appointees, well aware of the debt they owed to a figure readily acknowledged as the leading man in Rome. Titus had been thorough, which made Lucius wonder how all that had been happening in the interior had been missed by the governors of both Spanish provinces. So the leader Aulus Cornelius had been sent to fight ten years before had returned to cause more trouble! Lucius read the details of his activities with a jaundiced eye, knowing people paid for information often gilded the lily to enhance their tale. The way the traders and renegades had described this hill-fort, plus Brennos's plans to extend it, made the place sound unassailable. Lucius was less impressed; Numantia was too far away to bother Rome. If this Brennos was fortifying the place, surely it was as a defence against his fellow tribesmen, not against the Republic. As for the trouble on the frontier, it happened from time to time, and was thus no cause for special alarm. The threats of a great Celtic confederation he dismissed out of hand.

Domitius was careful to add that he had subsequently been left in relative peace, and having suffered no more than minor provocations he had not retaliated, but the wily old engineer added that additional troops would be welcome. Lucius, with his sharp eye for dissimulation, could read between the lines of that statement; Domitius knew as well as anyone the special nature of Iberia in the collective memory of the Roman populace, for the name Hannibal was still used to frighten children into good behaviour. The Carthaginian had come from Spain, crossed the Alps with his elephants, annihilated two Roman armies at Lake Trasimene and Cannae, then spent the next twelve years traversing the length and breadth of Italy, burning, looting and destroying. He was aided in his invasion, and sustained in the ravages he visited on the Italian heartland, by the Celtic tribes that hated Hannibal's enemies, clans that all around the northern provinces shared a border with Rome.

The only way to keep them at bay was to punish them for any transgression. Domitius should have abandoned his construction work and attacked at once, but the man cared more for his road than the fate of frontier farmers. He intended to press on with his work, but the old fox wrote that if the Senate insisted that he chastise this Brennos, then they must provide the means for him to do so. Such behaviour was not inclined to make the censor smile, yet he did now, for Lucius Falerius, on many occasions, had been given cause to wonder at the mischief of the gods.

That a despatch relating to this Brennos should come to him on this very day was uncanny. The shaman had been assumed to be history, yet it was clearly not so. The other part of that history was waiting to see him at this very moment. He rang the bell that would summon his steward, intent on giving him instructions that his caller, Aulus Cornelius Macedonicus, should be shown in forthwith, but he changed his mind and pulled himself to his feet. Given the circumstances a little magnanimity would not go amiss, so he walked out of his study to fetch his visitor himself.

Aulus was a punctual man in a city where many were not; being kept waiting was a thing to which he had become accustomed, if not resigned. Lucius Falerius was one of the worst, more easily forgiven than most, for it was not brought on by a lack of respect but by the fact that as one of the two censors – and the head of a strong political faction – he undertook the work of ten men, having reams of visitors who were either supplicants, or adherents needing to be reminded of where he insisted their interests lay. There had been a steady cooling of their friendship, though all the proper forms had been observed; no breach occurred, and all the courtesies were fully observed. They had congregated at all the festivals and religious ceremonies; met often, either at the games, in fellow senator's houses, or at the Senate. If Aulus found himself excluded from the more intimate political discussions that was only to be expected.

He believed friendship and that blood oath transcended politics and assumed his old friend felt the same. He had dutifully supported Lucius in his successful campaign for the censorship, lending him money for his games and accepting that as holder of that office he was made even busier, so that recently, socially, they saw even less of each other. Why Lucius had asked him to call he did not know, but he was sure it was not to ask his advice. Despite his loathing for gossip, he had heard nothing good from those closer to the man. He was, it seemed, becoming more and more secretive and authoritarian, demanding utter loyalty to his vision of Rome, which left Aulus wondering if he was in for an uncomfortable interview. Yet at that very moment, when he was ruminating on how he would respond, Lucius came out to greet him personally, with his fine-boned and weary-lined face wreathed in smiles, acknowledging both their companionship and their equality.

'My good friend, how pleased I am to see you!' he cried, arms outstretched. He gave Aulus a perfunctory embrace and, still talking, took his arm to lead him back to his study. 'Why is it, these days, that we see so little of each other?'

There was a slight trace of pique in the voice, as

though their lack of social contact was the fault of his visitor. Aulus fought the temptation to snap at him, keeping his tone even. 'You have declined more than one invitation to dine, Lucius.'

His host threw up his hands, exposing bony wrists in a gesture meant to imply frustration, though both men knew that Claudia was part of the reason. 'I know, my friend, and you have been most forgiving in not taking it badly. It requires the breeding of a true aristocrat to know when an apology is just that, and not some disguised slight. What Rome needs are more people of our stamp. The consuls we get these days are a sorry bunch.'

Lucius faced him, his hands on Aulus's arms, with a look in his eye that denied all responsibility for the dubious qualities of those who held power, men who could not have dreamt of office without his aid. 'If I have not apologised already, please accept one from me now. The pressure of work is so great that it leaves little time for pleasure.'

'I saw young Marcellus in the classroom,' said Aulus, in order to stem this tide of insincerity.

'Ah yes,' replied the boy's father, his eyes lighting up. 'A fine specimen of Roman youth, wouldn't you say. He makes his old father proud, though he sometimes angers me with his want of attention.'

Aulus produced a grim smile. 'He seems to make his teacher somewhat angry too.'

'Then I hope the fellow punishes him severely for it.'

Aulus had intended to intercede on the pupil's behalf, and suggest that Lucius curb the pedagogue, but those words made him bite his tongue. The punishment the man was meting out had the full approval of his employer, so he had only managed to save the boy one swipe of the sapling and he was not foolish enough to believe that his words would stop the teacher for long. The man would be lashing away again tomorrow, and with more venom to compensate for his humiliation.

'Pray, be seated,' said Lucius, waiting till Aulus had obliged before continuing. 'I asked you to call so that I could outline to you a matter that troubles me greatly. Yet I find that some information, just come in, may be of more interest to you.' With a grin, he threw the despatch from Domitius across the desk, the heavy scroll landing with a thud. 'Fresh in from Spain, this very day, and with a kind reference to your son Titus.'

The name Brennos leapt out at Aulus like a spear aimed at his innermost being. It was not just care that made him read the words slowly, his pounding heart and the need to disguise his emotions from Lucius made it difficult to concentrate. The renegade Druid was back with a vengeance.

'Interesting reading,' said Lucius.

'It certainly is.'

'Nonsense of course. Those Greeks are exaggerating. They always do!'

'Have you read what he is preaching at the tribes?'

'It's not something I haven't heard before, Aulus. It's a message repeated on every border we share with barbarians.'

The truth of that remark made Aulus check himself and he fought to bring his thoughts and his voice under control. It occurred to him to mention that eagle charm and relate it, as he had, to their joint prophecy. The thought died as he recalled that Lucius had never seen it in the same light as he, had always humoured him about his fears and right at this moment that was a reaction he did not wish to engender, especially since the charm and its wearer were so far away, too far to be any threat to either man. Unless, of course, Brennos succeeded in his long-term aims.

'Perhaps you're right, Lucius, but take the advice of someone who's fought him.'

'And what would that be?'

'Spy on him, bribe, threaten and cajole. Make sure you know what he does before he does it, what he thinks before he thinks it. Don't wait for him to act! Anticipate his every move. This man could represent the greatest threat to Rome since Hannibal.'

'This fellow has possessed you, Aulus.' He

reached over and took the scroll out of Aulus's hands. 'But important, no doubt, as he is, we have other matters to discuss. I take it that you are available, if called upon, to serve the Republic again?'

'As always,' replied Aulus, swiftly, his finger pointed to the despatch. 'With a strong preference for a return to Spain. Let me deal with this menace.'

Lucius threw back his head and laughed. 'Nonsense, Aulus. This Brennos, as a pest, ranks alongside a flea. Take my word for it, he is beneath your dignity. The problem we have is in Illyricum, which I hazard is a province with which you're even better acquainted. I need you to go back there.'

'I doubt Vegetius Flaminus would take kindly to that.'

'And what if he is the problem?'

'Explain,' Aulus said, without anything even approaching enthusiasm.

It took some persuading; nothing could be worse for a provincial governor than to be under the gaze of a predecessor. That lasted till Lucius showed him some of the things the locals had been saying about Vegetius, letters that made it obvious everything he had achieved in pacifying the place had been thrown away on the altar of the man's greed. Lucius wanted to send a commission out to investigate and he wanted Aulus to lead it.

'I think you'll agree he needs to be reprimanded.'

Aulus's expression, when he looked at Lucius, implied that he had in mind more painful punishments. 'But I cannot do anything with letters from disgruntled provincials, however true they might be, because I cannot lay them before the Senate as evidence. They will just throw such complaints out.'

'If there are enough of them...'

Lucius interrupted, but not in a rude way. 'You know our fellow senators as well as I do, Aulus. Some are honest, like you and I, but not enough of them. The rest will not take these as we would intend, rather they will think of what they have done in the past and what they might like to do in the future and judge Vegetius on that criteria rather than the truth. The man is making a great deal of money and few would wish to see the ability to make a fortune curbed. Also, I have to tell you that should you accept this task you will be part of a commission that has on it representatives who will openly admit to being the man's friends. I take it, if what these communications say are true, you would not wish Vegetius to retain his governorship.'

'I'm not sure I would want him to retain his head.'

'Then I must tell you that will not happen. Replacing him as governor will be hard enough.'

'It would be better if I went alone.'

'I agree, but that is not possible. Getting you as

head of the commission means I have to accommodate the views of others to maintain balance in the house. It will probably please you to know that even I cannot force through the Senate any measure I like.'

There was a temptation on Lucius's part to add that Aulus was partly responsible for that, but he held his tongue. His initial fear, when Aulus publicly separated from him was that he would become the focus of opposition. Lucius could guess how many people had tried to persuade him into that role. His hope was that his old friend stood alone and aloof, supporting those proposals with which he agreed, and staying silent when he could not. This was one he should be eager to back.

Smiling to take the sting out of a slightly barbed observation, Aulus replied. 'It will not please you to know that I think that is as it should be.'

'On the contrary, my friend. If I have fought for any principle in my life it is that such a situation should not only exist but be maintained.' Lucius paused, and looked Aulus in the eye. 'I am going to allude to something that perhaps would be better left unsaid. I sometimes wonder if you understand me, Aulus, just as I wonder if you think I aim for supreme power.'

'If I thought that I would be your enemy.'

'I know, and I hope you are aware that I respect you for it.'

'If I have sometimes failed to support you, Lucius, it is because my conscience had left me no choice.'

'And how can any honest man not praise you for that?'

'I dislike the idea of going to Illyricum without a proper mandate.'

Lucius allowed himself a ghost of a smile at what was nothing less than a deliberate change of subject. Honesty, or the lack of it, was not an area into which Aulus wished to enter.

'I have an idea to circumvent that.'

'Circumvent the Senate!'

'No. Do you really think I would ask you to do such a thing? What I propose is that you should send back to me whatever information you gather by private letter.'

'Why?'

'I will show these to certain of our fellow senators and I know before the commission report comes in that they will very likely be at odds with what it says. Vegetius's friends will force even you to compromise – to see his actions in the light of precedence rather than justice. Any attempt to dissent would make you a lone voice, and that, even from you, will not be heard. But certain people, primed, will know what questions to ask, questions which may expose the report as fraudulent. If you were then to voice your dissent on the floor of the house we might just bring about the downfall of a man who deserves no less.'

'How much of an enemy to you is Vegetius Flaminus?'

'He is an enemy of the Imperium of Rome, Aulus, and sometimes my likes and dislikes coincide with that. Besides, you mean rival, not enemy, and he is certainly not that.'

'Private letters? It smacks of chicanery.'

'Only if the truth comes out, which it will not, since I will return your correspondence to you as soon as you come back to Rome.'

'You know I will burn them?'

'Aulus, my old friend, you have no idea how you would shock me if you did not.'

CHAPTER FIFTEEN

The battle was reaching its climax. Marcellus Falerius, wooden sword in hand, had allotted himself the role of Scipio Africanus, while Gaius Trebonius had been given the role of Hannibal. Marcellus commanded his troops to open their ranks just as the slave appeared. He tried to ignore him – the man was interrupting their war game – but that proved impossible. When the slave, tired of waving at him, walked straight between the opposing armies locked in the mock battle of Zama, completely ruining, in the shape of the Calvinus twins, the encircling movement of Marcellus' cavalry, he had to call things to a halt.

'Your father has asked you to come to his study, Master Marcellus.'

'Not now!' cried the boy.

The slave just looked at him; with a father like Lucius Falerius, to state the immediacy of the summons would be superfluous.

'Ignore him, Marcellus,' cried the acting Hannibal. 'If you go now the Carthaginians will win.'

'Sorry.'

'Just tell your father this fellow forgot to call you.'

'What a thing to say, Gaius. How can you make a suggestion like that and call yourself Roman?'

Trebonius stuck his tongue out and blew a raspberry. 'Right now I'm a Carthaginian.'

'I don't think even they would sink so low as to inflict punishment on an innocent slave.'

'Don't be stupid, Marcellus,' said another boy. 'Who cares about slaves?'

Marcellus just fixed him with an icy stare, and adopting what he thought was a proper Roman posture, a pose that they had named his Horatius look, he followed the slave towards the back door of his house.

'Look at him,' snorted one of the Calvinus twins. 'You'd think he had a broomstick shoved up his arse.'

'Louder,' said Gaius Trebonius, since the other boy had made sure that Marcellus would not hear him.

'No fear. Let's get on with the fight. I'll be Africanus now.'

The boy took his place at the head of his small band of troops and issued his first command. 'On guard. Open ranks and prepare to receive elephants.'

Marcellus stood before the parental desk. Just turned nine, he was, even at that tender age, expected to confer with his father about all his recent decisions and come to a conclusion that pleased him, which Lucius never tired of telling his son was part of his training. His father was enlightening on the history of Rome, in a way that no Greek tutor could match, so it was not always a trial. He had been a power in the Senate, or close to it, for so long that he was steeped in knowledge of the leading personalities of the Republic, all the way back to the Tarquin kings. Such knowledge provided Lucius with his two guiding concepts; the first being that Rome should never again fall under the tyranny of a monarchy, with the caveat that he was no Athenian democrat, being equally opposed to sharing power with all and sundry. To his way of thinking, only those of the right class had the foresight, combined with the lack of avarice, to rule wisely. That was his second, and seemingly stronger, principle, one, as a patrician himself, he was prepared to sacrifice even his life to maintain.

As a dutiful son, far too young for independent thoughts, Marcellus shared his father's prejudices, so he too thought that the corn dole had made matters worse instead of better, dragging more people into Rome than the city could comfortably accommodate. He would scoff, just as derisively as Lucius, if anyone suggested that Rome's Italian allies should be allowed citizenship, or to plead in the courts against what they saw as the rapacity of her senators. The Republic was not greedy, merely victorious, a power more beneficial to the world than any that had existed before, something for which the conquered should be grateful. Because of Rome, these inhabitants of Italy enjoyed peace and prosperity while that unique and august body, the supreme forum of magistrates, better by far than any king, embodied in themselves the law that made Rome work.

Lucius sat back in his chair and folded his hands across his stomach, and smiled at his son. 'Now, boy. We have a problem in Illyricum. I believe I told you of it the other day.'

'Yes, father.'

'Never mind the "yes, father",' Lucius replied. 'Tell me about it.'

Marcellus tilted his head back and spoke like a soldier delivering a report, a pleasing pose. It took no great leap of parental imagination to see the boy a little older, talking in the same voice, and in the same posture, to a military superior.

'Following the outbreak of a rebellion a consular army of two legions, plus auxiliaries, has been in the province for four years. In that time it has engaged in no proper battle. Despatches from the commander Vegetius Flaminus state that the war is of a scattered nature and that the rebellious provincials will not congregate in enough strength to offer an opportunity to our troops.'

Marcellus looked down at his father, who merely said, 'Go on, boy.'

'He further stated that he wished to avoid exposing the legions to piecemeal engagements since this was more likely to reduce his forces than those of the rebels. Other letters from the province include numerous requests from the citizenry for something to be done, since their crops, cattle and mining concessions are under constant attack from marauding bands. They also hinted at certain irregular activities on the part of the governor.'

'I think you've forgotten something,' said Lucius, as Marcellus paused again.

'Forgive me, father.'

Lucius sat forward, fixing his son with a steely look. 'You really must pay more attention, Marcellus. If you miss such important points as the one you've so conspicuously left out of your report, you cannot hope for success in public life. In every case to be examined or pleaded there are salient points. Remember those, elaborate on them, and the rest becomes easy.'

'Yes, father.'

'None of this, or the conclusion we reached the other day, makes any sense, if you don't include the fact that the Dacian tribes are raiding across the border, in strength, and fighting alongside the

Illyrian rebels. Why does not the governor move to intercept them? What steps has he taken to gather intelligence that would allow him to do so? Without Dacian support, it should be easy to contain a few bands of Illyrian malcontents, should it not?'

'Yes, sir.'

'And what did we conclude?'

'You were of the opinion that Vegetius was sitting doing nothing, lining his pockets with bribes, content to avoid an engagement of any sort, especially one that may result in a check to his ambitions here at home. That forceful and swift action would have crushed the rebellion long ago.'

His father replied patiently. 'What I said was this. That Vegetius was unwilling to fight, more interested in using his proconsular powers to amass a fortune. Once he'd achieved that, he would come back to Rome intent on using that fortune to advance his political career. Since he is neither a friend nor a political ally of mine, that is not an outcome I welcome. So the nub of the problem is not what he is doing in Illyricum, so much as how his inactivity will one day impact here in Rome. You see the point?'

With Marcellus nodding, Lucius was wondering what someone like his son would make of a man like Vegetius Flaminus, a flabby individual, carefully barbered, and with an insatiable love of money. He had the reputation of being a bully and like all of that breed would lord it over the weak while wilting before anyone of strength; altogether a poor specimen. The house of Flaminus was an ancient one, but with the male line faltering adoption had been necessary to keep the name alive; common enough, and in some cases it had been spectacularly successful, but to Lucius it was a chancy business. It carried the risk that a noble family would bring into its protective fold someone like Vegetius, bred originally into a clan with an old Roman name, but no money to maintain their patrician status.

The reports told him that most of Vegetius's junior officers hated him for both his indolence and his peculations, but more for the man's utter lack of any trace of a backbone. He was a poor general who had let his legions go to seed, an administrator who sold his prerogatives rather than undertaking them, a man whose sole concern seemed to be for the comfort of his person and his belly. But he had friends, which was why he had been gifted the prized sinecure of Illyricum after Aulus Cornelius relinquished the post. It was a measure of the limits of Lucius's power that other factions in the Senate had to be accommodated, and having previously so favoured his own candidate, it had been politic to pacify those who opposed him by allowing their man the succession. Lucius sighed inwardly, saddened by the fact that all the good work Aulus had done was now in pieces. People who wondered why he toiled so long and hard had only to look at a man like Vegetius Flaminus, the nature of his appointment and the result, to see just how much still had to be done to protect the Republic. Not all Rome's enemies were external ones.

'Now, Marcellus,' he said, dragging himself back to the subject at hand. 'Having all this information at your disposal, you rise in the Senate to suggest a course of action, knowing his friends will speak on his behalf and that anything extreme could be voted down. What do you say?'

Marcellus, who loved the more relaxed atmosphere when his father talked of Roman history, hated these sessions, for he could never get them wholly right. 'Something must be done to either make Vegetius pursue the war, or he must be relieved.'

'That's obvious, boy. What I want is the means to achieve it.' Lucius waited for the youngster to speak. Marcellus stared at a point above his father's head, knowing that in his anxiety his mind had gone blank. 'My patience is not inexhaustible.'

'A commission,' said Marcellus panicking. It was the only thing he could think of and his heart sank. His father would forbid him to rejoin his friends playing outside; for such a miserable, catchall answer, he would be sent to his room to study. The actual response took him by surprise.

'Excellent! Now having suggested this, and with due eloquence persuaded your fellow senators to support you, who would you send?'

'Forgive me, father, I doubt I have the knowledge to answer such a question.'

Lucius finally smiled. 'A wise answer, Marcellus. You've done well today, but let us address that problem in the abstract. The whole question must be approached in two stages. First the commission must be agreed, without naming the members. That will pass easily, since the friends of Vegetius Flaminus will seek to get themselves appointed. Then we muster our forces, pick a time when they're unavailable, and make sure that at least some of the commissioners are people of the right sort. So we come to the next question Marcellus. The person empowered by the Senate to head the commission must be what?'

'A person with enough authority.'

'You're partly right, after all the authority of the Senate will travel with him, but it is often a good idea to send someone who has authority in his own right. Now, what qualifications does this powerful person require?'

'Would he need to be a client of yours?'

Lucius shook his head in slow disgust, unhappy that his son had reminded him that he was not all powerful in such cases, so diverse were the aims, needs and views of the members it was like trying to shape a particularly stupid form of quicksand. Certainly he had more clients and supporters than anyone else, but care had to be exercised in the marshalling of such forces and keeping them happy as individuals and groups was a full time occupation.

'I could get them to appoint an obvious client of mine, but the motion would face challenge at the next fully attended session. Understand Marcellus, that men who might back me in a crisis will readily vote me down in an area that is not seen as serious, some for no other reason than to show that they have a degree of independence.'

Marcellus now shook his head.

Lucius showed an unaccustomed degree of patience. 'Well, look at it this way. Since the matter under review is both military and civil, it would help if he were a successful soldier. That takes care of the military side. What would he need for the civil side?'

Marcellus, not really having a clue, pulled out of his memory one of his father's most frequently used words. 'Experience.'

'Excellent again, boy,' cried Lucius, genuinely pleased.

'Is there such a man, father? Someone who is the perfect choice.'

Lucius resumed his stern expression. 'Learn this, Marcellus, and learn it well. However many qualities a man has, he is never perfect. The Senate must send to Illyricum, not perfection, but the most suitable man they can find. That man was here today.' Lucius stood up and turned his back on Marcellus, reaching into the cupboards for a new set of scrolls. 'In fact he says he saw you.'

'Who is he father?'

'Aulus Cornelius Macedonicus. Not perfect as I say, but he's a very successful soldier and he was the previous governor of Illyricum. People say that the excesses of the man who succeeded him have sparked the rebellion. Apparently Aulus was much admired by the locals for his fairness, though I daresay he made a fair amount of money out of the place.'

Marcellus had heard of Aulus, had even studied his campaign in Macedonia. The man was a legend. 'If he defeated the Macedonians in battle as well, he sounds like a great man to me.'

Lucius still had his back to his son, so he did not see the gleam in his eyes. 'No, my boy, he hasn't the makings of a truly great man. I can tell you that I know him better than any person alive, and he has any number of Achilles' heels.'

As he spoke those words Lucius recalled Aulus's words about Brennos. Caution, in Rome's defence, was something that had paid dividends in the past and perhaps Aulus was right. It would do no harm, and cost little, to keep an eye on this Druid. He checked himself, having already begun to compose a cautionary despatch, and dragged his mind back to the present. The interview with Aulus had partly amused, and partly annoyed him, for he found it hard to sit opposite his one-time friend and not feel betrayed by the man, while he knew from the look in his visitor's eyes just how much his emotions differed from the tone of his voice. Aulus would gladly give up his eye teeth for a true reconciliation, but that was impossible; if he could not make matters good with a lie, the truth would not bring them closer, for idealistic Aulus would never accept that sometimes only pragmatic solutions would serve, never accept that such idealism was sometimes an abdication of responsibility.

It had not turned to hate on either side. Aulus was not given to that and he did not have time for such a useless passion and yet, as they had sat there, he had felt they were still inextricably bound to each other; he could not ignore Aulus and neither could Aulus slight him, for they shared too much past; indeed the bond they had formed as boys was still unbreakable. There was that prophecy of course, the remembrance of which only came to Lucius when Aulus was present. It was distant and toothless now; age and experience had made Lucius even more sceptical than he had pretended to be that night.

Even with his son present he again felt lonely;

how he longed to sit with someone he trusted absolutely, someone who would dispute with him and test his own internal assertions, yet at the same time understand his motives and thinking. Aulus should have been there for that, but he had detached himself so forcibly as to forfeit any position of trust. At least his famed independence would make him ideal to sort out the mess created by Vegetius Flaminus, and if he abided by that which Lucius had asked, he would, in his natural unwitting way, help to make good the damage he had caused so many years before.

Then Lucius reminded himself he had his son, too young now to fulfil that role, but who would grow to be first his companion, then his colleague, and finally his successor. With that in prospect he had no need of his old friend.

'Yes,' he said, 'Aulus Cornelius will do for the task in hand, notwithstanding his myriad faults.'

Marcellus did not dare to disagree openly with his father, even though he knew him to be wrong. How could a man who looked like Aulus Cornelius Macedonicus possibly be prey to faults?

CHAPTER SIXTEEN

Fulmina was getting older and was finding it harder and harder to control Aquila; not, it has to be said, that she had ever tried very hard, for the gods had spoken through her dreams, as well as the musings of the old soothsayer Drisia. A simple soul, Fulmina believed that fate was pre-destined, hers as well as that of the boy, so the gods would take care of Aquila without her going out of her way to chastise him. And really, the things he got up to were those that all youngsters of his age indulged in, just more so. Now ten summers old he was taller than his peers by a good head, stronger by far and leagues-away the most daring. He climbed trees faster, swam quicker and fought better without ever being a thug. Other mothers, who needed their sons to help in the fields were given to complaining heartily when Aquila, freed from such labour by Dabo's deliveries of household necessities, turned up and tempted them off to play in the woods.

Many days he was left to his own devices, which did not please him much. It was no fun following wild boar tracks alone; it could be tedious laying still on your belly for hours watching the weasels come and go from their burrows, often with a dead rabbit or bird in their mouths. Besides, there was greater danger in being alone; boar with young could kill if provoked; you had to listen out too for wolves in winter, though the bears were rarely seen now. They had long since retired from this cultivated part of the world and moved into the forests, higher up the mountains that stood tall and majestic to the east. The occasional big cat would come hunting in the lowlands and they were the most dangerous of all.

Sometimes Aquila would sit up a tree at the edge of the wood and look towards the distant mountains, which ran north and south like a great barrier. The eagles, his namesakes, nested there, ranging far and wide on the hot air currents in search of food. Occasionally one would come into view and he would sigh, thinking that it must be wonderful to be able to fly and to look down on the world from such a height. Like a god really. Perhaps those birds could comprehend the size of the world; he could not, never having been more than half a league from the hut he called home.

He was often lonely, but days spent in the woods gave him an affinity with nature, even if he did not quite know what to call the plants and trees. He knew the birds and the animals for they were a constant subject of discussion and pursuit amongst the locals. Birds you could eat, and the same applied to some animals and these, notwithstanding the fact that the woods were private property, provided most of the meat in the poorer families' diet. Occasional boar hunts were organised as winter approached, but that was an event for men, not boys. Other animals were identified as inedible but dangerous; they killed chickens, geese and the smaller livestock. He would lie still and listen to the hum of the forest, and in time he could sort out the sounds of the birds from those of the other creatures. He learnt to recognise the silence that fell when a larger predator entered the vicinity, then he too would fall quiet and seek a place of safety, usually in a tree.

The boy thought about and asked about Clodius all the time. Seven years his papa had been gone now with only the occasional word related to Fulmina by a passing soldier on leave. The toy uniform hung on the wall of the hut; too small now, yet a constant reminder of his absent parent. Even in the woods he missed Clodius, for he knew things that Aquila did not and would have taken much pleasure in teaching his son how to trap the birds and the smaller mammals. A father would have told him the stories that Fulmina avoided; she told tales of goodness and upright behaviour, or, if she thought he had been particularly wayward, of youths turned into donkeys or pigs. Tales of heroism she avoided, for her gods were all pastoral deities; Clodius would have told him of the lives of warriors and heroes. Other fathers were happy to include him when they were storytelling, but it was not the same as being curled up beside your own papa, with a fire blazing in the pitch dark forest on a chill night, and listening to the sound of a voice you loved tell you of myths, magic and martial deeds.

At times his meanderings took him close to the big villa by the road that ran south from Rome, but not too close in daylight, for he feared that those employed to keep the likes of him out of the woods, to stop the poaching, would come after him, and being distinctive had its drawbacks. He could only go into the compound in winter, when the nights were dark early, and he had become adept at getting to the rabbit hutches and grabbing one to take home for the cold-weather pot. His mama would happily eat what he brought home, but she would not be happy to see the steward of Cassius Barbinus at her door, the owner of the villa being the man she most hated in all the world.

'If you see him, Aquila, you will know right away it is he. Fat as a pregnant sow, he is, from too much good food stolen from the likes of us. All that land for his cattle and sheep, our old farm included, and him so full-bellied I would not be surprised if he eats them all himself.'

'Have a care Cassius Barbinus does not hear you, Fulmina.' She turned to see Piscius Dabo in the doorway, a bag of wheat in one hand and a bundle of kindling strapped to his back. He looked at the birds hanging head down on the line, and added, 'And if he sees those it will be even worse.'

'Barbinus come here, Dabo? That won't happen, and he would not get through the door if he did.'

'I can get through the door any time you like, day or night.'

Aquila saw Fulmina pull a face and he wondered at the look on the face of Dabo, yet he could not comprehend. All he knew was that Dabo came only second to Fat Barbinus in the ranks of those Fulmina loathed.

He laid down the sack of wheat and took the kindling off his back. 'Must be lonely without old Clodius here.'

Fulmina stood behind her boy and put her hands on his shoulders. 'Not when I have Aquila.'

'That ain't the kind of company I reckon you need.'

'Well you ain't the kind of company I want.'

Dabo looked disappointed and slightly angry. 'Suit yourself. Send the boy over tomorrow and I will fill your pitcher with milk.' Then he glared at

Aquila. 'And try not to get into a fight with my lads, this time.'

'They start it.'

'That's not what my boys say. Maybe you should come over and do some work, like they have to, then you wouldn't have the energy to scrap.'

'The day Aquila works for the likes of you, Piscius Dabo, is the day the heavens will fall in.'

'I know, I know. He's going to be a great man.' Dabo laughed as he departed, the sound echoing inside the sod hut. 'The only person who'll ever get on their knees to him is you Fulmina, and that's to tie the straps on his sandals. Great man, my arse.'

'Is Papa ever going to come home?' Aquila asked as Dabo disappeared from the doorway.

'One day, boy. He will be home one day.'

'I'll go with him to the woods, the day he returns.'

'Of course you will,' Fulmina replied, wondering how her husband, after such a long absence, would react to a boy now nearly as tall as himself.

He was alone again, barefoot and seeking animal tracks, when the forest, quite suddenly, went totally silent. Aquila was up like a flash and headed for the nearest large tree. His sandals were tied to his waist and being barefoot he shinned up the gnarled oak easily, his heart pounding. If it turned out to be anything like a bear or a large cat, they could climb trees better than any ten-year-old boy. He lay flat along a thick branch, his dark brown tunic and tanned skin blending in with the tree bark and when he heard the bells, he laughed, pushing his face into the wood to suppress the sound. A shepherd! He, Aquila, had run for cover to avoid sheep. He lay still, listening, as the sound of the bells grew louder, watched as the lead animal entered the clearing and walked right under his perch. As it left the clearing the shepherd entered from the other side. The man was tall and had long, near white hair poking out from under a battered straw hat. He shuffled rather than walked, head down and supported by a long staff, following his flock, paying no attention to his surroundings. An old man, doing an old man's job.

The boy realised he would pass right beneath him and with a delicious thrill of impending mischief he decided to deliver the shepherd the fright of his life. As the man came under the tree, Aquila slipped off the branch, and with a wild yell dropped right behind him, missing his back by an inch. The speed with which his victim spun round surprised him, as did the guttural cry that shot from his lips. Aquila had dropped to his knees to break his fall and found himself, frozen for a split second, staring up into the most alarming face; as he had turned, the man's straw hat had flown off. Underneath the huge mane of flying, flaxen hair, the skin was bright red, peeled in places where he had suffered from the sun. The mouth was open in a snarl, but it was the great gash, stark and scary across the empty eye socket, which frightened the boy most; that, and the plain fact that the shepherd was not an old man.

He tried to escape, standing up and turning as he did so. The huge dog was pounding across the clearing, fangs bared as it made straight for him. Again he froze, trying to decide which way to jump and mentally cursing himself for a fool. The forest would not have gone silent for sheep or a shepherd: it was the presence of this enormous dog that had made them still. With the speed at which it came for him there seemed no escape. The staff took him right on the ankles lifting his feet to near waist height and Aquila dropped flat on his back, the wind driven in a gush out of his lungs. He could hear the man shouting, though he could make no sense of the words he used. The staff came down at speed and was pressed across his throat just as the dog leapt. The paws hit him in the ribs causing him even more pain, but the huge teeth, instead of entering the soft flesh of his neck, hit the wooden staff.

The shepherd, still shouting, swung the pole and pulled the snarling animal to one side. As that huge canine face had come close to his, Aquila had shut his eyes in fear. They stayed shut and he listened as the voice, still speaking in a strange tongue, went from angry shouts, to normal tone, then finally to a soothing litany. When he opened his eyes and turned his head, the dog was sitting, panting slightly, its great tongue lolling out of its mouth.

'You hurt?' the shepherd asked in heavily accented Latin, kneeling down to look him over. The face, now that it was not reacting to a sudden assault, and was not quite so close, seemed a lot less frightening, though it was hard to avoid gazing at the empty eye socket.

'I'm sorry,' gasped Aquila, one eye still on the dog.

'I think you are. Minca killed you nearly. He protect his master, like good dog should.'

The voice was quite gentle, deep and rasping, but warm and friendly. He said something in the other tongue, patting the animal on the head and the dog whined and nuzzled his hand. Aquila pushed himself up until he was sitting. He still felt drained of air and he rubbed his chest where the huge paws had thumped into him.

'You like stroke him?'

Aquila put out his hand gingerly, stopping well short of the animal's jaws. The huge square head with its pointed ears was not something to inspire him with confidence, even if the enormous brown eyes looked friendly enough. The dog, near black, with lighter brown colouring around the muzzle and lower legs, pushed its head forward to sniff his fingers and Aquila felt the rough tongue lick the tips.

'You be all right now he know you. You stand up, he will not attack again.'

The man took Aquila's arm to help him to his feet, as the boy apologised again. 'I didn't mean any harm.'

The blond man smiled. 'You gave me fright.' He reached out with his free hand to touch Aquila's hair, a look of curiosity in his one good eye. 'What you doing in woods?'

'Just playing.'

The shepherd then touched the edge of Aquila's smock, so clearly the garment of someone poor. 'You have benevolent master, boy.'

'Master?'

The man smiled, then shrugged. 'A slave boy with time for play.'

'I'm no slave boy,' snapped Aquila, in a voice that brought the dog to his feet. 'I'm a free-born Roman.'

'Not worry,' said the shepherd quickly, seeing the boy back away from the creature slightly. 'Minca as gentle as a lamb.'

This seemed to remind him of his other charges and he let forth with a string of incomprehensible commands that sent the dog running off toward the sound of the distant sheep bells. Then he turned back, looking Aquila up and down before speaking.

'Free-born Roman, eh?' he enquired in his bad Latin, fingering Aquila's hair again. Then he touched his face gently. 'Your skin take sun well, unlike me. If you Roman, that means your father is free-born Roman too.'

'He most certainly is.'

He smiled even more at the emphatic way the boy spoke. 'So father toils in fields, while son runs off to play?'

Aquila puffed out his chest in pride. 'My father is serving with the 10th Legion of the Roman Army in Illyricum.'

'Has he same colour hair?'

'No.'

Aquila frowned, not making any attempt to hide his displeasure; all his life he had been subjected to taunts for his height and his hair, with more than the odd hint as to his dubious parentage. Few dared to let him overhear these days, since he would thump anyone who even suggested that he was different. The girls were the worst, but you could hardly just give them a buffet round the ear. Mind, recently, their remarks tended to be phrased in a way designed to catch his attention, rather than taunt him, and only turned nasty when he treated their interest with lofty disdain.

The one eye did not flicker, holding the boy in its solitary gaze. 'So your father in legions. Where does mother come from?'

'What do you mean?'

'She Roman?'

'Of course!'

'Father ever been to Gaul?'

Aquila spoke as if he did not understand. 'Gaul?'

The man pointed over his shoulder. 'Up there, north.'

'I know where Gaul is. It's full of blond giants who fight naked. The legions always beat them…' Aquila realised he was talking to a blond giant who spoke in a strange tongue and fell into an embarrassed silence as the smile disappeared and the rasp in the voice was less friendly.

'They not always win, boy.'

Aquila was now glaring up at him. 'You were taken prisoner?'

The shepherd nodded with some reluctance. 'So you a free-born Roman?'

Aquila replied defiantly. 'Yes.'

'You have name?'

'Aquila Terentius.'

The man raised his head to look at the sky, as if acknowledging the source. 'Well, young eagle, I too have name. It Gadoric, and I a slave, though I was once free-born like you.' Aquila held his hand out and the man took it with a grin. 'Free-born Roman shakes the hand of slave!'

'Is that the wrong thing to do?' asked Aquila, confused.

The shepherd laughed and picked up his battered straw hat. 'No, boy, that the right thing to do, but it not happen often. Let us go, see if I have any animals left.'

The sheep were huddled in a tight group, with Minca laying right in front of them, paws outstretched and eyes fixed for the least sign of movement.

'He's a bit big for a sheepdog.'

'He bred to hunt stags. Two-week-old pup when I was taken. Kept him inside my coat, next to the skin.' He called to the dog in his alien tongue and it ran over to join him, to have its ears vigorously rubbed. 'Now we look after sheep.'

Gadoric issued some more commands to the dog and it ran out of sight. Then he tapped the lead ram with his long staff and it immediately headed in the opposite direction, away from the canine smell.

'Where are you going?' asked Aquila.

'To field over there.' He pointed his staff to the south of the woods.

Aquila was curious about this man, Gadoric. He was a slave, but he had once been free and with that scar and his empty eye socket, he had probably been a soldier. He might have some interesting tales to tell. 'Can I come with you?'

'I just about to ask,' said Gadoric, clapping the youngster on the shoulder. Aquila might be curious about him, but that was nothing compared to the interest that the flaxen-haired Celt had in the golden-haired child.

As they left the woods the shepherd, with his hat back in place, bent his shoulders, once more adopting the shuffling gait of an old man. Aquila looked at him strangely.

'Can trust you?' asked Gadoric, stopping suddenly. Taken by surprise, Aquila did not answer and they gazed intently at each other, until eventually, not sure what to say, the boy shrugged. 'There be no way knowing, is there?' Aquila shrugged again. Gadoric leant on his staff, clearly unsure if it was wise to speak. When he did, he sounded just as uncertain. 'I could ask you swear on your Roman gods, but I not believe in them.'

'I do,' said Aquila quickly, silently evoking the name of *Sanctus,* the God of Good Faith.

'No. I know men swear on every god in world, plus father's life, that they not betray something, then watch them do it.' He put one finger to his scarred face. 'I prefer to look in the eye, my one against you two, and ask straight. Aquila Terentius, I tell you secret, can I trust you keep it?'

The boy threw his arm across his chest in a soldierly salute and used the words he had been told were appropriate. 'On the altar of *Sanctus* and on pain of death.'

'Not die to keep it, lad,' said Gadoric with a

smile, again touching Aquila's hair. 'Just not give it away to whole neighbourhood.'

'I won't!'

So Gadoric told him that his shuffling gait was a pretence to keep him here. He had pretended sickness when he was brought south, taking herbs that made him seem really ill. All the others, brought south with him, had been sent to Sicily, to toil on starvation rations in the cornfields. Too weak for such work, he had been kept here as a shepherd for the local magnate, Cassius Barbinus.

'Cassius Barbinus is a very wealthy man. He's very important round here. He bought my father's farm off him, which is why he had to go into the legions. Barbinus owns this wood, too, and it's rumoured he's told his overseer to flog anyone he finds taking game from it. Everyone is frightened of him.'

'I not frightened of him,' snapped Gadoric. 'But this part Italy closer to home than Sicily. One day I go back.'

'Will Barbinus free you?' asked Aquila.

'No boy, he not free me.' Aquila felt a trace of fear at the look in Gadoric's single eye. 'But maybe I cut out stinking Roman heart as souvenir to take home.'

He must have realised he had scared the boy, so he laughed again and patted him on the shoulder, then indicated, with his head, the sheep grazing happily on some long grass. 'Grass for the cattle, not sheep. The dog need get them moving, eh?'

He whistled. Minca came out of the woods and bounded towards them. 'You like tell Minca what do?'

'I'll be happy just as long as he doesn't attack me.'

The dog, tail wagging, leapt about excitedly and it was obvious he was not going to attack anyone. 'So you not want to?'

'Yes,' said Aquila eagerly. Fulmina would not let him have a dog, since she held that it would just take the food out of their mouths, and besides they had no work to justify keeping an animal.

'Minca not understand Latin. You need learn my tongue before you give him commands.'

'I'm a quick learner,' said Aquila eagerly.

'So we try, no?'

CHAPTER SEVENTEEN

Marcellus watched with intense fascination as the two gladiators circled round each other. They had come to proper combat twice already and the Bithynian, a professional fighter, had a large gash on his upper arm, bleeding copiously, but he had narrowly missed skewering his opponent, a Lacedemonian Greek, who now had a corresponding gash in his side, just below his sword arm. Neither had been able to gain an advantage in the fierce struggles, so they had been forced to part, just to recover their breath. He was aware of his father, glancing at him occasionally to see how he was reacting to the sight of proper fighting and real blood.

Marcellus wanted to yell encouragement to the Greek but he dare not; it was no part of a patrician boy's behaviour to show that he was partisan, especially when his father had been given the place of honour. A client of his, a man who was standing for election as one of the Urban Aediles for this year, had staged the games, of which this contest was the final event. Lucius, presiding, would have to decide if one of these men lived or died and the only criteria would be their courage and skill with the short swords and shields in their hands.

All of his school friends were there as well, with their parents and siblings, so he sneaked a look towards the Trebonius family, his eye catching that of Gaius's sister Valeria. She immediately gave him sight of her tongue, accompanied by a derisory shake of the head. Marcellus, who would have liked a brother, was grateful not to have a sister; those of his friends with female siblings seemed to suffer mightily for the privilege, none more than Gaius Trebonius, Valeria being a positive menace. Sharp-tongued and interfering, she could not leave the boys to their games. Worse, as far as Marcellus was concerned, she seemed determined to include him in her torments, as if his being an only child qualified him for her attention.

The mother was soft-hearted and indulgent, seemingly blind to her behaviour, while her father was away. Not that his presence would have made any difference; Marcellus remembered him as even less of a disciplinarian than the mother. He loathed nothing more than those occasions when whole families were invited to his house, since Valeria encouraged all the other girls, so that together they teased him and his friends beyond endurance. He shook his head slightly to clear her image from his mind and returned his whole attention to the fight.

Why did he favour the Greek? Marcellus did not really know, but the Lacedemonian was wearing a most handsome helmet, polished till it gleamed and crowned with stiff horsehair. Dyed deep red, it made the boy think of Achilles, Ajax and the other Greek heroes of antiquity, perhaps even Alexander himself. The Bithynian wore a drab affair, little more than a peaked metal skullcap, electing to fight in something light, rather than something impressive. To Marcellus, schooled in the historical works of Ptolemy, it was the Alexandrian hero versus the Persian tyranny. No Roman could place his support the other way, yet many did, no doubt because they had money on the fellow. He was quite well known, having survived several bouts at previous games without so much as a scratch and he should have seen off his less experienced Greek opponent well before this. In the first clash he had seemed content to demonstrate his prowess, exciting the crowd with some very fancy swordplay.

The Greek, fighting in a much more prosaic fashion, had parried the elegant thrusts with some difficulty and having proved his abilities to those in the crowd who supported him, the Bithynian had stood off to rest, circling round his opponent for a full minute before dashing in for the finish, his intentions plain; a couple of quick thrusts to disarm his rival, a hefty cut to draw blood and finally a stroke with the sword to bring the fellow to his knees, then he could hand the man's fate over to Lucius Falerius. But the Greek was not prepared to play and the nature of the contest had changed immediately, the Bithynian suddenly finding himself on the defensive, with his opponent thrusting past his guard to slash his arm. The spurt of blood added an instantaneous spur, the contest becoming immediately much more heated. The Bithynian attacked with great fury, returning the compliment by drawing blood, but he could not overcome his opponent and the frustration started to show in the way the fight developed.

The noise abated as they drifted apart, but it rose to an even higher crescendo as the two combatants, with a resounding clash of swords, rushed at each other simultaneously. They hacked away, the ringing sound of metal striking metal barely audible above the roar of the crowd. Their shields clashed as they sought to knock each other off balance, the prelude to a disabling thrust. The Bithynian, using his shield to protect his front, coiled his body to one side then swung his sword, neck height, with all his strength. The Greek was caught with his shield in the wrong place and had the blow connected it would have decapitated him. Marcellus heard his father speak sharply, complaining quickly about such a murderous cut, this as the Greek dropped to his knee, the sword lopping half the horse-hair plumes from the top of his helmet. He did not stay down, but used the spring effect, coming swiftly back to his full height. The boss of his shield, rising above his head, took the Bithynian's unadorned helmet on the cap, knocking the man's head back. The Greek's sword followed, and the roar of the crowd was near deafening as it sliced into his opponents throat, entering in the middle of the jaw, and exiting from one side.

Marcellus kept a keen eye fixed on the scene as the blood spurted out of the gorge in a great gush. The Bithynian's head, neck sliced through to the bone, fell drunkenly to one side, as though it was about to come off completely, the tendons and muscles looking white against the rushing, foaming blood that pumped out of the torn veins. His father, unusually for him, swore loudly, as the Bithynian dropped into the sand like a sacrificed bull, twitching and jerking as he died.

'This is outrageous, Hortensius,' snapped Lucius to the man on his left, the Aedile candidate who was paying for these games. The crowd had fallen silent, so the older senator's voice fairly boomed out, 'You really must speak to your gladiator manager about the way these fellows are conducting themselves.'

'I agree, Lucius Falerius,' replied the young,

would-be magistrate, aware that any offence to his honoured guest could put a serious blight on his future career. Marcellus wondered if he really did agree; it had been a very good fight and from what he had heard, such a thing as he had just witnessed, the killing of one opponent by another, common in the south, was extremely rare in Rome itself. It harked back to the origin of the contest, the funeral rites of great leaders, where selected warriors would fight to the death over their grave for the right to accompany them to Hades.

'We cannot have these fellows killing each other without permission, Hortensius. What is the point of having a presiding magistrate of the games?'

Hortensius looked very serious as he replied. 'We mustn't have them usurping your prerogatives, Lucius Falerius.'

'This isn't some left-handed way to save money, is it, a guarantee of saving a fee?'

Marcellus thought his father had asked a silly question and so did Hortensius judging by the look on his face. Luckily, Lucius had turned his attention back to the arena, and the sweating Greek who stood facing the platform, sword raised in front of his heaving chest.

Hortensius spoke quickly, eager to please. 'Since this fellow has deprived you of your right to choose life or death for his opponent, I think it only fitting, Lucius Falerius, that you decide on his fate. Victor he might be, but he's yours to dispose of.'

Lucius nodded once, his eyes still fixed on the man who had so angered him. Marcellus also had his eyes fixed on the Greek now, half in admiration, and half to avoid looking at the spreading bloodstain and the exposed organs of the Bithynian at his feet.

'This is my son's first visit to the games, Hortensius. Would you permit him a hand in the decision?'

Marcellus stiffened as the host replied. 'Gladly.'

'Well?'

Marcellus blinked. He barely understood what had happened but he knew enough to be sure of one thing; that his incensed parent had the right to take this Greek gladiator's life and why? Merely because the man had taken a meaningless decision out of his father's hands; gladiators were supposed to entertain the crowd. It was obvious that there should be blood to please them, but to deliberately kill your opponent, without permission, was seen as an insult and now Lucius would have the guards spear him to death. Why should he take part in such a charade or a consultation that was equally meaningless? Even later that day, when he had had ample time to think, and describing the exchange to his friends, he could not say what prompted the words he used, nor the insolent tone in which he said them.

'Am I being asked to decide his fate, father?'

'What!' said Lucius, surprised enough to take his eyes off the Greek and look at his son. He declined to speak for several seconds, but when he did, his voice had that tone which warned Marcellus of deep trouble in store. 'Do you feel qualified, boy?'

'Would I be permitted to answer a question with a question, father?'

'Yes,' snapped Lucius.

'Are you determined that this fellow should die?'

That took Lucius by surprise, a rare thing, and Marcellus knew he had the right of it for that very reason, but the question forced a denial. 'My mind is open.'

'Liar!' The word sprang unbidden into his mind and Marcellus felt his body go cold. He was still of an age to assume a parent omnipotent enough to hear even his most secret thoughts, so he chose his words very carefully. 'Then you, sir, will have to judge if I am qualified. If you feel I'm not, I would humbly beg your permission to take no part in the decision.'

Marcellus knew his father always saw dissent instead of discerning logic, so he had no hope of escaping parental wrath by pointing out the basic undesirability of the position into which his father had forced him. But Lucius was no fool either, and he had much more experience than his son at perceiving the truth behind men's words.

'You would let him live?'

'I would, father.'

'Why?'

'He fought bravely and I think he responded to the lethal blow his opponent aimed at his head. I think he reacted like a soldier in battle, sir, and not a gladiator concerned to survive and collect his fee.'

'Indeed?'

The thin smile on his father's face did little to reassure Marcellus. Then Lucius indicated that the Greek should approach the platform and the man walked forward, stepping over the corpse of his dead enemy. Lucius leant forward to address him, fluently, in his own tongue.

'Tell me, fellow, how long have you been a gladiator?'

'Six months, your honour,' said the Greek, his voice deepened by the metal guards on the side of his gleaming helmet.

Lucius tried to sound friendly, but given the nature of the discussion the effect was chilling. 'Only six months. Have you had many bouts?'

'This is my first, sir.'

That brought a frown, plus a sideways glance at Hortensius, with the implied accusation of parsimony quite evident, but the hesitation lasted only a second. Lucius returned to questioning the gladiator. 'Indeed. And what did you do before that?'

'I was a slave, but my master sold me to pay his debts.'

A slight note of impatience entered Lucius's voice, as though he suspected the Greek was deliberately indulging in conversation to add a minute to his life. 'And before that?'

'Twelve years ago I was a soldier, your honour, in the service of Macedonia.'

'May I ask a question, father?' said Marcellus eagerly, fired by thoughts of that once invincible Macedonian Army that had been defeated by Aulus Cornelius.

Lucius's head snapped round, his eyes boring into those of his son. 'No, Marcellus, you may not.'

Then he waved his hand in a gesture of dismissal. The Greek raised his sword in salute, and as he turned to walk away the crowd, which, mostly without the Greek necessary to understand the exchange, had been holding its breath, roared out its approval for this unexpected decision. Lucius frowned even more deeply. He hated anything that smacked of appeasing the mob.

Marcellus had been allowed to return home from the games with Gaius, careful, on the entire journey, to avoid the unwelcome attentions of Valeria. Fortunately she shared his aversion and had gone off to play with her dolls as soon as they entered the gate. The Trebonius household made Marcellus uncomfortable and just a little envious, since Gaius had many of the things he desired, possessions forbidden him by his father. There were several dogs and cats, as well as cages full of songbirds. It was a family house in a way that he could barely comprehend, full of noise and activity, with six children running around, all under ten years old, and to Marcellus's ordered mind, completely out of control. They drove their household slaves to distraction.

The dogs chased the cats who, in turn, could not be trusted with the pet mice, or the goldfinches. One child, at least, was always in tears, constantly pleading for justice against an older or younger sibling. Gaius's mother seemed oblivious to all this turmoil, smiling benignly if she could be made to bother at all, and reassuring her wailing offspring that things would look much better in a few minutes. She was invariably right, because the tribulations of another child took over, submerging whatever it was that was bothering the original complainant.

Gaius and Marcellus had been playing knucklebones, using walnuts as counters with which to bet, but his little brother Lineaus, only four years old, was having terrible trouble building a fortress with his wooden bricks. Marcellus went to help, despite his friend's protests that the little brat should be kicked out of the room so that they could continue their game, a remark which reduced Lineaus to a wailing wreck, though there was no sign of a proper tear. Gaius agreed to help, merely to secure some peace and they built Lineaus a wonderful fort, with battlements, towers and an entry port, then helped him arrange his toy legionaries, before going back to the low table to continue their game.

Valeria came in right in the middle of their next set of throws, her terra-cotta doll dressed like a high-born Roman lady, complete with curled wig. She wandered over to the table and stared at the boys for a while, no doubt hoping by her presence to interrupt them. Both studiously ignored her, even when she initiated an imagined conversation with her doll on the failings of Roman boys, compared to Roman girls. When that too fell on deaf ears, she wandered over to the squatting Lineaus, congratulating him coyly on the way he had built his fort.

'Marcellus built it for me,' lisped Lineaus, half-truthfully excluding his own brother.

'Did he?' she replied, her voice high with exaggerated surprise.

Valeria's foot swept in a wide arc, completely demolishing the fort and scattering bricks everywhere. Marcellus and Gaius were forced to pay attention as the little boy let out an anguished cry. Valeria stood, doll in hand, with a defiant and triumphant look, directly aimed at them. Gaius dived at her, but she was gone, loudly screaming as she went out through the door, calling to her mother to come and save her from her murderous brother.

CHAPTER EIGHTEEN

Midway through the next morning, Marcellus sat in his sparsely furnished bedroom pondering his fate, the rough wood of his cot scratching his legs painfully. Already in bad odour with his father because of his behaviour the previous afternoon at the Hortensian games, he had done something more serious, in finally reacting to the constant punishment from his tutor, Timeon, not verbally, but physically.

He must sit still and upright ignoring the cold and the discomfort, because his father would come at some point, entering unannounced. When he did, his son wanted to ensure there was no hint of slovenliness or an air of insolence that he would assume was aimed at him personally. He had worked out his defence using the very tenets of oratory his father so admired. If he could not persuade him that he, Marcellus, was in the right, then he must endure, unflinchingly, any punishment

Lucius saw fit to hand down. His father was not the man to portray anger in any form, so when the door did open, it was slowly and somewhat more frightening for that. Marcellus tensed himself and fought the impulse to look down. His father's unblinking stare held his, registering just the slightest flicker when Marcellus stood up. Then he saw the household slave behind his father; there would be a whip in the man's hand.

'This is not a duty that I find welcome,' said Lucius coldly. 'It is something for which I do not have the time. Yet I find I must undertake this task, since I cannot have you behaving like some drunken labourer. You are a Falerii. You've disgraced me.'

'Am I to be allowed to defend myself?' asked Marcellus. He could hear the tremor in his voice, so he assumed that his father had detected it too.

'What defence could there possibly be for such behaviour?'

'Is it not a cornerstone of Roman law that each man is entitled to a defence?'

That cracked the studied parental veneer. 'How dare you address me so!'

Marcellus took a deep breath, still holding the irate gaze. 'I speak out of admiration for everything you have taught me, Father.'

'I don't remember ever teaching you to use your fists. That is, outside the gymnasium.'

'Yet you have never tired of telling me that it's my duty to oppose tyranny.'

Lucius frowned. 'Tyranny! What are you on about, boy?'

This was his chance and it would be the only one. If he did not make the beginnings of a case in a matter of seconds, his father would set the slave to beat him, and Marcellus would have no choice but to submit. He told himself that it was the injustice that fired him, the need to right a patent wrong, not any fear of punishment, but there was a small voice within him that consistently cast doubt on that.

'Should I refuse punishment that I richly deserve, sir?'

'Of course not!'

'And what should I do in the face of the arbitrary abuse of power?' His father just stared at him and Marcellus wondered how long it had been since Lucius had been unable to reply swiftly to a question. He seized the chance afforded by the pause. 'Could I propose to you, Father, that opposition to the threat of tyranny is the first duty of a Roman citizen.'

Lucius actually blinked, wondering if he was being mocked, with his son quoting at him words he often used himself, but Marcellus didn't give him a chance to speak.

'Could I further propose this. That to expose a pupil to a regime which satisfies the basest instincts of a man who enjoys inflicting pain, just for its own sake, flies in the face of the teachings that you, yourself, have taken such trouble to instil in me.'

Lucius recovered his composure, then allowed himself a slight smile. There was a chair in the corner of the room, the only other piece of furniture apart from the cot. Lucius gathered up his toga in a most elegant gesture, then sat down. 'You wish to make your case, boy? So be it. Proceed!'

'Thank you, Father.' Another deep breath. He knew he was speaking too quickly, but he could not help it. 'When I was younger, at the very earliest stages of my education, I learnt, very quickly, that I could never hope to answer correctly every question put to me. I also discovered that the penalty for such inability was painful. This I accepted as quite proper, since the style of my education had been decided by you. It was my duty, not only to abide by the pattern you had set but to actively support it. I was set to learn things and if I could not do so, the consequences, very properly, fell upon me.'

Marcellus was terribly tempted to start using gestures, but he kept his hand as close to his side as he could so that his words would smack of sincerity as well as rhetorical flair. 'But I wasn't only taught by a pedagogue. It's also been my privilege to have you as a teacher. To be initiated by you into the mysteries of Roman law and politics. I have learnt that you have, through your abilities, which I as your son would give a great deal to emulate, raised yourself to a position in which you are considered as one of the leading men in the Roman state.'

Lucius bowed his head slightly in acknowledgement, for all the world as though he were sitting on his bench in the *Forum*. Marcellus felt the tightness in his chest ease slightly. He also silently thanked the gods for giving him the power, so early in life, of eloquent speech. 'You have taught me many things, Father, too many to enumerate here. Now I must concentrate on those teachings which are apposite to the dilemma I face.'

A frown came from his father at that, as though Lucius couldn't countenance that a boy of his son's age could have a dilemma at all.

'Firstly I wish to address the problem of respect. While I find respect for your person both proper and easy, I must confess that I cannot always extend that feeling to every adult.' His voice changed as he asked himself a question. 'Is that laudable? For me, Marcellus Falerius, respect for an older person should be my primary emotion. That is what I have been taught and I should find no difficulty in carrying out what is my duty.'

He paused again, wondering if he was using too much rhetoric. After all, his father must have guessed what was coming and there was nothing in the face to tell him how he was doing. The slave in the doorway was looking at the ceiling. Not that a look of approval from him would have raised Marcellus's hopes, so, still uncertain, he plunged on.

'But I must confess to such an inability. You have set me a standard and when I apply it, can I really say I feel respect for every adult I encounter? In truth, I cannot. Few equal you. That is point number one. The second point I wish to respectfully bring to your attention is the one I have already alluded to. Since the primary duty of a Roman is to oppose tyranny, can I sit still and observe such behaviour in action, and do nothing to curb it.'

Marcellus began to warm to his task, addressing an expressionless parental countenance. He spoke of the glory of Roman tradition, of the expulsion of the Tarquin kings, naming heroes and castigating villains to support his case. Of the need for the strong to protect the weak, which had been the basis of the expansion of the Republic from a city-state to an empire. Finally the time came for the peroration, the closing arguments, the justification for boxing Timeon around the ears. The man had used that vine sapling once too often. Since that day, months before, when Aulus Macedonicus had halted him in mid-swing, he had become even more free with the stinging sapling. The blows were heavier, more frequent, just as the pleasure he took in administering them shone on the man's face.

'As I have observed already, Father, it is my duty

to abide by the regime set by you, as well as to take my punishment without flinching. Yet I owe a duty to you that transcends even that. I cannot ignore one thing, that the lessons you favour me with are of a higher value than those of any Greek teacher, however able. When I am faced with a choice between acceding to your wishes on the one hand, and following your principles on the other, I can only choose one course. To put one on a higher plane than the other would be to insult you to an unacceptable degree. Timeon the pedagogue has so come to enjoy the vine sapling that he employs it without respite. I also cannot believe that it is part of the education you wish me to benefit from, to have me sit under the lash of a tyrant and do nothing.'

Marcellus, when he stopped speaking, was slightly at a loss. He might be addressing his father as though he was a fellow-senator, but he was still his son and he could not, like a member of that august assembly, end participation in the debate by merely sitting down. He knew, as he spoke his final words, that they detracted from the impression he was seeking to create, smacking, as they did, of the impertinence he had sought so hard to avoid.

'I yield the floor,' he stammered.

'An interesting dissertation,' replied Lucius, calmly. 'You seek to tell me that you have elevated my principles above my instructions, implying, as

you did so, that the punishment administered to
you was excessive. Tyrannical, in fact, so that you,
as a Roman, felt bound to oppose it.'

Marcellus didn't reply. In this game he wasn't
allowed to.

Lucius rubbed his chin thoughtfully. 'It's well
argued, boy, and it might be that you have the right
of it. Perhaps Timeon has become too fond of the
whip. If he has, you have the right to make this
plain to him in a manner that he will comprehend.
The question is, does that run to buffeting him
around the ears, to the extent that he required the
attentions of a physician?' Lucius stayed silent for a
second, but there was no doubt that he had yet to
finish. 'Perhaps it does, Marcellus. I would never
knowingly countenance a Greek thrashing a
Roman, especially if it was unjust.'

Again he paused, this time looking at the slave
still standing silent in the doorway. Marcellus felt
his hopes rise. His father would be persuaded, by
the power of his arguments, to order Timeon to
desist and Marcellus could then justly still that
insistent, internal voice, that whispered steadily the
accusation of cowardice. He could tell himself, as
well as his fellow pupils, that he had argued for a
noble cause and triumphed. His father stood up and
turned his back, as a prelude to leaving the room.

'However, Marcellus, you've ignored one very
important point. You're not the only boy in the

class. You see fit to attack your teacher. What will the others think? Marcellus Falerius can do this, why can't I? Perhaps you had good cause. It may well be that you adhered to my principles in this matter but in following one, you ignored another and that is the duty of a Falerii to set an example.'

He brushed past the slave, still talking as he walked away. 'So, Marcellus, much as I admire your rhetoric, I know I must curtail your spirit. If this hurts you greatly, remember I only do it to discourage the others. I shall not enjoy hearing you cry in pain but it is very necessary that you do so.'

The slave had obviously been given his instructions; as his master's voice faded, he entered the room and closed the door, with Marcellus looking at him unflinchingly. From behind his back came another vine sapling. No whip then, just the same tool as that used by his teacher. The slave held the boy's gaze as he raised it above his head. Marcellus continued to stare, fighting to avoid the blink that would come as a natural reaction to the blow as the slave hunched his shoulders and began his swing. He could not help himself; his eyes closed.

He heard the thudding sound and wondered why he felt no pain, then looked, only to find himself eyeball to eyeball with the slave as the dust from the coarse blanket rose behind him. Marcellus looked over his shoulder as the slave lifted the sapling from the bed. The mark he had made was deep. When Marcellus looked back at the man, he was treated to a broad wink.

'Now, if'n it was that bastard Timeon, Master Marcellus, there's not a slave in the household would hesitate. It would give us great pleasure to tan his hide. You'll have to yell a bit, like, or it'll look fishy, but how's your papa to know if the marks on your back are from me, or that sod who he's set to teach you?'

The slave raised the sapling again as principle fought with subterfuge in the youngster's breast. What would be the consequences of accepting this offer from the slave? Could he cheat his fate and keep his dignity? Then the round sweating face of his pint-sized teacher came into view and he treated the slave to a smile, which was returned.

'Now don't you go yellin' too loud, Master Marcellus, otherwise that will make your papa suspicious.'

The blanket was hit again, with all his might, that followed by a howl of pain.

CHAPTER NINETEEN

---·---

The flickering light from the tallow wads seemed to cast their own spells in Gadoric's hut, only adding to the power of his words as he intoned a long Celtic saga. Aquila listened with rapt attention; the words were not yet so familiar that he could easily follow this story and the shepherd had been talking for over an hour, never once pausing as he recited, from memory, a tale of war, fickle gods and magic. This was just one of many sagas the shepherd had imparted and Aquila had learnt all about the Celtic way of fighting, their tribal rivalries as well as their religion. Nothing was written; every potion that healed, or spell that damned, was committed to memory, as were the stories of a world at one with nature and the elements, where a tree could be a better friend than a fellow man. A world where earth, fire and water provided the means not only to live but to worship.

Gadoric's pastoral religion was very close to that

of Fulmina, who held herself untainted by what she saw as Greek imports, but some of the Celtic myths had echoes of the celestial heroes worshipped at Rome. There was *Dagda*, a God of the Open Sky to match *Jupiter*, *Taranis*, a God of War to equal *Mars*, male and female counterparts to the Greek deities of *Apollo* and *Artemis*. But given the sheer number of gods and sacred objects, this pantheon, to Aquila, seemed full of chaos, with no power great enough to impose order on a fractured world. Only the Celtic holy men could truly understand, which made the boy suspicious.

Fulmina hated augers and priests and had taught him to be sceptical of the breed. She was adamant; they only performed their rituals for money, position, or to gain power over their followers. The boy enjoyed Gadoric's tales, but not as much as he enjoyed learning how to throw a spear or fire one of the Celt's trio of flint-tipped arrows, weapons forbidden to slaves. Gadoric had stolen the spear from the guard hut by the road of the Barbinus villa; if found by the senator's overseer, it would be enough to see him crucified.

Even more pleasure came from occasional day-long trips into the foothills of the mountains, the sheep sent to crop overgrown grasses on steep hillsides. Leaving them to graze under the watchful eye of Minca, Gadoric and the boy would seek the spoor of larger creatures, bears and big cats, with the shepherd teaching him which signs to look for and how to track their routes. Close to the villa or in the hills they hunted for food daily, sometimes at night when the moon was full, and since Celtic traps were cunning, Fulmina's pot was rarely without meat. His mentor taught him all he knew, and the seasons passed in a blur of happy activity.

The first night-time expedition without Minca was no hunting trip, with Gadoric strangely reluctant to explain to Aquila what he was about. But the absence of the dog, left to guard the shepherd's hut, was soon explained by the destination, none other than the slave quarters of the Barbinus villa. One sniff of Minca's scent and the guard dogs would have raised the alarm and brought out men with flaming torches in case it was some kind of dangerous predator. The Celt, with the boy at his side, watched the compound for an age as the last light of the day disappeared. He waited until the barns were closed, the lanterns lit in all the occupied buildings and the moon up enough to bathe the landscape. Only then did he begin to creep forward to the wicker fence built to keep out stray animals.

'Follow,' Gadoric whispered in his broken Latin, making an opening where the fence was joined by knotted twine.

'Are we going to steal some rabbits?' Aquila asked.

The 'No', hissed over suppressed mirth, mystified the boy, as he followed Gadoric to the long building he knew to be the slave quarters. Halfway along, Gadoric stopped, and reaching up, tapped gently on a closed shutter, which was opened, just a fraction, a couple of seconds later.

'Stay here beneath shutter, Aquila. If anyone come, likely to get too close, throw dirt at it then get out sight yourself. Make for break in fence and wait for me in field on other side.'

The Celt stood up, pulled the shutter wide open, and jumping up, eased himself through, leaving Aquila, still mystified, crouching down on his haunches, his back against the stone wall. Through the gap between shutter and frame above his head he could hear whispering, that followed by a low chuckling sound mixed with soft female laughter. That was followed by silence, then the creak of something wooden, a sound that began to be repeated with increasing frequency. Then the moaning started, low at first, but getting louder, until it sounded as if it was being muffled. To the boy it seemed so noisy that everyone within the compound should hear it. Alarmed enough to stand, he eased himself past several other closed shutters towards the end of the building, looking round the corner towards the defunct fountain in the centre of a courtyard bathed in moonlight. Thankfully there was no one around. No one, not even the dogs, seemed to be alerted by the noise which he was sure he could still hear. Still, he felt it prudent to pick up some loose dirt, just in case.

'Hello, who are you?'

The shock of that voice was total, even although it was soft and female, and it froze him to the spot as every drop of his blood seemed to head for his gut. Slowly he looked up, to another open shutter and the girl who was leaning out. She was smiling and unthreatening, but that did nothing to make him feel safe. Caught in the compound he would be lucky to escape with a severe flogging.

'Who wants to know?' he asked, with more bravado than courage.

'My name is Sosia,' she replied in a gentle tone. 'Are you going to tell me yours?'

'Aquila...' He hesitated then, unwilling to add the name Terentius, which would make him easy to identify to the overseer.

'Are you with the shepherd?'

Another shock. 'You know about him?'

'Everybody knows about him.' There was enough moon to show how much that notion alarmed Aquila, so she added quickly. 'Well, not everybody, just the women. He comes to visit Nona quite often, but usually he is alone.'

'Who's Nona?'

'A slave.'

'What is he doing with her?'

Sosia chuckled, and said, 'Listen.' The moaning, for all the muffling, was loud and increasingly frequent, then came the first of a series of stifled cries and deep-throat groans. 'If Nicos, the overseer, catches them, he will be furious.'

'Why?'

'Slaves are not allowed to mate without permission.'

'Mate?' Aquila said, forgetting to whisper, which had the girl putting a finger to her lips. 'Is that what they are doing?'

'What else would they do?'

Feeling slightly foolish, Aquila looked up and smiled, realising, as he looked at the girl, that she seemed pretty, that she had a nice smile and that her eyes had a gentle quality that he found pleasant. Those thoughts were washed away by what seemed a racket, as the grunts and cries melded in one final outburst, which had Aquila back at the corner of the building once more searching the courtyard.

'No one will come,' Sosia hissed. 'The master is not at home, so everyone does as they please. The shepherd will tell you it is different when Cassius Barbinus is here. He would never dare come near the slave quarters then.'

'Are you a slave too?'

'Yes,' she replied, in a way that implied it was obvious.

'I'm not,' Aquila boasted. 'I'm free-born.'

A frown crossed her face, as though the notion of anyone not being a slave was strange to her. 'I don't think I have ever met anyone free-born, except my master and those he has as guests. If the shepherd comes again, why don't you knock on my shutter?'

'Why?'

That threw her slightly and she paused before replying. 'It's nice to talk to someone who is not a slave.' The slight creak of a moving shutter alerted Aquila to the fact that Gadoric was exiting, and he made to move away, followed by a slightly plaintive plea. 'You will knock next time, won't you?'

It was two weeks before Gadoric paid another visit to the slave quarters, weeks in which the boy thought a lot about the girl. This time Aquila asked no questions and as soon as the Celt disappeared into Nona's cubicle he made for Sosia's shutter. On that occasion the two youngsters just talked, but the third time they touched hands, which created a strange sensation for Aquila, one he had never experienced before, a sort of pleasant ache that ran down his arm then through his whole body.

'You must be careful, Aquila. We have been told to prepare for Barbinus coming from Rome. When he is here your shepherd knows not to come, and neither should you.'

'I'm not afraid of Barbinus,' he said. 'According to my mama he is a fat slug.'

'If he is here the male slaves act as proper guards.'

The idea of not meeting Sosia because of Fat Barbinus was, to the boy, ridiculous. 'Is there not a place we could meet?'

The speed of her reply told Aquila that she had thought about this; that it was no sudden inspiration and he wondered why she had obliged him to pose the question. 'Where the washing is hung out to dry beyond the barns. It is close to the woods, and far enough from the villa and the slave quarters to be unobserved.'

'I'll look out for you.'

'Be careful.'

That became a regular feature of Aquila's days; he still hunted with Gadoric, still learnt his skills and his tongue but now it was with one eye cast elsewhere. In the evening, instead of staying with the shepherd, he would dash back to his family hut, Minca at his running heels, to wash off the dirt of the day, before making his way through the woods to the lines of drying washing. Seeing her for the first time in daylight and standing was a pleasant surprise. She had a willowy figure and her hair, tied up during the day, hung long and light brown down to the middle of her back when released. Her face was smooth and unblemished and the smile was even more pleasant when it was lit by the dying rays of the sun.

It was only a few days spent together, time for Aquila to tell her his stories; of his legionary papa, of his mother and the arrangement with Dabo that gave him so much freedom plus the luck of having Gadoric for a friend. She had little to say to match that; born to the Barbinus household she knew no other life, yet she insisted it had been an agreeable upbringing. There were more than enough slaves to carry out the needed tasks, she was never overworked and had only been beaten twice in her life. Her father had been sent away to another property as soon as she was born, lest he neglect his duties, her mother some time later, but the females of the household had raised her as if she was their own.

'How can you be happy when you are a slave?'

'I know no other life, Aquila.'

Sosia and Aquila never exchanged anything other than a chaste kiss, but they did hold hands and, despite the obstacles, they talked of a future that could never be. She was a slave and he was free; Sosia belonged to Fat Barbinus, and unless Aquila had the funds to buy and free her, then that's the way it would stay. The girl adored Minca, whose nose and tongue tended, if they got too close, to come between their faces.

Fulmina sat down heavily on the side of the wooden tub; the washing would have to wait till she had more energy. Perhaps she could card some wool, anything, just to stay sitting for a bit. The ache in her lower belly was getting worse and she seemed to have less strength each day. At first she had put the pain down to some smelly pork that Dabo had delivered, months before, as part of his bond.

'Typical,' she said out loud, rubbing her belly, thinking once more it was possibly true. 'The richer he gets, the meaner he becomes.'

Dabo might not be getting richer but he was certainly acquiring more land. He had taken advantage of the call-up to buy, at rock bottom prices, the farms of other men who had gone off to war. There was much mumbling from the womenfolk about his ability to avoid serving in the legions, as well as the way he used his 'phantom' *dilectus* to avoid paying taxes – if he was not here, if he was serving in the legions, he was not liable. The men moaned too, but while most guessed what had happened, they did not let on, it being a bad idea to inform anyone in authority about anything, because once they started poking their noses in to people's lives, you never knew what they would turn up. And really, anyone who could get one over on those in power, unless they happened to be a miserable sod like Dabo, was openly admired rather than condemned.

She looked out of the door of the hut. It was getting late and she spoke again, softly. 'Where is that boy.'

Aquila was rarely home, up at the crack of dawn

and off to the woods. He had told Fulmina the day they met about his new friend, though not about his way of behaving like an old man and, at first, she had felt inclined to forbid him to see this Gadoric. After all, there were some undesirable folk about and those jokes the men made about shepherds were not always misplaced. Yet it soon became obvious that such a course was impossible unless she found something else for the boy to do, and in her more sanguine moments she was grateful; the slave/shepherd had, these last two seasons, given him an interest in things. That had stopped the boy moaning about the lack of friends to play and hunt with, Aquila quite forgetting, or not caring, that they did not have his freedom. The notion that he should work was never considered; having toiled all her life, Fulmina was not going to see her precious Aquila, bent over, doing the kind of back-breaking labour a boy his age would be consigned to by the likes of Dabo. He was destined for greater things.

But she could not keep him at home all day, so, if he went to the woods, even if he sometimes stayed out most of the night, she just had to trust him, with the help of the gods, to look after himself, something he was going to have to do anyway if this pain got any worse. She just wished he would give up bringing that huge dog home but there was little choice in that, too. Since he was often out till after dark, his shepherd insisted the dog escort him home. Not that he stayed at home; Fulmina was not sure, but she suspected that Aquila had acquired a sudden interest in girls. All he ever did when he came home was wolf his food and depart, but he had shown a sudden tendency to wash recently, which was not something he would do if he was going to be with boys.

Clodius knew he had struck a poor bargain, one that favoured Fulmina and Aquila much more than it advantaged him. Gone were the days when the Roman Army could campaign in the fighting season from early spring till late summer, then return to help with the harvest; the conquests and the responsibilities of empire were too great. Soldiering went on all year round, and not for a year or two either: even the standard six-year engagement had been broken and he was now in his seventh year. Worse still, for Clodius, the 10th legion, in that period, had been transferred to Illyricum from a comfortable life on the southern borders of Gaul, to put down an insurrection of the local tribes against direct Roman rule. To make matters dire they were now under the supervision of an indolent commander and governor called Vegetius Flaminus.

There was little chance of plunder or a bounty in either posting; riches came from new conquests, not old ones, so Clodius found himself scraping a living, in just the same manner as he had at home,

Vegetius being no more energetic in the matter of the prompt distribution of pay. The general preferred to lend it out for a while, pocketing the interest before passing the residue on to the troops. Clodius, not as sharp as some of his fellows at squeezing money out of the locals, wanted nothing more than to get home and tell Dabo that the deal was off, that it was time for the sod to do his own duty. Unfortunately that was a message that could only be delivered to Dabo's face and the only person who could make that happen was his centurion, Didius Flaccus.

'If only I could get home, your honour, I'd be able to sort things out. I have something of value there, something that would more than settle the debt for my leave.'

Clodius pushed all the sincerity he could into that last bit, aware that it was a debt that would fall on Dabo when he took up his proper duty and if it all went wrong then there was still that gold eagle pendant that Fulmina had stashed away. He had never been able to persuade her to tell him where it was hidden, let alone get her to part with it, just as she had never told him all the things that Drisia had prophesied about the boy's future, but at this distance, and in such a situation, the difficulties of persuading his wife of the need to finally surrender it looked eminently possible. Not for the first time in his life, desperation made Clodius an optimist.

'How long do you think I've been in the legions, Piscius Dabo?' asked Centurion Flaccus, using the name by which Clodius was listed on the company roll. He was a grizzled veteran who had the scars to prove it, with skin like well-worn leather, short, iron-grey hair, and a pair of eyes that seemed able to see right through a toughened leather shield. Clodius's immediate superior, he was mighty free with the vine sapling if the efforts of his men displeased him.

'Thank the gods you've seen a lot of service, your honour,' replied Clodius swiftly. 'All the lads say they feel safer under you than some of the pups they've promoted recently.'

Flaccus was well used to flattery, inclined to take it as his due in the way a wine shop owner believes the warm words he gets from his early morning customers. He smiled, showing the gaps in his teeth. 'Eighteen years, Piscius Dabo and ten of those in my present rank. If I had a silver sesterces for every promise of future payment I've listened to in those ten years, I'd have enough money to take my rightful place amongst the knights when I retire. And do you know how much money it costs to qualify for that?'

Clodius was aware that this was the prelude to a blank refusal. The centurion's smile disappeared, to be replaced by a look that chilled his blood. 'One hundred thousand sesterces, oaf. And what chance do you think I have of getting that in the year left to me, serving in this miserable hellhole. If you want leave it's cash on the table, so you best get to work and earn a little extra. Now piss off and leave me in peace.'

Clodius struggled hard to save up enough to satisfy Flaccus; there was no alternative. They had been talking of reform in the legions for years, it being a much abused system; but no one actually ever got round to changing anything. Only the centurion could grant leave and the longer you wanted, the more he charged to release you. In Flaccus, Clodius was stuck with a particularly avaricious member of that breed of robbing bastards who were put in authority above people like him. Pay did get through from time to time, but just when he was getting ahead, a drinking bout or a game of knucklebones would diminish his small reserve of capital. Actually when it came to gambling, knucklebones or dice, he usually lost everything he had saved and occasional trips into the garrison town cleaned him out just as quick. A night spent in the wine shops and brothels of Salonae left him with a heavy head and a very light purse.

His least successful idea was to gamble with his centurion in the hope of winning some leave. Flaccus scooped *Venus* so many times with the dice that Clodius now had a substantial debt to pay just to get even with the man, never mind acquiring the funds to get ahead and all the while his wife and the child were living in comfort, which was how the disgruntled legionary imagined it. It was not true, of course, and had Clodius been aware of Dabo's other proposals, made because of his absence, he might have been even more discontented. Not that these extra worries would have had any foundation; Fulmina had had her fill of men, knowing they would promise the earth to conquer and deliver precious little when the time came to pay.

'You're certain?' asked Didius Flaccus, his eyes fixed intently on the hunched old man opposite. Between them lay a set of small pieces of ivory with images, numbers and symbols carved into them. These had been selected and laid out, to be read by a man who claimed to understand the portents they contained.

'Nothing is certain,' replied the soothsayer, his eyes hooded in a heavily lined face. 'The gods speak to us in riddles.'

Flaccus had considered telling him about the others, for this was not the centurion's first visit to a seer; a deeply superstitious man he had consulted one in every posting he had ever had. But this Salonae soothsayer, the best in the city by repute, might ask him why he sought reassurance for predictions that had already been made. Didius

Flaccus could not admit he was prey to great doubts, half the time convinced that the gods, or the stars, determined everything, the other half only too aware of the evidence of his own eyes; that life was all chance. He still wanted to hear his future, but in plain language. Yet this man before him was like the rest, wrapping up his predictions in convoluted words and riddles that did not make sense.

'Tell me again,' he demanded.

The old man looked at the pieces arranged before him. 'I see a golden aura and I see you under a great and valuable burden. It consists of something you value highly, that you have worked and toiled to acquire. There are men around you, numerous and yelling.'

'Cheering?' asked Flaccus, sitting forward eagerly, to confirm what he had been told by others.

The soothsayer was wise in more than one respect; he knew enough to tell a customer what they wanted to hear, while at the same time keeping doubt in his voice, for too overt an enthusiasm would dent the aura of omniscience on which he relied.

'Perhaps cheering.' Then he bent forward to look again at the decorated pieces of ivory that covered the table, his voice becoming more eager. 'Cheering. Yes, definitely cheering.'

'And the golden aura?' asked Flaccus, his voice anxious.

'Great wealth, Centurion. A golden aura means great wealth.'

Flaccus slipped another coin across the table, gold this time, part of the money that came to him through his rank. 'Speak plain, soothsayer, and this is yours.'

The old man looked up, his pale watery eyes fixed on Flaccus, the voice as steady as his gaze. 'I risk damnation.'

Flaccus, his heart pounding, fished out two more coins, feeling that he was, at last, on the verge of hearing the plain truth. He laid the coins on the table beside the other one and the soothsayer's eyes flicked to the side, to take them in. Then having calculated the fee, he lifted them to gaze steadily at his excited customer.

'You will be covered in gold and men will cheer you. I can say no more.'

He reached out a hand to take Flaccus's money but the centurion covered it, gripped it tightly and pulled the soothsayer forward. 'A good future then?'

'Not good,' replied the old man, his lined face creasing into a toothless smile. 'Brilliant.'

Flaccus released the hand and allowed him to take his reward. Then he stood up. 'I shan't forget you, soothsayer. When this prophecy comes to pass, you will get your just reward.'

'If the gods will it,' replied the old man calmly.

As Flaccus left the soothsayer's house, he did not fail to say, as he passed though the door, a quick prayer to the Goddess *Cardea*.

Little interest was taken, at home, in the doings of the 10th legion. Conquest excited the citizens; what happened in a rebellious Roman province like Illyricum meant little by comparison, so Clodius and his fellow soldiers felt ignored and with good cause. To be away from the centre of attention was bad enough, but to then be cursed with a commander like Vegetius made things ten times worse.

'He don't give a fig about us,' said Clodius/Dabo, to the closest of his workmates. 'He treats us like a private work force, then pockets our pay for months on end.'

The vine sapling caught him across his naked back, for in the deep drainage ditch, shovelling the earth over the side above his head, he had not seen Flaccus approach. Clodius cried out as the thin, swishing length of pliant wood struck him.

'He might pay you out with a proper floggin' at the wheel.'

Clodius crouched down trying to get below the range of that vine sapling he saw swinging in Flaccus's hand. 'Save your wind to dig, scum, or you'll have no puff left at all.'

Clodius cursed under his breath, careful to

ensure that the departing Flaccus could not hear him. 'It's all right for you, you greedy bastard. Old Vegetius Flaminus pays you a portion of his take for our labour.'

'You need eyes in the back of your head when that sod's around,' whispered one of the men in his section. 'I hope something happens soon, or we'll have dug up the whole damn province!'

By keeping his soldiers from their proper occupation Vegetius Flaminus was able to hire them out, digging irrigation ditches and the like, pocketing the proceeds and while this pleased some of the absentee Roman ranchers, it failed to excite the ones who actually lived in the province, especially those on the borders. The rumbles of discontent were getting worse. Not that Vegetius cared; the need to confront the rebels and bring Illyricum back to peace and prosperity took second place to his own well being and the state of his coffers. He was selling the tax farming concessions at exorbitant rates, costs which only fuelled unrest since they were passed on to the already over-burdened provincials and rumour had it he was making a pretty penny from bribes paid by the locals for protection as well, parcelling out small pockets of troops to protect the outlying farms. Stands to reason that you only need protection from a threat, so it was in the senator's interest to keep the danger alive.

Some of this filtered back to Fulmina. Most soldiers had started off richer and were, in any case, less of a spendthrift than her husband, or perhaps they served under centurions who charged them an affordable amount to go on leave. Messages drifted back that Clodius was alive and well, if far from happy, accompanied by promises of his imminent return laden with booty.

'Never out of trouble, is Clodius,' was the basic refrain she heard from these itinerant messengers, to whom his true identity was no secret. Fulmina always took care to show them the golden-headed boy, thanked the messengers kindly, gave them wine, oil and freshly baked bread, and sent them on their way with a return message, this to the effect that she and Aquila were well and happy.

'Clodius Terentius must put his duty to the Republic before any thoughts of our welfare,' she would say, imbuing the words with as much sincerity as she could muster.

Clodius/Dabo was not fooled when this message returned. These high flown sentiments were just a barely disguised message to say that if he wished to stay away forever, she would not pine to death for the lack of his company. Of course the returnees would all praise the boy, saying what a fine lad he was, big for his age and lively. At first Clodius welcomed the praise, but time and the thought of the comforts of home made him less and less inclined to do so, until any mention of this changeling child was met with a growl. This would be followed by all his well-rehearsed grievances, most notably the lack of any prospect of plunder.

Thoughts of booty often turned his mind to that charm. To Clodius, the more he thought about it, the greater his sense of injustice. Damn Fulmina and her dreams; damn Drisia and her spitting; never mind her bag of bones. Here he was, on short rations half the time, stuck in the middle of nowhere, under a false name, at the beck and call of anyone who cared to order him to do anything, including die a painful death, all this while his wife kept the means of his deliverance locked away and lavished on a strange child the affection that should properly, as her husband, have come to him. It was hard to recall that he had once looked forward to raising him like his own son.

CHAPTER TWENTY

———◆———

The imminent arrival of the senatorial commission stirred Vegetius Flaminus to action. Now instead of boredom and digging ditches, Clodius was faced with danger and mutilation as the legions rushed from one place to the next, always in danger of ambush, in an attempt to flush out the rebels and bring them to battle, but Vegetius had left it too late and the province was still in turmoil when the senators arrived. Clodius was delighted that, at the head of the commission came the great Macedonicus himself. Now there was a proper soldier, a man who had made a mint of money, both for himself and the troops he commanded. Every legionary prayed that he would take things over, and they were not disappointed. Despite the very vocal protests of the titular commander, Aulus started to take a hand in the direction of operations. He was working through Vegetius, certainly, pretending to consult him at every stage, but they all knew, just by their nature, where these new instructions were coming from.

First Aulus instituted some proper training in field and battle tactics; then when he felt that the troops had relearnt their job, he let them loose on the enemy and, based on proper intelligence, things took a turn for the better. Rebel encampments were found and destroyed; treasonable chieftains taken and crucified until the insurrection seemed to peter out from lack of leadership. Those who survived the onslaught had apparently retired over the border, into barbarian lands, and the province seemed, finally, at peace. Clodius was not downhearted; even if he had failed to get his hands on any booty, at least he could look forward to going home.

The messenger that rode into the legionary camp at Salonae soon spoilt that notion. Vegetius Flaminus was with Aulus when the news arrived and the dust coated messenger was brought straight to the command tent by the oration platform to blurt out his despatch to the general.

'Greetings to the noble Vegetius Flaminus, commander of the illustrious 10th legion, from the noble Publius Trebonius, governor of the province of Epirus...'

The messenger seemed set to go through all the formalities, plus the rituals of address from one high-born Roman to another. Aulus, however, intervened. 'We're all noble, Tribune, but, by the state of your dress I suspect the message is urgent. Have a drink of wine to refresh yourself, then be so good as to deliver it.'

Vegetius frowned quite openly. This was his command tent; he had the right to offer or refuse hospitality to this filthy young fellow. Aulus Macedonicus had been behaving like this ever since he arrived and Vegetius was tempted to issue a reminder that the message was intended for him. Then he checked himself; Aulus had hinted that regardless of what his fellow commissioners, and Vegetius's friends, thought, he had enquired into certain allegations of bribery that were floating around. It would be a bad idea to upset him. The governor did not know that he had already upset his fellow senator more than enough. Having kept Roman soldiers here for years, rather than months, he had committed a cardinal sin in the Cornelii eye. Aulus was not only aware that the bribery allegations were true, he fully intended to have Vegetius impeached before the Senate when he got home and had privately sent Lucius Falerius as arranged, full details of what he had been able to find out.

The tribune drank deeply from the cup he was offered then brought himself back to attention and rattled out his despatch in a parade ground voice. 'Publius Trebonius sends to tell you that he has had to flee from Epirus, taking with him as many of the local Roman population as he could.'

'Damn these Greeks,' said Aulus. 'Will they never tire of revolt?'

'Perhaps we have been too lenient in the past,' suggested Vegetius, smoothly. 'They see us as simple barbarians, content to dress like peasants and worship at their shrines.'

Aulus ignored the allusion to himself. As an act of reconciliation, after his successful war in Macedonia, the victor had toured Greece, dressed simply, accompanied by just a personal bodyguard and his servant Cholon. He had worshipped at most of the major shrines and engaged in philosophical debates with the academics of Athens, all in an attempt to show the Greeks that if they stayed at peace, they had nothing to fear from the Imperium of Rome.

'We cannot rule the world by force, Vegetius. We lack the means.'

Vegetius continued in the same smooth voice, pitched just on the polite side of insult. 'It seems we lack the means to rule by consent.'

Aulus snapped back at him. 'Our task would be made easier if some of our generals were more diligent.'

That brought forth a gubernatorial flush, as Aulus indicated that the messenger should continue. The man looked from one to the other, confused, before addressing Aulus.

'Many of the outlying communities have been massacred. Publius Trebonius wishes it to be clear that Roman blood has been spilt, in some quantity, and that some form of punitive action seems appropriate. He also knows that the noble Vegetius Flaminus will be aware that Epirus lies on the direct route of Roman communications with the east. He feels that a swift example must be made and urges that, since he lacks troops in sufficient quantity, the 10th legion with auxiliaries should march south to restore order.'

'A request that should have properly been sent to Rome,' said Vegetius haughtily.

Aulus sighed, but felt it necessary to state the obvious. 'I daresay Trebonius, with a revolt on his hands, feels that haste in these matters often brings a swift conclusion. He will be concerned that the uprising doesn't spread.'

'Very admirable, but I cannot move my troops to another province without permission.'

'Leave us,' said Aulus, addressing the tribune. 'Give the details of what is required to the Quaestor, with a request that the troops be alerted to undertake a forced march as soon as is practicable.'

'You'll do no such thing. You go too far, Aulus Cornelius!' shouted Vegetius, for the first time stung out of his relaxed pose. The tribune, who had started his salute, stood rigid, not sure what to do.

'Better that, I think, than to go nowhere,' replied Aulus softly. Then, with a benign smile, he looked at the tribune, staring at the ceiling, still halfway though his salute, with his arm, fist closed tight, across his leather breastplate. 'You, young man, go to my tent. Instruct my servant to provide you with a bath. I'm sure the tribunes of the 10th will be happy to give you some food, as well as lend you clean clothes. When you have eaten, you will be provided with a fresh horse. Your orders are to proceed to Brindisium by ship, then take post horses to Rome with a message, from me, to the Senate.'

Vegetius sat silent, his fat face flushing a very deep red. The tribune finished his salute, turned on his heel and marched out. Aulus, still with the same benign smile, turned back to the titular commander. 'As you see, Vegetius, I am taking responsibility. If the Senate questions my actions, I feel sure that I'll be able to convince them of my personal probity. Not something I fear, however, that will be available to you.'

Vegetius felt a knot of fear in his stomach. 'I don't know what you mean.'

'I think you do. If you want to hang on to any of that money you've acquired these last few years, I should get hold of your Quaestor, right away, and confirm the orders that I gave to the tribune.'

Vegetius tried to bluff it out, but the words wouldn't come. 'I...'

Aulus finally lost his patience, and, in a voice that had addressed an entire consular army, he told Vegetius in plain language what his fate would be if he did not order the preparations necessary to march.

'I must warn you that my despatches concerning your actions, or rather the lack of them, are already on their way to Rome. Do as I say or I will personally see you impeached, stripped of all you own, and thrown into the pit of the Tulliniam to be consumed by the rats. You are a disgrace to the name of Rome. Do you think the locals don't know, to a man, what you have been about? I have already said we can't rule by force, we must rule by the respect of law, the laws of the city we represent. How can we impose respect for the Imperium of Rome with petty thieves, like you, lining your own pockets? You have a choice Vegetius, redeem yourself or I'll have you hauled back to Rome in chains.'

Vegetius positively ran out of the tent, and those officers who had little respect for him smiled to themselves.

'And who knows,' said Clodius, when the news swept through the camp that they were headed south. 'There might be a bit of loot to be had after all.'

Claudia would have readily admitted, had she been taxed, that she was probably on a fruitless search. Revisiting the villa was easy, since it belonged to a member of her own family and was, at present, as it had been the night of the birth, unoccupied. She had been tempted to come here so many times, but finding an occasion when Aulus was out of Rome, at the same time as both his sons, had proved an insurmountable obstacle and even now she risked discovery. It was a rare thing that someone as well-born as she should choose to travel with just her personal maid, Callista, and her maid's husband Thoas, in attendance.

Thoas, sworn to secrecy, had hired strangers to carry her litter instead of using the household slaves. This alone was bound to excite comment in the Cornelii abode and leave a trace that could surface in an accidental comment. Aulus and Titus would be gone for so long that her travelling would hopefully fade from the collective memory before either of them returned. Quintus would be back in a month or so, but he was so heartily disliked that she had every reason to believe the household slaves would ensure he remained ignorant of her strange excursion.

'I wish you to try and find a midwife who answers to the name of Marcia.' She took a small bag of coins from her chest and handed it to Thoas.

'Do you have another name, lady?' asked Thoas.

'No,' she replied with a slightly waspish tone. 'Nor do I wish you to enquire further. Merely find her, and bring her to me.'

The tall Numidian bowed, which at least brought his head down to her level and Claudia realised, with a start, that she did not know this man very well. He was not the type for domestic service, being tall and physically strong, surely more fitted for manual labour or as a protective body slave. But he was Callista's husband, so it made sense to bring him along to perform this task, since she could hardly go asking around the neighbourhood herself. He had married the person she had been most intimate with for the last eight years; Claudia trusted Callista absolutely, so surely she could trust him.

'This is a very personal matter, Thoas,' she added in a more pleasant tone. 'I am relying on you to be discreet. It's not something I would want discussed by the rest of the household.'

The Numidian bowed again. 'I am yours to command, lady.'

He found Marcia fairly quickly; there was a finite number of local midwives but Thoas was no fool; he added several more days to the search, purloining a fair amount of his mistress's money in the process, supposedly distributed as bribes to gather information, in reality spent on wine, women and pleasure as well as the greatest of all satisfactions; the ability to behave like a free man.

Those were days that dragged for Claudia, days when she relived every event in her life: her childhood, in the home of indulgent parents; her father an upright but far from wealthy senator, a good soldier who brought her up as a proud Roman; the flattery of marriage to a man like Aulus Cornelius Macedonicus, whose gravity, presence and achievements so impressed a sixteen-year-old girl. It was a match that shocked her friends, yet Claudia had sensed their jealousy too; had she not snared the city's leading soldier, as well as the richest man in Rome? And despite the age difference, he was handsome as well as gentle, showing to all with eyes to see that he was besotted with her.

Life after the wedding ceremonies turned her head even more; she was no longer a young girl to be indulged but had become the Lady Claudia Cornelia, a person of substance. People, certainly older women, who would have been condescending in her previous station, now showed due deference. She became the mistress of a great house instead of the child of another and Aulus had immediately signified his trust in her by giving her the keys to the strongbox and the doors, so that everyone in the household knew she was in charge of all the domestic arrangements.

Men of all ages, who had in the past flattered her

for her looks, now professed themselves amazed at her sagacity when she advanced an opinion. Her husband treated her with just as much respect and, with an almost paternal care, awoke in her the passionate side of her nature. To wound such a paragon was not easy and Claudia took no pleasure in it, but over the first weeks in the company of Brennos she had realised that she had married Aulus for his standing, not his person, as well as to please her father. She was in love with the image, not the man, and nothing proved that more to her than the physical reaction she felt to the Celt's presence, a vibrancy to their lovemaking so very different to the tender couplings she had enjoyed with Aulus. There were times she cursed the decision to travel with Aulus to Spain, something that had been brought about partly by her own pleading. Still young, she craved adventure, was in thrall to the notion of being the other half of a Proconsular Imperium. In her imagination, as well as lording it over the provincial Romans of Spain, she would comfort the great general at the same time as inspiring his legions to feats of arms hitherto unheard of. With Claudia by his side Aulus Cornelius Macedonicus would add even more lustre to his name.

She should have stayed at home! In Rome Claudia would have avoided temptation, bound by family, name and responsibility: she would never have met Brennos, never have experienced the all-consuming nature of true love, have remained content with her station; she would not have made her upright husband unhappy and never suffered the torment of losing the child of her Celtic lover. Claudia would not have had to live the lie that the child she bore had been unwillingly conceived. To tell Aulus otherwise, to proclaim the joy she felt when she knew she was pregnant by another man, would be to destroy him. She might have been happy, instead of tormented by the knowledge that, having compelled Brennos to break his vows of celibacy, she had failed him by her inability to protect his son.

Many times she imagined telling Aulus, only to recoil from such a thought; first of the battle that had seen the wagon she was travelling in taken by Quintus, of the look in her stepson's eyes when he had realised her condition. She had thought of killing herself then, in the time between that meeting and his arrival, but with a baby in her womb she could not do it, that followed by a determination to see the child born at whatever cost. Tell Aulus the truth and even he might, in a jealous rage, kill them both. Had that been the right choice? Once under her husband's care his desire to hide what he thought to be her disgrace had created a prison from which she could not escape. In guarding her from prying eyes, under the protection of strangers whose only task was to make sure she remained unseen, all choice had been taken away. Her heart was wrenched with fear as she heard of Roman victories, a terror that one day Aulus would walk though her door to tell her Brennos was dead. That did not come, but her lover's dream collapsed, and with a speed that meant the child in her womb was born here in Italy, instead of Spain.

When the legions came home, Aulus had to come with them. That he chose not to march with them, instead taking ship, was considered strange to troops who had been victorious. When they landed as Ostia the litter in which she was to travel was brought aboard so that no one on shore should see her and they had travelled incognito to this villa, where she had given birth on this very floor on which she now paced to and fro. So much for the pride of the Lady Claudia Cornelia! The image of that baby would be with her forever; the bright blue eyes and that hair, russet mixed with gold, wet from the waters that had eased his birth. Perhaps the charm she had placed round his foot was too valuable, but it was the only thing she had had that might save him, a talisman she had taken from his father the better to remember Brennos. That Celtic goldsmith had been clever, the replica he had made so perfect that had she not switched them directly, she could never have been sure she had the original. And Brennos had never noticed, even when he fingered the replacement around his neck.

She had felt something very strange at the moment when she put the charm round the baby's foot, as if her head was filled with flashes of lightning interspersed with fleeting images of her blue-eyed Celtic warrior, images that had subsided as soon as she let go. But then Claudia knew she had been exhausted, and could not be sure that what she had been vouchsafed were genuine visions, instead of hallucinations.

Claudia was so nervous her throat refused to function, sure that the midwife felt more at ease than her. It was way short of true, for in the presence of this high-born lady, whom she recognised at once, Marcia kept her head half-bowed, which hid the fright in her eyes. Each question was answered in a monotone, which suggested indifference.

'This is a matter of some importance to me.'

The lady's sharp tone finally made Marcia lift her head and look Claudia in the eye. 'You forget that I saw you place that talisman round the child's ankle. I knew you wished him to live.'

Claudia's voice was full of sadness. 'But he didn't live, did he?'

'Lady, the boy wasn't exposed around here. I asked everyone, even offering a reward. I knew you would repay me tenfold. Your husband and that

Greek slave used their horses when they took him away. You slept, so you did not see them return. They did not come back till after dawn.'

Claudia stood up quickly. If this Marcia had half a brain, she would be able to find out about her; who she was and, more importantly, to whom she was married. The family connection of the villa would ensure that. Since she could not be of any use, only her silence was valuable.

'Do you remember the oaths you swore that night?'

'Only too well,' the midwife replied, shivering slightly. Yet what she remembered was that look from the black-eyed man, one that threatened her with death.

Claudia gave her a very direct and slightly threatening look. 'That is good.'

'Can you not ask the Greek slave where they exposed the baby?'

Claudia treated her to a humourless smile, seized as she was with a vision of a small dead body, a skeleton now, with that eagle the only thing still intact in the tiny grave. Claudia shook her head violently, and reminded herself of the nature of her husband. Certainly he was a warrior and he could be a ruthless one, but for all Aulus's distress and anger at what had happened, she could not bring herself to believe a man like him could cold-bloodedly murder a new-born infant.

'No, Marcia. I cannot, any more than I can ask my husband.'

Thoas shot away from the doorway, scurrying to hide behind a pillar as Marcia and Claudia emerged into the vestibule. He did not have it all, there was still more of the mystery, but perhaps he had enough. The Falerii steward had promised him a rich reward for this secret. Over a decade, as he had steadily tired of his tiny wife, Callista, he had given up all hope of release from her tiresome embrace, but now perhaps that had changed. It would be interesting to see if the steward to Lucius Falerius still wanted this information after all these years.

CHAPTER TWENTY-ONE

Lucius looked at the despatches that Aulus had sent him, unaware that they were, in one sense, out of date. His correspondent had been thorough, not merely listing Vegetius Flaminus's various crimes but including a mass of attested evidence as well. In the seesaw world of the Senate, with its shifting alliances and constant battles, Aulus had provided Lucius with the political equivalent of gold dust. Impeaching a senator was a prospect often invoked, but rarely pursued; indeed Lucius disliked such actions, which only served to show senatorial shortcomings to the mob. Better to maintain the fiction of complete probity.

The impossibility of perfection, in anything, made him reach for another scroll, which his steward had given him just the day before. The man had been insufferably smug, hinting that he had surpassed his master in the way that his idea had paid off, many years after it had been initiated. The

Numidian slave, Thoas, had done well, and he deserved his reward, but Lucius could not believe that the information he had garnered could have taken so long to acquire. It struck him now that in all the despatches that Aulus had sent from Spain there had been no mention of his wife. Had he cared about her at all, Lucius would have noticed at the time, but to him she was no more than a minor irritant, a distraction that could affect the judgement of the man who had the Spanish command. What she did, and when she did it, was within the realms of gossip, and not something to demand attention from a man so deeply immersed in serious politics.

His mind went back to the day his son had been born and he remembered how angry he had been at Aulus's absence and wondered why. The childhood oath, taken in blood, of undying support, meant less to Lucius than it did to Aulus. He had known, even as he invoked it, that it was merely an excuse for his anger, not the cause. Then he recalled the turmoil of that day, with the Feast of *Lupercalia* in full swing, mingling with the tension in the streets. There were his own intentions in regard to Tiberius Livonius as well as the need to dispose of Ragas. He had been on edge, in need of Aulus, at a time when he still felt he could trust him. Perhaps he still could, despite the years of suspicion, now he knew for certain that Aulus had engaged in no conspiracy against him. The information in this scroll showed quite clearly that he had acted like a fool; why he should seek to protect an adulterous woman was beyond Lucius. The easiest solution would have been to toss Claudia overboard on the way back from Spain.

He allowed himself a smile; everyone knew the perils of an older man wedding a young, beautiful woman; indeed, he had made several jests in that vein himself. Idly, he wondered who had fathered the brat, considering if it was worth his while to find out. He was, very slightly, tempted to throw this information in Aulus's face, if only to see a man who's probity had become a byword stuck for a reply. But he put the thought aside and chided himself for such unkind thoughts. They had been friends once; perhaps they would be again. It all depended on how far Aulus wanted to take the matter about which he had written home.

Thinking about the two interconnected subjects made Lucius realise that they formed two parts of the prophecy he and Aulus had heard as children. Aulus, in humbling Macedonia, had tamed a mighty foe, while he, Lucius, had murdered Livonius. Was that 'striking to save Rome's fame?' He was less inclined to welcome the only line that stood out clearly in his memory. *'But neither will achieve their aim.'*

'I shall achieve my aim,' he barked out loud, in a

voice angry enough to make his steward step backwards.

'Master?' said the steward, totally confused.

Lucius looked up, realising that he had spoken aloud. He had been trying to remember the exact wording of the last part of the prophecy, something about birds that could not fly but it would not come, which was an annoying sign of age and to cover himself before his servant, he went back to examining his scrolls and ruminating on his old friend. He had always slightly envied Aulus, who had military prowess in such abundance where he had none, but that same onset of age meant Lucius was now old enough to examine that envy objectively. When young, he had been no different to anyone else; dreaming of a proper Roman triumph, with him in the lead chariot, face painted red and his brow garlanded with oak leaves, just like Aulus had been when he returned from Macedonia. To think that such a man, having achieved so much, should go to such lengths, should jeopardise his reputation, and for what? For a woman who was far too young for him in the first place.

His reaction to Aulus's non-attendance at the birth of Marcellus had been nothing compared to the way he had nailed him about the murder of Tiberius Livonius. That had really rankled, forcing him to tell a blatant falsehood. Lucius afforded himself a smile, knowing that had not been his first evasion, nor would it be his last. He wondered at the naivety of people like Aulus Cornelius, deeply religious fools, who thought that the world could be run by simple truth, backed up by a few military conquests. It was nearly as bad as the venal and blatant theft of hypocritical senators like Vegetius Flaminus. All the while they claimed as *populares* to have the interests of the dispossessed at heart, but in truth they took every opportunity to rob the state blind. Yet that very lack of honesty could yield political dividends. He could repose trust in neither; the honest man was as likely to cause trouble as the thief. He weighed the two scrolls, one in each hand, aware that the possibilities they afforded him were endless. Knowledge was power and here were two instruments that, played properly, could produce a wonderful result. He could live without prophecies and as for triumphs, his son would achieve those.

'The litters are ready, master,' his steward said. 'Shall I fetch Master Marcellus?'

'I doubt you'll have to. The way he was hopping from foot to foot this morning makes me think he will already be aboard.'

There followed a stream of instructions as Lucius made his way to the front gate: the need to ensure that mounted messengers knew his route to Aprilium, the location of the post houses in which he would be staying on the two nights of the journey; that all he needed had been packed in the spare litter. The steward replied in the positive, even though he had been asked and answered all these questions a dozen times, reflecting that his master had grown more fractious over the years, and not for the first time wished he had remarried, for a man with a wife was so much more amenable than a crabbed widower.

As he watched the caravan head off down the Palatine Hill he recalled with some affection the Lady Ameliana, dead these ten years. She had been a plump good-natured woman, much given to tolerance, who had made life in the Falerii house pleasant. Her death in childbirth had passed almost unnoticed in the joy over the birth of Master Marcellus: that had blanked out everything else, including, the steward ruminated, the disappearance of the Dacian body slave Ragas. They talked in the slave quarters of that fellow occasionally, though no one in the servants' quarters had liked him; he was arrogant and inclined to bully, not shy of waving those great fists of his to win an argument. There was no doubt he was, like all barbarians, capable of extreme violence, so when they talked, it took no great stretch of the imagination to add his disappearance to the death of Tiberius Livonius, and see there a connection.

The steward made a silent obeisance to *Jove*,

hoping that the impious thought that accompanied this train of thought was untrue. If Ragas had killed the plebeian tribune and his fellow worshippers of the Cult of *Lupercalia*, then it could only have been on the instruction of his master. If true, such a thing would curse this house and all who resided in it.

Gafon needed a drink badly, but there was nothing unusual in that these days, for it was the only way he could get any peace, the only way he could forget that he had once been somebody. He would tell them that often, his fellow imbibers, tell them of his gladiator school, of the gold he had taken off senators and how he had fooled them into thinking the fights they were paying for would be worth the money, when in fact he had sold them flabby sods who could scarce lift a weapon, never mind use it, or fixed the results in advance to his own advantage. Then he would hint at secrets, at deeds that could never be more than a finger to the side of the nose to imply to his listeners that it was information that would keep him out of the gutter. He would hint that there was a noble senator who would pay dear for this, but never would he mention the name. Occasionally, as proof, from inside his tunic, the ivory handle of the scroll he had taken from Ragas would appear, grubbier and grubbier from frequent handling, accompanied by the words that what lay inside would see him to a life of milk, honey and endless wine. Boasters themselves, as all drunks are, none of those companions who spent all day with him in the wine shops believed a word of it, too busy relating their own fantasies to give much credence to that of another.

He was angry too, for he had tried to trade the scroll for wine, his last possession offered up for a pittance compared to what it was worth, but two tavern owners had turned him down already, and the third one had offered him no more than one flagon, reckoning that the papyrus was used and worthless, though the holder might fetch something from one of the scribes who occasionally dropped in for a drink. There had been a time when Gafon could fight, a time when he had trained good gladiators with enough skill to make them fear him, but now his body was without muscles and his brain, addled with the effects of years of wine, could not tell his wasted arms what to do. To try to fight the tavern keeper he was certain had insulted him was a bad idea anyway, to try to hit him with one of his own empty amphorae was fatal.

For the price of the drink he had refused Gafon, two of his regular customers took the body, with the blood still streaming from the shattered skull, out into an alley. Let the watchmen find him. With nothing on the body to identify him, Gafon would be just another of those unfortunates who packed

Rome, some country bumpkin fleeced by one of the gangs who made their living by robbery and murder or who got beaten up by a roving gang of rich, drunken youths. They would burn his body, along with dozens of others, without ceremony. The scroll, picked up off the floor, was thrown into a drawer, and forgotten.

As the sun began to dip, Aquila, grazing the sheep on the slope between the rear of the stables and the water cistern while hoping for a sight of Sosia, put on his cloak to ward off the evening chill. The house was busier than usual, and he guessed, because he had seen it before, that Cassius Barbinus was in residence. With him around everything that needed to be done was accomplished with an air of bustle, and if there had been any doubt, the fountain that stood in the centre of the courtyard was on, sending a spout of water high into the air. From his position high on the hill he saw the caravan coming down the road from the north; several litters, two curtained, decorated and personal, another plain bearing metal-bound chests, and a heavily armed escort, some mounted and lictors out in front to clear the way, which indicated that whoever was travelling was an important official heading south towards Naples, not an uncommon sight on the Via Appia. That it turned to cross the bridge over the culvert that separated the road from the villa was less common.

Marcellus had never been this far from Rome and so had, on the road south, constantly pulled aside the curtains set to keep out the dust to look upon the route they were taking. There was much to see, not just in those using it but in the changing nature of the landscape. Sometimes it was flat marsh, at other times deep dark forests and here, close to their destination, good farmland mixed with woodland, the hills rising to the east to the white caps of the distant Apennines. His father was in the front, working as usual, a scribe walking alongside his litter reading correspondence that had just been brought to them by messengers from the city. Tonight, no doubt, he would dictate replies and these, signed and sealed by the reigning consuls, would be sent all over the empire by those very same messengers, riding on Roman roads and staying at Roman post houses holding a ready supply of fresh horses. This so that a governor as far away as Spain could write to the Senate and receive a reply within ten days. The soldiers fought to gain territory, but it was the system of consular messengers that kept it secure.

As they turned into the Barbinus villa, Marcellus closed the curtain tight, for his father would not be happy to see that a Falerii had allowed his dignity to be overcome by his curiosity. Staying on the right side of the parental temperament was important to

Marcellus, given he was rarely allowed to accompany his father on the few occasions when he left Rome. Just being away from his teacher was a bonus; not being at school at all doubled that enjoyment. The protocol was strict, with a slave given the task of informing both master and son that it would be proper for them to alight; that the owner, his wife and family, as well as his senior servants, were arrayed in a manner befitting the rituals necessary to greet such an elevated person as Lucius Falerius.

Barbinus himself came forward as the curtain was drawn back on Lucius's litter, his arms outstretched, the face wreathed in a broad smile. Marcellus examined him; fat, with a waddle of a walk and a gross head with features to match. The nose was big and so were the thick lips; only the eyes, deep in the puffy cheeks, seemed too small for their host.

'My good friend, I bid you welcome,' Barbinus cried, clasping the arm of the now upright Lucius. 'That you should come to me instead of summoning me to attend on you in Rome does me great honour.'

The words his father had used before leaving came to Marcellus. 'Barbinus is not the kind of person I wish to be seen with in the streets of Rome, nor do I want him knocking at my door. He must be one of the greediest men I know, with the morals of a snake. His family are poor stock, more Volscian than Roman, yet he is a senator, rich, without any power of his own and in need of a sponsor. He also knows that I have the power, and enough information on his peculations, to remove him from the Senate roll.'

'So you will attach him to you?'

'That I will decide, Marcellus, when we have concluded our business.'

The business was the sale of the last far-flung property that Lucius owned, farms in Sicily that had been a drain on his time and money, rather than an asset. They had been hard to sell, but Barbinus, who owned other Sicilian properties, had looked them over on his last visit then indicated that he would give Lucius a fair price. Lucius was not fooled; he suspected that Barbinus was buying a way into his favour, not farms from which he could make a profit.

'You must be fatigued after your journey. The bath house is ready for you.'

Marcellus looked around for a bath house but could see nothing resembling the public baths in Rome. Barbinus, he realised, must have one of his own, which was real luxury, even in a country villa.

'My son will need it, certainly,' Lucius replied, 'since his long nose, poking out endlessly from his litter, has covered him in the dust of the roadway. I prefer to get straight down to business, Barbinus.

Let any bathing take place after that.'

'As you wish, Lucius Falerius.' Barbinus tried to click his fingers, but they were too fleshy to make much sound. It mattered little; his steward stepped forward immediately. 'Nicos, take young master Marcellus to the bath house.'

Everyone else – lictors, scribes and escort – was sent to an empty barn, while Lucius was shepherded into the atrium of the villa, a substantial space with a smaller fountain playing in the middle. Marcellus, walking behind, heard his host snap at his steward, ordering him to get a rider on the road to find out what had happened to something, but he was unable to quite catch what it was as he was led down a corridor to his destination. With a plentiful supply of water from the mountain streams, and plentiful wood, Barbinus had made full use of what nature provided, so both room and pool were steaming hot. Feeling grubby after his journey he was happy to strip and plunge into the latter. When he emerged there was a masseur waiting to knead whatever strains he had suffered from his muscles and a very pretty girl with long brown hair to pour small drops of warm, scented oil onto his sweating flesh, which she then scraped to clean the pores. Such indulgence would never have been allowed in the Falerii household; Lucius, though often to be found at the public baths, frowned on such display, ever ready to accuse those who delighted in such luxury as vulgar and un-Roman.

At that time, Lucius was being very Roman indeed, trying to gauge just how much Barbinus was prepared to pay to get into his good offices. Like most rich men, the host hankered after more wealth and he had in his house a man who could not only secure his standing but provide him with more opportunities for profit than anyone else in the Senate. But Barbinus also craved respectability; he had reached his senatorial status because of his money, but had never served in any of the offices that fell to men of that rank and that left him vulnerable. Too old to begin the *cursus honarium* he still craved the eminence that went with such service to the Republic. Lucius Falerius was in a position to satisfy those desires.

CHAPTER TWENTY-TWO

The wagon, a barred travelling cage, that arrived an hour after these important visitors had Aquila on his feet, moving out of the shade of a tree and down the slope for a closer look. He was not alone, nearly every youngster in the village had followed it to the gate of the Barbinus property, jumping up and down and pointing at the two big cats. They paced back and forth in a restless manner, eyes ranging hungrily over the excited crowd. The sheep he had with him must have picked up a scent, because they were running up the hill, to huddle against the fencing that bordered the nearest wood. There were wildcats and lynx out in the woods he hunted in, but he had never seen anything like these. Their coats were yellow, the spots black and numerous and the bodies of both creatures sleek and lithe. Not as big as Minca they looked just as dangerous, baring teeth that were twice the size. Luckily the sutler brought his wagon past the front entrance to

the villa and manoeuvred it close to the rear
boundary of the property, thus affording Aquila a
good close look.

'Leopards,' the sutler replied when asked, 'from
Africa.'

'Fierce?' asked Aquila, coming right up to the
fence for a closer look.

'Can be, lad,' the man replied, as he unhitched
his oxen. 'But these pair have been tamed for
household pets.'

'Who tamed them?'

'I did.' The oxen were led to the stone water
trough as Aquila examined the cats more closely,
able now to see quite clearly the collars they wore.
He resumed his interrogation as soon as the sutler
returned. 'Easy, really. They have to be taken
young, which usually means killing the mother, then
they are reared by human hand so that they get used
to us. Keep 'em fed on milk and such like and they
forget they're hunters. Doesn't last mind. I always
tell my clients to keep them for three of four years
then sell them on to a stadium owner for a fight.
They get fractious as they get older and are just as
like to take a nip out of a human if the mood
changes.'

'Why not breed them?'

Both Aquila and the sutler turned at the sound of
the new voice. What they saw was a dark-haired,
swarthy youth in a fine wool cloak, open to reveal

a snow-white smock held at the waist by a rope of knotted leather, capped at each end by gold stops. Aquila could see that his sandals were as soft and well made as the voice, that his damp hair had been cut and combed so that the curls neatly fringed his forehead.

'Ain't worth it, young sir,' the sutler replied. 'You has to feed 'em while they breed and lay a litter and that takes meat which is dear to buy. Best to bring the creatures in from Africa. There's plenty there as well as locals only too happy to hunt them down for a copper ass or two.'

Aquila had backed away, turning to go back to his sheep. It was not fear that made him withdraw, more the natural embarrassment of a poor youth in too close proximity to one who was clearly the opposite. To the sutler he was 'lad'; the other boy was ' young sir'. It was impossible not to look on such a person and not feel inadequate, with his own messy hair, greasy leather cap and homespun clothes. He had no experience of rich people, only ever having once or twice seen Barbinus at a distance as he came to or left the ranch, but he knew he did not like them; they ordered folk about, and that was something Aquila did not fancy. But he did turn to watch him from a distance, noticing the way the sutler's shoulders dipped to acknowledge the rank of the boy with whom he was conversing.

For reasons he could not quite fathom he tried to imagine what it would be like to fight him; they were of a size, just as well developed even if the stranger's skin did shine. Aquila decided he liked the idea, and reckoned he could take him, even as he put the notion aside, knowing that even to raise his fist could see him flogged. That scented prick was one of Barbinus' guests; touch him and the consequences would be dire. He moved even further away when Fat Barbinus emerged, waddling his way towards the wagon containing the cats.

'Fine beasts, are they not, Master Marcellus,' Barbinus boomed, in a voice loud enough for Aquila to hear.

'Beautiful, sir,' the boy replied, his voice dropping as the fat senator came closer. 'They move with such elegance.'

Had his swarthy complexion not been tanned by a summer of sun, Barbinus would have seen Marcellus blush then. The contrast between the way Barbinus moved, legs thrown wide so each could get past the other corpulent thigh, was such a contrast to the easy way the cats slunk back and forth in their cage.

'Wait till you see them out, boy,' Barbinus said, nodding to the sutler to oblige.

From the moment he picked up the stout leather leads the cats grew excited, jumping about so much that everyone allowed themselves a safe backward step. The mobile cage had a double set of doors, the outer one of which the sutler shut before opening the inner. Both cats, as soon as he was close enough, began to rub themselves against him, purring loudly as he stroked them behind the ears, and allowing their collar to be attached with ease. It needed muscle to hold them as they emerged, but on the ground they ceased to strain, and stood together either side of the man who had reared them, proud, colourful and magnificent.

'Beauties,' Barbinus said.

'You should stroke them, sir. The sooner they get to know you the better.'

'They're not for me, fellow, they are a gift for my guests.'

It took Marcellus a second to register that he was a guest, a look of disbelief to realise that Barbinus was smiling at him and a jaw that dropped unbidden at the realisation of the truth.

'Me?'

'Strictly speaking, your father, but something tells me you may warm to the gift just as much as he.' Marcellus looked around then for a sight of Lucius, till Barbinus enlightened him. 'He has agreed to use my bath house after all, though being the man he is he has taken his scribe in there with him. I daresay the poor man is sweltering as he tries to write his despatches.'

'The farms?'

'Are mine,' Barbinus replied.

This time the smile was fixed and humourless. Lucius had fleeced him, selling the Sicilian property for an inflated price, making him regret sending for the gift with which he intended to seal the bargain. He consoled himself with the thought that they had been so badly run by the Falerii overseers that, even if he could not turn them into profitable plots, he could certainly make them pay more.

'You wish to take hold of them, young sir?'

Marcellus responded tentatively to that, the hesitation as he stepped forward obvious, especially as both cats strained to sniff at his bare knees and sandalled feet, their purring loud and vibrant. It took a hefty tug from the sutler to pull them close and make them sit, an act that had more to do with his tight short grip on the leads than obedience to the verbal command. Marcellus stepped up beside him, taking first one lead and then the other. The sutler kept the whip, which had been coiled in his right hand.

'Now young sir, walk slowly and they will do likewise.' The sutler was right. Sleek heads sniffing the air, the two cats matched his pace as he walked round the paddock. 'I'd be obliged if you was to keep them clear of my oxen. Tame they might be, but that is no thicker than the skin on their back.'

Barbinus barked to his own servants to get the oxen away from the trough and into a stockade, as

Marcellus, feeling like a Persian tyrant, paraded round the paddock. The sutler stayed close enough to talk to him, instructing him when it was safe to let go of a bit of slack on the leash, and when to pull them in as they fought against the constraint.

'Not much different to a dog, young sir. Check 'em when they're young and they'll behave ever after.'

Marcellus stopped a few feet from Barbinus, hauling hard to bring their collar right up to his knuckles, pleased with the way the cats sat down, one finger stretching out to stoke a short ear, which produced an immediate reprise of the loud purring.

'You have a way with them, young sir.'

'What happens if they are unleashed.'

'Indoors it don't signify and they are peerless in the guarding line. The gods help any felon who breaks into a house where they are inside.'

'They would attack him?'

'That they would, and like as not kill the fellow, but it would be a bad idea to let them roam, for they would be just as like to attack a stranger in the street, which would never do.'

'They look too tame to harm anyone,' said Barbinus.

'That's the training your honour, at which I humbly beg to say, I am an expert, but the wild creature lurks, and given a sniff of a chance they will revert.'

'Show me!' Barbinus snapped. Marcellus looked at the deep sunk eyes then, trying and failing to read what was going on behind them.

The sutler looked set to argue, but faced with the bulk of Barbinus he turned to a crouch and wheedling tone. 'Bad for 'em, your honour. If they are let loose now that fence twixt the cats and my oxen won't stop them.'

Barbinus looked out into the field where Aquila, back standing under his tree, leaning on a long staff, was watching, then to the sheep still huddled at the top of the hill against the fence that cut off the forest. There was a gate halfway along, which he ordered opened, a command that brought a look of alarm to the sutler's face.

'Marcellus Falerius. I bid you take them into that field. Let them sniff the presence of the sheep.'

Aquila was mystified by what was happening as the gate swung open and the cats were led through. Barbinus stayed on the other side as it was closed again, only the sutler and that rich boy with the cats this side of the fence. When the latter untied the leads his bewilderment increased. Neither leopard ran off, they stayed close to their human minder, sat at his feet, nuzzling his hands. It was as if freedom was such a strange thing that they had no idea how to exploit it, but that did not last. First one then the other sniffed the grass, no doubt picking up scents that appealed to their instincts. Slowly, as they circled the grass, the distance between them and the two humans grew wider. He could not know, because he was too far away to see or hear, that the sutler, who had loosed his coiled whip, was warning Marcellus to stay absolutely still, worried that, though the cats knew him well, they did not know this boy at all.

The leopards ceased to sniff the grass and lifted their heads to search for scents on the air. Then they began to lope around, heads jerking left and right, as the sheep at the top of the field began to bleat, a sound that attracted their attention. The flock began to break up just as Aquila moved, staff held out, his hat flying off as he sought to get between the cats and what was sure to become their prey. Concentrating on protection, he had no time to appreciate, as Marcellus did, the perfection of movement that followed. First the single stiff steps as each cat edged forward, which quickened into a loping trot as they increased the gap between them. Working together they cast left and right to isolate the now scattering sheep, selecting a target that because of their positions would have no chance of escape.

At that pace Aquila thought he had a chance to intervene but when the two cats had made their decision they leapt forward at a rate that turned them almost into a blur. He was oblivious to the shouts from below, from Barbinus a bellow of annoyance, from the sutler a shout to stop lest he become the prey. In the event Aquila was nowhere near the kill and had the sense to stop as it happened. One cat hit the running sheep just behind the neck while the other sank long teeth into the back of its leg, dragging it down. The animal was dead within seconds, with both leopards shaking powerful necks to rip into the flesh. As the sutler had moved, the rich boy, with the two leads still in his hand, moved with him, ignoring his instructions to stay put and walking up the hill.

Marcellus heard the man cursing Barbinus for undoing the work of nearly a year, words that the purchaser of these leopards could not hear. Realising that the young nobleman was still with him, he put up his hand.

'Best not go too close, young sir, they've tasted running meat.' Forward progress was then an inching forward, to the point where the nearest leopard lifted his head and snarled. 'That's as close as we dare get.'

'What happens now?' asked Marcellus.

'We have to let them feed, then let's see what happens. They might come back onto the leads. If not, then I'll have to net them, and if they rear up at me then they'll either have to be speared or let loose.'

'Cassius Barbinus won't like that.'

The object of that remark was smiling, still behind the fence, thinking that as a gift these two cats had taken on an added virtue. They could kill, and perhaps in Rome they would do that to the avaricious bastard who had just stung him for so much money. Perhaps, one night, they would eat Lucius Falerius.

Aquila took his cue from the sutler, staying the same distance as he from the cats gorging on the bloody carcass. Spying him, the man called out. 'Best get the rest of that flock out of here while you can, lad. And take them by a route that keeps them well away from this pair.'

As he walked across the slope, in an arc that took him round the leopards, Aquila glared at the well-dressed Roman youth with the two useless leads swinging free in his hand. He wanted to kill him now, not fight him. Marcellus, lifting his own eyes, observed a boy of about his own age, poorly dressed, but tall and quite muscular. The colouring intrigued him; golden hair tinged with red and fair light-brown skin. But the eyes did more than that; bright blue, they were fixed on his, and even at a distance he could almost feel the hate.

'Just some angry peasant,' he murmured to himself, as his attention went back to the sound of crunching bones and the sight of tearing flesh.

Barbinus, watching Aquila move away, wondered who he was. With so many slaves in his possession he had no idea what they all did, but he visited this place quite often and he could not recall seeing that particular youth. His overseer would know.

'There nothing about it to do, Aquila,' Gadoric insisted. 'You did well get the other sheep back to pens. Besides, they property of Cassius Barbinus. If he want to feed them to pets instead of guests, that his business.'

'If you or I did it, we would be strung up.'

'I no deny it, but that way of the world.'

'It would have been different if Minca had been there.'

The dog raised its huge head at the mention of its name, but dropped it quickly when he heard the harsh tone of Gadoric's reply, this time talking in his own language, slowly so Aquila could understand.

'The two cats like you've described would have seen to him, a bit slower than a sheep I grant you, but they'd have killed him nevertheless. I know because there are beasts like that in the mountains where I fought, maybe not the same colouring but the same nature. Don't you ever take chances just for pride, for there's precious little of that left in a carcass. With odds too great to conquer you withdraw and bide your time. Take your enemy when it suits you, not them. If the men who led us against the Romans had thought that way I wouldn't be here now.'

Reverting to Latin, he said, 'Now you best get on way home.'

Dinner with Barbinus proved to be an awkward affair; the fat senator looked even more gross lying on a couch than he did on his feet. Lucius had not enjoyed being told about the episode with the leopards any more than his host had enjoyed being fleeced over the sale of the farms. In reality the two men were so very different that they would have struggled in even better circumstances to agree about anything. It was instructive for Marcellus, who in his own house never met anyone but loyal supporters of both his father and his beliefs. Though Cassius Barbinus was trying to sound like an upright and honourable man, his natural sybaritic nature kept breaking through, made more obvious during the latter part of the dinner than the beginning due to the copious amounts of wine he began to consume.

A slave girl had the task of easing the gorge when guest or host were too full to continue eating, bringing forward the basin she was holding so that the person in distress could vomit. As she entered the circle of lamplight Marcellus examined her closely, recognising her as the same creature who had poured oil on his back that afternoon. She had a good figure and an alluring way of walking. There was something very familiar about her and it took him time, in this setting, to spot that she bore a striking resemblance to Gaius Trebonius's horrible sister, Valeria. The girl had a more developed figure, but dress her hair and put her in good clothes and the two could be near twins. Watching the submissive way she held the golden bowl, while her master evacuated, he reasoned that the similarity was only physical. Valeria would have emptied the contents over the fat senator's head.

Lucius waited until Barbinus was finished before continuing a homily on the need for patrician abstinence. Barbinus only half-heard that stricture; his attention was taken up with the way the Falerii boy was watching the slave girl as she exited to empty the bowl. The look in the boy's eyes, as he gazed at those swaying hips, was one that the host understood only too well. When he did give Lucius full focus he narrowed his deep-set eyes even further, reflecting that a bloodline as long as that of the Falerii did nothing to stop a man from being pompous or a boy from being lecherous. Lucius was reflecting on a set of rules, introduced as far as Barbinus could tell by noble skinflints, mostly impoverished, to stop their wealthier brethren enjoying the fruits of their success. The sumptuary laws had become a code that covered dress, the number of household slaves a man could have, what food he could serve as well as what kind of outward display he could indulge in right down to the decoration on his own litter. It was just as well most senators, while paying lip service, ignored them.

'I fear your leopards might lead people to fear you have succumbed to imperial pretensions.' It was the wrong thing to say, a remark brought on by too much wine and Barbinus knew it as soon as he spoke the words. His body went rigid at the look in Lucius's eyes and he added hastily, 'No one who knows you would think that, of course.'

'I was planning to say this privately,' Lucius replied, 'but since you have raised it, I find I must do so in front of my son. It is with regret that I have to decline the offer of your beasts.' Barbinus grunted and Marcellus felt his heart sink as his father continued; he had been looking forward to showing off the cats to his friends. 'I'm aware of the nature of what I say, but I hope you will not take it as an insult that I cannot accept. It is, I fear, because of that very remark you just made.'

Barbinus protested, but Lucius held up his hand to stop him. 'I am aware it was a jest, but you will readily see that it is one that others might make with real malice. It is, I know, a gross breach of propriety to refuse your kind offer, but I must.'

What Lucius did not know was that the gift would have had to be withdrawn anyway. The man who had fetched the cats was adamant; there was no way of knowing what they would do after having tasted that sheep so to gift them to a person unused to handling them was to court disaster. The cats could eat Lucius for all Barbinus cared, but they would more than likely take a lump out of a slave, or worse the man's son which would kill off any right he had to demand a future favour.

'You must let me give you something with which to replace it,' Barbinus insisted. Lucius nodded his head, acknowledging that having been rude enough to decline a gift, he had little choice but to accept a substitute.

The fat senator was thinking hard: for all his lard he was no fool; he would never have amassed such wealth if he were and so looking for advantage was something in which he was well versed. Barbinus could think of nothing to give Lucius that would in any way endear him to a man he considered a stuck up streak of piss. But what about the son? Lucius, for all his heavy fathering, clearly doted on the boy. Could Barbinus gain an ally in the Falerii household through a gift that would please Marcellus, one that would do nothing to offend the boy's father?

'A slave,' he said. 'A household slave.'

'I do not want for those, Barbinus,' Lucius replied doubtfully.

'You cannot decline me twice,' Barbinus objected. 'And if I may speak freely, you have been a bachelor these many years. I would guess that your household is well provided with male servants, yet light in the article of females.'

Lucius shrugged to acknowledge the truth of the remark. 'That is so.'

'Then I propose a female slave and a valuable one, who is young and will give your house many years of estimable service. I'm sure she will breed well if you wish her to and from that you can certainly profit.' Barbinus saw Marcellus wriggle in the corner of his eye. 'What do you say to the one who just attended my evacuation?'

For the sake of appearances, Lucius looked as if he was ruminating but he had no choice in the matter. To decline two gifts would be a terminal breach of good manners. The fact that Barbinus should not have offered him anything, leopards or a slave girl, made no difference. The overture had been made, and he must respond.

'You are most kind,' Lucius conceded. 'Now, since we need to depart at first light, I fear I must get some sleep. You too, Marcellus.'

'Yes, Father,' the boy said, before turning to Barbinus. 'And may I thank you, Senator Barbinus, for such an entertaining day.'

'Gods in the heavens,' Barbinus groaned, as soon as Lucius and Marcellus were out of earshot. 'That was a trial.'

His overseer, Nicos, was a man who was allowed

certain liberties, so he replied with an ironic grin and in a sonorous tone of voice. 'The most noble Lucius Falerius Nerva is famed for his probity, master.'

'He's Nerva all right, but he's also a prick, man, and a damned greedy one at that. Do you know how much the tough old bastard charged me for that Sicilian dustbowl of his?'

'I fear too much,' Nicos said.

'I've a good mind to turn the whole price into copper asses and drop it on his head.'

'Would that kill him, master?'

'It might.'

'Can I advance the opinion that might is not good enough.'

'You're probably right, Nicos. He's the power in the land and I, who own dozens of farms, must bow the knee to him. The gall! I had to practically force a gift down his throat.'

'To think, with those big cats it could have been the reverse.'

'You paid the sutler off?'

Nicos nodded. 'Half the agreed fee, master.'

'That much?'

'He threatened to go to a praetor and make a case. I reasoned that it was easier to settle for half than suffer the bother.'

'You're probably right. Anyway I decided to gift him Sosia to replace them.'

'Ah!' Nicos replied, looking away.

'That's not a problem?'

'No, master.'

Barbinus dug him in the ribs. 'Lining up to take her were you?'

Nicos looked shocked. 'Would I?'

'If my back was turned, yes,' Barbinus insisted. 'You will steal any of my rights as a slave owner that you can and you know it. If you weren't so good with money and ranch running I'd have strung you up by the thumbs years ago.'

'A gift of a virgin is very complimentary, master. A noble sacrifice indeed.'

'I think she's safe with old Lucius. He's so hung up on being snooty I doubt he knows he's got balls between his legs but the youngster had his eye on her when she was serving, so perhaps he might be the one to do the deflowering.'

'Two virgins,' said Nicos.

'Messy,' Barbinus replied, his eyes rolling in the fat that surrounded them. 'Perhaps she should be prepared.'

'May I humbly offer my services, master,' Nicos said.

'Offer away, man, but I do think that I should do the deed. After all, she's going to be patrician meat, so we should start her out as we mean to finish. Fetch her to the spare guest chamber. I'll go there as soon as I'm sure old Lucius is asleep.'

'As you wish, master,' Nicos replied, turning away, the curse on his lips hidden from Barbinus.

'By the way, how long have we had that young fellow who tends the sheep?'

'What young fellow?'

'The one I saw today. Nearly got in the way of the leopards, funny coloured hair, what I could see of it. Odd, I don't remember buying him.'

'We do breed our own occasionally,' Nicos replied, wondering who in the name of *Jupiter* his master was talking about. The man who tended the sheep was an addle-brained Celt. Not that he was about to say so; it would never do to show ignorance to someone like Barbinus.

Aquila had penned the sheep and returned after dark, something he had done before when the senator had been entertaining and Sosia had been kept back to serve. He waited, with Minca, sitting with his back to the part of the wicker fence that served as their meeting place, looking up at the star-filled sky and wondering that the heavens could contain so many gods. He was also wondering what it took to call them down to his aid. He would like to have done that today, perhaps a thunderbolt from *Vulcan* to strike down that scented prick who let loose those leopards, but as the thought came so did the conclusion; the boy was rich and he was not. Master Marcellus, Barbinus had called him. If he wanted the gods to intercede for him, no doubt they would queue up to do so.

Aquila shivered and stood up, realising by the position of the moon that it was much later than he had thought. Looking at the house he could see that the whole place was in darkness, barring the few oil lamps left burning for the watchmen to do their rounds. He leapt over the fence, followed by the dog and scurried over to the back of the slave quarters, to tap gently on Sosia's shutter. The lack of response made him tap harder, to no avail. Perhaps Barbinus was still up, and if he was then she might be too. He decided to investigate, and he edged round the slave quarters building and moved slowly towards the main villa, looking for the light of oil lamps that would tell him there was still activity, but there was no sign of that or Sosia, so Aquila, reluctantly, resigned himself to the idea that she was not coming and turned to make his way back to the fence.

The single scream that rent the air made him freeze, right out in the open, where anyone looking out onto the moon and starlit courtyard would easily see him. Was it animal or human, and what direction had it come from, the house or the nearby forest? Minca growled, one paw went up and his snout quivered. Aquila waited, his ears straining for another unusual sound, but there were no others, save those that belonged to a forest. The hoot of an owl, the swish of an autumn wind blowing through packed branches. He decided it was a fox in pain that had screamed, no doubt the victim of some larger predator. Aquila pulled at the dog's ears to make him follow, and headed for the fence and home.

CHAPTER TWENTY-THREE

Thanks to work already done by Aulus, the first units of the 10th legion could move out within the week. He gave up any pretence of working through Vegetius, and at the council of war no one was left in any doubt who had assumed command. He carefully questioned everyone present regarding recent intelligence, making full use of the map on the table before him. Finally Aulus made his dispositions and laid out both the routes, as well as the order of march for the main body.

'We have to go looking for our rebels but whatever happens our troops must not be caught in extended order in broken country. If our forward elements find an enemy force, they are to retire fast on the main body to give us time to be ready for battle. Our aim is to draw the rebels onto a position of our choice, preferably a spacious piece of flat ground with a single secure flank, where our superior discipline and mobility will give us an advantage.'

'We have a numerical advantage anyway,' said Vegetius loudly, seeking to assert himself.

In order to appear martial at this conference he had abandoned his toga and donned his armour, breastplate, greaves, his horsehair-topped helmet under one arm. Given his flabby body and weak countenance it made him look faintly absurd rather than military.

'Are you privy to some information that has escaped me?' asked Aulus, his voice as hard as the look in his eyes. A good head taller than Vegetius, even in a plain smock he looked every inch the Roman general set against a leather-enclosed tub of lard.

'Not that I know of,' Vegetius stammered in reply.

'So you don't actually know the strength of the forces opposing us?'

'A ragtag army of rebels and malcontents,' the senator protested, looking for support in the faces of the others present. None came as he added, 'What am I saying "army" for. I shouldn't dignify them with the name.'

Aulus gave a thin smile. 'I will treat them with respect until I'm sure that I can do otherwise. I suggest, Vegetius, that you do the same.' He looked around the room, full of the assembled officers of the 10th legion. 'Gentlemen, I have, as you are aware, a successful record as a soldier. If that sounds immodest, I apologise. Lest you wonder at these precautions I will tell you that I nearly lost two whole legions in Spain because I didn't treat my enemy with respect. It's not an error I intend to repeat.'

There was silence while all present recalled Aulus's hard-fought campaign against the Celt-Iberians ten years previously, which he had freely admitted to the Senate was a much more difficult task than he had originally anticipated. Far from Rome, even further from Spain, they, unlike the general who fought him, were not aware that the spectre of Brennos had risen again, nor could they know that the man talking to them now had determined, once this commission had done its work, to return to Spain, with or without the permission of the Senate.

Brennos, to him, represented more than a threat to Rome's Imperium, he was a personal enemy, the man who had destroyed any chance he had of inner contentment. Aulus knew, deep in his heart, that killing the Celtic shaman would not bring him peace and happiness, but leaving Brennos alive was even worse. Aware that he had paused for a long time, Aulus coughed loudly and recommenced his briefing.

'So I advise you all to follow my example. Don't assume that just because you're Roman these tribesmen will be frightened of you. After all, they've had several years to observe that, when it comes to the business of soldiering, Romans are no more perfect than anyone else.' This was delivered without looking at Vegetius, but they all knew what Aulus meant. 'Having said that, I intend that we should move swiftly so as to catch the enemy off balance.'

He looked around the tent, his eyes finally settling on the deep tanned and lined face of Flaccus, a senior centurion, commander of the *hastari*, who comprised some of the most experienced men in the legion. The look alone brought the man to rigid attention.

'Your name, Centurion?' demanded Aulus.

His fist crashed against his breastplate. 'Didius Flaccus, General.'

Aulus nodded to acknowledge the salute. 'You will command the advance guard, which will consist of one cohort for now. I shall join you as soon as we've got the rest of the army on the move. You're to act independently till then but you are not, under any circumstances, to risk your men. Your primary task is to go to the rescue of the Romans under Publius Trebonius fleeing north from Epirus. We have to presume that the enemy is pursuing them.'

He looked at the map again, running his pointer across the province of Illyricum. 'It is odd that such a revolt should break out just when this province is becoming peaceful. They could have linked up any time in the last five years, yet they chose not to. But, having said that, they've had ample time to coordinate their plans. Perhaps our recent successes have come too easy. I must therefore, merely for safety's sake, anticipate some connection. So, gather them up if you can. They are to join the main force without delay. We can send the civilians back here to our base camp.'

Aulus beckoned Flaccus towards him, pointing at the map.

'I also want you to take and hold the pass at Thralaxas. We need the lines of communication to the south kept open, so that we can get our troops through and confront the enemy as near as possible to their own base. I want them close to home so that their minds are on their wives and children. Provided they are still well to the south we can get the whole army through and deploy on the plains before they can interfere. I suggest that if you reach Thralaxas unopposed, you press on with one maniple and leave the other two to hold the pass. If, by any chance, you make contact with the enemy south of that point, you are to retire before them. I will come personally when the legions are assembled to assess what we must do. I take it you're ready to leave?'

'I am, General!'

'Then go. No heavy equipment, Flaccus! I shall bring that up myself.'

Flaccus said a silent prayer to the Goddess *Felicitas*, as he always did when he suspected luck might be needed. Those left in the tent heard him shouting as they went over the rest of Aulus's disposition, then the crashing noise of legionaries falling in and marching off at double pace, Clodius Terentius near the front. The years of discipline and the regular diet of very basic food had made him a much fitter man. Not that he had ever been a slouch, but drinking without working had given him a belly and over-ripe countenance, which humping sacks had left intact. That was gone now. He might be older than most of his fellows, but he had a hard flat stomach and a lean, tanned face.

Once they had left the settled part of the province behind there was no road in the Roman sense, just a cart track that was sometimes good and at other times non-existent. It skirted the coast where the landscape permitted, but the sheer cliffs and deep ravines often drove it inland, forcing them to advance gingerly through dense forest, with Flaccus, superstitious as ever, murmuring incantations to *Nemestrinus,* skirmishers out in front and everyone's javelins at the ready. They reached Thralaxas just as the sun went down and Flaccus, in line with his orders, detached two of his maniples to hold the narrow defile and make it as safe as they could while he pressed on, using the moonlight to guide him.

They had set out from Salonae briskly enough but having been on the march all day, and though it had clouded over late in the day, they had spent a long time under the blazing sun. Clodius plodded along wearily, just concentrating on putting one foot in front of the other, while mentally moaning like the good soldier he was. His tired mind told him he was too old for this sort of thing. Not that the younger men seemed to be faring any better; their steps, too, were punctuated with numerous curses as they slipped and slithered on the treacherous track, especially when the moon slipped behind the clouds. Flaccus was immune to blandishments, refusing to slacken the pace, issuing dire threats of punishment to those whose complaints reached his ears. Clodius was long enough, in both teeth and legions, to know that it was a dangerous course of action, marching along at this pace, in single file, with only the moon and the stars to light your way, for it could not be done in silence, and all Flaccus's praying to every Roman god he could think of would not change matters. An enemy, if they were close enough to hear, would have ample time to prepare for their arrival. Flaccus might think he was obeying the general's orders; to Clodius's mind he was exceeding them. It was hard to keep too many secrets in a legionary camp, and everyone knew that Flaccus had instructions not to risk casualties.

'Keep moving, you bonehead,' snapped Clodius, bumping into the man in front of him. The moon had slipped behind a huge cloud, plunging them all into almost total darkness.

'Quiet there,' called Flaccus, trying to shout and whisper at the same time and Clodius realised that the column had come to a halt. He heard several curses as legionaries who, like him, had been plodding along head down, crashed into those in front of them until eventually silence fell. Close to the front of the column, Clodius could see Flaccus framed against the clouded sky, which had a faint orange tinge, throwing into sharp relief the pines at the top of the hill they were ascending. The gap, where the cart track cut through, stood out clearly between the trees on either side. Flaccus came back down the line, stopping just behind Clodius, quietly issuing orders to his second-in-command.

'Deploy your men to one side of the track and stay out of sight. I'm going on ahead to see what's up. If we come back at a run, kill anyone who's chasing us.'

'And then?' asked the senior legionary, a man half Flaccus's age and with a tenth of his experience.

The sarcasm in the centurion's voice was so heavy Clodius could conjure up the hard look that went with it. 'Then? You must be hungry after a long day's march, lad. Light a fire and send some men out to hunt down your supper.' A thick growl followed that. 'If you're lucky you might have a few uninvited guests.' The man mumbled an apology and Flaccus relented enough to explain what should have been obvious. 'You follow us. We'll set up another ambush if we can. You keep moving. Don't stop till you get back to the pass at Thralaxas, even if that means leaving us to our fate.'

Flaccus brushed past Clodius, calling on him, and those in front, to move out. 'Quietly now.'

As they came near to the top of the hill, the noise, which had been masked by the hill, grew steadily louder. They could hear, clearly, the sound of the laughing, the shouting and most of all the screaming. Flaccus bade them slow down to a crawl as he approached the crest, dropping onto his belly and sliding the last few yards through the trees. The men with him followed suit, spreading out on either side of the cart track. They found themselves looking down into a well-lit glade, full to bursting with enemy soldiers. The fires came from the burning wagons and the heap of possessions that had been built into a bonfire.

Clodius could hear the women scream, see the queues of men waiting to take their turn in raping them. They lay, some held face up and others face down, their pale skins stark in the firelight. Trees off to the right were laden with bodies hanging from ropes. Dead, they swung in the faint breeze and judging by the number of wounds, these poor unfortunates had been used for target practice. The cart track ran straight ahead down the hill in front of them. Clodius, lying right beside Flaccus, could see the two files of men lining either side. Roman soldiers, stripped naked but for their leather helmets were being forced to run between the lines. Those at the far end had whips, those in the middle clubs, but the men at the end had swords. They watched as one unfortunate set off at a run, goaded by a spear in the backside. He tried to shy away from the whips, but with little success, then he came under a steady stream of blows when he reached those of his enemies with clubs, which made him stagger from side to side. His arms were raised around his head in a pathetic attempt to protect himself, and he was nearly down on his knees when he reached the swordsmen. They started by giving him gentle stabs, then one fellow, who had just helped himself to a swig from a wine gourd, slashed at the tendons on the back of his leg. The Roman fell forward, emitting a scream of pain and this seemed to excite the others, who joined in, cutting and stabbing, all the while laughing and taunting their victim who rolled on the ground in a futile attempt to avoid his fate. Clodius closed his eyes, not wishing to see the final agony of the fellow, as he was hacked to death.

'Over there, look!' said Flaccus.

Clodius raised his head to follow the pointing

finger of his centurion. Flaccus had spotted a solitary wagon, clearly Roman by its design, off to one side of the clearing, well away from those burning in the centre, faintly visible because it still had its white canopy intact. The clouds obscured the moon, so it was far from easy to make out anything else until one of the burning wagons in the centre of the clearing collapsed, sending up a great whoosh of sparks, which illuminated the whole area. The sun-bleached canopy of the wagon now stood out clearly, but his attention was drawn to something else. Just in front of that solitary wagon he saw, like a tableau, two naked men simultaneously assaulting a young girl. You could see by her tiny breasts and gamine figure that she was not yet fully grown. One had her hair in his hands, and was pulling her head ferociously into his groin while the other stood behind her thrusting forward with as much vigour as his companion. Their arms and armour gleamed dully in the grass beside them. The sparks died down, plunging the whole thing back into near darkness.

'I wonder if we could get down there?' said Flaccus, peering into the gloom.

'She won't be much use to no one by the time those two are finished,' said Clodius sadly.

'I don't mean the girl, you idiot. I'm talking about the wagon.'

'What do we want a wagon for?' snapped

Clodius, putting aside his normal deference, genuinely angered by his commander's indifference.

'No wonder you're poor. If that wagon ain't burning like the rest, that has to tell you something.'

'Like what?'

Flaccus leant close making sure that no one else heard. 'Like it might have something of value in it. If Publius Trebonius got out of Epirus on the double, I doubt he'd leave without taking his gold with him.'

'Gold!' Clodius replied breathlessly. It was a word that never failed to excite him.

'His treasury, you dope. The money he needs to do his job of governing. Look at the base of that wagon.'

'I can hardly see the damned thing.'

As if on command, a second shower of sparks shot up from the blaze to show another soldier staggering down the line, in much worse shape than the man who had gone before him. He fell to his knees having only covered half the distance. One of the clubmen stepped forward and felled him with a single huge blow that split open both his leather helmet and his skull. He was dragged out of the way and the twin lines of men looked away from the watching legionaries, waiting for the next victim. Flaccus had not taken his eyes off the wagon. Clodius, having had a quick look at the dying man, turned back and saw the two men who had been raping the girl reach for their armour. She lay face down on the ground now, her body racked with sobs. The one furthest away picked up his sword, raised it high in the air, and with one swift blow, decapitated her.

'Bastard,' said Flaccus without emotion. The fire died down again. He was watching to see if the men rejoined the others in the centre of the clearing, but they did not emerge from the gloom. 'That does it. Those two bastards are set to guard that wagon. It must have something of value in it. Come on.'

Flaccus slid back from the crest, tugging at Clodius to follow him at the same time as he called to the others to stay put. Once he was out of sight of those over the hill, he stood up, setting off at a run to a point further along the crest. Clodius followed reluctantly, grumbling under his breath. Flaccus had near thirty men with him, why collar him for the dangerous work? The centurion ran, crouched over, using his left hand to stop himself from sliding. His heart was pounding and his head was filled with the soothsayer's prophecy. Judging that he had gone far enough, he threw himself flat and slid back to the crest where Clodius joined him. They were now on the far side of the single wagon, which was silhouetted against the bonfire. Another great cheer rent the air as another mangled body was thrown onto the pile at the end of the twin files of death. Flaccus tugged eagerly at Clodius's tunic and whispered to him.

'I was right. Look at those two. They're guarding that bleeding wagon.'

Clodius could hear the excitement in Flaccus's voice, and he did not like the sound of it one bit. He too saw the men, leaning on spears, watching what was taking place at the centre near the bonfire.

'Come on.'

'What!'

Clodius tried to free the arm that Flaccus had grabbed, but he suddenly found the centurion's face pressed right into his own. He could feel the man's hot breath on his nose.

'You've always wanted to get hold of some loot, now's your chance. Maybe you can pay me back what you owe me. All we have to do is kill those two bastards and we can help ourselves to whatever there is in that wagon.'

'What about the rest of the men. Surely it would be better if there were more of us.'

'Oh yes. Let's all charge down there. It'll only take one of them sods near the fire to turn round and it'll be you and me trying to make our way down that line.' Clodius felt fear drain the blood from his face. 'This has to be done swift and silent.'

'Why me?'

'You was the one closest to me, mate, and I can't do it on my own. I'll wager there's enough gold in that wagon to see you into the senate.'

'But it's not ours.'

'Then pray to *Furina* for help, because if we can I intend to steal it.'

Clodius heard the slight scraping sound as Flaccus pulled out his sword. Then the man was over the crest, bent double to reduce his profile. The word gold reverberated around his head as he swallowed hard, pulled out his own weapon, and followed Flaccus over the top. The moon was out again, but their quarry were too intent on being spectators to see them coming, and the noise from the cheering crowds in the middle of the clearing masked the sound of their approach. They stood behind them, poised on tiptoe, and, at a nod from Flaccus, Clodius reached over his victim's head, grabbed the front of his helmet and pulled it back. The strangled gasp caused by the tightened strap died as the point of the sword cut through his windpipe, then he hauled hard, dragging the man down till he lay flat on his back. The sword plunged sideways, missing the breastplate, slicing into the man's heart and as he pushed, Clodius heard the ribs cave in. Flaccus stood over the inert body of his victim, who had suffered a similar fate. He lifted his lower tunic, and, with a swift motion, he sliced off his genitals, then stuffed them in the man's mouth. Clodius heard him, even if it was only a whisper, as he rubbed his bloody sword on the thick grass.

'That's for the girl, you bastard, and may the Goddess of Death show you her arse.'

Flaccus then headed for the wagon, jumping up and tearing back the flap. Clodius followed. It was pitch dark inside.

'We can't see a thing.'

The sound of ripping canvas was all he got as a reply as Flaccus stuck his sword through the roof of the wagon, then pulled hard. A faint burst of light from the moon lit the interior.

'Just as I thought,' said the centurion, kneeling down. Clodius looked over his shoulder. The white light from the moon caught the brass edges that bound the huge chest. Flaccus was running his hands over it, looking for a way to prise it open.

'Poke your head out the back,' he said urgently. 'Make sure no one's coming this way.'

Clodius did as he was told. He heard the scraping and cursing at his rear, then the snap that seemed to reverberate round the whole clearing as Flaccus used his sword to break the hasp that locked the chest. He also heard the clinking of coins a few seconds later.

'Money all right!' said Flaccus, 'but I'm buggered if I can see what they are.' Clodius, keeping his eyes on the enemy, felt the centurion squeeze alongside him. He was holding his hand out in front and the light from the fire caught the gold coins right away. It also caught the look of naked greed in Flaccus's eye. 'Just when we've got a chance to be rich, *Sors* be damned, we're stuck with more gold than we can carry.'

'We could get the others down here.'

'No!' Flaccus used his free hand to grasp Clodius's arm in a painful grip. He explained quickly about the various prophecies, especially the last one he had had from the old soothsayer in Salonae, his voice rasping and eager, rising when necessary to make himself heard over the sounds from the clearing. 'There's enough gold to cover me twice over and that sounds near enough like cheering to me. But this is Roman gold, mate, and you know as well as I do, by rights it should be handed in. If we let all the lads in on the secret, one of them's bound to croak, even if it's only through drink. Let's take what we can carry, scatter the rest, then set this wagon alight.'

'Seems like a good way to die,' whispered Clodius

'No. We've got to keep them occupied, even if it's just pickin' up money. Otherwise it might be that none of us get out of here. Come on.'

Flaccus was halfway up the hill with the two heavy leather bags round his shoulders when the thought came to him. 'We'll never manage this lot. If we need to run we'll have to throw it away.'

'So?' asked Clodius with a painful gasp. He liked gold, but he loved life more.

Flaccus was speaking quickly. 'We'll bury it on the other side of the hill, and still set fire to the wagon.'

Another great cheer rent the air. Another Roman soldier died.

'They're goin' to run out of victims soon, Flaccus. I say we should get out of here.'

The centurion dropped all pretence at being nice. His lined face, faintly illuminated by the firelight was screwed up in a passion, his eyes were like flints and his voice carried a snarl that made him sound more animal than human. 'Lily-livered son of a whore, do the gods ever do what I ask? I could have picked any one of thirty men and I got you. You just do as I say, or I'll personally add another Roman body to the casualty list.'

There was no doubt that he meant it, just as Clodius knew he could do it and, listing him as missing, never have to explain the casualty. They worked steadily, Flaccus digging a hole with his sword between the base of a tree and a thick thorn bush. Clodius, fetching the heavy bags from the wagon, heard him cursing as the thorns cut his flesh, that quickly followed by an apology to one of the three Goddesses of the Fates, or maybe it was all three, given the depth of Flaccian superstition. For all that piety, it was Flaccus who realised that the yelling and screaming had stopped and he shot back up to the crest and looked down, Clodius beside him.

'Something's up. Time to get out of here. You go down and fire the wagon while I fill in the hole, and be quick about it, for as soon as they're done over there, one of 'em's bound to come over and have a look at their booty. Don't forget to scatter some money about in the grass. Make it look as though we've headed south. It will slow them down, especially if they think one of their own has thieved it.'

Clodius slithered down the hill to the wagon. There were just two leather bags left in the chest, joined at the top by a strap. He took them out and slung them round his neck. A sword thrust into the base of each one was enough to ensure a steady stream of gold as he ran to the trees south of the clearing. As soon as the bags were empty he ran back to the wagon, reaching into his tunic for the two hardwood sticks. No legionary ever went anywhere without the means to start a fire, and long practice made them all adept. Clodius scrabbled around, found some dry wood and used his sword to make shavings. Having collected kindling and some dried ferns, he crouched at the back of the wagon, furiously rubbing his sticks together.

He blew gently as soon as he saw a spark and his heart leapt at the first light on the edge of a piece of the shavings. He picked it up and blew on it till it glowed, then laid it down, ferns on top. Blowing again, still gently, he fed more dried fern into the glowing area until they took, flaring slightly, enough to allow him to heap small pieces of kindling on top. Once that had shown the first signs of burning he added the more substantial twigs, pushing the whole lot against the side of the wagon and laid the tarred ropes that held the canvas canopy across the fire. Once a flame got going it would set light to the tar and soon reach the canvas of the roof. That would burn for sure, and if the timber of the wagon itself was dry, as he thought it must be, then the whole thing would be ablaze in no time.

Clodius leapt down as soon as he decently could. There was always a chance that he had left too early, a chance that the fire would go out, but he had no intention of leaving too late. He ran up the hill to where Flaccus was waiting for him and the centurion dragged him to the spot where he had buried their loot.

'Right,' he said. 'It's a bloody great pine, with a wild rose bush at the base, fourteen paces from the crest. We'll pace the distance back to the cart track together and compare at the end. Come on.'

Clodius counted silently. He could hear Flaccus talking softly to himself, tallying off the steps, and he fought to block the sound out. In less than a minute they were back amongst the others, still lying flat, still transfixed by the scene before them. A voice spoke out of the darkness.

'Quick, Flaccus, come and look at this.'

Both Clodius and Flaccus scurried back into their previous positions to see that the whole mass of men in the clearing had now gathered in the middle by the track. It was no longer two lines, more like two heaving crowds with the sandy soil of the roadway running down the centre. At the head of the crowd they saw him, a noble Roman, standing erect, dressed in his senatorial robes, looking neither left nor right. No one made a sound.

'Publius Trebonius,' whispered Flaccus. 'It has to be.'

Without prodding, the man set off down the lane formed by the two files of his enemies. No one touched him, the whips stayed loose at the sides of their owners, as though the sheer presence of this Roman noble awed them too much to strike. He passed on to those who held the clubs, as a few raised their weapons, but none dared use them. Clodius could see the smile on Trebonius's face, a smile that mocked these men who threatened him. The senator made it to the swordsmen and for a moment it looked as though he was going to get to the end unscathed, until a richly dressed individual jumped out at the very end, blocking Trebonius's exit. The old man walked right up to him and looked him straight in the eye. Trebonius spoke, his words rising up the hillside, clear to those hidden over the crest.

'You must stand aside. I represent the Imperium of the Senate of Rome. No man may block my progress.'

The whole place was silent as Trebonius raised his fasces, the bundle of sticks with the small axe inside, the symbol of his authority. In no way did it threaten harm; it was merely being used to gently poke the man's chest, but it was enough. His sword shot out from his side in an underarm blow that carried it into the senator's guts, right up to the hilt and Trebonius doubled over. A great cry went up and the crowd on either side surged forward to strike at him. Swords flashed and blood spurted as his enemies literally hacked him to pieces. They could see some of the blood-spattered tribesmen leaving the crowd, their teeth tearing at great chunks of Publius Trebonius's flesh.

'Time to get out of here lads,' said Flaccus softly. 'They've left old Trebonius till last.'

CHAPTER TWENTY-FOUR

Didius Flaccus and his men straggled back, at dawn, into the temporary camp at the pass, filthy, tired and hungry, to find their general had arrived with several wagons and was busy supervising the construction of some defences. Cholon, his servant, had tethered both their horses and was trying to arrange a space where, if he so desired, his master could take his ease. This involved the surreptitious use of some of the troops Aulus was directing. The wagons were being broken up to provide a fighting platform, trees were being felled and dragged into position to form a palisade across the track at the point where the pass narrowed. A few were diverted by the fastidious Greek for use as a bench on which Aulus could sit, the smaller branches going to feed the fire he had started. The servant looked at what he had laid out with something less than satisfaction, for no amount of pleading had ever allowed Cholon to travel on campaign with the things he insisted he required. Aulus was content to eat a soldier's rations, if nothing finer was available, a deprivation much resented by his attendant, forced to live off the same food as his master. Now all he had was the contents of two saddlebags, plus the leftovers from the meal they had eaten in the main camp the night before.

Flaccus, giving a crisp salute, noticed that, as the general broke off from his task, he first counted the number of men who had returned. Sure that all were present and showing no signs of combat, he nodded and ordered the centurion to breakfast his men, then get them into the small tents which had been set up, at the temporary camp, just to the north of the pass.

'Once you've done that, report back to me.'

Flaccus was as tired as his men but he knew he would be lucky to get any rest; the general would want to reconnoitre the situation as soon as he heard the news and logic demanded that he take with him the man who had seen the terrain. Not that the centurion was averse to a return; after all, the gold was there. A quick splash of cold water across the face revived him a bit, then he saw his men settled, with all their equipment neatly stacked, before returning to make his report. Aulus listened in silence as Flaccus told him of the fate of Publius Trebonius and those he had sought to bring out of Epirus.

'Were they Epirote?' asked Aulus.

'Can't rightly say, sir. I didn't get close enough to have a proper look.'

'No chance to take a prisoner, then?'

Flaccus had told lies all his life, no more necessarily than other men of his rank. You could not rise in any army without the ability to look a senior officer in the face and tell him a blatant falsehood yet even with all his wealth of experience, the centurion felt uncomfortable under this gaze. Aulus's eyes, boring into his, caused him to stammer out a reply, rather than answer in the crisp fashion that was required.

'Your orders, General, not to risk casualties. I couldn't see how to fetch back a prisoner without risking all our lives.'

The general said nothing; he just kept staring at the centurion. Flaccus tried to take his mind off the gold and the two men he had killed to get it, lest the truth somehow show in his face, feeling even more exposed, there being no god to pray to that dealt with untruths. He could easily have taken one of them prisoner. Damn it, he had failed even to examine their armour to try and find out where they were from.

'They're too far north for my liking,' Aulus said eventually, looking through the narrow pass. 'Trebonius got away quickly enough and the tribune he sent to inform us said that he had ample transport. They should have been able to outrun the pursuit.' The other man stayed rigidly at attention, eyes now focused on his commander's back, hoping to avoid another searching look. 'I can't go back to the main body without some more information.'

Flaccus had been at the original conference and he knew enough of the general's thinking to be able to essay a comment. 'There weren't enough of them to stop you if you want to push the legions south, sir.'

'But it doesn't feel right, Didius Flaccus, does it?' It was not for the likes of a centurion to answer that kind of question and Aulus hardly gave him the opportunity anyway. 'Ever since that tribune arrived at Salonae the whole thing has had a rank smell. I don't want to make any final dispositions till I know who it is I'm fighting.'

This sounded like excessive caution to Flaccus, but he could not say so. 'Then we'd best go an' have a look, General.'

Aulus glanced at the sky, thinking that the legions to the north would have broken camp by now; that is, if Vegetius had not decided to afford himself a morning in bed. He could send orders for them to stop, though he was reluctant to halt them too early in the day. Yet at the same time he was loath to try and push them through this narrow defile until he was sure what lay ahead.

'A dozen men, Didius Flaccus. The fittest you've

got. No armour and no shields, though they can make up their own minds about swords or spears.'

Aulus turned on his heel and made for the spot that Cholon had chosen as their temporary base. The Greek was heating several items on a hardwood spit. Being covered in leaves, Aulus could not see what they consisted of but he could smell it, which meant that the soldiers toiling with axes and scythes could do likewise. Given that they had breakfasted on a cold and tasteless pulse, washed down with water from a nearby stream, such a smell was likely to start a mutiny.

'Another few minutes before it's ready,' said Cholon cheerfully.

To admonish him would be pointless; his master had been trying to do that for years, with little success. The Greek made no bones about his feelings on the matter; wealthy men should behave as such, to do otherwise smacked of hypocrisy; a false act, designed to win a specious form of favour with the lower orders. They did not respect you for it, rather they despised you. Aulus was never sure if his servant was right or wrong.

'Get me out of this armour, Cholon,' he growled

The slave rushed to obey. 'Can I just loosen the straps, your honour. If I leave those birds too long, without spinning them, they'll burn.'

Aulus looked at the fire and spoke angrily. 'How many times have I told you, Cholon?'

'As many times as I've replied, master,' said the servant, totally unaffected by the tone of voice. 'It may suit your dignity to be on short commons, but it does mine no good whatsoever. I have the task of caring for you, something I shall do to my utmost.'

Aulus just sighed and lifted off his own breastplate as Cholon ran back to his roasting birds. 'I'm taking a dozen men out to scout the area south of here. Since they're unlikely to eat again today, we'll split the food amongst them.'

Cholon, leaning over his spit, sighed unhappily. There would be none left for him.

Deep, dreamless sleep. The kick brought him round quick enough and Clodius cursed and forced his eyes open, only to see Flaccus standing above him.

'On your feet, old lad. We're off to war again.'

Clodius groaned. 'I've only just got my head down.'

Flaccus sat down on his haunches and spoke quietly. 'You'll get no sympathy from me. I haven't had a chance to close my eyes, at all, so you best get up if you don't want another boot in the ribs. The general wants to take us back to the spot we visited last night. Now I've told him you're one of my best men and that I wouldn't dream of going anywhere without you.'

'You must think I'm dreaming if you expect me to believe that,' said Clodius, pulling himself up.

Flaccus was smiling, which was rare. 'Bit of luck really, when you think on it. Tunic only, no helmet or armour. Take a spear or sword, but not both. Seems we're set to run back.'

The vultures wheeled overhead, and carrion crow filled the trees, squawking noisily, angry at being disturbed and the ashes of the fire were still hot. Aulus looked at the pile of bodies, rigid now and drained of blood. All their weapons and armour had been taken and as a final insult the bodies of the women had been thrown on top of the men, arranged so that they seemed to be indulging in grotesque sexual couplings. Trebonius was in there somewhere; that is if enough of him had survived to be identified. They would need a proper pyre, of course, but that would have to wait. Aulus started to walk about the place, looking for clues as to the identity of the men who had done this. Flaccus stayed on the crest of the hill with Clodius, looking south, ostensibly keeping a lookout.

'Slip along the ridge and see if our loot's still there,' he said softly.

'What if the general sees me?'

'Then I'll tell him you've been caught short. Perhaps all that rich food he gave us didn't agree with you.'

Clodius dropped back out of sight and headed to his left, sword out in front, counting the paces as he walked. The disturbed state of the ground around the base of the pine tree told him all he needed to know but he went to have a proper look anyway. The hole that Flaccus had dug was empty, the earth scattered all around and the thorn bush had been hacked back to make access easier. He swore under his breath, not only for the loss of the money but for the fact that he would have to go back and tell Flaccus they were still poor.

'So much for all his damned prayers.'

Clodius turned and went up to the crest to look down into the clearing, with the charred frame of the wagon that he had set alight just below. He could see, in the long grass on the hillside, that those searching had left an impression and no doubt that was how they found the cache. Flaccus had not thought of that. Clodius had gone up and down from the wagon more than a dozen times. They could not see the result in the dark, but in daylight the flattened grass that marked his journey must have looked damn near like a proper path. It would have led those searching right to the spot and that made him curse under his breath again. Clodius would have been content to have what he could have carried in his belt; now, thanks to Flaccus's greed in trying to steal the lot, they had nothing at all.

His foot kicked the small pile of coins as he turned, causing them to clink. Someone had dropped them in the grass, and had either been unable to find them, or too laden to care. He bent and picked them up, gold, four of them in all, enough for a few good nights out, but a far cry from what they could have had. He put them in his belt and headed back towards the main body.

Aulus Cornelius looked at the small pile of evidence he and his soldiers had accumulated, and saw that everything pointed to the attackers being Illyrians, rather than the Epirotes from the south. Not that there was much; some cloth, a few bits of broken pottery, a buckle from a sword belt. The most telling thing was a decorated wine gourd. The carvings were quite distinctive, but if anything travelled far and wide, it was a flask made to hold wine. He disliked the idea, but he would have to go even further south to look for clues. The people who had left this clearing had gone that way; so must he.

One look at the centurion was enough. Clodius shrugged and opened his mouth to explain, but the general shouting orders for the two of them to join him cut off his words. Flaccus moved down the slope immediately and Clodius spurted to catch him.

'Gone,' he said.

'All of it?' asked Flaccus with a catch in his throat. 'That soothsayer...'

'Later,' replied Clodius, as they came abreast of their commander. Aulus turned and started to jog south, his men at his heels. They left the clearing and the bodies and as soon as the sound of their presence faded, the vultures came back to feed.

'That's not a bunch of rebels, it's an army.'

Normally sparing in his use of words, this statement from Aulus marked the level of his surprise, since those he had just used were superfluous. The road before them dropped away steeply, twisting left and right as it wound its way down to the plain below. The whole landscape was covered with marching men, all heading in their direction.

'Where have they all come from?' asked Flaccus.

'Dacia!' replied Aulus emphatically. 'They've been supporting the Illyrian insurrection for years. I knew it didn't smell right. They probably incited the Epirotes to rebel as well.'

'What about the lot we saw last night?'

'Poor Trebonius,' he sighed. They knew that their general meant 'poor everybody'. 'The tribesmen he ran into were Illyrians heading south.'

'To join up with this lot?' asked Flaccus.

'They can't know we're at Thralaxas, otherwise they would never have come on. Common sense would have told them to halt and fortify the pass, which means that we've moved a lot faster than they think. They expect to get back through there without a fight.'

The Illyrians had no need to come south at all, of course. They could have waited until the promised allies arrived. Did that mean they were prey to doubt, unsure that the promised support would be forthcoming? If so, that indicated a lack of trust, even the possibility of divided loyalties. Aulus did not analyse these thoughts in too great a depth, being experienced enough to know that war was an art most often conducted in a form of mental semi-darkness. He also knew that good generalship, once you had assembled all the available information, was instinctive. Without another word, he spun on his heel and started jogging back to the north. His soldiers dragged themselves to their feet and followed. They passed the heap of bodies again, but there was no time to bury or burn anyone. All they could do as they jogged past was offer a quick prayer for their souls to the Goddess *Dea Tactica*.

The sun was getting low in the sky; Flaccus stood beside his general studying the map he was tracing in the ground with the stick. 'Tell Vegetius Flaminus to send me two more cohorts to hold the pass, plus a couple of catapults and half the cavalry. I want him to force-march his army to the east, throw a bridge across the Lisenus river and make for that plain to the south where we saw the enemy today.

Once he's there he's to fortify a camp and let them know that he's behind them. If we've held them here they will realise that there's no way forward.'

'Which means they'll turn and attack our legions,' added Flaccus happily, so carried away by the flow of the general's words that he felt no qualms about speaking.

'They might,' replied Aulus, doubtfully. 'I'm rather hoping they will see that their situation is hopeless and try and disperse.'

The centurion was shocked. 'No battle, sir?'

Aulus gave him a wry smile. 'One of the advantages, Didius Flaccus, of serving under a general who's already had a triumph, is that he has no desire left to sacrifice troops in order to advance his career. I hope for a victory, I can forgo the battle.'

'What about the Illyrian rebels?'

'Probably the only thing that's sustained them is the hope of a general uprising in the whole region. Once this is over, I think their rebellion will finally collapse.'

He handed Flaccus a scroll tied with a red ribbon. 'Anyway, I've had Cholon write out the orders, so there'll be no chance of an error.'

Having lost one fortune, Flaccus was even more painfully aware than usual of the prospect of booty; it could be that the only fighting would be here at the Pass of Thralaxas. The enemy was coming this way, and they might have his money with them. He pulled himself to attention. 'With respect, General, could I detail someone else to carry your despatch.'

'You wish to stay and fight?'

'I do, sir.'

'Sorry, Flaccus. You're the most senior man here, apart from me. I can't go and leave you with such a heavy responsibility, nor can I deliver such a message in the hands of any old ranker. You are one of the senior centurions in the legion. You have enough weight to emphasise the importance of what you carry. However, once you have delivered your despatch, you may return with the reinforcements.'

Clodius had had no chance to talk to Flaccus. Not that either of them had much time now, with the centurion making ready to leave and, really, what was there to say? He told Flaccus what he had found and why he thought the cache had been discovered. The grizzled veteran just grunted, though the look he gave Clodius left the ranker in no doubt that he held him to blame. Stammering slightly, he opened his belt and reached into the cavity holding the gold coins.

'I did find this in the grass. One of them must have dropped them.' Clodius held his hand out, with the four gold coins gleaming in his palm, trying to sound cheerful. 'Not much after what we had, I know. But better than a poke in the eye, eh! He took two coins and offered them to Flaccus. 'Half each.'

The centurion took the coins, looking at those Clodius still held in his hand, then, with a swift motion he snatched them as well. Clodius made to protest, but Flaccus gave him a very hard look. 'That'll go some way to paying off the money you owe me. Let's hope you have some luck here as well mate, 'cause I retire soon, and I want that lot paid back before I go home. Every sesterces!'

CHAPTER TWENTY-FIVE

Aulus, having sent Flaccus off with his orders, inspected the fortifications, pronounced himself satisfied with the work, then set his tired men to collecting heavy stones for the catapults he hoped would arrive shortly. The part they would play in slowing down the enemy stifled any dissent. Aulus intended to site them so that the stones, thrown against the steep rocks of the pass, would bounce off the enclosing walls and carry on down the narrow defile. If both catapults could be brought to bear at the same time, it would set up a barrage that no troops could withstand.

'That's the first phase,' he said the following morning, to troops now rested and fed. 'When our reinforcements arrive, I intend to put one cohort on the top of each hill so that the enemy can't outflank us. I've asked for some cavalry, as well, to use as a mobile reserve.'

Clodius had never served under a commander

who took so much trouble to explain his intentions, and no high falutin' stuff either, just plain speaking. He had been in quite a few battles and the best he had ever had was a ringing declaration of the need to do his duty, usually delivered from the oration platform by a man who would probably be well back from the actual point of fighting.

'The Dacians are a Celtic tribe, and from what we know of them they lack discipline. Celts are all right if things are going their way, but the chain of command is usually a bit fractured, with various thanes vying for the leadership, so any reverse tends to lead to a lot of internal dissension. Their allies, both Epirote and Illyrian, can't be anything more than a scratch force of malcontents, not soldiers in the sense we use the term. They will outnumber us heavily, but we have several things in our favour. Training for one plus the fact that we are fighting in a strong defensive position and the knowledge that we only have to hold until Vegetius gets astride their rear.'

Aulus paused for a second, then smiled at the assembled men. 'And courage, of course, in abundance.'

He had skirmishers set well down the pass, with runners out even further ahead, to keep him informed as to what point the enemy had reached. They were coming on at a steady pace, probably still unaware that the Romans held the pass. If they continued their advance units would be upon him the following day. Aulus had to fight hard not to keep looking to the north. He had deliberately declined to say precisely when he expected reinforcements, so as to avoid a creeping sense of gloom overtaking his men as the day wore on. The nagging fear that misfortune could undo all his plans never left him. Should he have sent a strong party with the centurion? Flaccus, alone, even if he was on the general's own horse, could easily fall off. Rebels or just plain robbers could ambush him; enough people had been dispossessed by Vegetius' depredations. The countryside fairly teemed with them, half starving, and willing to kill for a bite to eat. Would they take on a well-armed man?

He had an odd feeling, for no prospective battle before had affected him like this. It was not that he was outnumbered – Romans usually were – nor that he was in an exposed position. It was really the idea of not being totally in control. His men, who spent a good deal of their time looking north, seeking the tell-tale dust clouds that would herald the approach of more troops, also glanced at him constantly, so that they could be reassured by his calm exterior. Cholon watched him carefully too, but he was not fooled, sensing that his master was troubled. Finally he decided to speak, as a way of breaking the growing tension.

'Might I suggest that we do a little hunting, your honour. It will relieve the boredom and stock up our larder. After all, we don't know how long we're going to be here.'

'If the men see me leave here, carrying my weapons, on your horse, Cholon, I hardly think it will make them feel secure.'

'Then let me take some of them.'

Aulus shook his head. 'They have a hard fight ahead, let them rest. Besides, the reinforcements will bring up supplies.'

Cholon paused for a moment, turning his head to look at the barren rocky landscape and the men dotted around it. 'They'd all like to know the answer to one question. Am I permitted to ask it?'

Aulus gave him a grim smile. 'If there's no sign of the men I've sent for by dawn tomorrow, I would say we are in trouble.'

'Dawn tomorrow?' said Cholon surprised. 'Surely they'll be here before that.'

'The cavalry, yes. The foot soldiers could take longer. I shall be annoyed if Vegetius has instructed them to stay together.'

'When will the enemy attack?' asked Cholon.

Aulus spun away, suddenly angered by the interrogation, his reply unusually harsh. 'Tomorrow, not at first light and before you ask what time, I don't know.'

He walked around the area, checking on his men, who sat in every patch of shade. One of them was using a stick to draw in the red sandy earth, exposing as he did so the darker crimson soil underneath and Aulus stopped to look. The blood drained from his face as he saw the outline and he stood, rock still, staring at it. The look brought the trooper jumping to attention and the stick dropped from his hand so his fist could crash into his breastplate.

'General!'

The sound, as well as the crisply delivered acknowledgement, seemed to break whatever spell gripped Aulus. He looked at the trooper, and fought with his tumultuous emotions in an effort to smile. These men needed reassurance, not their commander's probably groundless superstitions about an old prophecy.

'Sit down, soldier. Don't waste your energy saluting me. Save it for the enemy.'

The trooper had to salute again, regulations demanded it. Aulus merely nodded, looked at the ground again thinking that the dark crimson earth that stick had exposed looked very like blood, frowned, then walked away to continue his rounds. The soldier waited till he was gone before he sat down. He then picked up the stick and tried to add the finishing touches to the drawing. It was far from perfect, but it was a fair representation of the eagle charm that Fulmina had taken off Aquila's foot that day Clodius had found him in the woods.

Vegetius Flaminus, fresh from bathing, sat upright in his Curile chair, reading the despatch. He had a flagon of wine at his elbow and a richly decorated cup in his free hand. Flaccus stood to attention, covered in dust, dying for something to drink. If he had noted the centurion's condition, the governor had not bothered to offer him any refreshment. Finally he finished reading, took a large swig of wine, then looked at Flaccus.

'You've personally seen the enemy forces, you say?'

'I have, sir,' the centurion replied, adding a deliberate lie. 'I'd reckon that we're equally matched in numbers.'

Vegetius leant forward, rubbing his puffy cheek with one hand. The senatorial ring on his thick finger, gold instead of iron, flashed in the light. 'It seems very foolish to place ourselves on the other side of a force that size. They will be between us and our base at Salonae.'

'The commander, Aulus…'

'Not commander, Centurion!' snapped the man behind the table. 'Senator is the proper title for Aulus Cornelius Macedonicus. I am the commander in this province, by order of the very body he's supposed to represent.'

Flaccus said nothing for a moment, but his thoughts were in turmoil. Aulus should have come himself. The other senators, who had been part of his commission, were back in Salonae. Vegetius had no one to answer to but himself and he certainly was not going to be awed by a centurion, however senior.

'Is that clear to you, soldier?'

'Yes, sir,' replied Flaccus crisply, ignoring the insult that Vegetius had delivered by not using his rank.

'Good,' Vegetius continued smoothly. 'Please be so good as to continue. After all, I do need to know what is in the senator's mind.'

Flaccus outlined what Aulus had told him, trying, as he did so, to diminish the threat the enemy posed, without making them seem like a chimera.

'No battle? What a strange attitude to take, Centurion. It seems in my humble opinion, a touch over-sanguine to expect the enemy to melt away just because we are close behind them.' Vegetius dropped the studied languor and his voice took on a harder edge. 'It also seems to me a very foolish course to let these villains disperse, they'll only cause trouble at some future date. They have slaughtered a great number of Romans, including Publius Trebonius, so they need to be punished, and visibly so. A heap of bleached bones on the battlefield will do more to keep both provinces quiet than all of the blandishments of soft hearted, semi-retired administrators.'

A heap of bleached bones will earn you a triumph too, thought Flaccus, that is, as long as you fight the rebels in Illyricum. But he didn't say it. Vegetius Flaminus might be a slimy toad, but he had the power to break Didius Flaccus at the wheel. The man was not going to move out of his province, that was certain, since he saw no personal advantage in doing so. In that respect Aulus's plan was half-dead, but he would still need to be supported at Thralaxas, even if it was only to get away in one piece.

'It's not my place to suggest a course of action, sir, I know that.'

'But you wish to anyway,' said Vegetius coldly.

The tone made Flaccus change his tack. No point in making too overt a suggestion to this man. 'I wouldn't presume, sir, only, having been at the point where the enemy will attack, I feel I can help you come to a proper conclusion if I share what knowledge I have.'

Vegetius yawned, took a sip of wine, then spoke in a bored tone. 'Do go on.'

'Well, I doubt that the comm…senator can hold the pass without reinforcements.'

'I trust he'll have the good sense to retire in time.'

'That's just it, your honour. He doesn't know that you disagree with his instructions…'

The fist slammed down on the table, causing the flagon to jump in the air and fall over. The wine spilt out onto the floor. Vegetius, red in the face, ignored it, and shouted at Flaccus. 'Requests, Centurion. Not instructions.'

Flaccus cursed himself for using the wrong words. He did not like senior officers at all and cared nothing for their fate, and that included Macedonicus, but at least he was a proper soldier, unlike this ball of lard sitting there drinking wine and spitting venom at him.

'Those are my men up there, sir. The senior class in the legion, the best armed. The enemy will engage my troops long before they know you're not trying to outflank them by crossing the Lisenius...'

Vegetius adopted a mocking tone. 'Oh, dear me. Does the great democrat, Aulus Cornelius Macedonicus, tell his men all his plans?'

'Happen he don't but they'll guess the broad outline, your honour. They'll be well aware they're only expected to hold the pass for so long. And they're soldiers, sir, they'll know, just as I do, that if they are involved in a fight, they can't get away safely without help.'

'Your concern for your men is commendable, Centurion.' He waved the rolled despatch at Flaccus. 'My fellow senator has proposed a plan of action that I cannot agree with, not that I'm blind to his experience, you understand. I don't dispute everything he says. For instance, I agree that we must not split our army. I agree that we must fight the enemy at a place of our choosing. Where we part company is that I reserve the right to choose the place.'

He paused for a moment, as though he had not already made up his mind, but Flaccus knew that Vegetius had done that a long time before. 'Therefore, Didius Flaccus, I suggest you return to the Pass at Thralaxas. Tell Aulus Cornelius Macedonicus that the Governor of Illyricum declines to endanger his troops on this hair-brained plan. You may further suggest that the wisest course of action for the cohort at the pass would be for them to withdraw. Let the enemy through to the north, let them find a point where we can engage them in strength.'

Flaccus had to fight to stay at attention. His heart felt heavy and, being tired, he wanted nothing more than to let his shoulders slump. Even though he knew the answer, he had to ask the question. 'Reinforcements, sir? Perhaps some cavalry.'

'No, Centurion. I am sorry.' The insincere tone of solicitation in Vegetius's voice made Flaccus seriously harbour the thought of killing him. 'You look tired, my man. I think you should get some rest before you start back.'

'There's no time,' snapped Flaccus.

Vegetius smiled and spoke softly. 'You're very likely correct.'

Aulus could not sleep; that drawing, the eagle in the sand, haunted him, preying on the nagging doubts and making them worse. The words the Sybil had used, her rasping voice in that dank smelly cave rang in his ears.

'Look aloft if you dare, though what you fear cannot fly, both will face it before you die.'

There was no sign of the men he needed yet he had no idea if they were on the way. All his instincts told him that something had gone wrong and he now had to decide what to do about it. He had called in his runners and skirmishers at twilight so everyone was safe for the moment, but if they stayed here, without support, they would not last very long. Now it was dark the men had been fed and told to rest, though they had not been told how perilous was their situation, but Aulus suspected they had been in the legions long enough to have worked that out for themselves, especially since he had ordered them to sleep in their armour. He paced up and down the stoop at the rear of the palisade, perspiring slightly in the warm night air, exchanging the odd word with the sentries, mulling over his options.

There were really only two, without substantially more troops; to stay here and die, or to make a run for it at first light. Even that was a bit of a forlorn hope given some of the Dacian forces were mounted on swift ponies. Really, he had reached the point of decision; if he wanted to get away in safety, he had to go now, even if that meant a forced march in darkness. It was that eagle, drawn in the sand which decided him. If the prophecy was correct, he was endangering the lives of all these men for a curse that applied only to him. He turned to issue the orders, but the chink of metal against rock stopped him, just as it alerted all the sentries on the palisade. The men in the defile must have realised that further subterfuge was useless for whoever led them gave a loud, blood-curdling yell. This was taken up by the others, their war cries echoed off the narrow gorge, as a whole wave of attackers seemed to emerge from the gloom to assault the wooden wall. Aulus, sword out, yelled at the top of his voice, calling his men to arms. He switched the sword to his left hand and grabbed a spear from the pile stacked on the step.

A helmeted head appeared over the palisade, ahead of the man who was struggling to get up, his foot scraping the rough trunks as he sought a foothold. The butt of Aulus's spear took him full in the face, sending him spinning back onto those trying to follow him. The air was full of sound, metal striking metal, the thud of axes cutting toe-holds in the wood, all overlaid with shouting and cursing and the occasional screech as a man was wounded. Aulus shouted at the top of his voice to hurry the soldiers who had been asleep, then leant over the spiked top of the wall and jabbed furiously into the mass of attackers at the base. Dimly he heard the pounding feet, as the rest of the cohort rushed to arms.

'Secure the ends, men,' he shouted, knowing the insurgents would concentrate on the two points where the palisade joined the rocky sides of the defile. The spear was hauled out of his hand, the force his opponent exerted nearly toppling him over the edge and as the spikes raked his breastplate he felt himself falling forward. Aulus stabbed downwards with his sword and he heard the cries as he made contact, felt the jarring feeling, in his arm, as his weapon pierced soft flesh, to break the solid bone beneath. He was off balance and set to fall into the crowd of attackers until hands grabbed his legs and hauled him upright. Backing off, he looked along the stoop to see that all his men were now engaged, with no visible sign that the attackers were making any progress. Dimly, in his mind, he registered that the enemy had surprised him; they had come on at night when he had expected them to stop. Reinforced properly, it would make little difference, this first assault could probably be contained by the small number of men he commanded.

The other thought that followed was less pleasant. For some reason his mind turned to Leonidas and his Spartans, holding the pass at

Thermopyle. They had died there, seeking to hold the might of the Persian Army at bay. Leonidas could probably have got away, melting into the mountains to make his escape, but he declined to withdraw, and Aulus knew that was now the only course open to him and the men he commanded. He wondered if he had the courage to take it for this would be no paced withdrawal. Aulus Macedonicus would be forced to run away like a hunted fox, but there was no time for speculation.

First things first; once he had beaten off this assault he could look at the possibilities with more clarity. He leapt forward to the palisade, struck out again and again at his enemies, using the noise of battle to cover the shouts he issued to *Mars* and *Jupiter*, praying to them to send help. Combat, and the need to solve a constant stream of pressing problems, had driven all thoughts of that sand-drawn eagle from his mind.

CHAPTER TWENTY-SIX

The image of that eagle drawn in the sand returned to Aulus soon enough, though not to haunt him. The battle was over with few casualties and the enemy, judging by the bodies at the bottom of the wooden wall, had suffered badly. Aulus was surprised, himself, at the feeling of inner peace; he felt like a traveller who had come to a safe haven, after a difficult, dangerous journey. His fate was in the hands of the gods now and that one fact seemed to release him from all his cares and there was no time, before he called his men together, in which to review his life, to examine his soul. He would meet his destiny without that luxury, simply because there was too much to do.

'They'll come again during darkness, if only to keep us awake.'

Aulus paused because he disliked the words forming in his mind and was reluctant to use them, never having been comfortable with character assassination, especially with a member of his own class. Not that his opinion of their titular commander was a secret and these men had served under Vegetius for years, so any implied criticism of the governor would barely affect the deep contempt in which his soldiers already held the man.

'I don't think we can anticipate any help. For reasons I don't yet know, Vegetius Flaminus has not sent the troops I requested.' There was a grumbling in the ranks at that. He saw Cholon making his way amongst the men, doling out the remaining food. That alone would tell them part of what he intended, but not all. 'If we stay here we will die, and to no purpose, but to get away, in one piece, will be damned hard unless we can inflict some kind of check on the enemy. We have to achieve two things. The first is to make them think we're more numerous than we actually are and the second is to give them such a bloody nose, during one of their attacks, that they'll draw off until daylight.'

The men listened eagerly as Aulus explained his plan. They knew it was desperate, just as he did himself, yet they all accepted the fiction that success would save them. No one articulated the truth that they would not all get away; there would be casualties and even if they were alive they would have to be left behind, but the thought was present and that sent a shiver through the ranks. Those who had not seen the atrocities inflicted on Trebonius and his men had certainly heard about them.

'Once we're done, successful or not, those still fit and garbed are to immediately dump their armour. Everyone to take food, water and a single weapon, then head north. Stay together on the road until daylight. As soon as you can see enough to obscure your trail, split up into smaller parties and head inland. Make your way back to the legions as best you can.'

Aulus gave the orders that would split the men into two equal groups, then called on Cholon. Taking him by the arm, he hauled his servant out of earshot.

'I want you out of here.' He could see his servant start to protest in the glare from the flickering fire. 'You're no soldier, Cholon. Therefore, you are useless in a fight.'

'I am still your body slave,' replied the Greek.

'Do you realise that I cannot leave here?'

'I suspected as much, master.'

'Yet you still want to stay?'

'When they tell stories of the death of Aulus Cornelius Macedonicus, perhaps they will mention that his faithful Greek body slave…'

Aulus cut in. 'You will be freed in my will.'

Cholon swallowed hard, paused for a moment, then took up exactly where he left off. '…his faithful Greek body slave stayed true to his master. Perhaps, in legend, I will become a hero too.'

'Are you so sure that I will become a hero?'

There was a slight catch in Cholon's voice as he replied. 'You are now, and you always have been to me.'

'We're not so very different, we Greeks and Romans,' said Aulus softly. 'All we crave is the good opinion of posterity.'

Cholon would have loved the right to proffer one distinction. How very different things would have been if they had both been Greek. Aulus, less the upright Roman, would, in a Hellenistic society, have allowed the affection they felt for each other some expression. He had watched this man, whom he loved, suffer, just as he himself had suffered, seeing his love ignored. But at least Aulus had been kind to him, unlike his Claudia, whose coldness after the birth of that child had wounded Aulus cruelly. If only he had turned to Cholon then, he would have found all the solace he required. The Greek slave sighed inwardly. It was not to be.

'There is something I want you very much to do. It's important, and you are the only person I can entrust to carry it out.'

Cholon had known Aulus too long to be fooled. Whatever task his master had thought up, it had just this very second germinated in his mind, even if he did try to make it sound as though he had been thinking it all along.

'Some of these men will die, either here, or before

they get back to Salonae. I feel responsible for that. I want you to copy the regimental roll and note the names of all those who don't return.'

His servant cut in. 'That assumes I shall survive.'

A hard note crept into Aulus's voice but Cholon was not fooled by that either. His master would have to order him to leave and he was cranking himself up to it.

'You might not. You might fall off your horse. If you do, get up and walk. I want you to seek out the dependants of those who fall and make sure that they are provided for. Now be so good as to fetch something to write with, so that I can give you a codicil to add to my will.'

Clodius looked up at the stars. No singing now, but he was talking to his gods nevertheless. Would he survive the night? He would be lucky to make it through the initial attack. All very well for the general to say that slopes too steep to climb were not too steep to run down, but he could break a leg if he failed to find one of the enemy to cushion his fall. A whispered command was passed along the line and Clodius pushed forward to the edge of the steep incline. The torches on the palisade cast a strong light on the area just in front of the wooden stakes, at the same time throwing the stoop itself into darkness so that the spears and helmets lining the wall were barely visible. They didn't look like much from up here; perhaps, in the gloom, the attackers would think the wall was manned with the full Roman strength. He could not see any of the men crouched below the parapet. They were completely in shadow.

Noise travels upwards, especially in a confined space, so those attackers, coming down the gorge, gave ample notice of their approach. They would have to charge the wall but if Aulus was right it would be a half-hearted assault, designed to keep the defenders on their toes rather than to inflict any real damage. It was up to those left on the wall, if they did attack, to tempt them to a proper fight so that once committed, the men on the hills could drop behind them and hopefully kill the entire force. Clodius grasped his spear as the attackers crept forward; when they reached the circle of light they emitted a fearsome yell and rushed forward. They only made half the distance, threw a few untipped spears wildly, before immediately running back out of range. So far so good, the general had been right, they were trying to draw fire, keep the defenders awake and deplete the Roman stock of javelins. When nothing happened at all, confusion set in and they ran forward again, with still no response from those on the wall.

Would they fall for it? Would they look closely and see that the shields and spears were just that, with nothing behind them. A few minutes passed then suddenly, without any preliminary shout, a body of properly armed spearmen rushed forward. They got much closer, hurling their weapons with some accuracy before turning round and heading back quickly to join their comrades. Most of the spears missed, some flying harmlessly past, while others stuck in the wooden wall. But three or four struck their targets, and the shields and helmets, supported only by a thin piece of wood, fell clattering to the ground.

Someone had command down below. There followed a single shout as he ordered his men to take the palisade and suddenly the well-lit area was full of running, screaming men. The defenders, crouched down behind the wooden stakes, kept their places until the attackers reached the wall and started to climb. Clodius, tensed like a coiled snake, heard Aulus give the command. With his fellow legionaries he launched himself forward and leapt down the sheer side of the gorge, fighting to keep his balance as it steepened, feeling as if he was flying as his feet took what purchase they could on the near perpendicular surface. In a blur, he saw the Romans who had been hiding stand up and engage the attackers climbing the wall and saw the faces raised in panic at the sound and fury of a hundred and fifty men attacking from above. Clodius hurled his spear into one of those faces only a split second before he landed right on top of the man it had struck, his momentum carrying them both down to the ground.

The gorge was full of fighting men, with the original attackers not only cut off, but with a great number of their enemies actually in their midst. Some threw down their weapons, only to die unarmed; this was no time to give quarter. Others fought furiously, against odds that lengthened against them every minute. Clodius was on his feet now. One leg would not support him at all and he wondered if it was broken. His back was to the rocky side of the defile and he hacked and slashed at anyone who came within his reach. Time seemed to stand still and it was impossible to make any sense of the melee before him; what was happening beyond he could not see. Then a space cleared in front of him; the fight was slackening, as the enemy fell, wounded or dead. Those Romans who had dropped down into the gorge were pressing the rebels back against the wooded wall, there to die from overhead spear thrusts. The fight moved past Clodius and he tried to follow but fell flat, into the sandy, blood-soaked soil.

He hauled himself back on to his good foot and leant back on the rocks, cursing under his breath. Clodius had not even felt the sword slash across the back of his knee, but he could feel the pain now, getting steadily worse. His leg was gone; it would not support his weight and regardless of the fact that the general had not actually said it, they all knew that any one who could not walk, could not escape.

The dead, Romans and a number of their enemies, were lashed to the palisade in full legionary dress. The wounded lay on the step ready to haul themselves up when ordered. Futile in itself, any resistance they could offer would give to their departed comrades a better chance of survival. They had pulled the remaining bodies away from the base of the wooded wall and heaped them up in a pile further down the gorge. When their enemies came, they would need to clamber over their dead before they could assault the defences.

Clodius, lying back with his eyes closed, rubbed the rough bandage that encased his leg. Sleep was impossible with the pain he felt, yet he knew he was in better straits than some of his fellows. Aulus had put several of the more seriously wounded out of their misery, but the cries of suffering men filled the night air, despite the orders to remain silent. There was a space beside him and he felt, rather than saw, someone fill it, the air brushing against his shoulder. He opened his eyes to find that Aulus Cornelius Macedonicus himself had sat down.

'How long now, General?' he asked.

'It will be daylight in an hour. They're sure to attack at first light.'

'Just before's a good time,' said Clodius.

It was hardly customary for a ranker like him to talk thus to a senior officer but approaching death made such distinctions superfluous. Besides, this general seemed to be the most approachable of men. Aulus realised that he was sitting beside the man who had drawn that eagle in the earth. He looked at him, noting the grey in the hair and the lines on the face.

'How long have you been in service, soldier?'

'Seven years now, General. I was in the legions before that mind. Helped to capture this godforsaken place in the year of the Scipian consulship.'

'Recalled?' asked Aulus.

Clodius laughed. No point in keeping up the pretence of being Dabo now, so he informed Aulus about his background and why it had forced him back into the legions. Given a chance to moan he took it with a vengeance, though his normal bitter tone was gone. He told the general of how he had switched places with Dabo and the bargain they had struck. Clodius could not help noticing that this information seemed to distress him.

'I sent my slave, Cholon, away with instructions to seek out your dependants. If he's not careful, the man who's prospered by your service stands to gain even more with your death.'

'He wouldn't dare,' said Clodius, angrily, but without much conviction.

'You have dependants, I take it?'

'I do, General, three grown-up children. They've left home now, so they don't really count, but I have a wife and an eleven-year-old boy, though he's not my own flesh and blood.'

'Adopted?'

'Not proper, your honour. I found him deep in the woods one morning. Been exposed.'

'In the woods?' asked Aulus.

'That's right. Whoever left him didn't want him found. If I hadn't been drinkin' the night before I'd never have come across the poor little sod in the first place.' It was plain that Aulus could not make sense of this, so he explained. 'When I'm a bit the worse for drink, I tend to go out into the country and sing to the gods.' And a fat lot of good it's done me, he thought to himself. When he spoke his tone was hard. 'That's how I found Aquila.'

Aulus stiffened slightly. 'That's the boy's name, Aquila?'

All Clodius's resentment vanished, hearing the general say the name; there was no point in it now. Instead he recalled the little fellow who had relished being thrown in the air, who paddled in the river like a dog and called him Papa.

'Fine little fellow, your honour, hair like fresh straw and tall for his age. Just coming up four the last time I clapped eyes on him. I ain't seen him in over seven years on account of that bastard Flaccus, saving your presence, but I've heard he's growing tall and straight, head and shoulders above his mates. We tried to find out who he belonged to.'

Aulus's mind drifted back to that day, so many years before, when he had placed a small bundle in a thickly wooded spot. Nothing in his life had ever been the same since then. 'If he was left in the woods you might have been unwelcome.'

Clodius slapped the wood of the step with his hand. 'That's what I said but my missus wouldn't have it. You see, your honour, he had this charm around his foot, a valuable one. My missus, Fulmina, insisted someone wanted him alive and that charm was the signal. Happen she was right. We looked, but we couldn't find out who he belonged to. I wanted to sell that charm, it being gold, but Fulmina wouldn't hear of it on account of her dreams. Women!'

Aulus was still thinking of the night that child was born and the events leading up to it. His silence allowed Clodius to continue. 'Said our little foundling child was destined to be a great soldier. Fulmina, in her dreams, saw him in a triumphal chariot, with a laurel wreath round his head. You know what women are like about dreams. Any road, we stopped looking. Ask me, whoever sired him wasn't from round my area.'

'Which is?'

'Near Aprilium, General.'

'How near?' asked Aulus sharply.

'Half a league south, just off the Via Appia.'

'And the boy's how old?'

Clodius had to use his fingers to be sure. 'Eleven, since it's summer now. I found him in mid-*Febricus*, the morning after the Feast of *Lupercalia*.'

Aulus's voice was hard now. 'You're near the mountains, are you not?'

'Not near, exactly, your honour, but you can see them from my place. There's one, an extinct volcano, which has a top shaped just like a votive cup...'

Clodius stopped talking as he heard the general swear softly. It had no force in it, rather it was the curse of a man who had failed. All the eagerness was gone from his voice. 'Yesterday, I came across you when you were drawing something in the sand?'

'Well, I have to admit it's upset me. As I said, when we found the lad, he had this charm on his foot. Gold it was, with the wings picked out to show the feathers.'

'Wings?'

'Yes, General. Did I not say? The charm was shaped like an eagle in flight. If only she'd let me sell it, I wouldn't be here now.' Clodius finally put some passion into his voice. 'Damn Fulmina and her dreams.'

A great gust of air left Aulus's lungs. He recalled

Claudia, that day in the back of that wagon in Spain, and realised with a stab of despair that the truth had been there in her eyes for him to see, but he had been too stupid, or too relieved that she had survived, to see it. Like dice slowly rolling to show *Venus*, each act, each word, each long silence of hers fell into a pattern that represented the truth; that the child in her womb was there through desire not violation; that the infant he had tried to dispose of was alive. It was with a sense of despair that the one thing he had prized above everything, his honour, had made him a fool, such a one that the only word for it was *Hubris*.

'I shouldn't go sneering at women's dreams, my friend,' said Aulus sadly. 'They have a way of coming true.'

'They're moving, General,' called a voice from along the other end of the palisade. Aulus looked up. The first tinge of the false dawn lit the sky.

'You were right, soldier,' he said, pulling himself up. He reached down to help Clodius to his feet.

'Could you help me lash myself to the palisade, General? I can't fight balanced on one leg.' Aulus took the rope and wound it round the spiked top of the defensive wall. Clodius spoke again, bitterness in his voice, moaning to the very end. 'Don't suppose we'll get a proper burial either.'

'I've done my best, soldier,' his commander replied.

Clodius's thoughts had moved on, so he failed even to register the answer. 'General, I don't suppose you have a spare coin on you.'

Aulus could not know that for Clodius scrounging was a lifetime's habit. He reached into his belt and produced a gold denarii, placing it in the legionary's hand. 'Make sure you don't swallow it.'

Clodius looked down at the coin, winking at him in the light from the flickering torches. His voice was low and even. 'A piece of my own gold, at last!'

The enemy had removed their dead and in doing so had slowed their attack so, by the time they were ready, the sky was lightening to the east. They approached the palisade, stopping just out of range.

'Gold,' said Clodius in a louder voice to the man nearest him, holding up the coin. 'It's brought me nothing but trouble.'

He slipped it under his tongue just as the enemy started their charge. He wasn't thinking about approaching death, he was wondering what his general was doing carrying a torch, now that it was getting light.

The gaps were too big, they couldn't hold the line. The fighting was on the step now, with the wounded men at an even greater disadvantage. Aulus was bleeding from more than a dozen wounds, so there was no point in waiting any longer. He managed to stab the enemy nearest to him, creating enough of an opening, though it was hard to push his way out, with all these men intent on killing him. His mind registered the spear that gored its way into his side and the torch nearly dropped out of his hand, but he managed to hold on to it, long enough to drop it onto the oil-soaked brushwood stacked against the palisade. The flames shot up immediately from the tinder dry faggots.

'A proper burial, soldier,' he said.

No one heard the words since no Roman was alive to listen. Aulus died, as the flames licked around him, from dozens of sword thrusts, in his mind trying to conjure up an image of a small boy, with red-gold hair and a strange name, somehow mixed up with a prophecy he had heard when only a child himself. He saw the eagle, his destiny, drawn in the sand and his lips formed the word 'Aquila'. But there was no breath left to say it, only the vision of that same object round Claudia's neck, mixed with curses and another image; that of the man who had owned it originally, a man he would never now have the pleasure of killing.

Several leagues to the north Flaccus and Cholon sat quietly on their horses. The centurion was near dead with fatigue, the slave red-eyed from copious weeping. They could see, to the south of them, the smoke billowing up from the burning wall; smoke that marked the funeral pyre of Aulus Cornelius Macedonicus and his remaining legionaries.

CHAPTER TWENTY-SEVEN

'Kill them all, Trebener. Their skulls will decorate the walls of your dwelling and bring you much respect.'

The Roman soldiers trapped in the Iberian defile did not hear these words but they could see above them the man who had uttered them. Tall, with red-gold hair, he was armed only with a heavy *falcata*, simply dressed apart from one gold object at his throat, which caught the sun and flashed as he made a wide sweep with his arm to encompass the intended victims.

'I cannot do that, Brennos.'

The man who answered was very different; small beside Brennos, he had dark hair over pale facial skin and was decorated as a Celt-Iberian chieftain should be: on his head an elaborate helmet crowned with a sculpted boar, a thick and valuable gold torque encircled his neck and he wore several more on his arms. His chest was covered in a breastplate of hardened leather richly enhanced to exaggerate his muscular physique. Trebener, chieftain of the Averici knew the Romans well, he and his tribe living as they did in an uneasy peace, close to the settled plains which they inhabited along the Mediterranean shore. His reluctance to massacre those he saw as his enemies was not based on anything like mercy, but on self-preservation; if one thing was guaranteed to bring down upon his tribe massive retribution from the most powerful state in the world, it would be a pile of dead legionary bodies crying out for vengeance.

'It would be madness to kill them all.'

'Then let them all go,' Brennos replied.

Trebener looked around at the members of his tribe, in truth not one tenth of the warriors he could muster and of that number only a third had set out to raid some cattle from the coastal pasture. It was a common enough incursion, which usually resulted in a desultory pursuit, soon abandoned when the Averici got into the hills that marked the boundary between the interior and the Roman settlements of Hither Spain. If they had moved at their normal pace they would have easily outrun the chase. It had been Brennos's notion to move slowly, to see how far the Romans would come, and the fool of a centurion below had taken the bait and kept on after the raiding tribesmen, seemingly determined to teach them a lesson. In doing so he had led his men into a trap against numbers he could not hope to best, and he was now confined in a narrow defile that was the worst possible place to deploy the normal Roman tactics. The man was an idiot, but he was also one who had set the Averici chieftain a problem which he would rather not have. To kill eighty Roman soldiers would mean retribution at some point in the future; to let them go could bring trouble even sooner from the men he led, who would see such an act as one of weakness from a chieftain who was getting too old to properly command unquestioning respect.

'I cannot do that either.'

'You must do one or the other, Trebener, for no other course will make you friends, or reduce the number of your enemies.'

Brennos took the gold object in his hand, drawing Trebener's eye towards what he knew to be the Druid shaman's talisman. On a gold chain, shaped like an eagle in flight, it was recognised by those who saw him clutch it as a source of some kind of spiritual power. It had been in Brennos's hand when he went amongst Trebener's warriors and the ideas with which he seduced them were just as ambitious as those he had employed in the past; that Rome was mighty, but could be destroyed. It was twelve summers since Brennos had persuaded the tribes of the interior to combine against Rome and act like an army instead of a mob; twelve summers since they had so very nearly humbled a whole legionary army on the very plains they had just raided.

Had Brennos known this would happen, for he had the gift to foretell the future? It was telling that, even here, surrounded by the men of his own tribe, Trebener had too much fear of the power of Brennos to demand of him an answer to that question. He scanned the horizon to the east, seeking the tell-tale signs of the mass movement of men, a trail of dust that would signal a second pursuit. A wisp of a cloud was all he could see, a few miles distant, one caused by a small group, probably on horses given the speed of their movement – nothing for him to worry about. The Averici chief stepped forward and looked down at the Romans in the defile. Swords sheathed, spears and shields down, these legionaries knew that they faced death.

Damn them, he thought, why had they not stopped as they usually did; why did they have to face him with such a dilemma. 'Get me the centurion.'

Brennos was looking at the dust cloud thrown up by the approaching horsemen, sure in his mind that he knew who led them, the son of the Roman general he had fought and so nearly beaten years before. Aulus Cornelius had been the name of the father, Titus was that of the son. Not that he had met either of them, but just as they spied on him, he sought information on them, as well as the wife of the enemy general, whom he had taken prisoner. Claudia Cornelia had been as haughty as only an aristocratic Roman lady could be, prepared to die rather than show fear, but two summers spent together, constantly on the move to avoid her husband and his soldiers had, gradually but inexorably, changed that. First had come respect, then friendship, until finally they had become lovers, and no woman Brennos had lain with since had come close to the passion she had aroused in him.

The last time he had seen her was when he sent her to a place of safety to bear the child of their union, escorted by the men he trusted most. All he knew was that they never reached their destination; the wagon in which she had been travelling had disappeared; he found the bones of his warriors where they had died trying to defend her. Claudia Cornelia and the child in her womb would be dead; Brennos could not believe that a proud Roman general, finding his wife with child by another man, would do anything other than kill her. It was something he himself would have done had the positions been reversed.

Titus Cornelius reined in his horse as soon as he saw the flashes from the Averici weapons and from that moment moved forward over the uneven ground with extreme caution; with an escort of a dozen men he was not keen to get too close. How could the fool of a centurion lead his whole command this far into the hills, in pursuit of a few tribesmen and a herd of cattle? It was a standing instruction never to pursue the tribes unless their raiding became too troublesome, and then the Romans would mount a punitive raid in force to subdue them. Most of the time a little judicious bribery kept them in the mountains. The hope that he would come up with the soldiers and turn them back had faded as soon as he saw the sun glinting on the tips of what he was sure were tribal spears.

He stopped his horse abruptly, so quickly that the men riding behind nearly collided with him. A thought came that made, if not sense, certainly provided a reason as to why the pursuit had come so far. 'He's here.'

'Sir?' asked the rider behind him.

'Brennos. He's here. I can feel it.'

Those cavalrymen he could not see pulled faces, for the tribune's fixation with the Celtic chieftain Brennos was no secret. There had, it was true, been an increase in raids by the various tribes up and down the frontier, so many and so frequent that it hinted at some kind of coordination. No one doubted this Brennos character to be dangerous but the idea that he, who lived several weeks' march away in the deep interior, would be here, leading a cattle raid, was a joke.

'You mean that trickster, sir?'

'He's no trickster.'

'Happen he is your honour, seeing as how, if'n you're right, he has managed to disappear a hundred of our men.'

'More likely we'll find them up ahead, in a heap of splintered bones.'

Titus could feel the sentiment even if he was not looking at the cavalrymen; they had no desire to join that heap, nor had the man leading them, but he knew that he had to keep going forward, if only to find out what had happened. He held up a wetted finger to feel the wind, which with the heat of the day was in the west, coming off the land, then he dismounted.

'Stay here and rest the mounts, but don't let them feed.' The cavalrymen nodded, it being a bad idea to let a horse graze if you might have to flee at a gallop; a full stomach slowed them down. 'Gather some brushwood and tie it to their tails. If we have to run I want to set up a dust storm in our wake.' Seeing a look of curiosity he added, 'Only an idiot would ride flat out on rough terrain when he can't see where he's going.'

'These are tribesmen, your honour,' opined one horse soldier, in a voice that did nothing to hide his contempt.

'And that is a ruse they taught me many years ago.'

'Thinks he knows it all,' said one soldier as Titus went forward on foot.

'He knows a damn sight more than you or I, brother. He used to play with the buggers when he was a lad.'

That creepy feeling, that Brennos was close, grew more acute the closer he got to those flashing spears, but Titus was aware that he could be deluding himself. Part of it was the unusual situation; having spent a long time in Spain, both as a boy and a full grown soldier, he felt he knew the Celt-Iberians well, certainly better than most of his peers. They were excitable, boastful, warlike and drank like fish at the endless feasts which were the centrepiece of their existence. They sang, told endless stories and quite often fought bloody encounters if in receipt of anything perceived to be an insult, but Titus never thought of them as fools, which was why he had been surprised not to come across a hundred happy legionaries marching back to the coast. Raiding tribesmen would outrun infantry regardless of how many stolen livestock they were burdened with; if they had drawn that century on it could only have been as a deliberate ploy, but to what purpose?

Not to massacre them surely, for that would mean that they would be butchered in turn. They knew what Rome would and would not let pass. Steal cattle or pigs, but not too many; never kill a

Roman farmer and leave their women alone. The rules were not written, but Titus knew they were understood because alone amongst his contemporaries, and because he had a smattering of the language, he had visited the encampments of the border tribes and had made sure that they did. Yet here he was, within a tenth of a league of this particular tribe who were stationary for a reason he dreaded, and the men he had trailed here were nowhere to be seen. It was unusual, and in his experience, every time something out of the ordinary happened in this part of the world the hand of Brennos was around somewhere.

It was almost a relief when Titus saw him, standing on the spur of a rock, looking straight at the spot where he himself stood. That it was Brennos he had no doubt even if he had never seen the man; the simplicity of the dress alone was nearly enough to identify him, but what was most telling was the feeling that he was subject to some outside influence, that the man staring at him was trying by the powerful exertion of a mystical force to crack his will, to make him turn and run away. Titus held the stare, and prayed with fierce determination to *Strenua*, the Goddess of strength and vigour. His will nearly cracked when he heard the first of the screams, horrible in themselves and made louder by the way they echoed off the surrounding hills.

They were still ringing out when the first of the

naked Romans came stumbling down the track, soon followed by another, both hunched over with one arm couching the other. When they got close Titus could hear the sobbing and it was only another moment before he saw the reason. Both had had their right hands hacked off, and when the first man came abreast the smell of cauterised flesh almost made Titus wretch. With that knowledge the screams made sense; first they had sliced of the hand, then plunged it into fire to stop the bleeding.

The next hour, as the sun fell in the sky, was mental torture, listening to the suffering of Roman soldiers as each was subjected to the same treatment. Sure that he was not going to be attacked, certain this was a demonstration of cruelty to distress him, he had his men tether their horses and give what succour they could to their wounded comrades. One rider was sent back to the settlements to fetch wagons, for these men, naked and in agony, could not walk back to safety. Then he took up station again, eyes locked with those of the man on the spur, determined to show that whatever he chose to do would not make Rome bow the knee to him.

It was hardest when, with the sun nearly gone and Brennos a silhouette against the western sky, a group of tribesmen brought forth the centurion. They had not stripped him, no doubt so that he would be recognised, but they had strapped him to some kind of frame which almost crucified the poor fool, with his legs swinging loosely. Titus wondered if they were just going to throw him into the brushwood well below, where if he did not die he would be so broken as to do so soon. Within minutes the ridge was a mass of men, all seeming to look in his direction.

'You see, Brennos,' said Trebener, 'there is always a middle way. The Romans are alive, but they will never be soldiers again.'

'I would have killed them, you know that.' His head jerked towards Titus Cornelius, wrapped in his red cloak, now barely visible as the gloom darkened the lower ground on which he stood. 'Including him.'

'And then you would be gone, Brennos.'

'Yes. It was a Roman who said about one of their enemies, let them hate us as long as they fear us. It is one lesson I am happy to take from them.'

'I am minded to grant to you the fate of our friend here. I had in mind to remove his legs so that he would remember, and perhaps pass on to others, that had he used them a little less he would still have them.'

Titus saw Brennos turn, lifting a heavy sword as he did so, recognisably a *falcata*, the most fearsome weapon in the armoury of the local tribes. Too unwieldy for most, it was carried only by those of great strength and martial skill. The shaman raised it above his head and it took no great leap of imagination to envisage the fear in the victim's eyes.

'You are a fool, Trebener.' Then he shouted, in a voice that Titus heard more than once as it bounced and echoed around the surrounding hills. 'There is only one way to deal with Rome.'

With that he brought the blade down, striking at the join between neck and body, with such force that it crunched through bone and flesh as Brennos nearly cut the centurion in half. Another sweeping blow removed the lolling head, two more the legs twitching in the throes of death. Drenched in blood from the fountain that sprang from the victim's jugular, Trebener cursed Brennos, but he could say nothing. Even if he had, it would not have been heard over the sound of his own men cheering a man they saw as a hero.

It took two days to get the wounded back to civilisation, two days in which Titus Cornelius planned the revenge he would take on those who had mutilated them. For once he would put aside any thought of humanity or understanding and react as a Roman. He would surpass his father in the way he chastised the tribes, wondering if, years ago, Aulus had been too lenient. Let him hear of this and the great Macedonicus would want to lead another army to this place to finish what he had failed to achieve ten years past.

In his mind Titus imagined himself riding at his father's side again, saw slaughtered men and cattle, for no beast or man would live, and a line of slaves. The women and children they would march into captivity. If the enemy had fields of crops they would be sown with salt, if they had wells they would poison them, forests they would burn so that anyone surviving would freeze in winter for want of the means to make a fire. Each thought of retribution piled on each other, but at the head of it all was the image of that Druid shaman hacking the centurion to death. Brennos he and his father would burn, patiently, over charcoal, and watch as the flesh fell slowly in strips off his pain-wracked body.

His commander was waiting for him as he marched, tired, hungry and covered in dust, into the command tent. That he was standing was unusual, for he was a person to have a care that his rank should be recognised. Just about to make a report, a raised hand stopped him.

'Titus Cornelius, I have for you some very sad news. Your father, the great Macedonicus, is no longer with us. You are to return to Rome immediately.'

CHAPTER TWENTY-EIGHT

———•———

Fulmina rubbed her belly again, trying to ease the pain that had been with her for months, getting steadily worse as if some beast was inside her eating at her vitals. The visit to the local healer had done little good: it had cost her a big slice of her meagre savings to be told something she already knew; how to brew an infusion of herbs, something her mother had taught her when she was a slip of a girl. She had asked Drisia to cast her bones and look into the future, but the soothsayer had claimed she could not see anything. Fulmina knew, deep down, that Drisia was lying, though she did not say so since there was nothing to do about it; it would either get better or get worse.

She had a peasant woman's attitude to life and death, accepting the one with little joy and the other as inevitable, but she had realised that she was lonely; for all his faults she missed Clodius. He was not much of a husband, but he had a good, if wayward nature and he had never beaten her. She wanted him to come home, not just for herself but to take care of the boy if anything happened to her. As she cast her mind back over the last seven years she bitterly regretted the callous messages she had sent back to him. These had been carried by men who had had the money to buy their time off, unlike poor Clodius, who had forgotten to include that provision in his bargain with Dabo. Her mind turned to her own children. Demetrius, the eldest, had opened a bakery in Rome and was doing well.

'That's one in the eye to all those doubters,' she said out loud, pulling herself to her feet. They had laughed at him when he said what he intended to do, but he had been right: city folk were sick of baking their own bread, so they flocked to his little shop, morning and afternoon, to buy it fresh. 'Maybe Demetrius will take the boy in. He's only got two of his own.'

There was no chance of her daughter taking care of him. She had eight children already and a constant struggle to feed them and the youngest son was worse than his father, Clodius. He was a true drunkard. Fulmina put her hands over her face, pressing hard. 'Why don't you come home, Clodius. Why?'

Aquila raced through the door, early for once, the huge dog Minca at his heels. 'Guess what Gadoric taught me today, Mama,' he yelled, and started spouting at her enthusiastically.

Not a single word made any sense, since he spoke in that gibberish she had been told was the shepherd's native tongue, but it was some kind of poem. All this happened while he poured water over his head, which made it even harder to comprehend, then, in between mouthfuls of food, he was busy with the comb, Fulmina's wedding present, slicking back his golden hair. The kiss he gave her barely touched her cheek, before he was gone. A stab of pain shot through her lower abdomen, and Fulmina worried over whether it was time for her to speak for it was something she dreaded, but also a matter she knew could not be left to anyone else. Should she wait up for him, or leave it till morning, when the sun was shining and the boy would go out to a day filled with lots to do? That was a way of avoiding endless questions, as well as a dark night for both of them, lots of time in which to feel miserable.

Barbinus's overseer was not noted locally for his kind heart. He was, in fact, termed a miserable bastard by all and sundry. The fire iron he had in his hand, which was waving close to Aquila's head, did nothing to dent that reputation.

'Don't you think the other female slaves knew what you two were about,' Nicos yelled. 'Mooning over each other behind that fence, sneaking off into the woods? I had it out of them at the threat of my whip when I saw you hanging about.'

Aquila did not reply, since there was really nothing to say. Only his own impatience at not seeing Sosia for three whole days, with no response to his taps on her shutters, had caused him to flout the normal rules, and enter the compound to ask for her whereabouts.

'Just you thank the gods that she was intact. If you'd laid a hand on her, Cassius Barbinus would have strung you up and me as well, for letting it happen.'

The look of incomprehension on Aquila's face must have registered. The fire iron came down to chest level and the boy felt it nudge into his ribs. Nicos stopped shouting, and instead growled at him. 'When Barbinus wants a virgin that's just what he means. Not goods soiled by the likes of you.'

'A virgin?' asked Aquila, shaking his head.

'That's right, boy. He took her, as is his right, a couple of nights ago. And then, when he'd had her, he shipped her off to Rome. If Sosia's lucky and does what her new master wants he'll like as not keep her in comfort but if she weeps, the way she did when she left here, then he'll send her to the slave market for some other bugger to try, or even flog her to a brothel.'

The overseer had turned away, shaking his head and murmuring to himself about 'tears, never heard the like'. Aquila was rooted to the spot, his mind and body churning, until he remembered the single piercing scream he had heard that night and realised that it had not, in fact, come from the throat of a terrified fox.

He would have struggled to sleep that night, anyway, but any thoughts he had were driven from his mind as he lay there listening to the painful groans of his mother as she tossed and turned in her cot. Aquila was young and eventually slumber took him, blotting out a misery that only came back to him when he had been awake for several minutes, a feeling that destroyed any desire to eat. He signalled to the dog, up and ready even if it was barely light.

'Come back here!' said Fulmina, sharply.

'I've got to go, Mama,' he replied, listlessly. 'Gadoric won't let the sheep out till Minca's there.'

'Then he'll just have to wait,' she said, favouring the hound with a baleful expression. Minca might be big and fierce, but he knew who was the boss in this hut. Fulmina's look was enough to cause him to emit a small whine, wag his tail once, and sit down.

'Oh, please,' pleaded Aquila. 'It's nearly full daylight already.'

Fulmina ignored him and went to the big chest in the corner of the room and opened the lid. 'I've made something for you. A gift.'

The prospect of a present dented Aquila's impatience a bit. 'For me?'

'Yes.' With her back to the boy, bent over the open chest, Fulmina clutched at her stomach, her eyes shut tight. The pain was terrible and she fought to control her voice so Aquila would not notice. 'And I want you to have it now, before it's too late.'

'Too late?' he asked, confused.

She snapped to cover her mistake, turning round to berate him. 'When do I ever see you. You go off before dawn, you're here for all of a minute before you go off chasing girls, and you come back after darkness. I wonder that you still count this as your home.'

He blushed slightly at the mention of girls, but stayed silent, just staring at her with a hurt look. Fulmina melted, unaware that Aquila was concealing a pain of his own. 'You're young. Enjoy it while you can.'

'I'm sorry.'

'For what?'

'For not doing as Papa asked. I haven't looked after you.'

He was so serious, standing there with a genuine look of shame, that Fulmina clutched him to her, biting back the stinging sensation in her eyes. 'Oh, get on with you, Aquila. I wouldn't have you any other way.'

'I promise to be here more often, Mama. I would stay now but I have to take the dog back to Gadoric.'

'I know, son. And so you shall. Just as soon as you put this on.'

She held out a leather amulet. It was deep brown, rubbed with beeswax to make it shine and Fulmina had embroidered it with the outline of an eagle, wings outstretched. More than that she had managed to raise the bird so that it stood out from the background, giving it a sense of real movement. The thongs to bind the amulet were threaded through the eyes, and she slipped it onto his arm, pulling them tight and lacing them quickly.

'Do you like it?' she asked.

'It's wonderful,' he replied enthusiastically, fingering the eagle.

'Now sit down for a moment, while I tell you something.' He glanced anxiously at the waiting dog, then composing himself, he looked back at Fulmina. 'There is something of value in this amulet, something that belongs to you.' Aquila started to speak, to ask what it contained, but she put her fingers of one hand over his lips and clutched the other tightly. 'No. Just listen. When you are old enough to fear no man, you must unpick the stitching around the bird. There you will find another eagle, a valuable one. It is your birthright. The chain to hold it is sown into the leather that laces the amulet to your arm. You must guard it with your life.'

The boy fingered the stiff leather. Fulmina could

see that he was about to start asking a host of questions. 'Say nothing! But swear to me, by all the gods, that you will do as I ask.'

The silence lasted for what seemed an age. He looked into her eyes and his young face registered a look of surprise, as if he was seeing the ravages of pain for the first time.

'Why now?'

'You have brought me more joy that I can say yet now I have to tell you that I am not your mama, just as Clodius is not your real father.' The boy dropped his head, trying to hide his emotions. He kept it there as Fulmina continued. 'I wanted you to become a man before telling you this, but I shall not have the time.'

The sun rose high in the sky as she spoke, telling the boy how Clodius had found him; of the valuable token he now wore on his arm, and of their fruitless search for his true parents. All the time he looked at the ground, with only an occasional squeeze on her hand to indicate the pain he was feeling.

She touched the eagle gently. 'All this time, I've kept this, though it could have eased our lives no end. Clodius wanted to sell it and buy another farm.' His voice was hoarse. She did not quite hear what he asked but she knew the nature of the question. 'At first I wanted to keep it so that we could claim our reward for raising you. Besides, I wouldn't have trusted Clodius to get a proper price for it. Even if he did, I wonder how much of the value would have been left when he got home. If we'd had enough to buy another farm he'd have drunk that away in no time.'

'He wouldn't have had to go away.'

'It was the dreams, really, and once Drisia had done with her spitting, and cast her bones, I knew it was true, since she saw your future as I did.'

For the first time in an age the boy looked up. He was hurt, that was clear from his expression. But he had not shed a single tear.

'It happened more than once, Aquila. You would appear in my dreams, that eagle on your neck, a grown man, but no farmer toiling in the fields. Crowds cheered you, and you wore white robes tinged with purple and a laurel wreath around your ears. All my dreams spoke of greatness, of a destiny for you, in which you will take your rightful place in the world. That is really why I kept the charm. It's part of your path to that destiny. By raising you, Clodius and I have played our part.'

She squeezed his hand again, but this time he spoke. 'You're going to die?'

'Yes.'

'How soon?'

She shook her head and shrugged her shoulders. 'That's of no account, Aquila. What matters is this. You know that there's a path to follow. Drisia and

I have seen that it won't be an easy one. You face death many times.' She rubbed the leather amulet again. 'But I want you to swear never to part with this. I can't tell you how, but this alone will propel you to glory. In the bottom of the chest you'll find some coins, not much, but enough perhaps to get you to your papa.' Her face clouded at the mention of her husband. 'If he tries to persuade you to sell it, tell him to go jump in the latrine.'

The head was down again, the voice forlorn. 'He's not really my papa.'

'That won't stop him,' she snapped. Then her voice softened. 'He's not a bad man, Aquila, just a weak one. Take care of him, and if you do have some fortune, ease his old age. Now come over here with me and swear.'

She led the boy by his hand to the tiny altar stuck in the corner of the hut. Fulmina had decorated it with meat, fruit and flowers, each a votive offering to the deities that she worshipped. Farmers' gods, since she had held to the older beliefs all her life, the religion of the land from which life came. She made incantations to *Luna,* to *Conditor*, the God of the Harvest, *Volturnus* the God of the River and *Robigo,* Goddess of the Fields, using words that she had learnt at her own mother's knee.

'We need no priests, Aquila. No visit to the temple, with a fee for the augurs and a chicken sacrificed that they'll eat for dinner. No offering to the gods that rich folk worship, either. These are our gods. The sun that brings life and the fruits of that life, the moon that tells us of the change of season. Swear by these gods, the ones we raised you by, that you will abide by my wishes, that you will keep that charm safe and never sell it.'

The boy touched each of the offerings in turn then put his hand on the turf of the altar. In his mind he recalled Gadoric's voice, talking of the deities that his tribe worshipped. They were the same kind of deities celebrated at this turf altar, even if they had different names. Fulmina, having finished her prayers, nudged him. His voice was steady as he spoke.

'I swear.'

She fought back the pain in her belly once more, with greater ease somehow, no longer caring. She had done with her task. 'Now take the dog and go see your barbarian.'

CHAPTER TWENTY-NINE

There was an unnatural stillness to the woods, a lack of sound that made the hairs on Aquila's neck twitch and the dog sensed it as well, the usual ritual of sniffing, then marking every tenth tree forgotten. Instead he would run a bit ahead, stop and test the wind, before moving on again. They left the woods and crossed the open field towards the pens. The sheep were still there but he could see no sign of Gadoric. Minca yelped suddenly and raced for the tiny lean-to hut that, set hard against a wall of rock, served the shepherd as home. Aquila put aside the knot of fear he felt and ran after the dog. The rope-hinged door had been torn off. What few possessions Gadoric had owned were scattered around the place and his cot, fashioned from rough-hewn saplings, was broken. The pole on which he hung his gutted birds and small game was empty and the long shepherd's staff lay on the floor, the white wood of the sword cuts it had sustained stark and frightening. The dog was whining loudly, sniffing at the floor. Aquila bent down and rubbed his fingers over the hard packed earth. The blood was still wet so whatever had occurred in the hut had happened very recently.

Minca whined again, looking pleadingly at Aquila and the boy covered his eyes to fight back the unaccustomed tears, for his heart was as heavy as a stone. How much loss could he take in one day? First Fulmina and the story of his birth, worse still the words backed up by the lined and weary face that told him of her impending death. Now the shepherd, who had come to occupy the central position in his life; he would not have known how to say what Gadoric had become to him, a surrogate father, but that was what had happened. The flaxen-haired giant had refined his crude skills and taught him to hunt, snare and trap, had shown him which bait to use and how to fish, the proper way to catch a snake without being bitten plus myriad other ways to survive in the woods. Gadoric had set up targets and made him practice at throwing his spear until the boy could be sure to hit a wild boar in the right spot, even if both he, and his quarry, were running flat out. They had had sessions with wooden swords that went on till Aquila's arm ached, but he could thrust, cut and parry enough to occasionally force his tutor onto the defensive. The bow that the shepherd had fashioned, along with the arrows he had cut, feathered and trimmed was back in the hut. Gadoric had worked hard with the boy until he could down a flying bird.

More than that, he had taught him his own tongue and told tales of barbarian gods clashing in the heavens as they fought for power, of great battles and mighty feats of arms, of lands to the north where the forests ran on for days, inhabited by fierce tribes who burnt their enemies alive in wicker cages. Aquila fingered the raised eagle on the still unfamiliar amulet as if that would clear the rush of images that filled his mind. Blood, but no body; that meant that whoever fought Gadoric had not killed him, but had taken him away. The youngster leapt across the cramped space, pulling aside the piles of kindling faggots that Gadoric had heaped in one corner.

The spear was still in its place, the metal head gleaming and sharp. A slave could die for the mere ownership of such a thing, but Gadoric had stolen it nevertheless, knowing he would need it to help him get home to his own land and people. Aquila grabbed the weapon, spun on his heel and shot through the doorway, shouting for the dog. Out in the bright sunlight he had no need to speak as the animal cast around in the disturbed grass round the doorway, moving in an ever-widening circle, yelping occasionally. Then he stopped, one forepaw raised, his nose pointing away from the woods towards the larger fields full of cattle to the north. Minca looked at Aquila for a second, then he yelped again, and nose low, he set of in pursuit of Gadoric's scent, with the boy running at his heels.

They moved quickly, further proof, given its strength, that the spoor was recent. The dog vaulted over the fences that marked the boundary of the best pasture. The cows had watched their approach with a look of bovine stupidity, but once the hound was in the field they upped and ran to the furthest corner. Minca stopped for a moment because the trail went right through the middle of a huge cowpat and that smell had filled his nostrils, putting him off the scent. Aquila could see where feet had made a groove through the middle. He pulled Minca gently by the ear and took him to a point several paces beyond the pile of ordure. The dog sniffed again, still a little confused, but he found the spoor he wanted in less than a minute and they were off again.

Aquila realised that the trail was leading them directly to the Barbinus villa and the outbuildings that surrounded it. As he trotted along beside the dog, spear in hand, he speculated on what could have happened at the hut. Gadoric had not been attacked by a band of strangers for the shepherd had placed his hut well. It backed on to a thorn-covered escarpment at the furthest point opposite the woods and this gave him plenty of time to observe anyone approaching, and he had set up lines with sheep bells so he could not be taken unawares, even if he was asleep. The man had almost animal instincts; the slightest sound would register in his brain, awake or asleep so he must have known those who came to take him. He would have watched them cross the field, probably already on the lookout for Aquila and his dog so they could not be enemies, since Gadoric would have fought them and, given his prowess with the spear, at least one of his assailants would have died.

The boy stopped when he saw the red-tiled roof of the spacious villa, so he called Minca to heel and leant on the spear to think. Gadoric's words rang in his ears, for the shepherd, talking of battles in which he had fought, never tired of telling Aquila to look before he leapt. The man who had led him into battles against the legions had forgotten that lesson, and those of his men who were not killed had ended up as Roman slaves. He had drawn the engagements with a stick, showing in the earth the dispositions of the men who had fought and the reasons one side gained victory and the word surprise was paramount! The shepherd repeated it over and over to make sure the boy understood.

'Before you go trying to surprise an enemy, lad, just make sure he hasn't got a little shock in store for you, for if he has, it'll be you that dies and not him. Use everything, your eyes, your ears and your nose. Listen for the sounds that should be there, for if they're not, then something else is. But there's a sense in you without a name, a feeling when things are not right. Trust that too.'

Something was not right here, but this was no battle. He could hardly just barge in to the farmyard and demand an explanation. What have you done with your slave, the shepherd? All he would get for his trouble would be the toe of the overseer's boot on his backside. His eyes roved over the landscape, taking in the details, features he had seen time and again, yet seemed to him as if they were being observed by a different set of eyes. In his heart he wanted to attack the place, to storm it and set it ablaze. The house and the outbuildings were set on flat land, but that was man-made, excavated out of the slope of the hillside, and the stable roofs, furthest from the entrance to the property, on the other side of the slave quarters were a continuation of the slanting grassy field where the excavation ended. The whole landscape was on an incline, falling gently towards the road bridge that crossed the culvert. Aquila looked up the hill to his right to where there was a small copse from which he could observe the whole extent of the farm without himself being seen. He tugged at the dog's ear again, harder this time, for Minca was reluctant to let go of the scent, and hauled him up towards the trees.

The small wood surrounded the cistern that held the water that supplied the spacious villa, and fed the fountain, the canopy of trees keeping the contents cool. From this height Aquila could not see into the actual central courtyard of the house itself, the place where he had stood the night he heard Sosia scream, but he could see the tip of the water spewing from the fountain as it rose to a height near that of his own. He stared at the house for quite some time, forming, as it did, a complete square enclosing the courtyard. There was no sign of Gadoric at all, which was a relief; Aquila had feared almost as soon as he had realised where the spoor was taking them, that he would find the shepherd strung up from a gibbet or crucified, yet he must be there and if he was there was a good chance he was still alive. Aquila crouched, his cheek against the smooth shaft of the spear, idle finger stroking the leather amulet that felt so strange on his arm, aware that he had no idea what to do. After all, he was only a boy and Gadoric had obviously been brought here by force, so he would need to be rescued the same way. Aquila knew how many men occupied the Barbinus ranch, knew it was certainly too many for him and the dog to tackle.

He looked at the far side of the ranch, nearer to the Via Appia where the barns were situated and wondered if Gadoric had been taken there. Since he could see nothing from here he decided to take a look, just to reassure himself, so he left the copse and headed along the hillside, all the time looking out for some clue which might be afforded by the changing angle of the view. Once past the line of the buildings, he headed downhill, till he was on the opposite side from their original approach, encouraging Minca to cast around again for the spoor. The dog ran around in a random way, nose to the ground, covering a great deal of ground in a fruitless search. Suddenly Minca stopped and raised his head looking towards the nearby buildings and Aquila turned, still leaning on his spear. Then he heard the shouts and the barking dogs, the noise accompanied by the cracking of a whip. He threw the spear to the ground and raced towards the wicker fence that marked the perimeter of the farm buildings. Through a gap between two of the barns he saw the group of chained men in the middle of the courtyard, surrounded by armed guards, some of whom had fierce-looking dogs straining on stout ropes.

Gadoric stood head and shoulders above the others and even from this distance Aquila could see that his flaxen hair was matted with dried blood, but he stood erect, looking around with his single eye, unlike the others, chained to him, who seemed to be bowed under the weight of some great burden. He was not sure but they looked like the men who had worked on the ranch doing the most menial tasks, cleaning out stalls, shifting hay, keeping the courtyard clean; one thing he did know, if it was them they were all slaves. Aquila stopped at the fence, not sure what to do until he heard Minca growl beside him, and just in time he reached out and grabbed the animal round the neck to stop it diving through to rescue its master. Minca struggled in his arms, trying to break free without doing any harm, the boy holding him speaking rapidly in the strange, barbaric tongue it understood, using soothing words to try and calm the animal.

He knew that if Minca tried to get to Gadoric, it would have to fight every one of those other dogs. Thus occupied, any one of those armed guards could then spear him. He had to get him away for if one of those guards swung a whip anywhere near Gadoric he would not have the strength to hold him back. Grabbing both ears he hauled the dog's head round and pulled him away from the point where he could see his master. Aquila grabbed his spear and headed back up the hill at a run, the sheepdog right by his heels. He went higher this time, skirting the rear of the copse he had occupied earlier. Just before he lost sight of the farm he heard the crack of the whip in the clear morning air and he looked back to see the file of prisoners being marched towards the front gates, heading for the road beyond the bridge.

The boy ran as fast as he could and Minca must have sensed their destination since he sped on ahead, making for the hut. Aquila knew he could leave the dog there; given the job of guarding his master's property, he would not budge and added to that, he would tear apart anyone who tried to enter. They reached the hut in good time, and Aquila, having given Minca his instructions, made as good a job as he could of securing the place, well aware that neither the damaged door or even the walls would hold the dog if he really wanted to get out. He was halfway through the wood when he realised that the spear was still in his hand.

He cursed softly and turned back in the direction of home, knowing he would have to leave it there before going in search of the column of slaves. He might be a free-born Roman but no one would like to see such a weapon in a young boy's hand. Racing across the stream, he ignored the stepping stones and the water that, spraying up from his flailing legs, soaked him to the skin. Aquila rushed into the hut and threw the spear into the corner by Fulmina's chest and was halfway back out the door when he heard the painful sob. The hut was not empty, as he had first thought. Then Fulmina spoke his name and the boy went back in reluctantly. She lay wrapped in her bedding, her face full of pain and creased with the marks of dried tears. Aquila felt under the covers for her hand and as he took it she clutched it tightly, pulling him hard towards her body and emitting a strangled gasp. Total confusion filled his mind, for he could not go and leave her like this, yet he could not stay.

'Thank the gods you came, Aquila,' said Fulmina through clenched teeth. 'I have lain here praying that you'd return.'

'I must get help,' he cried, aware that half his mind was on the fate of Gadoric and feeling guilty for it.

'Help!' The laugh that came from her throat was horrible. He tried to pull away but he was still tightly held by her hand. 'I'm beyond help, son.'

'No!'

Fulmina's body arched over in agony, pulling his hand into her lower belly, then she raised her head and whispered in his ear. 'In the chest. Go to the chest.'

Fulmina released his hand and Aquila obeyed. She must have heard the lid creak open because her eyes were still shut tight yet she spoke in a staccato way, each few words punctuated by a small cry of pain. 'A small ampoule... Aquila... Dark brown it is...down the side by your right hand...under my mourning shawl... Quick, boy, quick.'

Aquila felt down the side of the chest, his hand closing over the small clay container and he pulled it up and held it out for Fulmina to see. Still she did not open her eyes. 'Have...you got...it?'

'Yes!' He jumped back to the bed, reaching again for the hand.

'Open...it, Aquila...but don't...spill—' Fulmina cried out in agony, unable to finish what she was saying as Aquila broke the wax seal on the small bottle.

'What shall I do?' he asked desperately.

'Help me...drink it.'

He put his hands behind her head and lifted it slightly, putting the ampoule to her pale lips. Fulmina's other hand came up, to hold the back of his, then she forced his hand up so that the contents spilt down her throat. Her body jerked several times and she gagged slightly, as though she could not swallow the contents, but she persevered, keeping it at her mouth until she was sure it was empty. Once she had finished Aquila took it from her, then held her head against his chest, feeling the spasms subside. He talked, as much to comfort her, as to remind himself why he had come home.

'Barbinus's men have taken Gadoric. They've chained him to some other men and they were marching them off towards the road the last time I saw. Mama, I must go and see if I can help him.'

'The money, Aquila,' she said softly, as though she hadn't heard him.

'Money?'

'In the chest.'

'It won't be enough to buy his freedom, Mama.'

She seemed at ease now, the potion she had taken having lessened her pain. 'No, boy. We never had enough of that to be free, any of us, but fetch it anyway.'

Again he went to the chest, Fulmina speaking softly to guide him. 'Take everything out, Aquila.'

Everything did not amount to much; a mourning shawl, two extra blankets, a clean white woollen smock for Aquila which she had made in anticipation of his putting on his manly gown, with a decorated leather belt to go round his waist. A small box containing the polished stones, plucked out of the stream over the years, that she had never quite got round to turning into a necklace, some oddments of clothing and Fulmina's winter bed socks.

'At the bottom, a false floor. You can just get your nail under it.'

The boy ran his fingers across the smooth wood until he felt the small indentation and prised the lid open with his fingernail. He pulled out the soft leather pouch, tied at the neck with a thong and took it over to where his mother lay, her eyes open now. It seemed as if the potion had worked and the pain had gone so he tried to give her the purse but she pushed it away. 'Yours Aquila. Take it.'

'Mama, I must go and see what has happened to Gadoric.'

She smiled, the eyes once more had that light of

love in them, then with a great effort she hauled herself up to a sitting position, bent forward and kissed the raised eagle on his leather amulet. Aquila heard the words of her prayer, calling on the gods to keep their word. Then she lay back again. 'Your shepherd? Of course, off you go.'

He stood up to leave and she spoke again. 'I wonder, Aquila, if you could spare me just one of those coins?'

'Yes,' he said, surprised and he pulled the pouch open.

'There's some silver ones. If I could have one of those.'

He tipped the coins out into his hand, wondering if the pouch contained enough to bribe one of Gadoric's guards. There was not much, only three silver denarii with the rest copper asses. He gave one of the silver coins to Fulmina, who clutched it in her hand.

'Now, boy, give your mama a goodbye kiss and go and see about your shepherd.'

Aquila had planted a perfunctory kiss on her forehead and was halfway out of the door before she finished speaking, calling his farewells. 'I'll see you soon, I promise.'

'I pray to the gods you don't, my son, just as I prayed, just now, that they grant you your destiny.'

Fulmina raised her hand and put the silver coin under her tongue, then she lay still, for the pain had gone, never to return. The potion, which she had prepared with her own hand, would see to that. She thought of the boy and of her husband and of the life she had led and when she died the small amount of tears she had summoned up filled her eyes, then ran down the sides of her face.

Aquila came upon the column of slaves in a matter of minutes, as they were heading south towards the Via Appia, past the dusty ill-defined lane that led up to his hut and again he saw Gadoric, head and shoulders above the rest. Other boys had gathered round, to follow and mock the straggling group of chained men. He was really close when he saw one of them pick up a stone, pulling his arm back to throw it. Aquila thundered straight into him, sending him flying and as they both fell to the ground he followed up with a punch on the ear. The others, once they had recovered, sought to pull them apart.

'I'll kill you,' he screamed, struggling in the arms of boys he usually called friends.

'Hold there!' cried one of the guards pushing between them. The column had stopped so Aquila pulled himself free of the restraining arms and looked round to see Gadoric's one good eye fixed on him. The shepherd gave him a single emphatic shake of the head and it was only then that Aquila realised that his friend had lost the shuffled gait he normally used when others could observe him. He stood to his full height, as Aquila had seen him many times, proud and magnificent, even dressed in bloodstained rags.

The guard laughed and called to Gadoric. 'Your little playmate has come to rescue you, Blondie. Now there's true love for you. Makes you wonder what you two got up to in that there hut.'

The rest of the guards laughed, adding ribald comments of their own. Aquila could not really hear them, his whole attention was fixed on Gadoric, who suddenly spoke quickly in his own tongue, knowing that only Aquila could understand him.

'I hope I taught you well. Look after Minca.' The one eye flicked to the side to indicate the guard, still laughing at his own joke. 'Perhaps we were seen, practising with the spear. It makes no difference, they know I'm not the witless idiot I pretended to be.'

'No talking,' growled one guard.

'What's he sayin'?' demanded another, confused at the Celtic tongue.

'No more shepherding, Aquila,' said Gadoric quickly.

The guard who had made the joke stepped forward and raised his club. If he had expected his prisoner to try and avoid the blow, he was disappointed. Gadoric just fixed him with a look and the club remained in the air. 'One more word out of you, you bastard, and you'll never get near Sicily.'

'Sicily!'

The guard, obviously senior to his fellows, turned round and pushed his face close to Aquila's, relishing his words as he spoke. 'Oh yes, lad. Our dumb shepherd here, who has so cheated his master, is set to grow corn. He'll not get much to eat, nor little water to drink neither, and in that heat, I don't suppose he'll last too long, which is all to the good, I say.'

'One day, Aquila,' said Gadoric quickly, still speaking in his own tongue, 'you must ask your mama if you are truly her son.'

The club of one of the other guards hit him on the back with a strength that propelled him forward and Gadoric tried to spin round, his face full of hate, but the chains that attached him to his fellow prisoners stopped him.

The other guard had his club ready again. 'Go on, you bastard. It'll be a real pleasure to sort you out.'

'No!' shouted the leader, so close to Aquila he made the boy jump. 'Dying means nought to him, but let him endure a slow death, toiling in the fields and see if he enjoys that.'

'Sir,' said Aquila softly but urgently, tugging at the overseer's tunic. 'Would money ease his journey?'

The eyes narrowed, and the man paused before replying. When he did speak his voice was full of doubt. 'It might, lad, but where's the likes of you goin' to get any money?'

Aquila pulled out the soft leather purse and pressed it into the overseer's hand. As his eye caught a hint of what the boy was doing, the man spun round and loudly ordered the column to proceed, an action that cut Aquila off from everyone else. Yet one of his hands stayed still, ending up behind his back and it was that which took the offering. Looking down Aquila saw the hand squeeze the purse a couple of times. He then made half a turn back towards the boy, speaking out of the corner of his mouth.

'Why, this will do your shepherd no end of good, lad. At least it'll make sure he survives to reach Sicily.' The voice lost the tone of kindness, becoming harsh again. 'After that, it's out of my hands, and from what I've heard, men like him don't last long in that part of the world.'

He stood over Fulmina's bed, looking into the peaceful face, his hand rubbing the amulet on his upper arm. It was as though the gods had combined to empty his life of everything he valued, for he knew he would never see Gadoric or Sosia again, just as his mama would never hold him in her arms. He was not given to tears, but Aquila cried now, the sobs rising in volume until he wailed in his grief, not able to tell which loss was the greater. Eventually the wailing ceased; it had to, since no human being could sustain such a sound and he knelt by the bed, his eyes tight shut, full of images that made him want to die.

That was how Dabo found him, hunched over, his hand still holding Fulmina's. The farmer, arms full of food, looked at the dead body without emotion, wondering how this would affect his bargain. He had known when he struck his deal that Clodius would be away more than one season, but he had never thought service would extend this long. Not that he himself had failed to prosper by it. What worried him most was the thought of Clodius coming home, on leave, and forcing Dabo to do his own duty, thus jeopardising his chances of increasing his wealth still further.

It would not take this boy's papa long to find out that during all the time Clodius had been serving in his name, Dabo managed to avoid paying any tax. What a potent threat that would be if it came to a dispute between them. He put his hand gently on Aquila's shoulder, tenderness brought on by necessity, rather than any finer feeling. Dabo had to create an impression in which Clodius, should he return, would think well of him.

'Come boy. Death takes us all. We'll see her a decent pyre and send her off properly.'

Aquila, red-eyed, looked up at Dabo. Fulmina had disliked him, so did he, blaming Dabo for his papa's absence. Then he remembered. Clodius was not his father, any more than the dead Fulmina had been his mother. He spun round, pushed past Dabo, and rushed out of the hut, heading for the river, the woods and that lean-to where he had had so much pleasure. He was also heading for the only thing in his life that seemed certain. Everything had been taken from him, everything except one thing, the dog, Minca.

'What if he takes off to join his father?' said Dabo. He knew his fat wife was not really listening, more intent on consuming the bowl of grapes on the table than listening to her husband's catalogue of woes, but really Dabo was just thinking aloud. If his wife had ventured an opinion, he would have probably told her to shut up. 'You might say that Clodius hasn't happened to come home yet, and that's true. But if the boy turns up he'll know our bargain's dead. What then?'

He paced the main room of his house, kicking up clouds of pale dust that had accumulated on the floor from the newly plastered walls. With open arms he spun round to indicate the under-furnished room. 'And just when I've built this place!'

'This place' had yet to be given a proper roof. The man who had been given the job of making the tiles had under-priced his products to get the work, now he was demanding more money to complete the bargain. Dabo knew he would have to pay in the end, but he would fight as long as he could, only giving in at the approach of winter for nothing marked the level of his success more than this building. Really it was only one side of a proper villa, but he had plans already drawn to extend it round so that it formed one of those fashionable courtyards, like the one at the Barbinus ranch, just up the road.

'Is that all you can do. Sit there and stuff yourself?' he snapped, allowing his frustration to get the better of him. His wife ignored him and took elaborate care in the choice of her next grape. 'We'll have to take him in with us. Keep him here.'

'And feed him,' croaked his wife, finally speaking. Her voice seemed to hint that any food vouchsafed the boy would diminish that left for her.

'I've got to go get him anyway, so he can light Fulmina's funeral pyre.'

'Pyre!' His wife put down the grapes in her hand. 'All you are planning to do is fire her hut, with the body still inside. I don't call that a pyre.'

'I suppose you'd have me build her a proper one,' he growled. 'Ten foot high and half a forest to rest on. A pretty penny that would cost.' Dabo jabbed his finger in her direction, leaning over the table to emphasise his words. 'Logs don't grow on trees you know!' He was out of the door before he realised what he had said, the sound of his wife's laughter echoing behind him in the barely furnished house made him even angrier.

Aquila was not at the shepherd's hut and the place looked as if it had been put to rights and found a new occupant. Given the sheep were out of their pens, Dabo surmised that Barbinus's overseer had got himself a new shepherd so he made his way to the woods knowing that the boy had always played there.

'Lazy little swine,' he murmured to himself, stumbling through the undergrowth. 'Never done a day's work in his life. I'll take him in all right and I'll have him out in the fields just as quick. He'll earn his keep in my house.'

He tried to put as much good feeling into his voice as he could when he called out the boy's name, even smiling as he did so, just in case he was being secretly observed. Dabo might be a mean-fisted sod, well past his true prime, but he had been a soldier, and he was a countryman to his fingertips. The hairs on the back of his neck, and the tingling sensation of his skin, told him someone was close, probably Aquila, so he spoke loudly, his voice echoing in the seemingly empty forest.

'Come on, lad. I know you're upset, bound to be. I'd leave you be if I could but what am I to do? I'm too pious a fellow to start your mother's funeral without you. It's your duty to see her off. She'd only suffer in Hades if you don't.'

The spear was twenty feet away from him, but he saw the flash of its silver head out of the corner of his eye, and the thud as it hit the trunk of the oak tree made him jump. He used the quivering shaft to aim his look. No sign of Aquila, but that huge dog had come into view, and had him fixed with a frightening stare.

'She's not truly my mother, is she?'

Dabo spun round, biting back the curse; how had this boy got round behind him, in such a short space of time, without making a sound? Aquila stood, arms by his side. There was no threat in his pose, yet he had managed to inform this adult that he could have killed him with ease.

'Well, that's as maybe,' replied Dabo calmly, aware that the dog was behind him now and the nerves in his back told him it had come a lot closer. 'But she raised you as a son, adopted you, even if it weren't sworn. You have to see her off, lad. I know you was fond of her.'

The boy's shoulders suddenly slumped and his head dropped so Dabo walked across to him, realising for the first time, with a slight shock, that Aquila was now a fraction taller than him. He was just about to put his arm round the youngster's shoulder, in a paternal gesture, when he heard the dog growl. It was very close by the sound of it and

Dabo half turned, to fix the beast in the corner of his eye.

'I'd take it as a kindness if you'd tell your animal I'm a friend.'

Aquila didn't look up, but he said something Dabo couldn't understand, and the farmer was relieved to see the dog sit down. He patted Aquila on the shoulder, his eye catching the leather amulet with the raised eagle, which he examined while he searched for the right words to use. To his mind it was an un-Roman object, not suitable wear for a boy Aquila's age. Idly he wondered if the shepherd had given it to him. If he had, it would just about sum up what he thought, along with the rest of the neighbourhood, about their relationship.

'You can't stay out here, in the woods, boy. You need a home. I made a pact with your papa to look after you and Fulmina. She might be dead, but I've still got you as a charge on my conscience.' Dabo's voice took on an encouraging tone. 'I've moved the few things she owned to my place. We'll fire the hut to see her off. Place is near to falling down anyway, then you can move in with me.'

'I was going to join Clodius.'

'At your age? You might be tall, but you're still a toddler. I can't have you wandering about, exposed to heaven knows what. How could I face old Clodius if'n anything happened? No. You come and live with me.'

He felt the boy stiffen, taking Aquila's upper arm, immediately below the shining leather amulet, exerting just enough pressure to move him slightly. 'I won't hear a word against it, lad, and I shall send a message to your papa to get himself home, so he can look after you himself. Now come along. You know it's the right thing to do.'

Aquila allowed himself to be pulled into motion and Minca stood up and slowly padded along behind them. The older man talked steadily, but Dabo's mind was elsewhere. Should he let Aquila go, and take a chance on him coming to grief on the journey? The road to Illyricum was long and dangerous, especially for a good-looking youth who had led a sheltered life. It was tempting, but Dabo knew he had no choice. Not knowing what had happened to the boy, should he fail to reach his papa, was the worst possible alternative, one that would make Clodius hopping mad. So, he would take him home and sort him out, though he would have to get that dog chained up, for Dabo knew he could not do a thing with the boy until that was achieved.

These thoughts had made him tighten his grip on Aquila's arm, though he relaxed it immediately, albeit his hand ached to take a real purchase. What this youngster needed was a good thrashing, possibly more than one. That, and a few backbreaking days toiling in the fields. Proper work! That would knock the stuffing out of him. First things first; get him home, see to Fulmina's funeral, get a rope on that animal and then, if Clodius ever did come back, it would be to a vastly different creature than this cheeky bastard beside him.

When Didius Flaccus and Cholon Pyliades returned a week later to the pass at Thralaxas there was nothing left to see, not even any evidence of a fight. Any trace of the ashes and bones had been removed on the rushing feet of the fleeing survivors of the battle against the legions. The rebellion was over, the enemy crushed. Their general might be a blubbery fool, but the training that Aulus had instituted in his army paid handsome dividends when it came to the actual contest. The field was heaped with Dacian bones, with Illyrians and Epirotes to make up the numbers. Vegetius Flaminus would get his triumph and he would also probably avoid any censure for his previous conduct, given it was hard to impeach a successful general. It was also hard for Flaccus, after so many years of service, to quite get a hold of the fact that he was now retired. The Greek servant would never get over the loss of a man he loved.

'What now?' said Cholon.

'The quickest way home, mate,' replied Flaccus.

'Which is?'

'The way of the legions. South to Epirus and a sea passage to Brindisium.'

Cholon smiled, though his heart was like lead. 'I would have thought you would want to get away from the legions.'

'I do,' said the newly retired Flaccus with feeling. He rubbed his hands over his short grey hair. 'But I have an even greater wish to shake the dust of Illyricum off my feet.'

Flaccus had avoided giving the old soothsayer in Salonae any time to explain. The man had tried to gabble something as Flaccus stabbed him repeatedly, the message lost in cries of agony, but the last words had been plain, and the old man had a gleam in his eye as he uttered them.

'Everything I have said will come true.'

'Tell the Goddess *Angita*.'

Flaccus had grabbed him to shake more information out, only to see the light of life fade from the soothsayer's eyes, leaving him in the same state of doubt about his future as he had been the last time.

'I must seek out the heirs of those who died here,' Cholon said. 'My master left instructions that they should be granted pensions.'

'Just how rich was he?' Flaccus demanded in wonder.

'His true richness lay in his character.' Cholon put his hands to his eyes, pressing back the tears. 'I think the dust of this place will cling to me till I die.'

Flaccus reached down into the sandy cart track and scooped up a handful. 'Then take some with you, mate. It's always best to be able to look at your enemy square in the face.'

With a quick incantation to *Janus*, the ex-soldier led the way south.

CHAPTER THIRTY

Quintus Cornelius was being sonorous in a theatrical way, over-indulging himself in the sadness of the occasion and for once his stepmother was not inclined to reproach him for it. There had been a moment, when he had heard of the death of his father, when Quintus had seemed, not happy, but calmed. He had, of course, come into his inheritance – he was now the head of the Cornelii household and he was describing, as he sketched his ideas for the sculptures around the tomb, the images the public would see as they passed it on the road in and out of Rome.

'I think your father would care more what was here at the family altar.'

'We have no death mask, lady, but one can be made from the best of his statues, the most striking likeness, and will stand in the place of honour.'

'No ashes,' said Claudia, ruefully. 'It is sad that such a man should have no ashes, no pyre with mourners weeping at his passing. I think we would really have seen his soul ascending to the heavens, not just a flock of doves.'

'Cholon brought back a handful of dust from the place where he died. I intend that should go in his sarcophagus and the written inscription on the outside will remind Romans as long as time exists that my father died as well and as bravely as Leonidas at Thermopyle.'

'Many men died with him, Quintus, do not forget that.'

'Ordinary soldiers, lady.'

'Roman soldiers, seventy-four of them. I wish to erect a plaque near his tomb listing their names, for they were as brave as their general and I will endow a memorial sacrifice every year so that the God *Aeternitas* is reminded of their bravery.'

The way Quintus said, 'As you wish,' left Claudia in no doubt that he thought her notion a trifle foolish, while she was sure that her late husband would have approved. He also thought any grief she showed at the death of Aulus was faked; being the kind of insincere person he was, Quintus was much given to labelling other people with the same shortcoming. Cholon might be sincere but he had no love for her, the wife who had made his master so unhappy, and both had stood in embarrassed silence when she cried at the felicitations the senior consul brought to the house

– a signal honour which showed just how Aulus was viewed by his peers. She hoped that Titus would come home soon – he was on the way, not that she would be open with him, but he would accept her sorrow as genuine, which it was, though she was honest enough in herself to see there was a degree of self-pity in her anguish.

She knew she should feel free. Quintus thought her unconcerned about the Cornelii family name, but she was; the memory of her husband was too strong for her to easily bring that into disrepute. Having wounded Aulus in life she was not inclined to sully his name in death and what of Brennos, now a big enough nuisance to be a subject of occasional conversation in the circles in which she moved, the most recent barbarity another example of hatred. His opposition to Rome had not mellowed and she knew he had several wives and a large family, even a numerous tribe of his own.

Should she leave everything behind and go to Spain there was no guarantee that she would be welcome and how could she tell him that his son by their union had been exposed by Aulus, and was certainly dead; that the talisman by which he put so much store she had not only taken but lost; that it was buried under moss in some field or forest still hanging on the bones of a new born baby? The images of that horrible year flashed through her mind. At least Aulus had died unaware that the boy had been a love child, and he had expired in the fashion he would have wished, as a soldier serving the Republic. It was odd to think, given their edgy relationship over the last eleven years, that she was sure she would miss him.

The slave had entered so silently that when he spoke to Quintus, it made her start. 'The most noble Lucius Falerius Nerva is at the gate, sir, and begs to be allowed to intrude upon your grief.'

'Show the senator in at once,' cried Quintus, almost beaming. 'What an honour, lady, what an honour.'

He was so eager, too puffed up that such a man was calling, that Claudia wanted to ask why he did not crawl to the gate and open it himself, but an unspoken peace had been declared until the funeral rites were over and she was not about to break it. Was it so strange that the leading man of Rome should call to offer condolences for the death of her most puissant soldier? It was unlikely to be prompted by affection; you could not live with Aulus and not know that he often despaired of his childhood friend, nor could you be unaware that Lucius had slighted him more than once, subtly for certain, for he was a master of that art, but snubbed nonetheless. Had Claudia been head of the household she would at least have made the dried-up stick of venom wait. As it was, he was with them quickly, his son in tow, wearing black instead of his normal toga.

'Lady Claudia, I know I can measure your loss, for it is set against my own and I do not know how it could be deeper.'

There were two choices, to mock him or accept his condolences. The way Quintus was hopping from foot to foot nearly made her employ the first, but her breeding won out and she chose the second. 'I know how my late husband esteemed you. I think that to see you here and in mourning, would ease his soul.'

'His soul?' said Lucius with a pious expression. 'Was there ever a man with one so pure?'

She could not resist it. 'I know that you, Lucius Falerius, can discern purity better than any man in Rome.'

'I feel I knew Aulus better than anyone outside his family, given that we were friends all the way back to childhood. We served as consuls together and no man could have asked for a more loyal colleague.'

'That was something my late husband held very dear. He often mentioned the depth and duration of your association.'

Claudia had picked the word 'association' deliberately and the way it was said was designed to let Lucius know just how much he had failed in that respect; that all the work to keep their friendship alive had come from Aulus. Quintus might not be sure precisely what was going on, but he knew his stepmother too well to trust her and he wasn't prepared to let this conversation run its course.

'We are very conscious, Lucius Falerius, of the honour you do the house of Cornelii.'

'Your father did most to honour that, Quintus, but I am sure his sons will add even more lustre to the Cornelii name. Can I assure you that your brother Titus will be home in time for the rites and may I bring to your attention my son, Marcellus, who asked to be allowed to accompany me and has his own words to say.'

With a gesture he brought the youngster forward, and he bowed to Claudia. 'Lady, I only met your late husband on one occasion but it was a memorable one. To me he exemplified the very essence of all that is best about Rome. With your permission I would like to take him as my example in life, along with my own father, in the hope that one day I may emulate his nature and his military achievements.'

The sincerity of the boy was obvious, and Claudia responded in kind. 'You are generous in your praise, young man, and I am sure that Quintus Cornelius would not object should you ever wish to seek guidance at the Cornelii family altar.'

'We would consider it an honour, Master Marcellus,' Quintus added.

'Would I be permitted to enquire about the funeral arrangements?' asked Lucius. 'I ask only so that I may tell my fellow-senators what is being planned.'

'Of course,' Quintus replied, moving towards Lucius, who turned away so that they were walking, heads together, in quiet conversation.

Claudia was left with Marcellus, who was obviously at a loss to know what to do, and was very uncomfortable under the scrutiny of a high-born lady who was looking at him intently, wondering how a creature like Lucius Falerius managed to produce such an heir; handsome, well-built for his years, and obviously someone who could speak without dissimulation.

'Come closer, Marcellus, and tell me how you met my late husband.'

They talked for a short period, time enough for Marcellus to tell her that he had studied Aulus's military campaigns long before the meeting; that the occasion was brief but in a few words a man he admired already had risen hugely in his estimation. 'It is true to say, lady, that Aulus Cornelius had the great gift of not only being a great soldier but looking like one.'

'I am sure that one day, Marcellus Falerius, you will share the same quality. I think I can already see the forthcoming man in the boy and it is most pleasing.'

It was the kind of conversational flattery used socially by adults and it was plain, by his stammering response, that it was something

Marcellus was unused to; what Claudia did not take into account was his lack of a mother as well as the constrained life he led, and the lowered eyes hid from her the fact that the young man's admiration was not confined to her late husband. The woman before him was not only aristocratic and sophisticated – she was, even in mourning, still young and very beautiful, and for a boy on the cusp of puberty, she had great allure.

Quintus's voice, with a distinct note of pique, broke the intimacy of their conversation. 'I cannot command that Cholon speak with you, Lucius Falerius. Besides he is no longer under this roof. My father freed him in his will, and left him a great deal of money, which I fear has gone to his head.'

'Then I shall appeal to him as a Roman citizen. Surely having just gained such a distinction he will take that seriously.'

'If I may be permitted to advise you, Lucius Falerius,' said Claudia, 'appeal to him as a person who served my husband, and can serve him still by telling you all you want to know about that slimy toad who betrayed him and left him to die.'

'I have no doubt that Vegetius Falerius deliberately sacrificed my master to further his own career and if you question my word, talk to the centurion Didius Flaccus, for it was he Aulus Cornelius sent to ask for reinforcements.'

Lucius knew all about what had happened in Illyricum, as well as at Thralaxas. He had read all the despatches and having questioned Vegetius's officers, he had a very clear story of what the man had done. He even had it attested by the gubernatorial priests that the abandonment of Aulus and his men was a deliberate act brought on by jealousy and anger and not some tactical mistake, for the governor had asked them to sacrifice a goat and read its entrails to ensure that his actions would bring him the success he craved. He had even spoken to Flaccus to find out what Aulus had seen and done on that reconnaissance to the south where he had first realised the extent of the revolt.

Nothing the ex-centurion said had been any more enlightening than what Cholon was telling him now but it was necessary to go through the motions of questioning this newly freed slave to get to the nub of what he wanted to know. So he let him ramble on, and even sat with an air of seeming compassion as Cholon wept, until the man had drained himself of any more to say about the nobility of his late master, or the treachery of Vegetius.

'Did your master ever mention to you anything about eagles?'

'Eagles?' Cholon sniffed, dried his eyes and looked confused. 'We saw lots. Illyricum, at least the mountainous part, is full of them.'

'Flying.'

'That is what eagles do.'

'Did Aulus refer to them in any way?'

'Not that I recall.'

'I was thinking perhaps of one that had had its wings clipped, one that might try to fly but could not.'

Cholon was clearly confused. 'I saw no such creature.'

'You were close to your master?'

Cholon wanted to say, 'Closer than you know,' but actually said, 'Every waking moment, and I slept in the antechamber to his tent. The only time I was not, was because he sent me away. Why do you ask?'

Lucius waved an airy hand. 'Nothing really, just something Aulus and I talked about many years ago. It was something we were told as children, and plainly the possibility exists that it was false.'

'Might I ask what?'

Lucius was quite sharp. 'If your late master declined to enlighten you, I think it only fitting that I should do the same.'

Cholon responded in kind, enjoying the new freedom that allowed him to address someone like Lucius as an equal. 'When are you going to impeach Vegetius?'

'You are sure he deserves it, Cholon?'

The Greek bridled. 'He deserves to be tied into a sack with a dog and a snake and thrown into the Tiber, yet where is he? Sitting outside Rome with his legion waiting for the Senate to vote him a triumph.'

'Trust me, Greek, the Senate will know how to do the right thing.'

'Greetings, Lucius Falerius,' said Vegetius Flaminus, his voice decidedly tremulous. 'And welcome to the camp of the 10th Legion.'

The ex-governor was curious about the box that his visitor's slave brought in but there was no way he could ask what it contained. He was hoping that Lucius had come to tell him he was about to support the motion to grant his triumph, which would guarantee acceptance, yet nothing in the censor's demeanour hinted at such a thing. But then, Vegetius reminded himself, Lucius was not called Nerva for nothing. He was famous for his ability to mask his thoughts; he might be contemplating that, or a ritual disembowelling, you could never tell. That he had come out of Rome to see him in his legionary encampment, without lictors or escorts, was a positive sign.

'I do what I must. Since successful generals are not permitted to enter the city without approval, I have to come to you, as I feel we need to speak.'

Vegetius indicated a table laden with fruit, bread,

sweet delicacies and wine. 'May I offer you refreshments?'

Lucius waved aside the offer, visibly disappointing his host who had put off nibbling at the spread so as not to disturb the careful arrangement. He was hungry and craved a glass of wine, but that was nothing new; to a man like him such desires were permanent. Lucius was thinking that Vegetius had got fatter since he had last seem him and he had, on the day he had been granted the governorship, been no slim creature. He had expanded especially in the jowls; the lips, red and wet, had always been unattractively thick.

'I take it you captured much spoils from the rebellion?'

'Cart loads. We stripped the living as well as the dead.'

You would, thought Lucius. You probably stripped every household in both provinces to make your triumph look more impressive. 'Good. I would like to examine them if I may.'

The 'why' died on Vegetius's fat lips. 'As you wish. Do you need me to accompany you?'

'No, Vegetius, I will be content with a man of lower rank to show me the carts. Meanwhile, you are obviously in need of food and drink, so you can indulge yourself while I am away.'

'I can wait,' Vegetius replied, unconvincingly.

'Open that box I brought with me while I am

absent, it may help to suppress your appetite. I will talk to you about what it contains when I return.'

Lucius was handed over to a slave, then to an old soldier who was responsible for the triumphal trophies. They were behind the Praetorium, rows and rows of carts laden with helmets, swords and shields, animal skins and tribal symbols, too many to examine individually. Fortunately the old man with him had helped to load them from the mess they were in when they first came into the camp.

'Eagles? Don't recall seein' any, your honour, it not bein' a symbol that the buggers use, beggin' your pardon. They're strong on wolves and bears, daresay 'cause they hunt and kill them, and I have seen the odd big-toothed fish, river sort, but not eagles.'

'Who helped you load these?'

'Praetorian guards, and a mighty moan I got from them for the order, they seeing it as beneath them.'

'Fetch them.'

'All of them, your honour? There be some on duty guarding the general.'

'Vegetius is safe enough here in Italy, don't you think?'

The old soldier would like to have replied that he was not sure, for he knew the man he served was a dab hand at making enemies, but that was not the kind of remark the likes of him made to Lucius

Falerius so he did as he was asked. The soldiers
came, all were questioned, and none could recall a
single instance of an eagle. Finally satisfied, Lucius
sent them back to their duties.

Vegetius, who had been reading the scrolls that lay
in the chest, the private letters of Aulus Cornelius to
Lucius Falerius, had nearly died of heart failure
when his Praetorian Guards were removed,
mystified when they came back and took up their
posts. Then he had the thought that he was not
much loved by his soldiers. Lucius did not need
replacement sentinels on the Praetorian tent; some
of his own soldiers would no doubt gladly take part
in his arrest. That he was about to be arrested was
obvious for everything he had ever done that could
be misinterpreted was listed in Aulus's letters, and,
typical of the stuck-up snobbish bastard, he had
seen it all in the worst possible light. Vegetius was
not vain enough to believe that he was wholly
innocent of the odd bit of self-serving, but that was
what it was, the kind of little peculations that any
provincial governor got up to. Not Aulus Cornelius
of course; his predecessor had been so rich he had
not indulged even in what was unquestionably his
by right.

'My, Vegetius,' said Lucius, looking at the well-
laden table. 'You've not eaten a thing.'

Vegetius waved a scroll, his face red and his

anger seemingly manufactured and insincere. 'I am too busy reading these lies.'

'Dismiss your slaves now, we need to speak alone.' When they had been sent away, Lucius added, 'Are they lies, Vegetius?'

'Of course.'

'So you did not lend out your soldiers' pay for months and pocket the interest, you did not sell their services as labourers, you never took bribes from the frontier farmers and mine owners to provide security.'

'I...'

'Have a care, Vegetius. I am not a man to whom you can lightly tell a lie and I have not even mentioned two other possible things which raise questions. The excessive taxes which you pocketed from your office, and the fact that the treasury of Publius Trebonius, which we suspect was taken by the Illyrian rebels who killed him, and would surely have been with the forces you defeated, is missing.'

The fat red lips were wetted several times before a reply came. 'I have done nothing of which I am ashamed.'

'Then you have little knowledge of what the word means, I fear. You have taken gubernatorial rapacity to a height I have certainly never seen before, made yourself rich at the expense of your office and the state. You have deliberately left my oldest friend and the best soldier Rome had to die so that you could seek enough dead bodies to get you a triumph, and we are about to have a debate in the house to decide whether that wish should be granted.'

'I deny everything in these letters.'

'I think I need a glass of wine and I think I should pour you one.' This he did, only to see it disappear down the man's throat in one gulp. 'Now what you are saying is this. That Aulus Cornelius Macedonicus, probably the most honest and upright man ever to put on a senatorial toga, has told lies, while you, a man known for the depth rather than the height of your standards, are telling the truth. I wonder how that will be received?'

'I have friends who will support me.'

Lucius smiled, but it was the look of a fox who had just found its way into the chicken coop. 'I too have friends, and Aulus? He had the good opinion of everyone except those too base to comprehend his nature. I think that should I produce these letters, then propose not only that you be impeached but that you be stoned then cast naked from the Tarpien Rock, that I might carry the day.'

'I made a modest amount, I admit.'

'Modest?'

'And I am happy to share it.'

'A bribe, Vegetius. I think I should call for a shovel, since in a hole your inclination is to keep digging. What you need is someone who can save you from the justified anger of your peers.' Vegetius was wise enough then, to stay silent. 'But of course, such a saviour would have a price.'

'Anything.'

'That is a great deal, but nothing I suppose, set against your life, and a very painful death. Have you read the report of the commission that Aulus Cornelius headed?'

'Not yet.'

'You would enjoy it, but then since it was written by friends of yours that is hardly surprising.'

Vegetius sat forward, and spoke with a degree of hope. 'It absolves me?'

'It does not even accuse you, so much is it a pack of lies. Keeping the soldiers pay is excused as keeping them from throwing away their hard-earned money, their labours as service to the provincial farmers, and your policy of guarding the frontiers in small detachments is described as masterful. Given the lengths you employed to pacify the indigenes, the Illyrian peasants are seen as ingrates for their revolt. When I read it I laughed until tears filled my eyes.'

'What do you want, Lucius Falerius?'

'A peaceful life, Vegetius, is that not what we all want? No more scraped votes in the Forum, no more having to cajole my fellow senators to do the right thing. It would be wonderful not to hear of land redistribution ever again, just as I would welcome an end to the clamour for the peoples we have defeated to be given citizenship. You and your friends represent a sizeable block of senatorial votes. If I can always count on those my mind will be at rest.'

'These letters?'

'Are copies. The originals I shall keep.'

'Who has seen them?'

'Enough people of position to ensure that I can introduce them to the house at any time I choose.'

'They will lose potency as time passes, Lucius, and then people will ask why you hung on to them and said nothing.'

'They might not result in your death, but ruin can be just as painful.'

'You're asking me to help you gain total control of the Senate.'

'Never fear, Vegetius. No one ever has control of the Senate and if I do have power, I intend to use it wisely. That was something Aulus Cornelius never understood. Now, about your triumph.'

When Lucius departed he was content. He had what he had sought when he contrived at the murder of Tiberius Livonius, the power to ensure that the Imperium of Rome would remain unchanged and unsullied. Aulus had taken that away from him the day he had mounted his defence; now in death, without knowing it, his old friend had created the circumstances that gifted it back to him. There was another thing to cheer him up; no evidence of any eagles appeared in Aulus's death, so perhaps, as he always half suspected, that Alban Sybil was wont to give her prophecy out for the money they brought in, not as true warnings from the gods.

The burning drawing was no more than a conjuring trick to terrify the gullible, and he could now dismiss from his mind the occasional fears it produced.

EPILOGUE

Claudia sat alone, as all over the house they prepared to commemorate, with prayers, the life of Aulus Cornelius Macedonicus. Senators were arriving and crowds had gathered in the street to mourn with the family. She knew once it was over she would have to decide what to do, and although not resolved, she had a fair idea of the course she should take. First, find the spot where her child had been exposed, then if there were bones, a proper, albeit secret burial, if not a priestly ceremony and a sacrifice to ease the passage of the child's soul.

If that talisman was still there she could consider a return to Spain. If not, she must track it down, working out a way to effect that without bringing disgrace on the Cornelii name. But let that wait; now it was time to see to the funeral rites of her husband, and to pray to the gods that he would have more peace and happiness in Hades, than he ever enjoyed here on Earth.

The golden haired boy, now near a youth, with the dog Minca at his side, stood by the side of the Via Appia, the road that ran north to Rome and south to Sicily. He, despite his inclinations, could not travel in either direction. Having given what money Fulmina had bequeathed him to the guard, he was stuck here until something happened. Perhaps, with the news of victory in Illyricum, Clodius would come home, after all; yet the boy was not sure if he could face him. One thing he knew, that he would take food from Dabo, but never work in his fields.

Aquila turned and walked away, past the burnt outline that was all that remained of the hut in which he had grown up. He continued on down the stream to stand, after a lengthy walk, at the spot where, according to Fulmina, he had been found. He stood there for an age, trying to conjure up an image of the woman who had borne him and the people who had abandoned him, a baby wrapped in swaddling clothes. Inadvertently, his hand touched the leather amulet, his fingers tracing the outline of the eagle's wings, wondering if what Fulmina had said was true; that his destiny lay with what was stitched inside.

Taking it off his arm, he looked at it intently, seeing the hooked beak and the wide wings of the eagle in flight. He would keep his vow to the woman who made it, and only open it when he feared no man; that was not now, but it would be soon. And then he would leave this place, to go where he did not know, and perhaps he would find the destiny that his adopted mother had seen in her dreams.